"Enjoy the Journey!"

Never Remove the Cornerstone

Byron Marcello Coleman

Never Remove the Cornerstone
Copyright © 2019 by Byron Marcelle Coleman

Library of Congress Control Number: 2018965299
ISBN-13: Paperback: 978-1-64398-469-8
ePub: 978-1-64398-649-4
Kindle: 978-1-64398-650-0
Hardcover: 978-1-64398-651-7

All rights reserved. No part of this publication may be reproduced, distributed, or transmitted in any form or by any means, including photocopying, recording, or other electronic or mechanical methods, without the prior written permission of the publisher or author, except in the case of brief quotations embodied in critical reviews and certain other noncommercial uses permitted by copyright law.

Although every precaution has been taken to verify the accuracy of the information contained herein, the author and publisher assume no responsibility for any errors or omissions. No liability is assumed for damages that may result from the use of information contained within.

Printed in the United States of America

LitFire LLC
1-800-511-9787
www.litfirepublishing.com
order@litfirepublishing.com

CONTENTS

PART 1 WHERE AM I?..1
   CHAPTER 1   HAPPY (SAPPY) NEW YEAR 3
   CHAPTER 2   THE BEARER OF GOOD NEWS? 17
   CHAPTER 3   MAMA SAID THERE'D BE DAYS LIKE THIS 35
   CHAPTER 4   CHER..43

PART 2 FOUND IN JULES BAYONNE..55
   CHAPTER 5   COSMIC PERSPECTIVES..................................57
   CHAPTER 6   BLACK SOLDIERS 67
   CHAPTER 7   SOMETHING OLD . . . SOMETHING NEW 73

PART 3 CLOSER TO HOME...77
   CHAPTER 8   COLOR STRUCK?...79
   CHAPTER 9   ALL CAUTION TO THE WIND 91
   CHAPTER 10   . . . STARTING FROM THE BEGINNING..................99
   CHAPTER 11   AHA . . . MORE CONNECTIONS.........................113
   CHAPTER 12   CODE NOIR...133
   CHAPTER 13   THE PROMISE 141

PART 4 THE JOURNEY...145
   CHAPTER 14   JULES AT THE HELM 147
   CHAPTER 15   WADE SORRELL 167
   CHAPTER 16   FAST FORWARD 177

PART 5 REFERENCE POINT 179
   CHAPTER 17   CHOOSE LIFE..181
   CHAPTER 18   MODERN TIMES...193
   CHAPTER 19   REVELATIONS OF A DOMESTIC SERVANT............199
   CHAPTER 20   NEVER REMOVE THE 'CORNERSTONE'
                        OF YOUR FOREFATHERS 207

| CHAPTER 21 | GHOSTS FROM MY (OWN) PAST | 217 |
| CHAPTER 22 | A RETURN TO HAPPIER TIMES | 223 |

PART 6 MY STORY: A PERSONAL HISTORY

CHAPTER 23	MY LETTER TO JULES	233
CHAPTER 24	ELOISE SORRELL	237
CHAPTER 25	THE MAKING OF BYRON MARCELLO COLEMAN	243
CHAPTER 26	THE MYSTERY:	257
CHAPTER 27	THE PARCEL	261
CHAPTER 28	B. M.	271
CHAPTER 29	THE REUNION	283
CHAPTER 30	GRANNY HATTIE	289
CHAPTER 31	TRISH	297
CHAPTER 32	AN AMAZING SECRET	305

Bret,

My journey began with you on that 'golden time of day' when you *shared* those Dicky's Potato Chips with me on a street corner in the 'Goose,' just yesterday! Such a phenomenal ride, don't you agree?

For you.

Love,
B

PART 1

WHERE AM I?

CHAPTER 1

HAPPY (SAPPY) NEW YEAR

New Year's Eve-2006

"Happy New Year!" My family toasted out the old and welcomed in the new. As was the custom in my home and my mother's before me, we saluted the New Year with celebratory eggnog (heavily spiked with rum or scotch), tasty snacks, and the traditional black-eyed peas and greens for 'good fortune' and 'prosperity' for all present. While best wishes were generously shared among all family members; spiked eggnog was strictly reserved for the adults; though I'd caught a kid or two trying to sneak a sip of the potent libation!

The 'Big Apple's' ball drop, and then the New Year's celebration with Dick Clark, a number of very bad live performances at Time Square, always a good kiss from my wife was as familiar as it had been in previous years. But, this time it was different. I don't know how to explain what was different about *this* time, but still, it was, very different.

* * *

Run!

"Run baby!" I yelled to my wife, Janice, who had walked a few feet ahead of me, and having failed to look up, didn't see the five rough-looking men rushing directly towards us. Instinctively, I turned and ran in the opposite direction. I know what it looked like, but not intending on leaving my wife to fend alone, I had hopes that I could make the 911 call on my cell phone as three of the men closed in on me. Curiously, I was keenly aware of several others—maybe fifteen or twenty people, who had also turned in the same direction and were fleeing ahead of me, chaotically screaming in terror. Four gunshots rang out—two men on either side of me simultaneously pitched forward from the violent consequence of the shots which had only moments before been discharged from a yet unidentified source. I didn't stop to look, but from the angle they fell, I could quickly surmise that the bullets had found their way to the back of the men's heads. Where's my wife! As if answering my inquiry, at that very moment, I heard Janice scream. Fear had rushed over me to an incomprehensibility I had never experienced before. I shouted desperately to my wife, with great dread, not knowing what had happened to her. "God, help us! I love you baby, keep runnin'!" I fumbled through the phone's menu, and after finding the dial pad, punched in the numbers, 911 . . . stumbled on the uneven pavement . . . at last an answer.

"What is the nature of your emergency?"

"Help! "We're being attacked! I'm on Market Street, running southbound between Sixteenth and Seventeenth Streets!"

Keep running Levi!" I yelled to the tall, young, black man almost disappearing in front of me by more than one-hundred fifty feet. Why was I worried about Levi instead of Janice? . . . *Where's my wife?* . . . This time, only the unfamiliar chaos of running feet and unidentified shouts and muffling were my answer. Two more shots cracked. This time, the shots sounded a lot closer. *Oh my God, where's my wife?* This time, my answer came just as suddenly as before. I felt the grip of one assailant tugging on the back of my sport coat. Simultaneously and equally abruptly I felt a horrible, sharp pain in my head as I was struck repeatedly by something in the hand of one or more of the men. My fear now turned to terror as it dawned on me I had been overtaken by the very men I was trying to get away from. I don't know what scared me more; the impending pain that was sure to follow or the fact that I hadn't a clue why this was happening. Already in their grasp, the phone shattered as it was knocked from my hand and struck the damp paved street. The rapid spin of the moment cranked up my adrenalin about ten notches, way past the point of chaos, as by now I plummeted to the ground in a confused daze. Faced down in the warm, harsh surface; the last thing I recalled was the dusty smell of concrete and grit . . . as everything faded into a dark abyss, my final, uninterrupted, sluggish thought was: *Where is my wife?*

* * *

Full alertness evaded me as I struggled to awaken from the faint feeling that accompanied fear's piercing talons, which continued to maintain its tenacious grip. Not fully awake, I struggled to gain full consciousness. The horror in my mind seemed to increase exponentially. I blurted an uneasy moan, as my mind kept reeling over and over, *Oh no, no, no, they got Jesse on East Colfax!*

It occurred to me that this very vivid nightmare had paralyzed me on *this* night before the dawn of *this* brand, new and otherwise unadulterated New Year's Day with brutal and surreal detailed wonderment: *Why Colfax? . . . Who were Levi and Jesse?* I couldn't remember the faces of these two men, but their names lingered clearly in my mind after awakening from the horrible dream . . .

* * *

New Year's Day, 2007

Finally, I bolted out of the horror of the nightmare and looked around the white-noised, hushed serenity and safety of my own familiar bedroom. Happy New Year? Yeah right. I was so exhausted, emotionally drained and left with an excruciating headache from my nocturnal episode. Relieved, but still shaken, I clutched the fragrant softness of my bed linen as I reached over and touched my beautiful wife who was now breathing with the most peaceful and sweet rhythm of a newborn babe. I snuggled closer to her warm, welcoming body. Glad that last night had only been a dream, I could now force happiness back into my mind. Eventually, I resumed a restful, pre-nightmare, peaceful sleep.

* * *

I never mentioned this particular dream to anyone, not even Janice. Instead, I met the day with conflicting thoughts about the meaning of the dream. *Where had it taken place? What was of value to the attackers? Why were we there? Why was my wife walking ahead of me instead of at her reserved spot at my right side when the incident occurred?* Perhaps there was no meaning to the dream—maybe no more thought should be wasted on the whole damn episode. The most amazing and disturbing thing about the nightmare was my ability to recall so much detail—the physical surroundings, and even the names of those in harm's way with me. I saw their faces, but as I recall in the dream, I couldn't remember their faces. I still couldn't the next day; presumably, I didn't know who they were at all. However, in my gut, I sensed they were tied to me in some way and that we shared a common plight. One thing for certain was that we were all fleeing some strange, but common evil. As hard as I tried, I couldn't erase the dream or its effect. It was like having a front-row seat in a three-dimensional thriller and as the warm blood was splattered during the slaughter, I felt the splash and the smell of death with a frightening reality. Just then, I shuddered and hoped it had gone unnoticed by those family members present. It had. I quickly murmured, "Thank you, Jesus," as I breathed a sigh of relief that no one had approached me with the proverbial, "Are you okay?" at the slightest sign of a loved one's apparent distress.

No longer wishing to relive what I didn't want to experience in the first place, I willed my consciousness to a better place. This was the year to change my life, a sort of New Year's Resolution. This wasn't the first time or the first year that I had promised myself to *'come into my own'* in *this* New Year. But *this* time I was determined to succeed, I will be what *I* want to be, at last. I alerted no one about my plan, but then, my plan was simple—do nothing, say nothing, don't make waves and go through life with a spirit of 'peaceful coexistence'—live and let live! *I know—boring!*

Well, what I wanted to do and what was expected of me over the next few months was to be quite different than I could have ever dreamed of. Those dreams, incidentally, would contain the mysteries serving to shape my understanding of what it meant to survive life's madness, as well as, a tremendous preparation for an intriguing journey. *Okay, I warned myself, enough already! Today I'm gonna start living out my self-promise; to relax; no heavy duty thinking. PERIOD!*

The day proceeded with sleep on the sofa in the den with the door firmly closed; eat, then sleep again, intermingled with television—silver screen mysteries and 'my secret weapon' were among my favorites. They really helped dull the *(my)* senses . . . Just what I needed right now.

* * *

"A Hundred Yards Over the Rim"

I am almost ashamed to admit this but, usually I could blank out all of the world's cares by playing a *Winnie the Pooh* video *(okay, okay, so this is my secret weapon)* and gently falling to sleep with the sound of the lulling animated bear or donkey playing in my subconscious. I found this to be a most acceptable alternative to smoking a little *cannabis (which was my favorite method of stress relief some thirty-five years ago)*. Nevertheless, by this time in my life, I had become a more law-abiding, and productive citizen—a much better person, to the benefit of all, including myself. I was well on my way towards the difficult process of personal growth and change . . .

Instead, I had decided to snooze through the old black and white Twilight Zone Marathon episodes being aired on the television's Sci-Fi Channel. The sound of the heavy Georgian rainfall, coupled with those old black and white *reruns* provided the perfect sleep setting. Before long, I ceased to even see the flashing dullness of the programming through my closed eyelids, and as I attempted to reach a soothing slumber, the sound of the narrator, Rod Serling, was beginning to enter the depths of my subconscious. As I began to drift off, I remembered hearing his faint words:

"The year is 1847, the place is the (desert-terrain) territory of New Mexico, and the people are a tiny handful of men and women with a dream. Eleven months ago, they started out from Ohio and headed west. Someone told them about a place called California, about a warm sun and a blue sky, about rich land and fresh air, and at this moment almost a year later they've seen nothing but cold, heat, exhaustion, hunger, and sickness. This man's name is Christian Horn. He has a dying eight-year-old son and a heartsick wife, and he's the only one remaining who has even a fragment of the dream left. Mr. Chris Horn, who's going over the top of a rim to look for water and sustenance and in a moment, will move into the Twilight Zone."[1]

While scouting over a rim (sandy ridge), Christian Horn sees a paved road lined with telephone poles. A huge truck rushes by and scares him. He tumbles faced-down into unfamiliar and uncharted territory to the ground and his rifle accidentally fires a shot into his arm. He makes it to a nearby diner, Joe's Airflite Café, where Mary Lou, a former nurse's aide, treats his wound and gives him a bottle of penicillin. As Christian's eyes begin to focus on the contents of the room, a calendar becomes visible to him on the diner wall, and he reads that the current year is (month of September) 1961. A doctor is summoned, and he finds Christian's story credible, considering his clothes, gun, and old-fashioned fillings in his teeth. The doctor realizing this is beyond his

---

[1] Excerpts from The Twilight Zone, Second Season's *A Hundred Yards Over The Rim*-Writer: Rod Serling, Director: Buzz Kulik, Producer: Buck Houghton, Director of Photography: George T. Clemens, Music: Fred Steiner, Cast: Christian Horn: Cliff Robertson, Joe: John Crawford, Martha Horn: Miranda Jones, Charlie: John Astin

ability to comprehend the events before him calls the sheriff. Christian emerges from the back room. He has read an encyclopedia on one of the café's shelves and learned that his son grew up to be a famous physician. Before the sheriff and his deputy arrive to investigate the doctor's claims, Christian bolts from the diner. The sheriff and deputy give chase, but Christian tops the rim before they can apprehend him. Suddenly, Horn is whisked back to 1847, carrying the bottle of penicillin for his sick son; but without his trusty rifle. His rifle, looking like it has been rotting in the desert for a hundred years, is all that is left in 1961.

Mr. Christian Horn, one of the hardy breed of men who headed west during a time when there were no concrete highways or the solace of civilization. Mr. Christian Horn, family and party, heading west, after a brief detour through the Twilight Zone."

I continued to drift in and out of my slothful slumber during Mr. Horn's exploits until the incessantly, jarring, insistent ringing of my cell phone rudely announced that my nap time was over.

* * *

The Phone Call: On New Year's Day!?!

"Bringg, bringg," the cell phone resting on the glass shelf of the wrought iron baker's rack in the family room yelped like a puppy who'd suddenly been torn from its mother's tit, just as the meal was getting good and really 'hitting the spot.' It was only four o'clock in the afternoon but already the room was cast dark gray, gradually becoming slightly lightened near the large picture window on the east side of the room. On the exterior side of the window, rain that had come down so heavily for such a long time, revealed the tender turmoil of a mid-Georgian, winter thunderstorm. Despite the storm's somber dreariness, I was actually enjoying the peace and solitude an occasional crack of thunder brought just seconds after the sky had been fully lit up. Sounds of everything and everybody else had been merely a distant muffle; until . . . "Bringg, bring." Again, the obnoxious nuisance of the mobile phone ringing struck a nerve, so much so that I really wanted to throw the wretched thing against the wall, smashing it into more pieces than a sane person could count. Only the fact that it would cost me another $600 plus to replace the stupid thing, stayed my hand . . . and my sanity. Maybe it was the constant staccato of rain; or maybe it was just my 'I don't want to be bothered' attitude; or my kicking myself for not having turned the blasted thing off; I couldn't be sure at that point, but the ringing of the phone still really annoyed me, maybe even more than it should. Maybe it was my imagination, but its constant assault seemed to be ringing in sync with the rain, which had now pummeled the earth and now was beginning to assault my house as well. *I wished this ringing would stop . . . and SOON!* It was certain that no one else in the house would answer *that* particular wireless phone because it was reserved strictly for *my* business use. By the process of elimination, I could only assume that any incoming calls to this particular phone on New Years' Day would have to be from a business contact or a very 'tenacious' relative who had managed to secure the number from my business's website. My initial guess at who was calling was the latter . . . someone I had no desire to hear from at that moment *(or anytime soon, if the truth be told). Despite my annoyance, I had to smirk a little at the audacity of the caller. Business or otherwise took a lot of guts; especially if it were kin folk who knew either personally or from reliable 'hearsay' that I'm not (nor ever was) the most personable individual in my family.*

In fact, it has been often said that I am moody and sometimes intolerable. So, I admit, and without shame, that my wish to be left alone on that most inclement of days was not uncharacteristic for me. My mother often referred to me as being *'uncongenial,'* particularly as a youth. A neighbor, who had struggled with extending me a welcome to the neighborhood, recently indicated that based on my facial expression I was *'unapproachable,'* so for several years, he had been reluctant to initiate any conversation with me. Even my wife and children nicknamed me *'Shack Bully'* (which is loosely translated to mean *boss of the household*). I guess not much had changed; I was still 'uncongenial' and downright moody at times. Moreover, it didn't help much for me to have found favor in Ishmael

Reed's *'cowboy* in *Ra's Boat*,[2] or that I really could relate to actually being the 'Big Luke' I imagined in my version of the story:

* * *

'Big Luke,' Et Cetera

In an old western town near Denver, Colorado, around the mid-1800's, a group of the locals file into Jackson's Saloon. The chatter and murmurs among this small group of men seem to center around this one man . . .

. . . it's about midday and there's three locals at the bar casually sipping on whatever libation their money can buy, when, suddenly the saloon doors are flung open and a muscular, tall, bearded ruffian enters the saloon and strides briskly to the bar. "Bartender! Whiskey!" the man barks, causing the proprietor to nervously pour the first thing he could get his hands on in a shot glass to its rim. The man gulps it down and motions to the bartender to refill the glass. He polishes off the second shot, even more hurriedly than the first and then just as quickly loudly announces to no one in particular, 'Big Luke' is coming to town!" With the same deliberate urgency in which he had entered the saloon, the bearded man strides toward the swinging doors (with neither payment nor excuse) and exits.

'Big Luke,' represents the 'dread' of any small western town in those days. 'Big Luke' is 'known' to have been a 'bad' man. Although not many townspeople can specify what caused 'Big Luke' to be one to fear; nor can any person cite an incident in which 'Big Luke's' 'bad man' reputation was warranted. As a matter of fact, no one—living or dead-had ever admitted to even having laid eyes on him.

Still, whether the personage of 'Big Luke' was real or mythical, the appearance of fear on the faces of those remaining few was obvious as the men rambled: "Have you heard? 'Big Luke' is coming to town," one

---

2 From New and Collected Poems by Ishmael Reed, published by Atheneum. Copyright © 1989 by Ishmael Reed

fellow whispers to another as the others strain to listen to the hushed conversation. Panic surrounds the town as many of its people scurry to find not easily discovered hiding places . . . "'Big Luke' is coming to town!"

Just outside the saloon door, the dust bellowing in the distance captures the unified gaze of a few remaining men who have yet to find a place safe enough to shield them from the awesomeness of 'Big Luke.' Afraid, but still routed in the same spots, as the approaching figure becomes more visible, the onlookers begin to debate, "It's a stagecoach," one man blurts out! "No, it's a horseman!" another emphatically announces. "Too big for a horse!" another younger man contributes to the debate.

The figure, once too obscure to describe, advances close enough to finally be recognized. What emerges from the midst of the cloud of dust is a burly man, mounted on and fiercely whipping an unusually large beast of burden, now galloping full stride with his rider into the little dirt, road leading into town. The animal which the man is mounted on is a twenty-four-hundred-pound, snorting Brahma bull! Amazing . . . they are a long way from home! These animals were first introduced to the States in Texas only a few years ago! And to add further to this oddity, the man's 'whip' is actually an eight-foot rattlesnake! The man had a firm grip on the snake—which appeared to still be alive; from the tail end just above the rattler segment, the head of the snake viciously strikes the hide of the bull with each lash cracking by the hand of the large man saddled on its back.

Upon arriving at the saloon, the rider is somehow able to dismount the still snorting bull—obviously unaffected by the rattlesnake's venom. He loosely ties the reins to a post, and then he strikes the beast with his gloved, closed fist, squarely on the 'mug' and yells. "You'd better not move!" Like a well-trained dog in response to a master's "stay commands," the beast remains in absolute obedience where the man hitches him.

As the big man enters the saloon, for some unknown reason, he picks up a large spittoon that is stationed on the floor just inside the saloon's swinging doors; and without much caution nor ceremony, empties its putrid contents on the floor. The saloon's occupants can't believe what happens next. Taking the spittoon, the man saunters over to the bar as he, suspiciously eyes the small, crowd who is now cowering and afraid to openly look in the large man's direction.

"Bartender, give me a whiskey!" The scarred-faced, rugged, big man commands.

The bartender's anxiety is obvious. His hands are shaking so badly that he almost drops the shot glass he attempts to fill, when the man abruptly grabs the bottle of whiskey and pours the entire bottle into the spittoon. In one motion, without 'coming up for air' the man drinks the whiskey from the spittoon. Slamming the empty bottle and the completely drained spittoon on the bar, the man flips a large silver coin in the bartender's direction. He makes no effort to either catch nor otherwise retrieve the coin as it clatters to a final stand still on the bar's surface. Instead, hoping that the man is about to leave, he and the others in the bar breathe a common sigh of relief at the sound of the man's loud, almost visibly (though they didn't see) repugnant, lion-roaring belch. The bartender, still pop-eyed from the man's robust action, but somewhat less nervous retrieves a fresh bottle of whiskey, as he offers, "Sir, would you like another?"

The large man, quickly arising from the barstool, having now started for the door retorts, "Ain't got time, friend! Ain't you heard; 'Big Luke's' coming to town!"

* * *

By the time I was forty-one years old, Keyser Söze[3] was my hero. I relished in the idea of being the unknown, unseen, mysterious renegade. I related to the well-trained mercenary, placing emphasis on the 'task' or deed at the highest priority level. Quite frankly, I felt very comfortable in my own skin. I didn't have much use for 'leaders' nor was I interested in being a leader. My natural instincts overrode the need for a healthy self-image and the result was to revert to 'predator behavior' in order to survive the life in the environment I had to contend with. Given the choice between chickens and eagles, I picked eagles—their solitary trait being my attraction, versus

---

[3] The fictional villain character in the 1995 film *The Usual Suspects* by Christopher McQuarrie, directed by Bryan Singer.

'flocking' characteristics. Eagles and other animals of prey were my life teachers. Watching the chase of the 'big cat,' running down an antelope or wildebeest on a National Geographic program was (and still is) one of my favorite pastimes. I admired the dangerous 'bull-of-the-woods,' rather than the 'safety of the herd.'

It has been said that "everybody's looking for a hero—people need someone to look up to." So, it seems that characters borne from the imagination of writers, directors, comic book creators, and the like, appealed to my needs for defining positive moral qualities. My heroes sought justice and battled against inequities between people without regard to any disruption or devastation they might cause in the process. 'Big Luke,' Keyser Soze, Muhammed Ali—possessed all of the defining character elements I looked for in heroes!

* * *

Finally, the cell's chime indicated that a voice message had been recorded. *Good!* I thought.

The rain was falling even more heavily by now, and I kept wondering, *who could it be? Perhaps it was someone wishing me a Happy New Year? Well, I could always use a blessing, but the lull of the relentlessly rainy day, or perhaps it was simply my own laziness convincing me to reject the idea of checking the message right then.* And, just like my recently discovered personal, favorite (the unnamed boy) protagonist in the Seuss story: I Am Not Going to Get Up Today![4]

Stirring and restlessness, and perhaps a little bit of nosiness won out. I couldn't simply ignore it any longer! After what seemed like a few hours later; turned out to have been less than fifteen minutes since the first ring, I forced myself to sneak a peek at the caller ID all the while cussing under my breath and dreading the thought that I just might have to return an immediate greeting to someone. "Forget it!" I blurted aloud as I eagerly sought the button that allowed me to view the phone call's details. The

---

[4] A book by Dr. Seuss, entitled: *I Am Not Going to Get Up Today!* Text copyright 1987 Theodore S. Geisel (Dr. Seuss) and Audrey S. Geisel. Illustrations by James Stevenson. The protagonist is the unnamed boy who vows not to get up on that particular day.

message left from the caller ID indicated that the call was from Grady Memorial Hospital in Atlanta, Georgia.

Obstinately, I shrugged off the idea that the call was related to a 'real emergency,' and having done so, thoroughly convinced myself that I was merely exercising my previously self-declared intention of not answering any calls on New Year's Eve or the following day. It was my strange and twisted way of making a drastic 'resolution' change for the new year. Still, talking to myself, my rhetorical pondering left me wondering, *Now, who in the hell is calling me from there? Humph,* I snickered; *perhaps one or more of them crazy folk in my family finally got picked up and carted away to the 'loony bin.'*

I supposed from the symptoms just set forth, I may have been experiencing, what most normal folks would describe as nothing more than 'burnout.' Maybe my neuroses were directly related to those awful dreams and nightmares I had experienced of late. Maybe it was the overload of the media that was to blame for the *funk* I couldn't seem to shake. However, I am convinced, in due time, after I have presented the entire details of my most peculiar experience related to this New Year's Day phone call, you too will come to the conclusion that an incredible and bizarre encounter actually occurred.

* * *

CHAPTER 2

THE BEARER OF GOOD NEWS?

Jeffrey Harris

The following day, Tuesday morning, January 2 . . . My resolution did not extend past midnight on New Year's Day. I grumbled as I checked the voice mail and retrieved the strange but simple message: "Mr. Coleman, this is Jeffrey Harris, calling from Grady Health System. Happy New Year to you and your family. Please accept my apology for troubling you on New Year's Day, but we were desperately trying to locate a relative for a patient here in the hospital with the last name, Bayonne. Through our search on the Internet, we found reference to the patient's last name and alleged place of birth on your website. We are trying to locate anyone who might be able to help us complete our records and place Mr. Bayonne back with his family. Please call us at our main number (404) ###-#### and ask for me, Jeffrey Harris. I would appreciate any information you might be able to give us. Thank you very much, and again, Happy New Year."

I grappled with the idea of whether or not I should return the call. I wasn't entirely convinced that the intelligent, business-like voice I heard on my voice mail, allegedly belonging to a Mr. Jeffrey Harris of, for all I know, a mythical Grady Memorial Hospital, actually existed. (My suspicions were in part based upon the fact that during his initial call-the one I didn't answer-the caller ID indicated that it was from the Grady Memorial Hospital, not the Grady Health Systems as his actual voice message stated). The call sounded legit enough, but you still had to be so careful nowadays. I was keenly aware of the numerous scams conducted over the phone, the internet and/or other means of non-personal, face-to-face communications on the increase these days.

This was especially true since the paradigm shift in how we now communicate; exploding in the late1970's continued to culturally steamroll worldwide right through the new millennium, with the advent of the handheld mobile phone (0G, 1G, 2G, 3G, 4G, et cetera), digital pagers, e-mail and social networking, with absolute disdain. *Why would I want to be accessible (legitimately or otherwise) any more than I had been up to now?* I strongly felt that an all-out attack had been declared on man's personal freedom and everyone, except me, seemed to be okay with it. I hated the idea that most people thought it was all right to "just call me anytime." I was appalled by the whole "hit me-up," "follow me on . . . ," "text me at . . . ," "tweet me . . . ," "comment at . . . ," blah, blah, blah. *People! Shut up!* In my opinion, this new 'pollution' is a bunch of superfluous stuff billowing from millions of mouths, through the atmosphere and the ether, to millions of ears—junk having not the least bit of any resemblance to what was once recognized as nourishing (and sought out, I might add) qualities of true and meaningful communication! Time is *still* man's most valuable commodity, but boy, we have learned how to *'murder the clock'* in so many ways now!

I hated to admit it, but I was also faced with another complexity! My personal finances were becoming a nightmare (*like I need another nightmare—one to match those which lately, had plagued my sleep far too often*) and required my undivided attention. Nowhere on my agenda called for responding to entities or establishments soliciting money, to which I had no access to anyway. After all, I was broke. Nevertheless, the oddity of the message needled my imagination and once pricked, my curiosity got the best of me. Besides, Harris had not directly or indirectly, mentioned money . . . *yet*. Figuring I'd covered all the bases, and without 'further ado,' I punched the redial button and held my breath, as I listened to the familiar variety of tones that signaled my call was being connected.

The phone rang four times before a pleasant voice; I assumed to be that of a woman, possibly a receptionist, answered, "Good afternoon, Grady Health Services, how may I direct your call?"

"Oh, yes, hello. This is Mr. Byron Coleman and I'm returning Mr. Harris' phone call of yesterday."

"Great, Mr. Coleman, we were expecting your call. Please hold a moment while I connect your call."

Really? How'd they know I'd be calling back? After waiting, for what seemed to be a very long time, listening to a *Muzak*[5] instrumental version of Michael Jackson's *Remember the Time*, Mr. Harris finally came on the line.

"Mr. Coleman, thank you for calling us back so promptly. We had nowhere else to turn in hopes of finding out how we might help our patient, Mr. Bayonne. He appears to be experiencing a form of source psychogenic amnesia[6] and is only able to provide us with sketchy and most unusual details about himself."

---

5   Also referred to as elevator music, Muzak Holdings Corporation supplies business background music while a (phone) caller is on 'hold' status.

6   **Source amnesia** is an explicit memory disorder in which someone can recall certain information, but does not know where or how it was obtained. The disorder is particularly episodic, where source or contextual information surrounding facts are severely distorted or unable to be recalled.
   Psychogenic amnesia results from a psychological cause as opposed to direct damage to the brain caused by head injury, physical trauma or disease, which is known as organic amnesia. This can include:
   - **Dissociative amnesia** is used to refer to inability to recall information, usually about stressful or traumatic events in persons' lives, such as a violent attack or rape. Persons retain the capacity to learn new information.
   - **Fugue state** is also known as dissociative fugue. It is caused by psychological trauma and is usually temporary. The Merck Manual defines it as "one or more episodes of amnesia in which the inability to recall some or all of one's past and either the loss of one's identity or the formation of a new identity occur with sudden, unexpected,

"Can you come to our office and meet for lunch this Wednesday so we might be able to sort out some of our most intriguing patient's puzzling issues?"

"I'm sorry," I queried, "But *who* did you say had amnesia?"

"B-a-y-o-n-n-e is how he spells his name, Mr. Coleman." Harris quickly replied.

Harris' response caught me completely off guard. I couldn't help but thinking how he needed information from me, but now I'm the one puzzled . . . *thoroughly.*

"I apologize, Mr. Coleman," Harris continued. "But I have a call on hold and I'm due in a meeting in five minutes and I really could use any assistance you can provide. Lunch is on me, okay?"

I wanted to say, "Hey, wait a minute, I can't let you go just yet. I got too many questions!" My mind was reeling, but not so much so that I didn't realize that he probably couldn't provide me with the things I wanted to know anyway; which was the reason he contacted me in the first place.

"Ok, that sounds good to me." *I wondered if he could sense my newly found urgency to meet him and satisfy my curiosity regarding this mysterious Bayonne character? I hoped he hadn't, as my intentional lack of self-disclosure was perhaps one of my least flattering character traits.*

"I think that works for me." *I knew it would work, but didn't want him to know that lately, I'd been experiencing lots of 'idle business' activity.*

Almost as soon as our conversation was completed, Mary, the receptionist was back on the line to confirm our luncheon date.

"Thanks, Mary, I'll meet Mr. Harris tomorrow at noon at Afrodish's on Sweet Auburn Curb Market."

---

purposeful travel away from home." While popular in fiction, it is extremely rare in 'real' life situations.

- **Posthypnotic amnesia** is where events during hypnosis are forgotten, or where past memories are unable to be recalled.
- **Lacunar amnesia** is the loss of memory about one specific event.
- **Childhood amnesia** (also known as infantile amnesia) is the common inability to remember events from one's own childhood. Whilst Sigmund Freud attributed this to sexual repression, others have theorized that this may be due to language development or immature parts of the brain. This is often exploited by the use of false memories in child abuse cases.

Well, well, do wonders ever cease to amaze? I certainly hoped not because after hanging up, I was overcome with an unfamiliar state of euphoria. I wanted to jump up, click my heels and yell "Yippee!" I talked myself out of the jump and kick and settled on the "Yippee!" After all, I was way past a youthful twenty-year old and I certainly wasn't Dorothy, lost in the Land of Oz and needing to get back home to Kansas.

I was amped up! What I really needed to calm down was a glass of Pinot Noir and a short nap, in that order . . . and so I did.

* * *

Later that evening as I pondered the earlier events, I reasoned that the only male person I knew named Bayonne had to be my cousin, Harold. I was aware that he had been struggling with health issues, particularly after Katrina[7] in 2005. I had met Harold Bayonne Jr. only a few times; the very first time was in October 2002 during a family business meeting. At that same meeting I also met his sister Annette. Later, in July 2003, at our first family reunion (on my mother's side of the family), I was reacquainted with Harold as well as meeting his other sisters, Carol, Jacqueline and Patricia (Pat). I couldn't recall meeting any other Bayonnes at the reunion; nor was there any mention of any others at that time.

I know what I'll do, I mused. *I could always rely on my wife to jog my memory. I'm gonna ask Janice. She's good at remembering and reciting family histories. Guess I'll just have to wait 'til tomorrow when I meet this mysterious man who answers to the name, Jules Bayonne. Janice didn't know any more than I did. She must have been having as good a time as I was. I thought I was the only one 'meeting and greeting' with my never empty rocks glass of Johnny Walker Black* (without *the 'rocks,' of course).*

* * *

Mr. Harris, a soft-spoken tall, slender African-American man of about six-foot, three or four inches, roughly forty years old with a warm smile

---

7   Hurricane Katrina caused catastrophic damage in the Gulf Coast area, claiming the lives of more than 3,000 people and displacing hundreds of thousands of residents of Louisiana and Mississippi in September 2005.

and friendly demeanor met with me entering the restaurant. I could have picked him out of a crowd. His appearance matched his voice to "a tee," as my mother would say.

His soft hand greeted me with a hardy, firm handshake as he began to get directly to the point for our meeting. "Mr. Coleman, I don't quite know where to begin to tell you about this case. The patient has given us permission to release and discuss his details with you; however, I am not certain we have full legal clearance due to Mr. Bayonne's state of mind."

I assured Mr. Harris that I would do whatever I could to help and that the events to this point had me quite interested.

Although I had offered to help in any way, a looming thought continued to needle me. *Why on earth am I involved in this thing with Harris, Bayonne, or whomever? If this guy was Cousin Harold, his sisters, whom I assumed were alive and well, knew a heck of a lot more about him than I did. I'd met the man less than a handful of times!*

We followed the host to our seats located in the rear of the restaurant and were handed a couple of menus, impressively designed to match the restaurant's, equally designed 'to impress' blue and gold interior. The intrigue of meeting Jeffrey Harris had stymied me briefly and the mounting, unexplainable apprehension that I alone seemed to possess made reading the 'impressive' menu relatively unimportant.

As if anticipating my first question, Harris took the lead by, saying: "He was brought to us by a local ambulance service in response to a 911 emergency call on Sunday evening about 4:25 pm from a resident living in Atlanta, somewhere near Turner Field. The caller reported a man lying on the ground next to the sidewalk in front of their home. It had been raining most of the day and Mr. Bayonne was admitted through our emergency entrance, wet and barely conscious. We feared he was in shock from hypothermia so our medical team treated him based on his apparent symptoms. He was administered oxygen throughout the night and by midnight, according to the nurse on duty; he began to regain consciousness and seemed to express some objection to the sounds and visual discomfort he was experiencing from the television. The nurse assumed that the programming of the local celebration at Underground Atlanta was too loud and, used the bedside remote control to lower the volume. Immediately, Mr. Bayonne began to protest loudly in a mixture of what seemed to be French and English, "S'il vous plait, s'il vous plait, stop it!" Not knowing what else to do, the nurse called in one of the resident doctors and an intern to help calm Mr. Bayonne from what appeared to be a hysterical episode. He was given a mild sedative which was enough to calm him without the need to forfeit his 'alertness.' Our late-shift nurse, Jeanette DuBois, who could also speak French, spoke with him at length, and was able to explain to him how he ended up in the hospital. This somehow seemed to put him at ease and he soon drifted off into a peaceful sleep, without further incident."

Finding just the right moment to interrupt Harris, I asked, "Where does Mr. Bayonne come from? Is this why I was called at my home around 7:45 am on New Year's Day?"

"Now Mr. Coleman, (Harris obviously sensed my impatience) one of our senior medical staff members, Dr. Paul Garnett, asked if I could join him as a professional observer along with several other members from our Emma I. Darnell Geriatrics Center and Psychological Services while interviewing Mr. Bayonne."

Well, if I didn't learn anything else that day, I learned why the facility was sometimes referred to as Grady Health Systems, where Mr. Bayonne was a patient, which is separate from the hospital's primary care facility, Grady Memorial Hospital.

Our lunch hadn't even been ordered before the predictable happened: Harris excused himself to take a call on his mobile phone, but not before shooting me an apologetic look before rising from the table and stepping away to complete the call in private. It was as if he was trying to get my approval before conducting what I could only guess was a necessary part of his taking care of business . . . *The 'hallmark' of a true professional.*

"Mr. Coleman, please accept my apology for the interruption. I forgot to turn my phone off at noon. Everybody *knows* that I turn it off between noon and one thirty, so you can imagine my surprise when it rang."

Hmm, seemed as though I wasn't the only one who forgets to turn off their phones when they don't want to be disturbed!

"Anyway, as I was saying, I arrived at the hospital on New Years' day at 9:00 am for briefing with the doctors and was delighted to see an alert and awakened patient at 9:25 am. His vitals were checked and aside from a slightly higher than normal blood pressure reading, we began to talk to a relatively healthy African-American male, who appeared to be approximately fifty-five to sixty years of age. The doctors recorded no visible signs of physical trauma or injury. Dr. Armand Monroe, one of the three doctors conducting the initial interview was the first to introduce himself and offer his hand to Mr. Bayonne. The patient responded in a like manner. 'Bayonne,' he replied, as he leaned forward and offered his own hand in response to Dr. Monroe's welcoming gesture. Dr. Monroe paused, as if he was unsure what he should do next. His response, or more accurately stated, his lack thereof; and I'm only surmising here, was that given the patient's state upon his admission, Monroe was surprised he was so alert, let alone be able to carry on a *cogent conversation*. On the other hand, perhaps he was hoping to ease the subtle tension his mundane questions appeared to be causing everybody in the room. It very well may have been to give the other two doctors an opportunity to assist with the inquiries. The other doctors seemed content to allow Monroe to continue. I began to wonder why they were there in the first place, since their presence offered 'nada.' After a few awkward moments of silence, Dr. Monroe started to speak again, continuing his attempts to explain the oddity of the situation to this point."

"How old are you?" Monroe asked.

"Fifty-nine," Mr. Bayonne replied.

Dr. Monroe continued, "Additionally, he told us that his last memory had been of being very tired and lying in his bed going to sleep."

"When was this—on what day?" I asked.

"He told us that it had been on Friday evening, shortly after sundown." Harris paused a moment, as if he expected more questions from me before he continued.

"Though a remarkably cooperative patient, it was obvious Mr. Bayonne's attention was focused on the TV to such an extent that he was actually taking over the interview; if the truth be told. He inquired if the box, he repeatedly referred to as a 'bwat' on the wall was some type of weapon. The term he used for it was 'zam.' He seemed unusually curious about everything; especially the 'bwat' on the wall, which suggested to the staff that he had never seen a television before and did not know what its purpose was. He had previously observed the hospital staff or the nurses using the remote control to mute the volume, change channels and turn the television on and off. I was convinced he had reasoned that the remote control unit held special and unusual powers because he whispered to me asking me to tell that the *'woman,'* (the nurse) not point the 'device' in his direction. He acted as if the hospital was foreign to him referring to these unfamiliar 'lights, bells and voices' coming from walls and ceilings. I called Nurse Barnett in, and with her assistance, explained to Mr. Bayonne how the remote control device was part of the television unit. He asked detailed questions regarding the invention of television, transmission of the programs, the relationship of radio and electricity and just about everything else we cover in the two-hour session we'd set aside for his initial interview. Still, the caliber of his questions prompted us to ask where he was from, whereby; Mr. Bayonne then told us he resided in Livonia, Louisiana."

Harris paused as the server brought two glasses of water and while placing them on the table, introduced herself with the smile and cordial manner expected of her.

"Hello, my name is Olivia and I will be your server. Are you gentlemen ready to order or do you need a few more minutes to think about it?"

I fumbled through the menu and apologetically I asked, "Do you have fried catfish fillet on the menu?"

"Yes, and it is a very good choice!" Olivia pointed to the item on the menu as she spoke.

Duh, why'd I ask such a stupid question? It's right there on the menu: Catfish with Fries, prominently printed in English. . . . guess this news about Jules Bayonne affected me more than I was likely to admit.

"Then I'll have the catfish—but can I substitute fried okra for the French fries?" I blurted, as I returned the menu to our finely covered, linen table top.

This time Olivia only nodded an assent. But still, she maintained that gorgeously brilliant smile of hers. I guessed it was because she was sparing me the embarrassment of her having to again point out what I wanted was already on the menu.

Double Duh! Again, all I wanted to know was on the menu . . . all I had to do was to follow the asterisk which clearly indicated that the French fries could be substituted with fried Okra.

Well, anyway, I still felt kinda proud of myself, that I'd chosen vegetable over potatoes. But then who am I trying to fool? Potatoes or okra, both dishes were 'fried' and had to be drained of excess grease before serving.

"I'll have the crab cake lunch special and a Dasani—thank you." Harris said, offering both of our menus to the server.

Hastily, Harris began speaking again as if he expected another interruption might further 'high jack' the rest of what he needed to share with me before he could finish. "Now that leads me to the point of how we were able to find you: One of the nurses, Emily Mack, conducted an online white pages search for *'Bayonne'* in Louisiana. About thirty minutes later she returned to apologize for not having found anything in Livonia or Point Coupee Parish except for a minor reference to a fictional place called *Bayonne, Louisiana,* utilized in several writings by an author[8] currently residing in Oscar, Louisiana. This online search led us to your company's website and ultimately, to your business phone number. I apologize again, for any inconvenience we might have caused you, but we were desperate to get any information on who initially seemed to be a 'John Doe.' It might surprise you how many of these 'John' and 'Jane' individuals actually show up on our 'doorsteps' over the course of a year! So, it's not too hard to see why we try to locate family and friends as expediently as possible!"

"Mr. Harris," I took a deep breath and asked a question I wasn't sure I wanted answered. "Do we know Mr. Bayonne's full name?"

Harris hesitated for a moment as if he were trying to recall the name which had momentarily evaded him and said, "I think he said his name is Jules Bayonne."

Before I knew it, I blurted, much louder than I had intended, a whole slew of the most awful profanities that you only think aloud to yourself! *Was this all a big joke? If so, I found no humor in it! At all!*

Harris shot me an astonished look, and leaned back, away from the table. *I wasn't sure if he were ready to 'fight or take flight.' I don't think he'd made up his mind to do either, given my sudden explosive rant. Hell, I wasn't*

---

8 Referring to writer, Ernest J. Gaines, Pointe Coupee Parish, Oscar, Louisiana.

even sure what my next 'move' should be! Fortunately, I made a 'speedy recovery' which must have encouraged Harris to continue.

"Mr. Coleman, I apologize for offending you, as your reaction suggests that I somehow find this whole situation humorous or that we are attempting to make you the butt of some horrific practical joke. I assure you, that it is not my intention. Certainly, I don't find humor in this situation nor am I given to playing the 'Joker.' We just need some help in trying to find out how we may solve this quandary—Mr. Bayonne insisting he knows nothing of his family in Atlanta or how he arrived in the city, and so on. However, considering what Mr. Bayonne told us, and now, what you seem to be implying, I should be more shocked than you are, having now heard both sides of this incredible story directly from you and Mr. Bayonne!"

"No apology is *necessary* from you Mr. Harris," I reasoned a little less excited. "Please excuse my poor choice of words. Profanity is one my many bad vices—I should exercise better self-control." Still 'smarting' from my outburst and thinking about how glad I was my Momma would never learn about it, I continued my redress in the most apologetic tone I could muster while still trying to absorb the embarrassment of my previous action. "Please, let me explain, if I may. It's just that a person by the name of Jules Bayonne happens to be my great-great grandfather," I murmured.

"What?" Harris exclaimed. Disbelief was written all over his face: "Mr. Coleman, one of the reasons I wanted to meet with you before bringing you to meet with Mr. Bayonne is, he insists that he fell asleep at his home Thursday, the 20th."

"Well", "he *has* been away from home for a few days, I guess." *I rationally assumed he was referring to December 20, 2006.*

"No!" You don't understand, he insisted he fell asleep on Thursday, August 20th 1903! Does this make any sense to you?"

Holy Moly! Move over Christian Horn, I'm comin' over the rim!

Olivia returned with our meals. I hardly noticed her reappearance or what was on the plate she set before me, I stared at Harris. *How could any of this make sense? It didn't even make sense that I was entertaining the possibility that any of all this could even warrant the 'possibility' question!*

Trying to answer my own question, I reasoned that this man might be one of Jules Bayonne's—my great, great grandfather's descendants;⁹ perhaps a great-grandson I had yet to discover. Certainly there had to be a reasonable explanation as to this man's true identity, but deep down inside my mind, I *knew* there were no others in the family bearing that name.

I had difficulty blessing my food as I wondered when I would get something of importance (*that I could believe*) from this lunching date, as Harris had turned to making small-talk about everything except Jules Bayonne. *He probably thought it was a lot safer to talk about anything else, now that he had twisted my mind! Besides, what else could he say, given the 'bombshell' I just laid on him?*

As much as I loved catfish and fried okra, especially the way it was prepared it at Afrodish's; I might as well as have eaten a nondescript variety of cardboard of unknown origin after hearing Harris' wild story.

We finished our meal and in my foggy state-of-mind I thought I heard Harris say we would visit Mr. Bayonne briefly today in an attempt to find some answers to him and his staff's questions with my help. As the minutes clicked by, I slowly returned to the 'land of the living.' It became clear that I'd heard Harris correctly. He was very keen on the idea of havin' me accompany him to his afternoon visit with Mr. Bayonne—Just as I'd hoped.

"Well, Mr. Coleman, ready to go meet the Mysterious Jules Bayonne?" I nodded a gleeful assent, even though I'd lied to Harris about his inquiry concerning if I had enjoyed the catfish. The truth of the matter was that this Jules Bayonne thing had invaded all of my senses, having waged a personal attack on my taste buds—quite a coup, given my finely tuned, sensitive palate. *Besides, my Mom had taught me to always be gracious to the host, especially when they were paying a hefty price for the meal. I didn't see the bill, but I'm convinced it cost a pretty penny. At Afrodish, even its hamburgers started at $20; and that was lunch special price!*

Harris looked at his watch and started to get up from the table as if he had something pressing to do. I anticipated his next move as he spoke saying: "Mr. Coleman, I have to get back, now. I will be sure to see that

---

9   The author had noted that the 1900 U.S, Census provided for an eight-year old son of Jules Bayonne listed as Ferdinand, later detailed as Jules François Ferdinand Bayonne, born October 4, 1881. The initial thought was that "Ferdinand" had children and grandchildren bearing the name Jules Bayonne. Note that Ferdinand had no recorded offspring.

you are given the tour the facility by one of our more senior staff people. That will give us enough time to prepare for your initial meeting with the Jules Bayonne. There are a few things we must agree to before you are allowed to talk to Mr. Bayonne. As I stated before, he was found without identification and due to the abnormal behavior he has demonstrated; he may be subject to mental stability testing administered by state social services. We have scheduled a series of examinations and any references in discussions that may excite him or adversely impact the progress made by the doctors must be avoided. Therefore, for the time being, we ask that you not refer specifically to or address dates or imply that he might be related to you as an elder family member. Based upon what I've already told you, you can imagine how fragile the patient might be and how delicate a situation the hospital is relating to Mr. Bayonne. I think and hope you can understand and appreciate our position and the care we are taking for Mr. Bayonne's well-being."

"Rest assured Mr. Harris; I fully understand and respect your situation in this matter. As a matter of fact, for me to breach any confidence you've shared by suggesting to him that he might be my great-grandfather might cause him to wonder why I'm not in the hospital, instead of him; especially since it's evident that we're around the same age. On further note, I also find that such a suggestion would be impossible since *my* ancestor named Jules Bayonne died on August 20th 1903 at the age of fifty-nine!"

As adamant as I secretly pretended that Mr. Bayonne's implication was not possible, the idea was so maddening that I wondered if someone were watching me at this moment would conclude that I was gullible and/or crazy for even considering the possibility that this situation had the slightest degree of merit *(possibility)*. I believed only *black and white*—no *gray* areas—in anything. If it couldn't be seen, touched, tasted, heard or smelled, then it (except for God, Himself) simply didn't exist! Well, at least that's what life meant and held to me and for me—calculable, explainable, orderly and logical. Oh, I had considered the scientific likelihood of parallel universes and the studies conducted by Einstein, but as usual, I quickly dismissed the notion: I was NO EINSTEIN I had no trouble dismissing the thought, *at least that's all I was 'copping to.'* If it were possible, then someone like Hawking or Sagan,[10] obviously would have already discovered how it came to be. Not Jeffrey Harris, and for sure, not me. No matter, I concluded, but the strange thought persisted . . . Could this event fit the description of something like 'The Grandfather Paradox?' As I mulled over the question, I thought to myself, I, much like Prince Hamlet's friend, Horatio, could not rationally accept this sort of being as part of my 'philosophy' as readily after those eerily famous words echoed in my head— **"There are more things in heaven and earth, Horatio, Than are dreamt of in your philosophy."**[11]

As 'out of kilter' as I was at that moment, mental clarity competed robustly for factual stability. Suddenly, I was reminded of reminiscing; only a few days earlier of the completion of one of my high schools' class review of Shakespeare's play! *Coincidence? A premonition? Or, I had become the perfect candidate for a modern-day 'haunting?'* I hoped none of this was true, especially the latter. *My 'tough guy' persona has been suspect at times and subject to challenge. This just might be one of those times.* I believe in the existence of the spirit world, but I don't play around with that stuff!

"Come on now! This is a bit of a stretch (even for my imagination)!" I muttered half to myself and to whomever else, seen and unseen who might have heard me. *I'm still 'tripping!'*

I even recalled that I had once watched a documentary on the Science Channel, and that Mallett[12] had said that our universe would not be affected by what one does when visiting the past. But what about when one visits the future? My understanding was fair with regard to the 'Grandfather Paradox' in the world of physics, however, I wasn't prepared for *this* puzzle, presenting itself in the personage of my great-great grandfather, one Jules Bayonne. What if there was an intrinsic divine order guiding *all* life? What

---

10   Renowned scientists, Stephen William Hawking and Carl Edward Sagan are referred to by the author in an attempt to note their incomparable abilities in solving difficult issues, particularly as related to supernatural concerns.

11   Hamlet Act 1, scene 5, 159–167, William Shakespeare. Hamlet is confronted by the ghost of his father, the King, now joined abruptly by Horatio and Marcellus.

12   Ronald Mallett, University of Connecticut, Professor of Physics. Dr. Mallett was inspired to study 'time travel' when he was ten years old after witnessing his father's death from a heart attack.

if the statement made so often by Napoleon Hill[13] (*Whatever the mind of man can conceive and believe, it can achieve*) could be taken literally? *What if Jules Bayonne turned out to be 'proof' of Hill's oft quoted statement?*

Although, I was not aware whether proof existed regarding the concept of moving between and within the time and space dimension being a possibility, my faith was founded on the principle that spirit beings exist. And it was my faith that troubled me the most. It was my very faith which alluded to the idea that those very spirit beings created everything and *moved* among and between periods of time. Again, it was my faith that suggested we humans possess *some* of the elements of the deities our beliefs are founded upon. Therefore, the possibility of Jules Bayonne's present day appearance, in the flesh could at least, be a consideration.

I read where Dr. King, in his 1959 book,[14] in summarizing the sermons he had preached the prior year, contended that the mind of man is so marvelous as to afford him the ability to '*travel*' from the present to the past and into the future, employing his own imagination as his vehicle.

Here we go again, I thought to myself. *Would you listen to me—stuff ramblin' around inside my head. Shakespeare, Mallett, Hill and now King? I felt like a fool—no, more like a certifiable idiot!*

The fact of the matter was that I couldn't explain why I was having all of these strange thoughts about time travel and alternate dimensions. In addition to this strange pattern of thinking were the increasing episodes of detailed 'flashbacks' to my past. I could not get them out of my mind. The more I tried to clear my mind, the more thoughts of how *this* could be possible would creep in and dominate my thoughts.

Because of the anemic status of my personal debts and liabilities, incurred in the last few years' business cycle downturn, I had become reluctant to communicate with many of my creditors. Actually, I had successfully managed to avoid them altogether. So, I wondered if this strange set of events was the result of some elaborate scheme by collectors to catch up with me. *Paranoia? I might as well throw in the 'Conspiracy Theory' as well!* I

---

13 Author, journalist, and attorney Napoleon Hill (10-26-1883-11-8-1970) writer of Law of Success, Think and Grow Rich and Success Through a Positive Mental Attitude.

14 *The Measure of a Man* Martin Luther King Jr. 1959 "... This is man. He is God's marvelous creation. Through his mind he can leap oceans, break through walls, and transcend the categories of time and space." (page 18)

became sickened with the mounting suspicion and thought I would not be able to make the twenty-minute walk back to the hospital without *losing my hastily-eaten lunch along the way*. I hoped that the underlying cause of my feeling slightly ill was because I was trying to keep up with Harris' brisk pace. I didn't dare ask him to slow down; even a tad, even though it was obvious that he was in much better shape than me, *Just look at what the guy had for lunch: crab cakes which were probably baked, though I don't know that for sure; and bottled water. Besides, I don't think Harris would take too kindly to my regurgitating that pricey lunch he'd paid for not even a half hour earlier. . ... Talking about making a bad first impression!*

I had never experienced such intense anxiety before. Could all of this stuff be happening to me as a result of my own personal stress? Of course, the inevitable and immediate meeting with the man who might turn out to be my long ago, deceased great-great-grandfather greatly contributed to my present state.

So now, the meeting with the *patient* was set to happen shortly. The closer we came to the Grady Memorial Hospital, the more it seemed the earth under my feet gave way. I moved clumsily towards our journey's end as though I were walking on a cushioned surface. The concrete sidewalk eerily absorbed my footfalls which suddenly gave way to a strange silence, despite the fact that a noisy world was 'carrying on busy as usual' all around me. Just as suddenly, the extreme anxiety I had been experiencing just moments earlier melted away, almost without notice. It felt good. *I hadn't experienced such calmness for a long time. Decades had passed since I ceased to meditate daily, yet an involuntary, but much welcomed calmness took me back to those peaceful, uncomplicated days in my past.* I smiled a 'thank You, Jesus. Amen!'

Perhaps it was the faint fragrance of 'remembrance' that had sneaked in to permeate the air—the enchanting smell of the sweet olive shrubs, intermingled with rose blossoms which catapulted my memories to the Garden District in New Orleans during the 1970's. It was that familiar smell *that* reminded me of those wonderful, lofty sessions I attended to learn the meditation technique I had all but abandoned by now, some thirty-four years later. The pleasant rush of memories added to the euphoria I was experiencing as we approached the hospital's front steps. Nevertheless, I was mesmerized and haunted by my past, yet strangely aware of events and places I had never personally visited or been a part of before.

Harris had been kind enough not to do much talking or at least much that had required a response on my part. I'm sure it was because he couldn't help but notice my somewhat labored breathing. Or maybe I'd just been too caught up with my own ruminations that I'd tuned everything out, including him.

Harris' easy conversation about the changes in the area surrounding the hospital and Sweet Auburn may also have contributed to the comfortable physical change (including a return to regular breathing) I was experiencing. We arrived at the entrance and all my senses became acute as I walked in unison with Harris as if I knew each step he was going to take. I knew instinctively that we had to check in with Harris' assistant, who would provide me with the promised tour of the facilities, while Harris stopped by his office to check for any important messages, and anything else he needed to do in preparation for our meeting with the legendary, Jules Bayonne.

CHAPTER 3

MAMA SAID THERE'D BE DAYS LIKE THIS

Mr. Bayonne?

We walked in silence as we proceeded to Mr. Bayonne's room. I guessed that all that could be said, had already been said, given the little information we knew about this enigmatic patient. Mr. Bayonne's room was located on a huge winding hallway to the left of the main corridor, not far from where Harris and I reconnected after my tour. I was glad that it wasn't too far from the meeting place, as the short distance we had to travel didn't give rise to the resurgence of my 'shortness of breath' brought on by my trying to match Harris' brisk pace.

After a soft three rap knock, Harris pushed open the door to the patient's dimly lit room. I later learned that the darkness of the room was due to requests made to the hospital staff by our *special* patient. The far west end of the room was inhabited by two young male patients to whom

I paid little attention. My mission and only interest that day was to see this man who called himself Jules Bayonne. I focused immediately on his coarse-textured, gray hair and matching beard and his complexion which resembled smooth caramel. The wear of the years marked his skin at his brow and around the corners of his mouth, but even with the feathered lines, the contours of his face still held firm. Absent was the sagging, leathery flesh I was accustomed to seeing on the face of most aged people. Then I remembered that this man was claiming to be fifty-nine only a few years older than me. That 'fact' had somehow eluded me for a moment, as I had reverted back to thinking he had to be a much older man if in fact he truly was my great-great grandfather. As I drew closer to the man, a new panic welled inside of me. I wasn't sure what to make of all this, now that I was actually in the presence of this anomaly who called himself Jules Bayonne.

Jeffrey Harris stood just behind me, whispered softly, yet audibly enough to stir the man reclining before us.

"Mr. Bayonne?"

The man opened his eyes slowly and peered directly at me and said, "How many doctors will I need to see today?"

He looked a bit groggy. I supposed he was probably still experiencing the effects of the sedatives used to calm him down. I struggled to get the response out and after stammering clumsily, I finally blurted.

"I am *not* one of the doctors!"

He raised his head slightly and spoke softly with a confident voice: "I had a pretty good notion dat you were not, somehow, but den . . ." After an unusually long pause, he continued speaking. "You seem very familiar to me, somehow. So, den, if you are not a doctor, den am I to assume you are *da* person da doctors insisted dey would find to help me determine wat is happening to me?" *His statement was unanticipated in view of the caution and prohibitions Harris had warned me about earlier. No, it was not directly a question having to do with dates or implying that he might be related to me . . . but . . . close enough. I don't think Harris anticipated Mr. Bayonne's response to meeting me for the first time either. Now what was I supposed to do?*

Before I could respond, Jeffrey Harris intervened. "Mr. Bayonne, this is Mr. Coleman, a very considerate gentleman, also a native of Louisiana.

I contacted him hoping that he as a fellow Louisianan, could help us locate your folks. Meanwhile we will continue to use our best efforts to locate your family."

Hoping my awkwardness was not obvious to everyone, I hurriedly added, "Mr. Bayonne, I believe I know some of your *people*."

The Twilight Zone— *'Over the Rim'* episode ricocheted, wildly in my head. It was as if it were hollow, with nothing to stop the incredulous 'emptiness' and 'ping pong' effect of time and space. I didn't know where to go from here; particularly as I attempted to formulate some meaningful questions for the old man. Old man, it occurred to me at that moment, he's probably only a few years older than me. But that's not possible! I have a photo of . . . I needed to look at the photo once more, as if that would solve what I knew to be true. The photo was decades, if not hundreds of years old; but the man whose presence is now, lying in a hospital bed is in the present; and not some decades earlier. *This is more than weird because he is the man in the photo! Despite my doubts and fears, I knew sooner or later, I would have to show the photo to Harris. Even more frightening: who's going back over the rim. . . . him or . . . me?*

In a way, I was glad Harris had set out the guidelines of what I could and could not discuss with Bayonne because it allowed me to get a closer look and to make some observations; but not necessarily any sense, of this whole situation . . .

I studied this individual purporting to be Jules Bayonne with the intensity of solving a calculus problem. I couldn't be certain because he was partially reposed on his hospital bed, but he did not appear to be much more than two or three inches taller than me (*and in substantially better physical condition*). He 'sported' a well-groomed beard which was a bit more than an inch long at the point just covering his throat. His hair had been recently cut, as evidenced by its deliberate sharpness that framed his face and ended in a linear perfection at the back of his neck. I noted how he used his well-manicured hands to accent his essence as a man of few, but well-spent words. My mama used to refer to these types of individuals as 'those genteel folks.' The confidence he exuded told me he was accustomed to being highly respected and was no 'stranger' to sharing the presence of a room full of other *men of means*. In short, he appeared to be one who had possibly possessed a fair degree of material wealth, and for certain he was *not* destitute or homeless as I was led to believe. All my observations, though cursory, suggested that another layer of mystery had just been laid . . . And I wondered: *How in the Hell did he end up here?*

Much too briefly, my time with Mr. Bayonne was over. As I extended my hand to shake his as I was preparing to leave, he attempted to get out of bed. *At that moment, I could hear Momma's voice bragging an "I told you so . . . another sure sign he be one of them 'genteel folk.'"*

"Mr. Bayonne, please stay put, don't get up! There'll be plenty of time for us to stand on ceremony at our next meeting. No pun intended." We laughed at this shared bit of humor.

"When might dat be? He questioned"

I know you have a lot of questions for me and I have much I want to ask you as well. I didn't mention this earlier, but you probably do know some of my people. And, I have to admit, you look familiar to me too. But I still didn't want to admit I had a photograph of him when he was at the age he claimed to be in the present day.

"Yeah, I saw dat look on your face wen you walked into da room dat seemed to say: I've seen dis man before, I just can't recall when or where, right now." *He was correct . . . but I still kept silent about that photograph. Besides, how could I ever address any questions that this bit of info most certainly would generate? I'd made a wise decision by keeping my mouth shut!*

"Well, Mr. Harris has informed me that you're going to be transferred to Riverwoods Psychiatric Center's inpatient program for an extended evaluation. That's great because the Center is located in Clayton County, a bit closer to home. So, I will be back by Friday afternoon, once you get settled in at the treatment facility."

He softly spoke again, this time with a question, "Can one of you arrange for a message to be sent to my wife, Victorine at home, telling her where I am and dat I will be home to see her soon?" I looked at him with a reassuring stare, but hesitated to answer. *Had he remembered where he lived? I wondered why he didn't ask for someone to telephone his wife earlier instead of 'arranging for a message to be sent to her.'*

I left Mr. Bayonne's room with what seemed to be thousands of thoughts bombarding my mind all at once. That 'ricocheting' effect was again trying to resurface; for the second time today. *Perhaps if I left the hospital, my brain could relax and things would return to 'normal.'* On that note, I hurried down that long, curved hall to the hospital's main entrance.

As I exited the hospital I didn't know what to think or feel, for that matter. My first encounter with Mr. Bayonne was very impressive, however, still a bit more than unsettling.

One thing for certain, this man was not my cousin, Harold Bayonne—the man I had half-heartedly expected to see.

* * *

Where Am I and Where Do I Go From Here?

I panicked for a moment as I perused the hospital's parking lot looking for my car. Then I remembered, wishing it weren't so, that I had that twenty-minute trek back to the restaurant's parking lot where I'd left my car during my lunch with Harris. *Undoubtedly, it's going to take longer to get back than it did reaching the hospital, now that I was walking at my own pace and not trying to keep up with Harris' 'briskness.'* On the other hand, it's better this way because I had to try to mentally digest what just happened: *My first visit on the afternoon of January 3rd, 2007 with Mr. Bayonne, the most fascinating person I had ever met, marked the beginning of a profound personal change in my life, and unmatched to this date.*

Finally, before I knew it, and much to my surprise and delight, I was back at Afrodish's. I was glad I had only to press the hand held remote control to locate my car in Afrodish's now-packed parking lot. The alarm located my car; my second press of the remote opened my car's door. And, finally as I was on my way home, thoughts from my past began to flood my consciousness.

I had achieved many successes in the last thirty or so years of my professional career and as would normally be the case for a 'go-getter' personality, I had also experienced a number of failures, particularly after 2001. It seems that the impact of the terrorist attack against America on September 11th had adversely affected more of us, who initially thought the event would not have *a more enduring effect, than we thought. So, this wrestling with these economic cycles greatly contributed to my personal bouts with life's ups and downs, now compounded with the angst of worldwide threats. I was a 'mess' by anyone's definition. I suppose the last six years would have defined my professional business performance as mediocre at best. The fact that I had generated so little money in that period directly caused an anemic free-fall of my self-esteem. (Thank God for Janice. She never complained, was always supportive—both physically and spiritually. In her eyes I was still 'King of the Castle' and she took every opportunity to tell me and show me that this was her own personal truism (regardless of whatever anyone else said or thought!)*

As a result of my pitiful state of mind, in my weak attempt at a resolution to not get involved with complicated issues, and to avoid other people's problems, I had decided to do as little creative work as possible. No doubt, the decision to selfishly minimize contact with the world played a significant role in my own (mind's eye) seemingly insurmountable challenges. Nevertheless, the new change for the coming year, based on my self-determined *rules of resolution* required that I communicate with no one until after Monday, January 1st 2007—for which I had already reneged!

Presenting this next comment will sound a bit cliché, but I know you've *'heard that one before!'*

Suddenly my mind turned to thinking about my recent 'telephone' experience; I *too*, had heard stories of how a phone call to a person at the most precise time saved that person's life. They'd been contemplating some grisly act—suicide, or maybe murder when, just as the person was about to . . . , the ring of the telephone distracted their contemplated action(s); and the telephone, or at the very least, the person calling became the 'hero' of the day! Perhaps it was the mere sound of the ringing interruption of the phone call that might have altered the course of events of that time. Maybe such diversions caused a chain of events yielding a substantially different outcome from what might have otherwise occurred if there had been no diversion, such as *that* timely phone ring. And although, in my case, this incident (Harris' phone call) would prove to be far from being a life or death situation, I must confess to you I was not prepared for either the magnitude nor the impact this simple, annoying phone call would have on my life's 'present' . . . or future. Nor would I have ever dreamed that this occurrence would subsequently impact future events affecting several other people I had not yet come to know.

* * *

Home at last . . .

The remainder of the evening was not without incident, as I returned home to learn that the driver of a delivery truck attempting to back into my neighbor's driveway to return to the main road had accidently struck a utility pole, disabling a relay transformer and rendering a few residents in the subdivision without electricity . . . Somehow my home was not affected. For the second time that day, I again found myself thanking God for the little nicety of sparing me the inconvenience of having to search for flashlights that had been stowed away in a safe, secret, 'handy place' for just such an unfortunate event as this; not to mention having to endure the nuisance of hearing kids 'belly ache' all evening because they couldn't look at TV or otherwise engage in some activity which required the 'hunky-doriness' associated with the complete dependence on the marvels of modern day electricity.

CHAPTER 4

CHER

"Your people come from the islands"
— Ma Mere-Dolores 1974

Boy, my mind was in overdrive! Crashing between 'now,' 'then' and wherever Mr. Bayonne was from. No sooner had I finished visiting the recent past, which seemed to signal my economic downward spiral when my mind took a few steps back to my meeting with Mr. Bayonne. I had no sooner spoken the words to this man who referred to himself as Jules Bayonne, saying: "Mr. Bayonne, I believe I know some of your *people*," when it occurred to me that those words "your people" had been used before—the meaning of which was more defined by now. My recall of the incident where I had heard those words before poured from the past like the flood which had rushed over the levees during "Betsy."[15]

My mother, Dolores Mae, (née Washington), of New Orleans, Louisiana ... never spoke much about her family—even less regarding her mother's

---
[15] Hurricane Betsy, a category 3 storm affecting the Gulf Coast in 1965

people or her father's people (my grandparents on both sides). Interestingly enough, it never occurred to me to ask her about any of our family, so I was totally ignorant about our family's history, and as a result, I had little knowledge as to our family's origins. (*I jokingly refer to myself as the family historian because even the little I knew was a 'hecka lot' more than any of my sibs knew. Besides that my mother actually discouraged us kids from trying to search our family roots. Whenever it did come up in an accidental comment or conversation, my mother would summarily shut us down with that look we all knew too well: "kids should be seen and not heard!"* I should also add that despite what most Northerners thought about Southern folk, many of us, due to one reason or another were ill-equipped to run through a complete genealogy which 'outsiders' mistakenly thought could be passed down from one generation to another.

But, during the late summer of 1974, during my sophomore year at Southern University, I had just come home from a Saturday afternoon visit at the St. Louis #1[16] in New Orleans, to take photographs of Marie Laveau's tomb[17] I intended to use the photos as part of a class slide show presentation outlining the *Impact of Voodoo Worship in Louisiana*. It was customary for visitors to place ash-marked X's in groups of three on the tomb, believing that Laveau's spirit will grant them a wish. This custom, originally established in 1974, still persists to this present day. However, I did not indulge, opting to *not* leave the X or any other evidence of my visit. After all, I did not subscribe to belief in the custom—at least not at that point (or to that extent, particularly with respect to the 'rumor' that if people wanted Laveau to grant them a wish they should draw an 'X' on the tomb, turn around three times, knock on the tomb, and yell out their wish. If it was granted they had to return to the tomb, circle their X, and leave Laveau an offering—a string of Mardi Gras beads being the most common, animal teeth, spent lipstick tubes, old bus tokens, and other inexpensive trinkets have been served as 'acceptable' offerings). It

---

16   St. Louis Cemetery No. 1 is the oldest and most famous of the three Roman Catholic cemeteries in New Orleans, Louisiana. Opened in 1789, it replaced St. Peter Cemetery as the main burial ground when the city was redesigned after a fire in 1788.

17   **Marie Laveau** (1801?-June 16, 1881?) An American practitioner of voodoo.

all seemed a little too spooky to me and I wanted to get out of there as soon as I got what I came for.

As I entered the kitchen of my mother's house later that day after leaving the cemetery, I found her seated near the doorway leading into the den where she was intensely stitching a friend's wedding dress on her old Sears's sewing machine.

My mother was very often seated at that old sewing machine, particularly on weekends. She seemed to have an endless 'line-up' of projects, whether it was for an upcoming ball, costume party, wedding, or any other 'last minute' event.

My mother looked up from her work long enough to flash me her wonderful smile as she greeted me with her usual, "Hey Cher! How're doing?"

"Real good, mom." I replied as I returned her greeting with a flashy smile of my own.

"I see you've been at it for a while." I could smell the motor burning on that old sewing machine! "It might be a good idea to give that ole thing a break. And you could probably do with a break yourself. You look a little tired."

"Yeah, baby, I am tired a little bit. I been working since early this morning, but I need to finish Cookie's dress before tomorrow morning. Hmph, you should be the one to talk, you sound and look like you're a little run down yourself." Mom replied, in *that* inquisitive tone, she was so good at without actually posing the question.

The *inquisition* had begun. I really didn't want to tell her what I'd been doing, but damn, I hadn't been smart enough to think up a good enough story before I faced my mother. I tried to ease into the subject by explaining how the research for the class project was progressing and in doing so 'tiptoed' cautiously toward the nature of the study. I didn't do as good a job as I had hoped. I could immediately tell that I'd failed. She rose from her sewing machine so quickly I thought the chair she'd been sitting in would crash to the floor. She spun around just as quickly, paying no attention to her upended chair as she glared at me with one of the most frightening expressions of anger I had ever seen on her face. I was expecting her to be upset, but not explosive!

"You keep that voodoo shit outta my house! I don't want to hear it!" My attempt to assure my mother that I had no intention of adopting any cult practices *personally* went nowhere fast! I don't think she even heard my protest that my visit to Marie Laveau's tomb was nothing more than a study for school. Instead, she became more adamant than before, "I don't care what you are doing, I don't want to hear about it!" I knew better than to say anything further on the matter, no matter how 'innocent' it happened to be. All I could do at that moment was to run over to set the chair in its proper position and watch her, feeling like the rejected 'runt-of-the-litter,' as she returned to her sewing task. I ventured no more on the subject. I was looking at her back, but her rigid posture clearly signified what I'd already figured out: "Discussion Closed!"

I decided that changing the subject would be a good idea; and refocused on the dress she was sewing. I could tell by the way she started to explain the upcoming wedding event and the obligation to complete five bridesmaids' gowns and the bride's wedding dress, that all was forgiven. She became calmer . . . apparently all was forgotten as well. Or, maybe it was just because sewing always seemed to soothe her; even though I thought she did too much for too many undeserving people I personally thought took advantage of her. My mother was often the target of somebody taking advantage of her kindness. Oftentimes, she would purchase cloth, design and sew complete garments for others at no charge. She sometimes referred to this 'gratis' benefit as a gift for which God would reward her in one way or another; not to mention the pleasure and respite sewing brought her. Her sewing seemed to offer *her* own form of nirvana. She would look at me with soft, smiling eyes and say to me, "Cher, don't fret. When I'm working at sewing I can, at least for a short time, put life's challenges '*on hold*.'

I took this *perfect time* to beat an apologetic, but somewhat hasty retreat. My mom sighed almost imperceptibly as she moved into my proffered outstretched arms. I knew it wasn't quite safe yet, but I ventured on still shaky ground to bring the subject one more time. I needed to do more than merely change the subject. I needed to say the words. "Mom, I'm sorry to have upset you so much. I really didn't want to tell you what I was doing, knowing how you feel about the subject; but didn't want to lie to you either. I promise to try to never do something that angers you this way again."

* * *

"Your people come from the islands"

My mother stopped sewing, looked at me for a long time, as if she was carefully weighing her words before she finally said, "Cher, I did not mean to yell at you that way, but I want you to know that "***your* people**"[18] come from 'the islands' and they practiced that stuff! They call it a 'religion,' but I don't like that stuff at all! Maybe it's because I don't understand it—and don't want to. But, I can tell you this one thing about it . . ."

. . . Your aunt Bertha and her sister, Shosh (Dorian) both were raised devout Catholics, but they used to get 'advice' " from this old man who lived a few blocks from where we lived on Governor Nicholls Street.[19] One day, your Aunt Bertha decided to go and get some 'advice' from the man and insisted that I go with her. I protested to no avail, and instead, joined her to walk over to this place that had its entrance in an alley between his house and the house next door where roosters and hens were running around loose clapping and flapping and fluttering all over the place. I hung back a little when Aunt Bertha entered the alley and quickly closed the chest-high gate behind her. I didn't want her to go in alone, but I was too spooked to go in with her. This time I 'stuck to my guns' and told her I wouldn't go inside. It was about twenty minutes before she came back out the side entrance of the house, this time accompanied by the old man. I was glad to see her but noticed she

---

18   My people at the time of this discussion (1974) were thought to have been only my biological father and his parents, however by 2003; I came to discover that my "people" were also my mother's people, referring to her maternal grandmother and great grandfather (Bayonne).

19   Governor Nicholls Street is near the downriver end of the French Quarter, in the Treme (historically sometimes called Tremé or Faubourg Tremé) which is a neighborhood in the downtown portion of the city of New Orleans, Louisiana. It is one of the oldest neighborhoods in the city, and early in the city's history was the main neighborhood of free people of color.

had to slow down her usual brisk pace to match the old man's snail-like gait as they approached the gate. He walked slowly but talked loudly. I heard him say to her, 'don't worry about your sister, she's not going anywhere, anyway she's got that bad leg, so she needs you to be there.' Then he peered over the gate, giving me an 'all-knowing' look as he said to me, 'I know you don't believe, but that's okay 'cause I know many things and I know you are pregnant!' I was quick to answer him back saying, 'You got it all wrong this time, I'm definitely not pregnant!' He then smiled and said, Well then, 'It's your Mamman!'

Baby, I couldn't believe that I was with child. I had used every precaution to make sure I wouldn't get pregnant, but when my monthly visitor stopped, I thought about what the old man had told me. I couldn't deny it any longer. He had been right. I was pregnant with you. But, I didn't know I was expecting until I began to show and even then I didn't really believe it until my doctor had me pee in a jar to confirm it. What really bothered me about this is that your aunt (Monalisa) is two weeks older than you! So the old man, who I never found out his name, was right! Me and Mamman was pregnant at the same time!"

I never brought up the subject of voodoo or any religions other than that of Christianity with my mother again. We had many discussions about bible philosophy over the following seventeen years after that Saturday discussion, and I kept my promise about not provoking her to the degree of anger I had witnessed on that summer day in 1974.

The memory of this incident, some thirty-three years ago was vividly reenacted in my head as I walked out of Mr. Bayonne's room at Grady Memorial that early January evening of 2007.

* * *

More Memories of New Orleans

Still, my mind wouldn't let go and return to 'normal.' More memories of New Orleans surfaced in my mind. For the rest of the evening, I was unable to focus on any of the routine tasks I usually performed, almost mechanically; without much thought or problem. Finally, I threw my hands up in awesome surrender. I let the thoughts flow and have 'their way.' I seemed to have a stream of past reflections 'pop' in and out of my mind, beginning with that particular evening which followed my first visit with Mr. Bayonne. It was a new experience for me, but one that I *had* to accept, as they (those reflections) continued for several weeks, and occurred more frequently and intensity. I didn't know it at the time, but 'new' was 'good.' Heck, it was more than 'good!' It was exactly what I needed to jump start my life again and to get back on track!

Ironically, late that evening, I recalled that sometime around December, 2002, I had come across photos taken of me in the Tremé,[20] when we lived in a little yellow duplex on the corner of Ursulines and Villerie Streets. I came across them again, just a few years ago (in 2005) when I took on the long overdue and unrewarding task (until you're finished with it) of cleaning out the attic. I was about to throw them out, thinking that they were just collecting dust, but something told me that that might not be such a good idea after all. It'd just be my luck that as soon as I'd disposed of these photos that no one but me, had looked for or, at for decades somebody would want to know whatever happened to that photo of Uncle 'Who' or Aunt 'That'—which later nominate me to be the 'one' putting out an 'APB' for their 'recovery.' And, I didn't want to have to 'fess up' to my sister, Deborra, who had entrusted those old photos to me for their safe keeping.—even though she was the one who had gotten rid of them in the first place. So, without further thought, I returned them to the well-worn, cardboard box where I found them. I hadn't thought much about them until now, as their 'rediscovery' caused me to recall more of the details surrounding the time and place when and where the photos were actually taken! These thoughts hung onto a persistent lingering, even though I'd put them back where I found them. Much to my dismay, no 'outta sight, outta mind' relief was forthcoming!

---

20 The Faubourg Tremé or as it is more frequently referred to, The Tremé, is not only America's oldest black neighborhood but was the site of significant economic, cultural, political, social and legal events that have literally shaped the course of events in Black America for the past two centuries. http://www.neworleansonline.com/tools/neighborhoodguide/treme.html

My mind drifted back to the time we lived in the corner-end unit of that small creole-style house (duplex) through the end of 1964. Just before planning a visit back to New Orleans, in 1997, I discovered the photo taken of me, around 1961 on the front steps of the house across the street from that little duplex. During that trip to New Orleans, I learned that this house, located in the fourteen hundredth block of Ursulines where I posed on those steps, was once owned by Marie Laveau (the subject of that big 'blowout' between me and my mother during the summer of 1974 concerning the practice of voodoo) . The house had been purchased in the '80's by the African American Museum, located at 1418 Governor Nicholls—which is located just around the corner from the little yellow duplex. It was being restored prior to its suffering extensive damage by hurricane Katrina in September 2005. I am certain my mother never knew she lived across the street from one of the most famous voodoo priestesses of all time. *Did these tidbits of information hold some special meaning? I wondered why they were now becoming so vivid in my recollections of the past.*

Mulling over those old photos, in late 2005 caused me to reminisce about details most people would consider insignificant. Digging through those old photos I thought of things such as, those colorful Arborite or Formica-topped cracked-ice print dining tables with their heavy chrome borders and curved, chrome tubular legs complemented by those six matching padded chairs which were so stylish during the 1950's. I mused at how heavy those things were, not like the cheaply made, but expensive renditions of today's poor excuses of 'fine dining' furniture. Slashed and torn red vinyl upholstery oozed unrefined cotton that seemed to have no end—another testimony as to how well-made those things were. My Great-Aunt Bertha kept her particular dining set, albeit slashed and torn, well into mid-1960. Even after we moved into East New Orleans, just over five miles from our beloved Tremé, I thought that is was unbelievable that in the 1990's anyone would attempt to reintroduce that awful style of dinettes using the retro-pattern. It didn't go over very well the second time either. Nevertheless, it was this detail and others that streamed through my mind which I later learned were necessary to prepare me for upcoming discussions with Jules Bayonne. Still, I wondered why so much of the past fifty years seemed to consume so much of my thinking, particularly since I never experienced a whole lot of 'good old days' between 1954 and 1976 (my entire life up to that point). In other words, not all the 'good old days' were what I experienced as 'good.'

Sometimes, prompted by staring at those old photos, flashbacks heightened my senses of sight, smell, and hearing as I vividly recalled the 1960's and how Lincoln Beach was built for blacks and Ponchartrain Beach for the whites. Signs posted in public places that shouted, "WHITES ONLY" clearly personified the state of segregation in the '60's, and persisted through the 1970's, made it quite clear that separate was not equal. Regardless of the obvious limitations many of us (blacks in the southern states) were exposed to, most of the people we knew experienced similar fond, but oftentimes bittersweet memories of those years growing up in the 'Crescent City.' If you lived in New Orleans during the 1960's, a visit to the French Quarter, fondly referred to as '*Quarter*,' was always a welcomed treat. There, you would literally bask in the unmistakable, delectable aromas of the rich coffee blended with chicory. *You couldn't claim yourself as a New Orleans native* if you didn't know the origins and possess the knowledge of what the *Quarter* is. Although being in the *Quarter* meant different things to different people; but most everybody would agree that the *Quarter* was 'the place that had it going on.' For some of our people at that time, the *Quarter* captured an undeniable and unique 'atmosphere.' 'Street performing,' shining shoes, and the bold and brassy music that emanated from many restaurants and bars hung in the air for *all* to hear and enjoy (even street 'meanderers' like me and my brothers or cousins or some other combo of kith and kin who just happened to be hanging out in the *Quarter* we all loved).

I stared at an old photo of one of my elder cousins enjoying a six and a half ounce Coke which triggered a memory about life in the Tremé. In the 1960's, those who had fewer resources than others found creative solutions to overcoming the lack of money. We often engaged in 'bottle hustlin'' or scavenging the neighborhood for returnable empty soft drink bottles which could provide the finder with enough to get a small candy treat or two. The local grocery store owners would pay as much as two cents for recyclable bottles. Those same grocery store owners decided certain bottles were *not* subject to deposit refunds—at their discretion, of course—still they took (and kept) all of the 'non-refundables' too. Although we knew we were being 'swindled' for pennies, there was little we could do about it anyway. So, there wasn't much reason to kick up a fuss. Instead, we just continued to hustle for empties and hoped for the best, even if that meant we had to share a Coke with one or more of our sibs (kith and kin). The added insult was that often the kids who 'hustled' bottles and endured the scandalous grocery owners' piracy, were *required* to share a Coca-Cola with one or more siblings. But the kids who didn't have to scrounge for 'penny capitalism' seemed to always be able to drink the whole Coke! Funny how staring at that photo of my cousin with the 'Coke' reminded me about the Woolworths on the corner of Canal and North Rampart Streets and how even by 1962, mom said "we couldn't go there for lunch"—a real bummer since mom had been employed in that very kitchen at Woolworths a few years earlier!

The Tremé, my home for the first decade of my life, located west of the French Quarters, melded the cultures of the old city into a mixture of exotic, ethno-cultural soup. The Irish, Jewish and Italian inhabitants infused food, art and other cultural condiments to the existing base of the Creole[21] people, yielded a unique blend of citizens who contributed to the highly magnetic and romantic flavor loved by most who have sampled the taste of the 'Big Easy.'

If the kids in my family weren't hanging out in the *Quarter* or up to some mischief, we made sure we were within earshot of the great-aunts (Bertha, Dorian and Delean, who primarily spoke creole[22]) hoping every now and then they'd let something 'slip out' in English. They spoke creole

---

21 Louisiana Creole is a term used to describe people whose ancestry traces back to the state of Louisiana prior to the territory being acquired by the U.S. in the Louisiana Purchase (1803)—persons descended from the inhabitants of colonial Louisiana during the period of both French and Spanish rule. These people are mainly of French, Spanish, Native American or African heritage or a mixture of these heritages. See footnote 22 below for details related to creole language.

22 Louisiana creole (language) is a French-based vernacular tongue that developed on the sugarcane plantations of what are now southwestern Louisiana (U.S.) and the Mississippi Delta when those areas were French colonies. It had probably become relatively stabilized by the time of the Louisiana Purchase in 1803, although it was later influenced by the Creoles (people) spoken by slaves brought to North America from Haiti (formerly St. Domingue) and the Lesser Antilles by emigrating francophone planters. See footnote 21 above for details related to Creole people.

when excited, agitated, or sometimes simply to discuss topics they didn't want my mother or her children to know about. Those great-aunts frequently spoke about New Roads[23]—often in their creole dialect—so we, kids wouldn't know things they wanted to keep secret. I could never figure out why this topic was such a big deal. Kids don't care about 'no New Roads'! A better topic, at least for me, would have been about the magical allure of sugarcane. Oh, how they loved the taste of raw sugarcane. Although, to me, the raw cane seemed to be nothing more than unpleasant-tasting, non-aromatic sweet grass. However, an almost tribal tie to sugarcane seemed to take up residence in the back of my mind . . . *Sugarcane? Really? Perhaps I was remembering the 'lip smacking' the great-aunts made when savoring this obvious delicacy. Other than the fact that cane sugar was/is an ingredient in Coca-Cola; I saw no connection to the frequency or intensity of the numerous recollections of these past events, people or places which lately, seemed to have captivated me . . .*

My mind continued to 'sprint' back to the past, covering many details I had initially considered to be random and meaningless flashbacks. Yet, I held onto a strong hint that these thoughts must mean *something*; and would serve to remind me of just how much my world had changed in a few short years. The more I thought about the past, the more vivid details about specific events seemed to fight their way to my conscious state of mind. I had narrowed down the point in time to approximately mid-September 2002 when my recall process began to be almost hyperactive. At first, I was a bit unnerved by how increasingly acute these memory 'bursts' became until I slowed the pace down a bit to accept the looming thought that all of this cerebral activity was about to 'come to a head' anytime at any moment. Intuitively, I knew that events about which I knew nothing were about to unfold; and there wasn't a darn thing I could do about it . . . I just wasn't sure if I was ready for the inevitable . . . it didn't matter . . . the inevitable spoke to me clearly: "Ready or not, here I come!"

I had reasoned that perhaps these thoughts were occurring to open a pathway—a kind of necessary *preparation for things to come*, making it

---

23   New Roads (historically French: Poste-de-Pointe-Coupée) is a city in and the parish seat of Pointe Coupee Parish, Louisiana.

easier for the interaction awaiting me with this peculiar personality I had recently come to know as Jules Bayonne.

Maybe I just needed to define what it was to be a "Son of the Creoles" (a phrase used by my mother on many occasions to declare a male descendant from the inhabitants of colonial Louisiana during the period of both French and Spanish rule) in New Orleans during a rapidly changing period. Anyway, I couldn't help but think that maybe this whole thing with Jules Bayonne was one of those unexplained events tied somehow to the supernatural world. But, I had never taken much stock in superstitious stuff and I never allowed myself to dwell on confusing religious theories. So, even the recollection of the voodoo stuff began to make me wonder if there was something I was missing related to this mystery surrounding *our* peculiar visitor. But this, such a puzzling set of circumstances, challenged my sense of logic. How could this be? *This* Jules Bayonne is real and he *is* here!

* * *

PART 2

FOUND IN JULES BAYONNE

CHAPTER 5

COSMIC PERSPECTIVES

On Friday, January 5th I returned to see this mysterious man who insisted his name was 'Jules Bayonne' in his new digs at the River Woods Psychiatric Center. Visiting hours began at 2:00 pm and having arrived promptly, I was promptly led to a room where Mr. Bayonne was sitting in a wheelchair in a private room. *I wonder who's paying for all this. . . . sure hope they're not going to try to make me 'spring' for it!* He looked good, as if had been groomed from head to toe. His hands suggested he had been given a decent manicure and his hair had been recently brushed. One of the on-duty nurses, Mrs. Hayes joked that the old guy was pretty handsome and was worth taking out to a fine dinner now that he 'cleaned up real good.' The room was depressingly dark, lit only by the afternoon sunlight struggling its way through the sheer curtain which barely covered the room's only window. Inadequate as this was, the menial light was enough to cast a golden tone to his face and arms. His skin hue reminded me of a school mate from Andrew J. Bell, Junior High School—we all knew as

'Cherry Top,' a red-headed, light-skinned guy I hadn't seen since 1968. In addition to the age difference, 'Cherry Top's' trademarked red hair was substituted with a distinguished graying, wiry, textured, smoothly combed hair cut—neatly parted above his left ear. I became intrigued with his wily disposition and his choppy southern creole accent, dripping throughout his speech as though he had been personally trained by Samuel Clemens.[24] Maybe the way he spoke further intrigued me as to his origin and, I must admit, I had begun to develop a keen interest in *everything* surrounding Jules Bayonne.

"Mr. Coleman," he announced as I entered his room. He seemed glad to see me and in fact confirmed as much with, "It's good to see you. Come in, please! I promise to be better company for you today—hopefully much better dan wen I last saw you." *No doubt, already I could see that his language usage was more English than French.* "You see, I have been learning quite a bit from da television since I first met you. What a remarkable invention, don't you agree?" *I agreed that it was a remarkable invention; but couldn't quite reach his level of apparent excitement about something I'd been around all my life.*

I slowly replied, "Yes, it is Mr. Bayonne; however, I must confess that, until recently, I hadn't considered how important an invention it really is. TV, as we call it for short, has been around since before I was born. We always had one, so it doesn't hold the same novel entertainment for me as it apparently does for you. But, I understand that you have developed a great fondness for it." He nodded, in acknowledgement then paused for what seemed like several minutes.

Suddenly Mr. Bayonne inquired, "So, do you find da television serves as a necessary source of education too, Mr. Coleman?"

I wasn't exactly sure how to answer his question; I don't think I really understood what he was getting at, but took a chance as I studied his question, and then replied. "I suppose television could be useful with some respects to education, depending on the programming selected. Particularly in the case of the Discovery Channel or the History Channel, perhaps even the National Geographic programs. Though admittedly, I

---

24   Samuel Langhorne Clemens (1835-1910), U. S. author and humorist, wrote under the name of Mark Twain

think we probably tend to use the television more for entertainment than for educational purposes."

I breathed a sigh of relief, as my answer seemed to satisfy him. He deftly changed the subject to a more personal nature. Mr. Bayonne didn't take his eyes off me as he eased into the next question, just as easily as he had changed the subject. "We? I take dat to mean you have family."

"Yes sir, I do," I replied. "My wife, Janice and I have been married for more than thirty years and we have two great children. Derek, our son is the oldest and Erin, our daughter is the baby. My wife is on an extended, but well-deserved cruise with several of her friends and family. I thought it might be a good idea for her to relax and to get away of the routine and sometimes 'hum drum' of everyday life. The kids are away at college. My wife and children pretty much view television for entertainment purposes . . . That leaves me as the 'odd man out' in my household. They even refer to me as the 'odd man out,' among other things. I personally enjoy educational programs, particularly the history presentations."

Mr. Bayonne repeated an earlier comment. "What a remarkable invention!" He then queried, "Hey, do you understand how it works enough to explain it to me?" I almost chuckled out loud. I had misjudged the old guy. He wasn't yet done with talking about the TV.

"I don't know that I understand exactly how it works, but I'll do my best. Can you understand how a photograph is made?" He responded with an astonished look on his face. "Well yes, I suppose I understand, since I have had some experience wit photography. But da motion and sound . . . and da colors! How is it possible to experience today, wat happened days, a week, or many years ago from inside dis device?"

"Actually, with current technology, it is possible to capture up-to-the moment occurrences. I mean things that are happening right now." I continued my attempt to explain. "Mr. Bayonne some of what you see as motion photography was once stored on film somewhere other than this or a similar device; filed for later viewing and then later presented through electromagnetic transmission of a true recording, very similar to that of a still photograph. What you see now is sort of a 'finished product.' When I was growing up, there was no color TV, only black and white, until 1953. And even then, most blacks did not enjoy the luxury of color TV in their homes until the 1970's. When they first became available, they cost over $1,000. There have been significant improvements to the process in more recent years, which lends even more credence to its 'remarkability.' Things usually get more expensive with improvement, but the TV was just the opposite, like I said before, most blacks didn't have a TV in their homes until the 1970's. At that time, depending on the brand, screen size and whether it sat on the table (table model) or the floor (floor model), prices ranged from $125 to over $900. Need I say more about why a lot of people, including whites, didn't have one in their homes? I know I got a little bit off the subject, but it could be that because you made me realize that the TV is more remarkable than I had realized until now. Anyway, the ability to record events and capture the vision and sound has advanced so that now color and accurate sound can be presented by a complicated process of image capturing, storing, recording, transmission and receiving referred to as *digital* processing. Current technologies have made better use of airwaves, satellite transmissions and energy sources which enable us to provide a very accurate image of events, as they occur. The professional people refer to this as *'real time.'* Now, much of what you view from the television are enacted programs, which may or may not represent actual events. Such is the case of previously engaged battles, wars and the like, where all that is true is the written or oral history that is scripted, then acted out before movie cameras by professionals we call actors and actresses. What you have been viewing on the television has been transmissions of moving picture enactments of someone who has written or orally assessed what actually occurred."

Mr. Bayonne stared at me for a moment, nodded his head slowly to show me he comprehended my answer, and then asked, "Do you tink your television's version of history is *accurate* as it relates to da northern states' conquest of da south?"

"Are you referring to the Civil War?"

Mr. Bayonne again nodded; this time with a little more vigor. "Yes, dat's correct! I am referring to the *Civil War!* A history television program, as you refer to it, was recounting some of Uncle Willy's[25] battles just dis morning! It was most impressive!"

I wanted to answer his question sooner than I did, but was so amazed that he had gained so much from a television program; for a minute, I was more pensive than verbal. I wondered *who on earth is Uncle Willy?* I regained some of my composure quickly enough to reply, "I believe that much of what was presented is true, based on the evidence captured in photographs and written accounts in newspaper articles as well as the firsthand reports by the soldiers, inhabitants and the aftermath itself which required so much rebuilding. The television programming you have been viewing is called a 'documentary.' It's based on photographs taken during much of the actual battles which are included as part of the broadcast to serve as recorded evidence required to classify it as a documentary. Although I have to admit there is still some evidence of technological enhancements, specifically added to create an interesting appeal and attraction to the dramatization, for the sake of its viewing audience."

Mr. Bayonne paused before he asked, "You mean such as in da *music* playing? I assure you; I never heard music playing during any of da battles I witnessed. Also, it seems dere was this idea dat dere was tremendous courage by men, who more dan likely was faced wit da kind of uncontrollable fear dat made grown men soil dere pants. My recollection . . ."

His recollection? Was he intimating that he was actually there?

". . . of da events was dat most of dose *boys* was scared to death—not so much wanting to run headlong towards da fire! No, music playing is not wat we heard. But wat I *do* recall hearing is a lot of screaming, wailing and moaning wen young boys, too young to have yet reached da age to be called *sir*, being hit by da barrage of hot metal coming fast and furious from da *other* side!"

I tentatively added to his observations, "Narration by a powerful and convincing voice was added to the enactment and near perfect costumes didn't occur during the actual event, either. I didn't think much about it before, but war *is* a dirty business . . . much too dirty for sustaining

---

25 William Tecumseh Sherman was often referred to by his troops and sometimes slaves expecting the North's victory would secure liberty.

a rationale for those near perfect and pristine uniforms we see in those documentaries."

Mr. Bayonne declared excitedly, his voice filled with what could only be recognized as first-hand knowledge: "Photography is a most fascinating invention! It too, came wit reluctance and superstitious sentiments, however. One of my closest friends, François,[26] refused to have a photograph or a portrait made of himself, insisting dat his soul would transfer to da image. Da most damaging blow dealt to photography may have occurred wen it started to be used in place of artist illustrations and drawings of da war. Da detail captured in da photographs was very troubling for most people *at dat time*, and dese did not even have da color you are using in your television recordings. Even da men who made da invention of da photograph famous from da effects of da war are said to have been cursed by da very souls of da images dey captured. I hear tell many of dem photographer fellas died broke.[27]"

"Those alternative uses of recording—artistic illustrations in particular may appear to distort *how* those events really occurred. The captured images from a camera and the stark reality may appear somewhat different than what is perceived by the artists' rendition. The story teller is often allowed *some* creative *license* to generate interest in some attempts to record an event." Mr. Bayonne rose from his wheel chair, quickly turned away, paced a few steps, and when he faced me again, he did so with a furrowed brow. Instinctively, I knew he was about to parcel out one of his 'nuggets of wisdom.' Unconsciously, I returned my own furrowed brow in anticipation of what I was about to learn from one who had witnessed the gore and the glory of war, first-hand. As if he could read my mind, Jules set me straight on the 'glories' of war: "Da war was not so glorious as dese men make it

---

26   Francis François was a friend of Jules, possibly a relative for whom very little is known, except that Francis François originally was a half interest owner with Jules in the sixty-six acres purchased in Livonia in 1870 as evidenced in the original deed for the property. Later, in 1874, François sold his share to Jules for two-hundred dollars.

27   Jules may have been referring particularly to Mathew Brady. After his exhibit of "The Dead of Antietam" was presented in New York, (October 1862), the shock of the realities of war depicted in the graphic photos of dead soldiers contributed significantly to the loss of interest by the general public in war photography. Records reflect that Brady died penniless in the charity ward of Presbyterian Hospital in New York City on January 15, 1896. His funeral costs and burial in the Congressional Cemetery were paid by the Veterans of the 7th New York Infantry.

seem. Seeing dose young boys take a lead ball to da gut dat blew a hole in dem through and through; or dere arms or legs blasted off as easily as snapping green beans wasn't at all inspiring in a good kind of way. On da contrary, da whole ting of war was horrid! It was heartbreaking just tinking about da loss of all dem young lives; not to mention da devasting effects on der families and even on da land itself! But, on da other hand, I still find it fascinating dat dis invention could conjure da image in such a way to record da war as some glorious and generally accepted event! I find it even more interesting, Byron, dat you seemed to have intentionally avoided da issue of da *soul*. I had hoped you might express your viewpoint, but seems you either didn't pick up on my hint or chose to ignore it."

Jules sat down again and stared at me intently as he waited for my response. I knew I might be on shaky ground; but Jules' stare required—no demand for an answer.

"Now, with regards to the *issue of the soul*, again, your perception Mr. Bayonne is not completely unfounded. Your reference to the souls of those who were photographed—at least of those who were in battle, I suppose you're referring to—so, yes, I sort of avoided the subject due to the degree of my lack of knowledge. That being said, I too, tend to fear the things I don't understand. I have heard that some cultures—certain religious and some tribal groups have indicated that their exceptions to photographing people originate with the '*graven images*' biblical reference; while others believe the nature of the process involved—the manipulation of light in preserving a person's likeness, *removes, depletes or steals* some part of that person's life-force or *soul*. It sounds as if your friend François may have believed this as well based on what you say regarding his refusal to have himself photographed. I personally have a greater appreciation for the invention—almost a reverence for the idea of preserving a moment in time. With respect to the impact a person's photograph, or for that matter, a good painting or portrait, I suggest the 'essence' of that person enhances the *memory* for others who are fortunate to gaze upon the image for as long and as often as they choose to do so. For as long as any person has access and can view that image, the precise moment that image was produced is preserved for a very long time, barring some catastrophe or natural decay. My understanding of that fact is one of the most fascinating things in the world of inventions!"

I hoped my awkward attempt to stall or 'buy time' would slow the pace of our discussions. I was totally unprepared for Mr. Bayonne's comment regarding the soul and his expectation that I'd have a response to it. In my attempt to avoid revealing my incredible deficiency on what I believe to be a most complex subject (the human soul), I had inadvertently introduced another, equally complex subject—*memory*.

"I do hope we can spend a bit more time talking about what you think about the soul as well as the process I referred to as memory. Both of those are of great interest to me, but excuse me, I didn't mean to interrupt your assessment of the advancement in communication through photography and television. Please continue, Mr. Bayonne."

Mr. Bayonne seemed to agree. He nodded as he continued. "Advancement in *communication* seems a good description for television. It seems dat history books could be replaced by dis better form of story-telling. I suppose dere is an opportunity to rewrite da facts in a more stimulating way. I suppose written history may have been embellished by da men doing da writing back den, so any improvement can't be all bad or so very far from da truth. Anyway, we can only *hope* for da best as time goes on. I had hoped dat through da television I could view a recounting of General Banks[28] or General Taylor,[29] since both men were hosted by Madam Parlange[30] while I was at the plantation. You know, I think General Banks was da first Union soldier to use colored men in battle up dere in the Port Hudson battle. It might be something to see how your television recollected dat battle. Somewhere around ten thousand men perished within two months of da battle in Port Hudson. I surely hope television writes dat tragic event correctly."

---

28   General Nathaniel P. Banks, a Union general during the American Civil War.
29   General Richard Taylor was a Confederate general in the American Civil War. He was the son of United States President Zachary Taylor and First Lady Margaret Taylor.
30   Marie VirginieParlange, referred to as "Madame Parlange" was the owner and manager of the Parlange Plantation, where Jules was "employed" as a Domestic Servant. Formerly, Marie Virginnie de Ternant (née Trahan), the wife of Claude Vincent de Ternant, 3rd Marquis of Dansville-sur-Meuse. Later, married Charles Parlange, for whom the estate is named.

Hmm, looks like I 'dodged the bullet' concerning further discussion about the soul, after all . . . at least for the time being. But as I was beginning to learn more about this man, called Jules Bayonne, I was certain I'd be faced with Mr. Bayonne bringing it up again . . . still, I just bought myself more time to get ready for it.

I thought about how I might respond to Mr. Bayonne's comment about how historical events might be recollected through all the other current forms of modern communication, other than television; such as radio, cell/mobile telecommunications, and now the internet. But I had the more fundamental problem of having just learned the history about General Banks, General Taylor and even the Port Hudson *fight*. Up to that point, I'd only heard about the Battle of Antietam (Colonel Robert Gould Shaw) and the role of the all-black regiment as they were depicted in the movie, *Glory*. Granted, this battle occurred the year before (in 1862) the one fought at Port Hudson, but it seemed as though history was no longer willing to publicize or acknowledge the vital role of the Civil War's black soldier. Before Mr. Bayonne introduced me to these warriors and events, I had no knowledge about them, let alone being able to engage in an intelligent discussion with him (or anyone else for that matter). I began to ponder about whether I was beginning to acknowledge (to myself) if Mr. Bayonne was who he said he was and where (the time period) he said he was from. *This guy couldn't be making all this stuff up. And, he didn't seem to be crazy!* The more I thought about it, the more complicated thinking about this entire situation became. I inhaled deeply, and then audibly exhaled the deep breath in preparation for my next comment. "Mr. Bayonne, I may need a little help from you now." I had his undivided attention. He waited for me to speak, but the words got 'stuck' somewhere between my brain and my vocal chords. The thought occurred to me again, this time I felt more troubled, that Mr. Bayonne's discussions with me suggested that *he* actually was physically present during the 1860's, in the heat of the Civil War! Although, Mr. Bayonne was no longer in the care of the personnel from Grady Memorial Hospital, I still felt obligated to consider Jeffrey Harris' caution at our first meeting: *"Therefore, for the time being, we ask that you not refer specifically to or address dates or imply that he might be related to you as an elder family member."*

I found myself in a 'bind' again. For the 'nth' time, I kicked myself for leaping before I was ready to jump. I should have planned on fully articulating what I wanted to say to Mr. Bayonne before opening my big mouth . . . and nothing came out of it but a pitiful sigh.

CHAPTER 6

BLACK SOLDIERS

More than you thought you knew

I decided to ask Mr. Bayonne a question I thought would lead to an extended discussion on a subject other than the technological advancements of 2007 until a bit later, *since I had my doubts of whether or not I possessed enough knowledge to properly satisfy his curiosity.* Maybe, I reasoned, we could avoid that discussion altogether. Maybe, I reasoned, I could buy some time to brief myself on the Generals, Parlange, Port Hudson and the like. Anyway, the question . . .

"Mr. Bayonne, can you tell me what the sentiment of the people was regarding black soldiers in the battle at Port Hudson?"

"Oh my, yes! Certainly I can," he said in an eager, yet obviously frustrated tone. "Port Hudson is only about thirty-five miles from my home,[31] so I know quite a few of dose boys' families."

---

31   Jules was referring to Livonia, Louisiana

Mr. Bayonne paused, took a deep breath and then sighed, "I find your concerns regarding my knowledge of the war and of my home somewhat strange and peculiar." *He's probably wondering why I don't already know these things, given that I'd already told him that it's very likely we are kin folk.* "Yet I must admit, your company is quite pleasant. So, yes I can tell you wat happened, inasmuch as I can recollect."

As he leaned slightly forward towards my chair, which I had positioned a few feet closer to him, he also lowered his voice. "White people did not tink very highly of colored men carrying weapons. It made no difference if dey were freed slaves or free blacks. Dey were frowned upon for taking up arms. Of course, white people never tink very highly of black people wit respect to anything is da bigger issue. Anyway, dose boys were faced wit trying to kill da very people who had owned or controlled dem up to dat point in der lives. Most of dose boys didn't relish da idea of taking da lives of men dey knew and, who in many instances, most likely were blood relatives to dem. General Banks (Union) also seemed reluctant to arm dose boys. I know he didn't want to have anything to do wit black officers. If black soldiers came through battle alive, even if dey were seriously wounded, dey had to go 'up north' afterwards anyway, leaving behind family friends and familiar places. White people, seeking revenge after da war ended, looked for blacks who had taken up arms against dem over in Port Hudson. It wasn't likely dat dose boys could settle on land in da south after dey fought against whites for dere freedom. A greater portion of da nearly two-hundred 1st Louisiana Native Guards who were killed in late May over in Port Hudson, were from da north. Quite a few of dose boys were already free and some even owned property; but dey joined up nonetheless. Much of dere motivation for joinin' up was dat dey merely wanted to dispel da myth dat black soldiers would not and could not fight as well as da white Union soldiers."

Jules nestled back in his chair allowing me to quickly seize the opportunity to question him about a fairly recent subject of debate occurring in America regarding the alleged (significance in numbers and importance) participation of blacks who fought in the Confederate ranks during the Civil War.

"But, what of black soldiers who supported the Confederacy?"

Mr. Bayonne looked a bit puzzled. "You mean 'Reb-uniformed,' armed *colored* soldiers?"

"Yes, for starters, but *any* participation by blacks perceived to be in support of the Confederate cause is also part of my question."

"Hmm," Mr. Bayonne suddenly became more pensive as if considering the question for the very first time. He finally spoke, "I don't rightly know for certain if I ever saw a colored man dressed in a rebel uniform as such. Nevertheless dere had to have been some, I suppose. But, den again, who would have tended to da needs of da plantation if all da male slaves followed dere masters to da battlegrounds?"

I waited, hoping that Mr. Bayonne was going to eventually continue his answer. I did not think he required an answer from me addressing the rhetorical question he had just offered relative to slaves following their masters. After a long pause, Mr. Bayonne continued.

"Da truth of da matter is dat da South did not possess da resources to properly outfit most of dere own white boys and also care for da needs required to sustain dere plantations, so I can't imagine how da Confederacy could provide guns, ammunition and uniforms to *Negroes* as well. I'm certain dat some Negroes were taken from dere duties on the plantations to serve as cooks, valets, and whatever other menial tasks required in da conduct of war; the tasks dat most white boys, even da poor ones considered beneath dem. Dey more dan likely required somebody to wipe der asses and noses just as dey had wen dey were on da plantation. I reckon dat your television could make dat kind of participation appear as though Negroes would fight to keep status quo (slavery) on da plantation. My personal observations indicate dat most Negroes hoped, dreamt, believed and fought for da change dat would yield freedom—a very complicated concept not thoroughly comprehended, but desired nevertheless."

Mr. Bayonne had responded to the question I posed to him, yet my gut instinct told me he wanted to continue his discussion regarding black soldiers. I looked at him and waited for more. I sensed his apprehension from the quiet shallowness he now wore on his face. Then, after the silence seemed to have almost become a thick vapor in the air, he emerged in full bloom.

For the second time during our conversation, I wanted Mr. Bayonne to clarify what he meant by "personal observation" but quickly decided that I had so much more to learn and so didn't chance taking the 'mental detour.'

"Well I would like to know wat da great invention of television has to report about *our* boys? Wat da moving pictures have to say about da courage of Cailloux and Crowder?"[32]

I shrugged (as far as I knew no such motion picture had yet captured the subject), hoping Mr. Bayonne would continue. With some patience and an inquiring stare into the face of this man who was still very much a mystery to me, he did as I had hoped, weaving his vast knowledge with wisdom of a sage. I was mesmerized . . .

"If you ask me, I tink freedom cost a lot more dan anyone expected; for certain, with respect to da Confederacy. A great number of whites never returned; dere families depending on dem to labor in place of da departing slaves were disappointed, heartbroken or held bitter resentment towards everyone and everyting. Da loss of men's lives, dere property and dere way of life changed and hardened da disposition of otherwise fairly decent people. A good many of da whites who fought didn't even own property, so dose few who had owned property, wen dey returned, came back to nothing anyway. Dese former landowners were probably da most bitter since dey now had to struggle to get farm land and den, dey had to work da land demselves. Not to mention the fact, dat now dey also had to compete wit former slaves who had also survived da war; just to eke out a living! Now, da richest whites lost sons in some instances as well, but mostly, dere boys held rank and took on less heat of battle dan dere white foot soldiers brothers. Wen da rich boys did come back, dey hired out some of da same blacks dey had once held as slaves, only dis time dey had to pay dem as *sharecroppers*. Da days of free black labor had finally become a ting of da past! "

As I listened to Mr. Bayonne's version of Civil War history, I recalled that the main theme of a dramatization of the black regiment, focused

---

32   Documented black officers Captain André Cailloux and Lieutenant John Crowder of the 1st Louisiana Native Guards, were killed in the battle at Port Hudson. Cailloux was educated in Paris and fluent in both English and French, and was considered a man of great intellect and property, and a pillar in the free black community of New Orleans. Crowder, the young second lieutenant, came from a poor but free black family and learned to read and write through the efforts of his mother and a prominent black clergyman.

on the story of the 54th Massachusetts Volunteer Infantry. As portrayed in the movie, *Glory*,[33] the director[34] had taken some creative liberties in suggesting that The Massachusetts 54th regiment was largely composed of ex-slaves, who had developed a great hatred for slavery and based on their personal experience, compelled them to an intensive level of gallantry. This, however was not the case, as approximately 1,100 of the recruited blacks of the 54th, were from the northern states, the greater portion of whom were free born; and thusly, had no direct, personal experience (or knowledge) associated with the atrocities and injustices associated with slavery.

The film's apparent intent was to point out that of the more than 170,000 blacks who served in the *Union* army, nearly 100,000 were recruited from Louisiana, Mississippi or Tennessee and were predominately slaves. Ironically, these were among the first southern states occupied by the Union Army. "*Glory*, thus merges the story of the free blacks of the Massachusetts 54th with that of the former slaves who were from the Deep South."

He then asked if I had ever heard the comment made by the first 'colored' staff officer to serve in the Union.

Genuinely ignorant of both the individual and the comment, I had to fess up a 'qualified,' "No I don't think I know."

"His name is Martin Delaney!"[35]

"Major Delaney spoke to his troops encouraging dem to be strong wit da knowledge dat had it not been for da efforts of da colored troops fighting in da war, da Union would not have prevailed in victory. Furthermore, dose efforts won da very freedom of enslaved colored people in da South. Of course, Major Delaney was a *Gullah*[36] and him being from Virginia and

---

33 *Glory*, (1989) excerpts from *Re-Viewing the Past* Eleventh Edition, The American Nation: A History of the United States. Copyright 2003, Mark C. Carnes/John Garraty.

34 Edward Zwick, American filmmaker, producer and director. Some films include *Glory* (1989), Legends of the Fall (1994), The Siege (1998), The Last Samurai (2003), Blood Diamond (2006), and Defiance (2008).

35 Martin R. Delany, a black major, the first black staff officer in the U.S. military, in a speech given in late 1865: "Do you know that if it was not for the black men this war would never have been brought to a close with success to the Union, and the liberty of your race if it had not been for the Negro? I want you to understand that." Excerpts from: *The American Heritage new history of the Civil War*. Narrative by Bruce Catton, Edited with an introduction by James M McPherson 1996.

36 The Gullah people are descendents of enslaved Africans from various ethnic groups of west and central Africa. They were brought to the New World and forced to work on the

me from Louisiana, I never personally met him, aldough his war successes, particularly in South Carolina, are well-known. "

"I am excited to learn these kinds of details, Mr. Bayonne. I will certainly pass this important piece of knowledge on to my friends and relatives."

He smiled ever so slightly, bit down on the right corner of his lip momentarily, and then he said: "Byron, you should see to it dat your television records dis detail for da benefit of others like *you*."

It occurred to me that Mr. Bayonne appeared to be suggesting that I might have some influence over how historical 'programming' is recorded via television, or maybe he had a more basic understanding that I had enough influence on my peers, friends and family to 'set the record straight' for those in my own 'sphere' of influence. In any case, the task seemed monumental—at least at the moment he made the comment.

Nodding in agreement, "It seems as if the question as to the competency of black men in the military has been asked of you before," I added, hoping to have prompted a continuation of the discussion.

Mr. Bayonne continued, somewhat matter-of-factly. "Da discussion of da ability of da black soldier proving worthy will continue to be in dispute as long as black people are regarded as inferior to white people. President Lincoln hesitated to admit to da capability of black soldiers, but he had to consider da advantage accrued to da Union by promoting dere enlistment.[37] Even Toussaint[38] was asked da question. And da obvious answer is found in da liberation of black Haiti."

---

plantations of coastal South Carolina, Georgia, North Carolina and Florida,

[37] " . . . Lincoln also ordered that freed slaves should be encouraged to enlist in the army. In August 1863 Lincoln wrote to Grant enlisting them "works doubly, weakening the enemy and strengthening us . . ." The Story of America, John A. Garraty Copyright 1991 by Holt, Rinehart and Winston, Inc.

[38] François-Dominique Toussaint Louverture also known as Toussaint L'Ouverture or Toussaint Bréda, was the best-known leader of the Haitian Revolution (21 August 1791— 1 January 1804). L'Ouverture was a former slave who rose to become the leader of the only successful slave revolt in modern history. The question of whether black soldiers possessed equal ability to that of qualified, trained white soldiers had been posed to L'Ouverture during his rise to leadership in the Haitian Revolution. Jules Bayonne suggested that the successful outcome of that conflict affirmed that black soldiers were always worthy when provided equal training and equipment necessary to engage in battle.

CHAPTER 7

SOMETHING OLD . . . SOMETHING NEW

Telephones

Mr. Bayonne's appetite for knowledge was very inspiring, but phenomenally strenuous. Although keeping up with his curiosity and our shared quest for understanding each other's worlds was brutally tiring, I gained so much 'richness' from our discourses. Just as I decided this was a good time to 'call it a day' until my planned next visit on Monday (January 8th), my cell phone rang. I pressed the 'silence' button and allowed the caller's message go to voicemail. I wanted to say my proper "goodbyes" to Mr. Bayonne; but his eyes locked on my phone as I fumbled to put it in my pocket, told me he wasn't quite ready for me to leave.

"So wat is dat ting?" He queried, pointing his index finger directly at my pocket, which now housed the silenced device.

"This is my mobile phone—nothing more than an advanced, portable form of the phone on the table next to your bed." I responded, as I motioned to the beige, push-button, hard-wired telephone on the small table in the corner of the dimly lit room. Almost as if the room had a spotlight aimed directly on the phone in that corner, we were now focused on what was an ordinary, old object to me; but for Mr. Bayonne was another new and seemingly fantastic curiosity!

Mr. Bayonne walked slowly towards the telephone in the corner and excitedly exclaimed. "I suspected dat was a telephone! But it don't look noting like wat have at home! At one time, I tought it would be nice to have one, but nobody else had one in Livonia or Mix anyway, so even if I had one, dere was nobody else to talk to until two or three folks in New Roads got one." He shook his head in obvious bewilderment. "Dis is very different from wat I know as a telephone, aldough I have only seen a few of dem before."

Curiously, I watched him gently run his fingers across the telephone's handset receiver, causing it to move slightly in its cradle. Mildly startled by the resulting loudness caused by the phone's motion, he hurriedly retracted his hand, as he softly murmured, "I don't want to break it."

Astonished at his almost child-like excitement, I suddenly realized that this was the kind of behavior one should expect from an individual who had limited exposure to the magical world of communication, and its complementary hardware, though it had been available to most people over the last one-hundred years! I tried to imagine what the introduction of the telephone in the early part of the twentieth century was like. As he walked towards me with his finger pointing again, this time aimed straight at my pocket.

Eyes sparkling, he asked, "May I see your telephone—da one in your pocket? Where are da wires?"

I pulled my battered Nokia 5300 cell phone out of my pocket, handing it to Mr. Bayonne, answering simultaneously, "Of course you can, by all means take a look! This particular phone is a wireless—there are no wires." *I half-expected a witty Bayonne 'comeback': "I may not understand it, but I know wat wireless means"* Surprisingly, none was offered.

"Most of the phones in use today are wireless. These pocket varieties are called cell phones. We also have them in our houses. They are generally referred to as cordless phones. As a matter of fact, except for public phones, you rarely see hard wired phones anymore. Also, we used to have coin-operated phones on many street corners, which were 'housed' in rectangular structures called phone booths. To use those phones, you had to step inside the booth, close the bi-folded doors, lift the receiver, deposit coins and dial the number of the party you wanted to reach. I can't remember when they disappeared from street corners. It just seemed like they vanished in a puff of smoke. I guess the powers that be decided it'd be a waste of money maintaining them and collecting the deposited coins with the advent of the cell phone, as most people have them nowadays."

Carefully cradling the device in both hands, he rolled it over, inspecting the back, and then returning to the front he gently touched the keys, not firm enough to activate any of the applications. I was impressed by the care he took handling the little mobile phone with the respect I had long ago forgotten; now taking its remarkable advancement for granted.

"Oh, I see. I must remember to try and account for da passing of the years since *my time*." Mr. Bayonne added, now less animated, *(I suspected that he was getting tired)*, he handed my cell phone back to me. Extending his hand to offer an apologetic handshake, Mr. Bayonne graciously spoke, "Please forgive me for delaying you. I realize dat you were just about to leave when I asked you about da telephone."

Firmly shaking his hand, I noted assuredly, "No apology necessary! I am honored by your allowing me to spend time with you."

The twinkle returned to his eyes, and still firmly grasping my hand, he asked, "Then you'll come back to finish this discussion very soon?"

"Is Monday evening too soon?"

Smiling widely, he quipped, "Not soon enough! But I guess dat will have to suffice. I eagerly look forward to our visits!"

"As do I. Then, Monday, it is! Mr. Bayonne, I'll see you then." I waved at him as I exited his room. My heart soared with warmth and humility and a tiny bit of reluctance at the thought of leaving the presence of this very special spirit.

I floated home, not fully conscious of everything around me, I didn't recall passing most of my usual landmarks; you know the ones, that tell you home is just around the corner. As I pulled in my driveway just after 9:45 p.m., I let out a well-earned sigh. I needed a minute to unravel and make the transition from the cerebral workout I experienced, which was truly requisite when dealing with one, Jules Bayonne. I think I deserved one minute of down time before going inside. I breathed out another sigh. This time it signified "welcome home."

PART 3

CLOSER TO HOME

CHAPTER 8

COLOR STRUCK?

Sorrell and Pourciau

I arrived at the Center just after 5:00 on Monday, January 8th, looking forward to continuing our discussions from Friday evening regarding technological advances. We had already discussed the evolution of television from the cathode ray process to the current flat-screen technology, and the evolution of the telephone. I had been very careful not to offer too much detail and cause more confusion rather than a clearer understanding. I was pretty sure Mr. Bayonne had grasped a great deal of my explanation, but he seemed more astonished and concerned that his discovery of technological advances had exceeded his own personal experiences. I began to fear he might become overwhelmed, so I decided it was time I change the subject, although it was clear that Mr. Bayonne would have wished to continue the discussion on the merits of television and the telephone much longer. I had a feeling the subjects would resurface again later. It had also become apparent that *I* was accepting the notion that Mr. Bayonne was not from this time. After all, I came back to see him (a few times now) and at this point, I had ceased questioning *who* he was. The more pressing question in my mind now was *why is he here?*

"Mr. Bayonne," I inquired, selecting my words, carefully and intentionally, "Do you know any persons bearing the last name of Sorrell or Pourciau from the Point Coupee area?"

Mr. Bayonne gave my question much thought as he replied equally as slowly. "I know of a Sorrell who comes from New Roads."

He seemed to ponder the question for a few moments longer before continuing. All at once, his countenance changed, resulting in a gray tone on his face. I sensed he was troubled by the questions related to Sorrell, Pourciau, or perhaps even to Point Coupee.

"In fact, *da* Sorrell I had occasion to meet wit was a peculiar gentleman." Mr. Bayonne's reply had come quickly, and then just as quickly, he changed his direction of thinking. "Da name Pourciau comes from all over Point Coupee-both black and white folks." Mr. Bayonne continued, and then suddenly, he blurted "Why don't you call me Jules? We seem to be around da same age. Besides, we've spent enough time together by now dat we should be on a first name basis, don't you tink so?"

I couldn't help but wonder why Jules avoided talking about the man named Sorrell, though he seemed okay with talking about the Pourciau name and even mentioned Point Coupee. But that little, still voice inside of me told me to just 'hold on; that all would be revealed at some point.' For the moment, I' been willing to be patient.

I looked into his eyes and answered very slowly, "I'll give that some thought, but I still hold you in high esteem as my elder even if you are only a day older." I realized that Jules had successfully avoided my question regarding our being related and instead, further compounded the mystery surrounding who he was (or how likely he is who he claimed to be).

Jules shifted his position slightly towards the front of the chair he was seated on. "You said you weren't no doctor, and I believe it. Again, I tink we should dispense wit da formalities. Please feel free to call me

Jules if we gonna chat about False River.[39] Everybody dere who knows me, knows me as Jules!

I agreed, nodding as he continued.

"What you call yourself aside from Coleman anyway?" Jules questioned.

"Well Jules," I grinned, still a bit uneasy using his first name. "My friends know me as Byron or if you are comfortable with it, you can call me 'B.'"

"Dat's a peculiar name ain't it?" He asked as he studied me with up and down glances. "Hmm . . . Byron. Who dey named you after?" I don't know no Byron from where I come from. Well, aside from da last name of da *promiscuous fellow* dat was the inspiration or instigation for da young Shelly girl's[40] demon story, you are da only Byron I know of. Why do dey call you Bee? Do you have some fascination with insects?"

I replied with some embarrassment. "Not as in the 'insect', but as in the 'alphabet'—B. My father was simply referred to as 'B.M.'; and his father's name is 'N.Z.' I have no answer as to why their mothers' employed initials only. However, I adopted the practice of using initials *only* a very long time ago; well that is long before I knew anything about my father or his father."

"Well, dat certainly is interesting dat you chose da same habit as your father without having da benefit of knowing him firsthand. Anyway, continue please." Jules urged.

I don't know much about my father's side of the family, but on my mother's side of the family, however, I am the fifth generation born of free people in the United States.

---

39   False River (Fause Riviere) is an old Mississippi River bed resulting when the river followed the narrow stream over a neck of land (Pointe Coupee Parish) used in 1699 by Iberville (French explorer, Pierre Le Moyne d'Iberville) and party to shorten their route up river. The locals from New Roads, Louisiana and all of the towns in Point Coupee Parish, directly adjacent to the "oxbow lake", running the length of Highway 1/ Main Street, often refer to their towns as "False River." The town of New Roads, the parish seat of Point Coupee (see footnote 21) and the center of population of Louisiana is the northernmost town adjacent to False River and because the post office, opened in 1858 was named False River, renamed in 1875 to "New Roads", the names are used interchangeably to the current day.

40   It appears Jules was referring to Mary Shelly (still Mary Goodwin then) and her book, Frankenstein, written in 1818, allegedly after George Gordon Byron (Lord Byron) suggested during that fateful summer of 1816, that Mary, her fiancé, Percy Shelly and he write their own supernatural tale.

Oops, I thought, surely, Jules will ask about the time period and how could that differ from *our* (current) time period since Jules and I appeared to be close in age. I stopped talking for a moment, hoping Jules had not heard my comments about my great-grandparents. Somehow it seemed as if Jules was *more* aware that things were not normal or usual at all!

Jules chimed in abruptly, "Pourciau is a name of a people, both black and white, dat all came from *my* father's country. Most of da black ones are gens de couleur[41] because dere white French ancestry provided for dem a different status for dem in Louisiana. Da different status may or may not have been better because dey were gens de couleur. Often da *girl* children who could 'pass' saw economic advantage by being in a plaçage[42] 'arrangement', but da criteria for being a placée, had more to do wit da desire of da white man wit da wealth dan da color of skin. Dark-skinned gens de color women or dark-skinned mullatoes[43] were not usually considered 'suitable' for 'left-handed marriages[44]', so dere fate was more like dat of the male gens de couleur. Den, most of us free people 'joined' wit each other or da 'freed people' when *we* could."

Obviously, Jules wasn't yet ready to talk about the Sorrell name. He had completely strayed from any discussion of the Sorrell name. In fact, he seemed to have become slightly agitated by the mere mention of the

---

41 Gens de couleur is a French term meaning "people of color," It is a shortened form of 'gens de couleur libre's (French meaning "free people of color"). The mixed-race children resulting from plaçage relationships in Louisiana is deemed to be the nucleus of the class of free people of color or 'gens de couleur libre's.

42 Plaçage was a highly-developed and formally organized system in Louisiana wherby, ethnic European men entered into the equivalent of common-law marriages with non-Europeans, of African, Native American and mixed-race descent. Another important element in promoting plaçage were the quadroon balls, were social events designed to encourage mixed-race women to form liaisons with wealthy white men through this system of concubinage.

43 A mullato is defined as a person of mixed white and black ancestry, especially a person with one white and one black parent. Note that mullato does not infer that one is of a particular skin tone, as they may be "dark-skinned", "light-skinned" or any shade in between.

44 Jules Bayonne's use of the term, *left-handed marriage*, probably was meant to indicate that certain marriages were considered by Louisiana society to have been extramarital or unsanctioned unions, particularly in the instance of plaçage 'arrangements.' It is doubtful that he was referring to *Morganatic marriage*, historically (European) deemed 'left-handed marriage' means a marriage of unequals in class.

Sorrell name. I wondered if I should have asked specifically about Sorrell again when suddenly, out of the blue, Jules asked a strange question.

I was glad, I'd continued to listen to that still, small voice, especially since merely mentioning the Sorrell name seemed to cause Jules some uneasiness. Besides, I thought it better to let Jules take the discussion in the direction he wanted to go. There was no good reason to stop that flow at this point.

"Do dey have all dere '*Dots*'?" I gave him a puzzled look and questioned, "Dots"? He quickly responded, "Yes, dat's right, your folks?" Jules then asked, "Wat about *you* Byron? Do *you* have all *your* '*Dots*'?"

Before I could have him clarify this peculiar query, he reverted back to the discussion of the Pourciau origin. I was disappointed that Jules had changed the subject (again), especially since I really didn't know how to get him to refocus on a subject that I knew absolutely nothing about. For now, I just had to go with the flow and wait patiently for the opportunity to revisit this sometime in the near future. I had learned enough about Jules to know that if 'Dots' hadn't been an important "piece" he'd never had brought it up in the first place.

"Pourciau is a French name," Jules said sharply. *I already knew that, being a native Lousianian, but I didn't comment. I wanted Jules to stay on whatever "track" he was on, pretty certain that he'd return to the topic I was really interested in . . . about the 'Dots'"*

"It is likely dat all da Pourciaus from Pointe Coupee are related. Are you kin to da Pourciaus?"

I was still trying to recover from Jules' casual introduction about 'Dots' when just as casually he started talking about the Pourciaus, particularly since my favorite uncle, "Jimmy" bears the last name 'Pourciau.' I decided this might be a good time to tell him what *I knew* about the Pourciaus, including the fact that *I knew* it was a French name. Still, I wondered why he was so willing, perhaps even eager to talk about the Pourciaus while seemingly equally as resistant to talk about the Sorrells?

Now it was my turn, "Of the Pourciau family, I am the (great-grand) nephew of Samuel James Pourciau (Jimmy) and his younger sister Delean

Pourciau Evans (Dee). Both my Uncle Jimmy and Aunt Dee could 'pass'[45]—a pretty controversial situation as I recalled growing up in New Orleans."

The controversy associated with 'passing' was that the advantages gained when departing from one's race to embrace another, often caused disappointment as well as division amongst family members who could not or would not cross 'this threshold.'; These were those who felt as if they had been left behind—not granted 'admission', left awaiting the return of the one(s) 'admitted.' Fear of being 'discovered' by whites discouraged some individuals who could but chose not to from attempting to access a 'whites only' establishment. Meanwhile, the 'passing' individual wrestled with feelings of guilt associated with the decision to play the 'imposter's role' of a white person. Interestingly enough, the universal question among and between those passing and those who could not or chose not to 'pass' was exactly the same: "Is you is or *is* you ain't" (white)?[46] The answer to which could have legal, but most assuredly moral consequences.

It occurred to me how effective Jules had been in avoiding the question regarding the Sorrell name. I wanted Jules to be aware that my Uncle Jimmy and Aunt Dee were, in fact, the younger siblings of Peter Wade Sorrell, my maternal great-grandfather. I also wondered if Jules knew this as well; and if not, why not; but if so, why was he avoiding talking about the Sorrells? It seemed to me that you couldn't talk about one without talking about the other?

Jules interrupted, "Why are we here asking and answering all dese questions? I'm beginning to tink dat da doctors and dat Mr. Harris put you up to dis whole ting, including trying to get me to take you into my confidence . . . Where is da list of questions? It seems you are more den just curious, Byron. Maybe you have a prepared list of tings you are required to ask."

---

45   One who could 'pass' refers to racial passing—a person classified as a member of one racial group is also accepted as a member of a different racial group. In this context, Samuel J. Pourciau and Dellean Pourciau Evans, due to their light skin tone, both were referred to as 'passe en blanc' (or 'passe blanc'), meaning they could "pass for white." It should be noted,that although in Louisiana, people of color who passed as white were referred to as passe blanc, any person of a race not considered Caucasian, but able to appear so would be passe blanc.

46   A 'play' on the title of Louis Jordan's song, **Is You Is or Is You Ain't My Baby**, recorded on October 4, 1943.

Jules paused briefly before forging on, "Now, I have some questions for you. Why can't I go home, Byron? My wife is probably worried 'bout me, you know."

I answered, already knowing for certain he wasn't going to buy into my hasty, insufficient answer. "The doctors are just making sure you are okay before they release you, Jules."

"Well, Byron," Jules replied, "Some of dis don't make sense to me, you know. So many bright tings, lights, strange and unfamiliar sounds—tings not of *my time*, I must not be so okay. I saw so many shiny buggies when dey brought me here. I know someting has happened to me and, watever has happened has been very difficult for me to explain *to you, and, I suspect, you are having as much difficulty explaining wat has happened, to me.*"

I slumped down in the comfortable upholstered seat and clasped my hands, and as my elbows settled, resting on the arms of the chair, I gave serious thought to Jules' last comment. He nodded slowly, in agreement as to our lack of a rational explanation regarding the peculiar situation of Jules' presence. We sat in complete silence for a while; just how long, I couldn't recall. Jules had posed the last question, the ball was now in my court, but I refused to audibly comment.

I wouldn't know how or what to answer anyway, instead I waited for Jules to present me with more of his reasoning regarding how and why he came to 'my world' now—I needed more perspicuity to 'marinate' in my mind before I could continue. I could hear my momma say: "Take your time, son, let him tell you what's on his mind—wait, be patient!"

"Uh, Byron, are your people creole speakin' folks?" Jules asked. (He was 'fishing' now)

"Yes," I quickly replied, hoping to change the direction of the conversation.

"My maternal grandmother was the last of the creole-speaking folks in my family. She died more than thirty years ago, Jules."

"Was she a slave?" Jules asked with his eyes fixed on me, obviously as if to see if I would give him a clue to his strange query.

"No Jules, she was from the *'gens de couleur libré* like you." I answered, knowing that the reference to free people of color would cause him to focus on a subject other than how I might be a part of his 'puzzle.'

I erroneously thought that Jules had become slightly distracted, perhaps from the comment regarding the 'gens de couleur libré', but after a long pause, he returned to the subject with an almost renewed vigor.

Jules stood slowly, then clasped his hands together and after blowing a sigh into his closed hands, he began again.

"Byron, yes I am da son of da 'gens de couleur libré' through my father, but da union between my mother and father, resulting in my birth, determined wat and who *others* say I am. You see, my father belongs to a peculiar group of people. On da *island*, he belonged to da *family* of the 'gens de couleur libré' because his father was a white man—da son of a French planter from da southwestern region of France, near da Spanish border[47]. Dis unique group of people bore much of da blame for da revolt due to da nature of dere origin. Dey were deemed a "cursed" race by da whites, whose guilt arose from dere role in da "mixing of blood," granted limited advantages and freedoms to dere "forbidden offspring," including a trickling portion of dere obscene wealth, gained substantially from da efforts of dese wretched people's black ancestors. Also despised, often by dere own relatives—blacks, enslaved by da same whites, further enraged by da instinct-influenced sense dat da "forbidden union" spoken in da same breath with da master's justification for da horrible institution of slavery. Dis brought about a resolution dat da 'gens de couleur libré' were an abomination to da blacks—despite da fact dat dem same black folks' very existence was often da result of rape, incest, deceit and lust on da part of da white perpetrator and da victimized black. Seems like to me dat dey placed da blame on da wrong people. Any advantage accruing to da free peoples—mulattoes and da like, was tarnished in da eyes of dose from whom dey was a product of. Dis problem affected people like my father, and even me, sheds a different light on da prideful lips of the 'gens de couleur libré', no?"

As Jules spoke of the challenges of the mixing of races he experienced firsthand, I couldn't help thinking of how even though things had changed, some things never change at all. The complex issues related to blacks,

---

47 Bayonne is a city in the Basque Country region of southwest France, where the Nive and Adour rivers meet.

browns, and particularly those having hues leaning towards white skin pigments, are still adversely affecting people today.

I responded to Jules' summary question in a resounding "yes!"

Continuing my response, I was fully aware that Jules would probably offer more to help me comprehend the complex issue of racial strains amongst *my own*. All I had to do was to just stay with the flow of his thinking and as my mother often reminded me that one could learn much more by keeping a closed mouth and open ears!

"Though I never comprehended how we came to have so much animosity between people originating from the same root, I was (and still am) keenly aware of the conflicts that exist. Yes, most definitely you have shed light on where (and how) the brown to the passé blanc[48] originated. I wonder if the union between your father and mother bridged the gap between *black and brown* for you."

I had almost forgotten we had begun this conversation with Jules inquiring whether or not Theresa—my grandmother had been a slave. In my attempt to keep Jules focused on *his time*, occasionally I had referred the 19th century. Soon I would discover that Jules was far from distracted by the change in direction of our discourse and the departure of the earlier comment regarding my grandmother. Jules suddenly did comment, this time about where *I* wanted to go: "Byron, you refer to da 19th century as dough it were so long ago! For me, it was not so long ago. I was told in the hospital, dat right at dis moment, we are living in da second millennium, dat is to say, da year of 2007! Yet I have no recollection of wat transpired between the end of 1903 and da present day. Wat seems odder to me is da notion dat *I* am alive in *your* new millennium! So, your grandmother is younger dan I am—she is of a time after 1903 and *so are you!*"

Now, *it was out on the table*! Jules posed the intriguing question we all had been skirting around; hoping it would just go away—*how is this possible*? Out on the table, yes, but the subject was still not approachable, as we agreeably, but silently changed the subject instead.

We spoke uncomfortably about things such as the food that was served to Jules at the River Woods facility and how nice the room was arranged.

---

48 One who could *"pass"*, meant pass as a white person. Also referred to as passé en blanc or passé blanc.

The *small-talk* allowed the intensity of the earlier conversation to fade for the moment. Jules became quiet and stared at me for a moment, but for what seemed to last a much longer time, then he picked up a book from the small mahogany table next to his wheelchair and began reading silently to himself until a few minutes later when he began to doze off. *His sudden dozing off made me wonder just what was going on with him. Was he bored, disinterested or merely tired, or perhaps even overwhelmed by trying to dodge certain issues? With Jules you couldn't be sure, heck for all I knew, he was faking the whole dozing off episode.*

After about ten minutes, I decided his apparent slumber was legit and took the chance of to approach the man who now displayed the regular breathing pattern of slumbering individuals. I leaned towards Jules, now well into his slumber. I could see the book's title—*Dreams From My Father* . . . I later learned the book had been left by Harris a few days earlier. On the table next to the book was a slightly worn Rawlings official major league baseball Harris had been using to test Jules' grip strength.

I left the room, quietly while Jules slept. I started to leave him a goodbye note, but thought better of it. After all, I was planning to visit him again the next day. For some reason, I wore a strange, little smile on my face as I exited out of the front entrance, even though I was dreading the walk to my car parked in the lot not more than sixty yards from the building. The damp, cold of the evening pierced my leather jacket, making it feel more stiff than usual.

Throughout the forty-minute drive home, I was perplexed by this meeting with Jules Bayonne, particularly since I was still *conflicted* as to where he *really* came from. I sensed Jules' reaction to my queries related to Sorrell, Pourciau or Pointe Coupee stirred something in him that caused him to avoid some answers and prompted him to attempt to change the subject. Furthermore, why was he here? I knew there *had* to be a simple explanation to what seemed to be an incredible series of events; and that somehow, the man could not possibly be who he claimed to be. He had answers that seemed to make sense relative to the past period he insisted he was from; nevertheless, the whole incident was not quite right. Then there was this one more thing—my senses had never been so keen. By the second week in January 2007, my cognitive process was in *hyper drive*. I saw it and understood it. I had a "moment of clarity"!⁴⁹ Perhaps, like Jules Winnfield, God was trying to tell me something and I just needed to *chill* and let Him handle it! I sure hadn't done a very good job up to this point!

I arrived home as the sky was darkening into night as the evening neared its end. I ate a quick, simple meal of eggplant parmesan and attempted to read a book. I found myself reading the same four lines of the book, my thoughts returned to Jules as if I were hypnotized by his last words to me: "I have no recollection of what transpired between the end of 1903 and da present day." The night ended with me falling asleep watching the Daily Show with Jon Stewart, but not before, I wondered if he were speaking directly to me as I heard him say, " . . . and now, your moment of zen . . ."

---

49   Jules Winnfield, a character in the 1994, film "Pulp Fiction" coined the phrase after being shot at, but miraculously uninjured during a *collection* job on behalf of his employer, Mr. Marsellus Wallace. The experience of the shooting incident leaves Jules somewhat reflective about his life of crime. "God came down and stopped the bullets from killing me!" That's it! I'm going to deliver this case to Marsellus, then I'm going to retire . . . I had a moment of clarity."

CHAPTER 9

ALL CAUTION TO THE WIND

Dots

During this meeting with Jules, the format appeared to shift slightly in that, I felt more like an interviewer, gaining new insights from a *true* celebrity. This particular visit on Tuesday, January 9th with Jules Bayonne proved to be one of the most fascinating lessons about nature I had ever learned.

At last Jules was ready to explain 'Dots!' The way he put it, 'Dots' are like signatures, specific and uniquely identifiable. "You know, Byron I could see how puzzled you were wen I bought up 'Dots' da other day and I need to apologize for not clearing up wat I was talking about at da time. But sometimes it's hard to keep it all straight. So, if I go off da rails in the future, please chock it up to trying to get a lot in before I go. I don't know how I got here and don't know how long I'm gonna stay. You do understand, right?"

I did understand where Jules was headed. I quickly nodded an affirmative and hopefully reassuring response.

"You see Byron, certain birds were known to have a defined number of markings (he referred to those markings as 'Dots') and da male species of dem birds are often brightly colored or adorned wit feathers not usually seen in da female."

I thought Jules had taken another turn off the road we were on when he started to speak at length about childhood discussions he had with his father and how sometime between 1821 and 1823, his father, Theodore Bayonne, came to know John Audubon[50] during Theodore's visits to West Feliciana Parish several years prior to Jules' birth. According to Theodore, Audubon was a 'birder', in that he was a studier of birds.

Apparently, Audubon had recently completed his incarceration[51] the previous year (around 1820) and was then residing at the Oakley Plantation completing some bird paintings. Theodore met him when he was delivering a couple of saddles to the plantation. Jules claimed his father had told him, based on discussions with Audubon, that some male bird species, usually identified as the most colorful of a mated pair, engaged in elaborate mating rituals, accentuated their markings—'Dots' as it were, to attract the attention of the female species. He also noted that the female usually chose the most beautiful male of their species, the one with **all** of the appropriate markings, spots or 'Dots.'

Suddenly Jules confronted me with *that* most interesting question, *now*, for the second time.

"Byron, you got all your 'Dots'?"

Before I could digest the question, Jules continued, "You know, most birds won't mate wit a bird of da same species if dere is a visible flaw such as, a missing tail feather, a bit of molting, or unusual markings unfamiliar to the species." As if to provide a required added emphasis, Jules tilted his head slightly to his right and with his left eyebrow now raised, he

---

50 John James Audubon, French-American ornithologist, naturalist and painter. Born April 26, 1785; died January 27, 1851.

51 After the "Panic of 1819", the first major financial crisis in the U.S., John J. Audubon, like a large portion of the population, was unable to pay his debts. Many people, including Audubon, were imprisoned for debt delinquency.

continued. "Even da birds are equipped by *Our Maker* wit da instinct to select da most suitable mate available."

Jules eventually came right out and asked what he really wanted to know, "Byron, do you really have da 'intestinal fortitude' it takes to survive in dis life?" I took this to mean that the 'Dots' were usually hereditary and if my ancestors had them, then I should have them as well. He alluded that 'intestinal fortitude' is as much of a learned trait as it was an inherited one; forged by the heat and pressure of life's most difficult experiences.

Jules confirmed my expectations. "You see, Byron, I got all of my 'Dots' and I'm proud of it too. It come from both my mother and my father. Dey come from good stock!" Dat's where my 'intestional fortitude' come from; dey had it and passed it down! I don't want to get into it right now, cuz you like a baby. You ain't ready yet! First you got to drink milk 'fore you can learn to chew and digest meat. But I will tell you dis much "Dots' is not only a ting, it's also an action—you got to connect dem 'Dots' to before you can see da whole picture. You got to learn how to connect dem 'Dots' together . . . and in the right order, too. Da sooner da better!" Let me explain it to you a little more using birds again as an example. I know a lot 'bout dem and tink dey really help to explain lots of tings 'bout heredity, intestinal fortitude and life, in general. When it comes to birds of prey, my favorite is the eagle, aldough I'm personally more familiar wit owls and hawks. I got to admit to having only seen a bald eagle a few times, once or twice in flight; and once in a nest located in a large cypress by a stream near my farm. But I was very impressed at da size of dere nest; more than five feet across, it was. And boy, can dat ting fly. Soar is actually a better description!"

About then Jules uttered a strange, but general statement related to birds. "Birds fly, Byron, Dat is wat dey do!" He continued enthusiastically, "You know a bird dat can't fly is faced wit a serious problem," he added.

I wondered why Jules made that statement further without offering more. However, a glance at the clock reminded me that today's visit had to end earlier than usual, as I was scheduled to be in Atlanta before 5 p.m. to meet with Janice. Jules also appeared to be fast-approaching weariness. As usual, the visit had passed by too quickly, but it was time to go. I wanted to continue the 'bird' discussion with the hope of acquiring a better understanding of Jules' 'Dots' proposition. Little did I know at the time how quickly that desire would be fulfilled (at least in part).

* * *

The irony of this bird discussion appeared that very afternoon on my drive into downtown Atlanta to pick-up my wife, Janice from work. While passing Hartsfield-Jackson Airport, I spotted an injured black vulture on the highway in the emergency lane. He was walking just inside the yellow line, next to the concrete barrier divider which separated opposing flows of traffic. It was apparent that his right wing was broken, because it hung limply as he dragged it along. *Not to be facetious, but given his obvious debilitated status the emergency lane could offer him no safety.* I wondered what Jules would make of all this as I added this 'event' to my mental list of things to talk to him about during our next visit.

* * *

I told Jules during my next visit, the following day, about the vulture incident. The discussion of this strange encounter seemed to hold a peculiar interest with Jules. I could tell by the excited look on his face that he was anxious to embark on this discussion, which indicated an 'expecting' of our usual exchange of ideas and theories.

"Byron, more please, such as, the size of the animal and the color of its feathers! Dis is wat I was talkin' about wen I said, "You got to learn how to connect dem'Dots'"

I was just the teensiest bit sorry I'd brought it up! Just how much did he expect me to observe while driving on the road at more than 55 miles per hour. Then I remembered that in Jules' day, vehicles were restricted to a speed limit of around 10-15 miles per hour a whole lot less than 55 miles per hour!

Before I could offer my meager response, he offered interpretations of what he had once experienced in a dream involving a large black bird.

"I am told dat dreams where blackbirds are involved, suggest good fortune in one's future," Jules noted.

While listening to Jules during this visit, it seemed he was absorbing a tremendous amount of information from television programs, newspapers and our visits, I thought it was very strange that the subject of birds carried over from my previous visit with Jules. Suddenly Jules' previous comment, "Birds fly, Byron, dat is wat dey do. . . . a bird can't fly is faced wit a serious problem," made sense to me.

That vulture was screwed! His future was predictable; and it was grim. He was unable to defend himself by flying away; his ability to hunt for food was restricted at best.

"Dat 'po thing can't even make a sound. Every grunt and struggle to make noise could prove to be fatal (you see, according to Jules, New World vultures are like most other bird species faced with a similar problem—any distress calls would prove futile, particularly since Black Vultures revert to predatory tactics when presented with the 'gift' of an extremely sick, injured or infirmed animals—the injured 'one of their own kind' is no exception—he's food too!"

I wondered what squawking or being able to 'make a distress call' has to do with flying? As usual Jules' uncanny ability to 'read' me and to kick start my thinking about the relationship between the two actions began posthaste.

"You know, Byron, I hadn't thought about it before you tol me dat story about dat bird. We talked 'bout this one particular animal—a bird. We talked about what it duz—fly. We talked about how some have special ways of attracting mates—'Dots' on birds. I brought it up to show a 'likeness' 'tween birds and people—the rules of survival is wat I been aimin' to get across to you! Dere's 'extra' rules for decent people too! Aside from 'jus survivin,' we ought to be more! Dat's why the need for intestinal fortitude. No! It's much more dan dat! It's essential for da self-perpetration of da family!"

I looked over at Jules and I could tell from his expression he was still musing over his new found 'revelation.' I was glad for the 'reprieve,' as I'd been entertaining my own 'revelation!'

Hmm, with all the problems I thought were major to me at that precise moment, witnessing that bird put my problems in perspective. I had a lot more *good* going for me in life then, than I had realized. At least

I could squawk or otherwise make my needs known! A moment of clarity had arrived! The vulture incident revealed what, I'd already surmised: Jules had 'struck a nerve' with just about everything he spoke of so far! My life, the 'Cornerstone,' 'Dots'! All of it!

As usual, the visit ended too soon. I wanted more, but it was time to go. I finally realized that all of this mental 'marination' had exhausted me. I couldn't wait to get home to try some of that new wine Janice bought the other day. I couldn't think of its name at the time, but it didn't matter. All I cared about right then was that it be chilled and waiting for me to pop that cork.

I called Janice to tell her to put the wine on ice. I was on my way home.

* * *

The following day's commute to downtown proved the imminent demise of the vulture was now a fact. Remnants of most of his feathers were still attached to his tattered remains, but a good portion of them were also strewn along the dividing wall of the same segment of highway I had observed him the day before. Jules' comment (" . . . a bird can't fly is faced wit a serious problem!") resounded in my head—the rule for that bird had been followed without exception. He could no longer function as he was 'designed' to be. He was no longer able to fulfill his primary purpose—to fly . . . death was inevitable for that Black Vulture!

I believed I had some of my 'Dots!' With some effort, I could 'earn' the remaining missing ones—'intestinal fortitude' was my new quest!

This was the lesson for me that day and the first of many such lessons to come through talks with Jules. I had surmised that *that* lesson's purpose was to teach me that there is a particular *order* to and purpose for everything we humans define as 'life'—there is purpose and design for all creation—the rule as exemplified through birds is simple. We, humans would be wise to grasp this 'edict.': Basically, if you don't (can't) use it, you lose it—undoubtedly, the sooner the better. Amplification of the ideas that we should "Behold (consider) the fowls of the air . . ." is a definite truism. The understanding that; **to have, and use** all of the talents and abilities afforded to most human beings is deemed much more miraculous in us than in any other animal (including birds). It is a divine blessing which should never be taken for granted. Accordingly, I'm of the opinion that the misuse or failing to use a given talent would result in the ultimate forfeiture (again, use it or lose it) of the talent, rendering one useless, and wasteful!

The discussion on this visit with Jules taught me that there would be no better person I would ever personally know who could provide an example of the complex nature of human survival instincts than Jules. I was blessed and I knew it. I was learning one of several precious—'can't survive without it' lessons of a lifetime.

I began to contemplate the idea of disregarding Harris' warnings and decided that this had to be a once-in-a-lifetime opportunity to explore strange and unexplained mysteries of life firsthand. I also thought about how much I would have missed out on, if I'd chosen to take Harris' advice. To that end, I threw all caution to the wind and began to ask Jules questions I needed answers to if I were ever going to successfully continue this journey we call 'life.'

"Jules, tell me about your mother, what is her name and how does she come to live in Point Coupee?"

"My mother? Why is Fanny a concern of yours?"

"Jules", I said, "Look at me. You have been hoping that I would be honest and straight forward while talking with you, right?"

Jules answered slowly, "Byron if you got something on your mind you want to tell me, it's high time you start, okay?"

Boy, this guy must own a Ph.D in flipping the script to gain control of the conversation . . . He's so good at it! I think I'm in control of the 'interview' and before I know, it the ball has been volleyed back across the net into my court!

Jules had 'won' once again! I took a pen from my jacket pocket to take notes, but not before Jules stared at me and my pen. Finally, he commented, "Dat's a fancy *instrument* you got dere. You can write notes with dat ting?" I must have given him a quizzical look by what came next, as Jules insisted that he was accustomed to using quills and early forms of fountain pens and appeared to be amazed at the advances in pens.

I handed Jules the pen for his closer inspection as I attempted to explain to him something I had taken for granted my entire life—the major improvements in how one writes. I watched him closely with a sense of my own curiosity as he rolled the gold Cross pen between his fingers and thumb, cradled it in both hands and then eventually twisted it to reveal the ball point. I watched in amazement at his attention to the detail. It occurred to me as I watched him use the pen to scribble something on a half-used writing pad laying on the little table, doubling as a night stand, that Jules *had the ability to write, as well as to read writing*. This ability placed Jules among the elite of his time—an anomaly, considering that less than five out of every one hundred black men over the age of twenty-one in the State of Louisiana could read and write by 1900!

"Remarkable!" Jules exclaimed. "C-R-O-S-S, Made in USA, 12 K-T Gold Filled—it's inscribed on da end! It feels rich, undoubtedly a pleasure to use?"

"This is a more recent development in writing tools, Jules. You do understand that many things will be new to you because of the differences in where you live down in Louisiana and I, here in Georgia?" I remarked, weakly in my deliberate and somewhat desperate attempt to avoid a discussion on the advances in technology by focusing on the difference in our geographical locations instead. I knew (actually hoped) this 'strategy' would be short-lived at least, for the moment.

I suggested we go back to the subject I had initiated before. "So, now about your mother . . ." Much to my surprise, Jules acquiesced.

CHAPTER 10

...STARTING FROM THE BEGINNING

Fanny

Jules began. "My mother, Octavia—called Fanny by everyone, was born in Norfolk, Virginia 'round 1825. Her grandmother, Ndidi—called Dee Dee, one of seven of children, gave birth to, Adaku—called Addie (Fanny's mother) in Africa. Dey were taken from Nigeria (from the Ibo tribe) and brought to America through da middle passage[52] 'round 1774 wen my great-grandmother, Dee Dee was only 'bout twenty-tree years old. My mother did not recall knowing any of her mother's seven siblings, except one of da younger aunts dat she was told had been sold to a 'nother planter 'round da time she was nine years old. Dee Dee, 'long wit Addie, who

---

52 A function of the Atlantic Slave trade, whereby millions of people from Africa were shipped to the New World, whereby commercial (finished) goods shipped from European countries were sold to Africa and traded for enslaved Africans. The African slaves were then traded in the region referred to as the "triangular trade" for raw materials sold back to Europe, completing the voyage.

was 'bout seven years old, was brought to dis country wit at least tree other sisters whom she never saw again once dey were taken off da boat. Addie was Dee Dee's only child to live wit her in Virginia. According to my mother, great grandma Dee Dee died shortly before she was twelve, sometime 'round 1837. Addie died four years later.

Fanny believed she was da daughter of dere plantation owner's oldest son, Robert Campbell Jr, aldough, Addie never confirmed wedda Campbell was her father. I guess you could say ole Junior Campbell was a 'rolling stone;' it was rumored dat he fathered at least four other children between Addie and two other slaves who were owned by his father, Robert Campbell, Sr.

About a year after, the senior Mr. Campbell died, and shortly after Addie died da following year (about 1841); Robert Jr sold Fanny to a trader operating in New Roads, Louisiana, who den sold her to da Decuir family at Riverlake Plantation in Oscar, Louisiana. Robert Jr sold Fanny because da new Missus Campbell became uneasy with da rumors spreading regarding Robert Jr's involvement wit da female slaves. I guess ole' Robert Jr needed to keep da peace in Virginia, so Fanny *had* to go."

As that night's visit came to an end, my tired mind began to envision a sturdy but small young woman in a worn, faded, white cotton slip-over-the-head, dress. On a crisp, cool morning in May of 1842, this beautiful, frightened young girl, known as Fanny, estimated to be in her mid-to-late teens, and a group of other slaves owned by Robert Jr had come from Virginia, and sold at auction to a plantation in Point Coupee Parish, Louisiana. Jules had mentioned that his eldest daughter, Edwige was the 'spittin' image of Fanny."

* * *

I couldn't think of much else, as I hurried home to look through some old photos given to me in July, 2003 at our first family reunion in New Orleans. I anxiously searched through the group of photos, hoping to find a picture of Edwige—there she was, just as I'd envisioned! Edwige appeared to have been in her early twenties in this worn, black and white photograph which probably was taken around 1905. Based on Jules description and from viewing Edwige's photograph, I now had a fairly good idea of how Fanny may have looked.

* * *

I returned to the Riverdale center on the evening of January 10th, just before 5:00 p.m. I was anxious to hear more about what Jules had to offer in the way of "briefing me on family history," among other things. . . . Things that I'd only heard about or imagined . . . until now. *It occurred to me that Jules had appealed to my love for learning new things and his lessons were more intriguing and insightful than anything I could have learned in a course in any major university in America. Stored in his mind were amazing history lectures related to the Red River region, including accountings from much of the northwest part of the State of Louisiana, and knowledge of facts from areas, extending eastward, all along the Mississippi River through New Orleans. I was captivated by the details of events that came alive as he unfolded each recollection. More importantly though, I was fused and intertwined in this interesting man's complex and fascinating story, apparently by a birthright, particularly in light of the fact that I had only recently been made aware of Jules' twelve children.*

I had met some of his and Victorine's surviving heirs four years earlier (2003) at a family reunion held in New Orleans, however, it wasn't until the tenth of January, 2007 that I realized four of Jules and Victorine's children (Olympia, aka, Elizabeth; Noel, aka 'Man'; Edwige, and Marie, aka Florence) were represented at that reunion.

And . . . 'All' The Great Men . . .

Jules and I greeted each other in the usual, familiar way we had in my prior visits; and wasted little time getting started in our 'lesson for the evening.'

"You know Byron," Jules slyly commented, "Atlanta fixed up *tings* real good since da war from wat I read in da newspapers. I'm told da land in Georgia and South Carolina was pretty beat up by Uncle Willie and his boys."[53] Dat's another *'ting'* I can't understand. I had once hoped to visit wit two men who were in Atlanta a few years ago to get some help in gettin' my children some help wit dere education. William Du Bois is a teacher at a school in Atlanta somewhere and Booker T. Washington comes to Atlanta a lot from Alabama I'm told. Since I'm here, maybe I can get to meet dem."

I realized that William Tecumseh Sherman's infamous 'Atlanta Campaign' devastated the city in the summer of 1864. I had also heard and sometimes, employed the nickname 'Uncle Willy,' referring to Sherman on those occasions whenever I was faced with subtle racial comments infused with the idea of a rebirth of the Confederacy. A clever reminder that 'Uncle Willy' left Atlanta scorched the last time, 'in case they had forgotten!' However, Jules' reference to the educators, Du Bois and Washington led me to believe that he strongly favored and sought education for his children. This impressed me tremendously and I hoped to hear more about his position on education as well as all he knew about these two great men.

"You know of these men (DuBois and Washington) personally?" I queried.

Jules stroked his graying beard and replied. "Most *other* folks know about dem as much as I do, I suppose, but, I have never met dem *myself.* There is so much news written 'bout dem and a lot of talk about all da good dey do. William Du Bois recently wrote in a book recommendin' colored people buy land as a priority to stay free citizens. I tink he is right. Dat is one reason I bought land. Dat way, I could raise and grow food for my family. It was one of the most fulfillin' tings I ever done."

I mulled over and over, the question of why the man who insisted he was Jules Bayonne 'showed up' in Atlanta, of all places. Jules and I had just discussed how much he had longed to someday meet with W.E.B. Du Bois, an Economics and History professor at Atlanta University in the early 1900's. Perhaps this 'quest' had prompted him to travel to Atlanta in hopes of finally meeting this great man face-to-face.

---

53   Apparently, the "war" reference to Atlanta was due to news Jules had read about General William Tecumseh Sherman's notorious "Atlanta Campaign" and the eventual burning and fall of the city to the Union during the Civil War.

Never Remove the Cornerstone

I suggested that Jules' being in Atlanta was a 'strange coincidence' with respect to his desire to come in with contact Du Bois and Washington. It seemed as if those words struck a nerve, as his response was urgent and unequivocal!

"Strange coincidence? I believe dat is wat your namesake also said about 'strange coincidences'![54] Aldough, I don't tink he really believed in da concept of 'coincidence.' By da way, dis is da second time I heard you use da word—'coincidence.' If wat you call coincidences continue to occur wit any frequency, you probably will have to refrain from definin' such occurrences as bein' coincidental, yes? I suggest you try to find another word more suitable. I tink you can be more imaginative."

I'm certain I appeared startled to Jules; and he was right . . . I was startled, as I was genuinely stumped by the brilliance of his reasoning regarding the comment about my overuse of the word "coincidence." There was *something* special about this keenly intelligent man which magnetically and somehow magically, drew me to his gentle wisdom.

I listened intently as Jules continued on about Du Bois with some reverence and how he was so intrigued and impressed to find that Dr. Du Bois was the first black person to be awarded a Ph.D. from Harvard. I could tell that Jules was well on the way to full recovery by the way he became more excited as he paced the room (no longer needing a wheelchair) and noted how he had been inspired by Du Bois' own educational achievements and his position on the educational process for black people (Du Bois believed that black people would have to first educate themselves, and then teach others[55]). I was amazed that Jules knew so much about these men and how he seemed to be submerged in wonderment as he spoke of them.

As Jules continued to discuss details of both men he became a bit animated, as he stood up gesturing with his hands and pacing back and forth in the small area at the foot of his bed. He talked about how he wished he'd been present when Booker T. Washington, the founder of Tuskegee Institute had made his famed speech, the "Atlanta Compromise Speech"

---

54 A "strange coincidence," to use a phrase by which such things are settled nowadays—Lord Byron. Don Juan. Canto vi. Stanza 78.

55 "If the Negro was to learn, he must teach himself, and the most effective help that could be given him was the establishment of schools to train Negro teachers." *The Souls of Black Folk*, W.E.B. Du Bois, 1903.

in 1895. Washington urged black people to accept discrimination for the time being and to concentrate on elevating themselves through hard work and material prosperity—"pull yourselves up by your own bootstraps." Du Bois' position, on the other hand, urged blacks to educate themselves, was adamantly opposed to that of Washington.

Once again, Jules demonstrated his inherent wisdom in arriving at his own 'compromise:' "You know Byron, dere's some truth and reasonableness in both men's idea on how blacks can better demselves. Even dough I was unable to acquire a formal education, I did learn how to read and write, and I'm proud to say dat my economic status was accomplished by acquirin' and exercisin' sound business skills 'long wit wat I already knew 'bout agriculture. Any way you want to look at it, dat's wat's called using 'mother wit!' But still, I could also identify with Washington to a larger degree. If possible, black people could acquire formal education, political savvy, economic position and social equality simultaneously!"

Jules also noted that he believed most blacks would be inherently better off if they applied either position or *both* as opposed to doing neither. One thing for certain, Jules reiterated that he had learned a valuable lesson from Du Bois[56] by purchasing farm land in 1870.

"I had conversations wit Dunn and Pinchback[57]—both great black men in da political circles just before I bought my farm. Dey were very pleased wit da idea of da progress many of *us* were making since da *liberation,*[58] even dough dey were experiencing heated resistance from white politicians and da 'terror knights'[59] in dere own attempts to gain rights to vote and to achieve citizen status in America. Like Du Bois and

---

56 "... And what do the better classes of Negroes do to improve their situation? One of two things: if any way possible, they buy land; if not they migrate to town ..." Souls of Black Folk, W.E. B. Du Bois Excerpts from Of the Quest of the Golden Fleece. Published 1903.

57 Oscar Dunn and P.B.S. Pinchback were the first African Americans (and granted American citizenship by the 14th Amendment, , ratified in Louisiana,1868) to serve as lieutenant governors of a U.S. state. Pinchback succeeded the late Mr. Dunn as Louisiana's lieutenant governor in a mysteriously sudden, unexpected illness and death after serving from 1868 to 1871. Pinchback, then a state senator, served as acting lieutenant governor. Later Pinchback would become the first African American to serve as the 24th Governor of Louisiana for a short 35 day interim.

58 A subtle reference to the emancipation in America of January 1, 1863

59 Although not verified by Jules Bayonne, it was assumed his use of the term; 'terror knights' was his personal alternative to the use of Ku Klux Klan.

Washington, Dunn and Pinchback did not agree on much either, but dey too saw da importance in ownership of property for black folks. I had great regards for Dunn, dough he died too early in life, and under some very questionable circumstances, I might add. I shall sorely miss his robust way of standin' up against oppression of any kind.

Shortly after Pinchback came out of the governorship, white folks became as barbaric as ever. The year after we harvested our first crop, less than a hundred-twenty miles northwest of my farm, dere was a slaughter of black people, whose only 'crime' was *to hope* to participate fairly in the voting process."[60]

As Jules spoke, it occurred to me he was speaking as though Du Bois and Washington (as well as Pinkney) were still alive. I didn't have it in me to tell him that these men had long since passed away. So, I also hoped to get him back to the original conversation about our family tree. But then he began to speak about *others* who somehow seemed to invoke a feeling of familiarity and uneasiness. . . .

"A young man, Jessie McKinney who I met in New Orleans two years earlier before all dat mess got started, dough he was not involved in da actual conflict, still met wit misfortune. Dat poor boy was counted among da innocent. He got caught in da hateful crossfire of da ring leaders, Bill Cruikshank, Alphonse Cazabat and Christopher Columbus Nash, a mere few days before da major killings dat ended on dat bloody Easter Sunday. Levi Nelson[61] survived da onslaught, but was unable to make tings right,

---

60   The Colfax Massacre, or Colfax Riot occurred on Easter Sunday, April 13, 1873, in Colfax, Louisiana, the seat of Grant Parish. In the wake of the contested 1872 election for governor of Louisiana (between John McEnery, a Democrat and Republican Gov. Henry C. Warmoth) and other local offices, a group of white Democrats, armed with rifles and a small cannon, overpowered Republican freedmen and state militia (also black) trying to defend the Grant Parish courthouse in Colfax. Most of the freedmen were killed after they surrendered; nearly 50 were killed later that night after being held as prisoners for several hours. Estimates of the number of dead have varied, ranging from 62 to 153; three whites died but the number of black victims was difficult to determine because bodies had been thrown into the river or removed for burial.

61   From the infamous Colfax Massacre, only one black from the group, Levi Nelson, who was shot by Bill Cruikshank, but managed to crawl away unnoticed. He later served as one of the Federal government's chief witnesses against those who were indicted for the attacks in the controversial case of *United States v. Cruikshank*, which is said to had effectively enabled political parties' use of paramilitary forces, leaving Southern blacks helpless and at the mercy of increasingly hostile state governments, who did little to protect them for nearly

even in da 'high court.' Tings never got better for years later. But me and Victorine, we survived dat mess okay, I guess, 'dough tensions rose in most of da parishes for da next several years after dat."

I listened intently as Jules spoke of Jesse McKinney, Levi Nelson—hmm, I thought briefly. *Where had I heard those names before? Well, I thought, forget about it for now; surely it'll come back to me.*

"Wait a minute!" I blurted out suddenly and loudly. It was beginning to all come back now, but I needed a little more clarification from Jules before my recollection could fully resurface. "Jules, can you tell me who Jesse and Levi are one more time?"

Jules repeated his comment from before. "Jesse McKinney was a young fellow from Colfax in Grant Parish who had been in da town near da courthouse earlier in support for da defense of da Republicans guarding da courthouse. After a while, deciding dat *real* concerns were over, and he wasn't needed no more, he left to return home. He was working on da fence surroundin' his farm, minding his own business, wen he was struck and killed by gunfire from an unnamed, but identified, horseman who was 'mong Sheriff (Christopher Columbus) Nash's mob. It was generally tought to have been someone tied to Bill Cruikshank's group, as he was named in da final appeal (United States v. Cruikshank) to da federal government. It was bad enough that Jesse was killed, but da additional horror was dat it was done as his wife, Laurinda and his boy, Butler watched the horror from dere front porch as da rider dismounted his horse, and fired a sure shot at Jesse's head, point blank. He screamed and fell as his wife and son huddled together in an icy fear dat dey would be killed nex. And, as if dat wasn't enough, dey had to watch as da mob cheered at dere horrible deed. Da U.S. Supreme Court's ruling had a devastating and lasting effect on da black folks in most of da parishes in Louisiana at dat time, particularly from da Ku Klux Klan whose participation continued to grow by leaps and bounds. Levi Nelson, who was wounded during da raid on da courthouse, survived and escaped to recount da story to da courts to no avail. He eventually left Grant Parish not long after da case was concluded. No one

---

one hundred years, ending in 1966 with (United States v. Price; United States v. Guest) when the Court vitiated Cruikshank.

has seen or heard from him since. Some folk tink dat da Klan got him after all, but no one knows for sure. It's all speculation."

That's it, I knew it would come to me sooner or later! Jesse and Levi were the guys I had dreamed about in that horrible New Year's nightmare! Now how am I supposed to make sense of all this? How could I possibly dream about people I'd never met and a situation I'd never heard of, let alone had ever encountered? Things were getting stranger and stranger. Humph, and I foolishly thought things were getting clearer and clearer. I'ma just have to take a chill pill and ride this thing out. Whom I trying to fool, what else can I do but ride it out? . . . Absolutely nothing other than turning my ownself in to the loony bin . . . and that sure ain't gonna happen. Besides, I had some kinfolk I wanted to avoid at all costs who are or should be there already!

I didn't tell Jules about the nightmare, partly because I was very confused as to what it meant to have two people whom I did not personally know manifest themselves in *my* dream. Moreover, these men, Jesse and Levi, were present near downtown Denver, Colorado in an area where I had once resided with my family (from 1976 until 1990) quite a few years ago. I really did not make the connection between Colfax Avenue in Denver and Colfax, Louisiana until now, after hearing Jules' account of the Colfax Massacre. *Another thing that occurred to me was the fact that it had been no coincidence that I ended up residing in Denver, Colorado for a bit.* Furthermore, my disturbing dream had occurred (several days) before I *even* met Jules at Grady Memorial. No matter, since I was convinced that Jules, somehow *magically knew* about my dream, the connection, and whatever else relative to those poor men; and whatever the event meant, was certainly not coincidental! . The more Jules talked, the more the eerier déjà vu not only surfaced, but securely 'attached' to my psyche. I began to feel very uneasy about the strange discussion and the near panic attack I felt creeping slowly, but surely, into my soul regarding Jesse McKinney, Levi Nelson, and my dream's manifestation of the brutal attack on them. So, forcing myself to calm down and to forget my thoughts about the horrific Colfax *Massacre (including my nightmare about it)*, I decided, with some degree of urgency that now would be a good time to change the direction of the conversation.

"You were saying about Fanny, your mother," I reminded him. I succeeded, for the moment in diverting Jules' attention from the question I knew he wished to ask.

"No, *you* was sayin' 'bout my mother, but since we agreed to be straightforward about everyting as you put it, I'll answer you, but first you tell me dis: Are your questions and da answers I give you goin' to determine how it is I am here and dat I am who I say I am?"

"It is certain you are who you claim to be." I said in a tone I hoped sounded convincing. "But as for how you come to be here, I hope that whatever you tell me helps *both* of us answer that question.

I felt as if Jules Bayonne could see right through me and the feeling of guilt overwhelmed me because I didn't *quite* believe he was who he said he was. At that moment, I didn't feel as if I was being honest with Jules and it was obvious that this obstacle would prove to be a hindrance to any meaningful discourse between us. My gut instincts told me that I would soon have to dispense with my skeptic dishonesty, despite the apparent irrationality of the situation.

Jules stared at me for a few seconds as if he wanted to tell me something related to being this mysterious 'guest,' but instead resumed the conversation, regarding his mother; this time from a different perspective.

More about Fanny

"Like I told you before, Fanny came from Virginia by way of slave auction and worked on da farm as a young girl. She worked in da kitchen and in da gardens at Riverlake[62] where my father met her around 1841 or 1842. I don't know if my mother was freed before or after she met my father, but he married her wen she was around twenty-four years old, and by den she a freed slave. She had tick curly dark brown, mixed wit polished bronze colored hair dat she kept in a single braid, which extended almost to da middle of her back. Rarely did we ever see her hair uncovered, probably due to old habits from her days in bondage. Da custom of most slave

---

62   Riverlake Plantation in Oscar, Louisiana, was a large functioning farm in the early 1800's, primarily growing sugar cane.

women was to have dere hair under a tie or bandana of some sort. She stood just a little over five feet tall and was of slender to medium build, but don't let her small stature fool ya. She was sturdy enough to handle da plow from time-to-time.

Now 'bout dose laws in dem days. I guess da laws 'bout Creoles from Saint-Domingue make it so dey known as 'bebe ti gason'[63] can be born free from slavery, so I'm free *dat* way. Fanny was a pretty brown girl, and of course, her daddy was probably white. Dat was a common ting in dose days.

My father, who was fair-skinned and of French blood,[64] married my mother, Fanny, a much darker woman than he was, very likely due to da nature of da free peoples' reasoning. Da free men of color were of less value to free women of color who looked to wealthy white men as dere suitors and benefactors. Rarely would a free woman of color seek a free man of color, as such a union would not improve da lot of dat woman. To da free woman of color, da men of color was wat was referred to as 'Ils sont si dégoûtant!'[65] I hadn't tought of it until now, but it was probably da reason I was so attracted to Victorine, my beautiful mate."

I didn't quite grasp what Jules meant by the "nature of da free people' reasoning or what was the "reason I was so attracted to Victorine, my beautiful wife," but I surmised at the very least, Victorine was a darker-skinned woman— that was the only common 'thread' of similarity I connected with during this discussion. He may have been trying to point out that much like his father (Theodore Bayonne), married a 'darker-skinned woman—Fanny, Jules in turn was attracted to a 'darker-skinned woman—Victorine.' The underlying complexity of this issue seemed to make this conversation a bit ambiguous. Nevertheless, I didn't inquire further as to why Jules was so attracted to Victorine.

"As I grew older, I didn't see much of my maman (a term used by children referring to their mother) 'cause she stayed at da farm while I worked on Parlange land until I got my own farm almost thirty years ago."

Thirty years ago! It was apparent that Jules was still referring to his time—sometime around 1900.

---

63   Creole-"bebe ti gason", meaning "baby boy."
64   His father's ancestral lineage included French-Europeans.
65   Translated to mean: "They are so disgusting!"

I realized that the visiting hours had been over for nearly an hour now, so around 8:30 p.m., I bade Jules farewell, with a promise to return the day after tomorrow.

* * *

Homebound

As I walked out of the building to my car, I whistled a little tune that I could neither name nor recognize. All I knew is that it made me feel happy and somehow 'accomplished.' Then when I turned the ignition on starting my little green Jeep, without warning, the all too familiar thought popped into my mind at that instant:

"... Fifteen-hundred years ago everybody knew the earth was the center of the universe; five-hundred years ago everybody knew the earth was flat and fifteen minutes ago you knew human beings were alone on this planet. Imagine what you'll know tomorrow!" [66]

Agent K's proverb spoken in the movie, as the protagonist, James Darrell Edwards, III, gazed at bike riders in tandem on a neon lighted vehicle as they puttered away. As I drove away, unlimited possibilities began dominating my mind. I could now comfortably and competently accept the idea that nothing was impossible; especially about things humans *think they know*. The earth turned out not to be the center of the universe; the earth turned out not to be flat; and in Agent K's case, humans turned out to *not* be the only inhabitants of planet earth. Ergo, as I considered a reverse analogy, Jules *was* definitely who I *knew* he was, yet the part of me that still struggled to hang onto the rational world, wrestled with the weirdness of how the beginning of 2007 had unfolded up to this point.

But, why was that particular quote from a crazy movie firing my synapses so persistently? Oh yeah, I was keenly aware of the answer to those strange and difficult questions I had posed to myself! I simply refused to admit

---

[66] Quoted from *Men in Black,* a science fiction comedy action film released in 1997 starring Tommy Lee Jones and Will Smith. Agent K, portrayed by Jones is recruiting James Darrell Edwards, portrayed by Smith and reveals to Edwards the agency—MIB.

that there had been hints of spiritual properties functioning during every visit with Jules. Moreover, I had been stubbornly unwilling to reconcile Agent K's seemingly *random words of wisdom* into anything meaningful. Nevertheless, there *was* meaning to each word he uttered and the more I fought and struggled internally, the more my pitiful stubbornness became obvious to me and that I had nothing to gain by trying to hold onto this now fading state of 'rationalization.' If I kept going down the road with Jules the way we had gone up to that time, what more amazing things would I learn? Right then and there, I decided to no longer fight what I did not understand, but rather to embrace the adventures of the unknown . . .

Tired and mentally used up, I gobbled my palatable dinner, consumed the usual late night television routine and settled to a troubled, stirring sleep blended together with anxious unrest . . . *I was still tripping even in my unconscious REM. . . .*

CHAPTER 11

AHA ... MORE CONNECTIONS

Theodore Bayonne

Jules and I exchanged our usual greetings, but as we began our dialogue it seemed somewhat strained on this visit. Perhaps it was just my imagination, but I did not sense the high level of anxiety I had come to expect based on my previous visits. Instead, on this Friday evening (January 12, 2007), I sensed a distinct calmness from Jules, which seemed to almost dim the atmosphere around us. I wasn't sure if it was Jules or the steel, gray sky peeking in from the window of the small room, or the slight breeze causing the gentle sway of the trees which caused me to talk about the weather instead of what I really wanted to know.

"It looks like we're going to get some rain this evening."

"You didn't come to talk to me about the weather, did you now, Byron?"

I shrugged my shoulders. *How does this guy know me so well? As far as I could tell, he'd never laid eyes on me before a couple of days ago! I guess there is some validity to that old saying about someone knowing you better than you know yourself!*

"No, not really, I do have another question for you," I whispered. "Can you tell me about your father?"

Jules nodded in agreement as he answered. "I will, but I hope that you will grant me the same consideration and tell me of your father as well."

Jules waited for my response. I wasn't sure why he was even posing this question. I didn't think we would really *ever* have any discussion about my father, especially since I didn't know much about my father anyway. I'd already told Jules that, but then again, that's Jules for you; you never knew where he was going . . . but, for certain, he was going somewhere with this, as with all his queries . . . I just didn't know where. Eventually, I gestured in kind, a nod of my own as a means of acknowledging our quid pro quo agreement to share information about our fathers. I was hoping that he would forget about it later . . . *Yeah, right, fat chance of that happening.*

Interestingly enough Jules didn't know much about his father, Theodore Bayonne, either. He had to depend on what he learned as a youth:

"My father's name is Teodore (Theodore) Bayonne. I don't remember a lot about him. He passed away wen I was quite young, so I'm jus relating wat I was told. He was born on April 18, 1793 on Saint-Domingue, da small island in da Atlantic Ocean, now known as Haiti. His father, Ferdinand Philippe Bayonne, was a French planter who grew cane, coffee, indigo and cotton on da island. My father shared several brothers and sisters sired by his father, but none of the others were born from my father's mother.

Teodore Bayonne came to Louisiana two months after his twentieth birthday in da spring of 1813 and spent da first 12 years in New Orleans. Wen he came to Louisiana, he made several acquaintances while he was on board da ship from da island. One woman, a fair-skinned woman of nearly forty years old named Madame Azelia Faisse, accompanied by her 15-year old daughter, Celanise, adopted him as dere male protector. Madame Faisse's treated him like her own son, but she was adamant about him not having any contact whatsoever with respects to da beautiful Celanise. Celanise was as fair-skinned as any white woman Theodore had ever seen. Her European facial features were obviously passed down from da side of her French, planter father.

Upon his arrival in New Orleans, Teodore secured work wit a blacksmith at da Glapion Plantation. His duties did not limit his ability to come and go as was da case for many free blacks, so he visited da Faisse's as often as he could. Madame Faisse was more like family to Teodore dan anyone else since da death of his parents. Aldhough he was forbidden by Madame Faisse to socialize with Celanise, he caught a glimpse of her youthful body one morning while she was preparing for her daily bath. He recalled dat Celanise stared at him, and den purposely untied da loop at da neck of her dressing gown, allowing da translucent cotton gown to fall, encircling her feet, and exposing her perfectly curved naked body. As he approached to pour da hot water in da metal bathtub, she turned away from him, allowing Teodore a view of da back of her fair-skinned, well-formed buttocks. He said dat she was angelic in form, having da matured body of a woman of at least twenty.

Theodore admitted dat Celanese's physical features were da most appealing and perfect of any he had ever seen and doubted that he would ever witness such perfection again in his life. He said his level of arousal on dat occasion; was never matched by any woman again, until in his later years wen he met Fanny, of course. All of Teodore's fantasies about Celanise went, unsatisfied. He was never to experience da warmth of love from da goddess, Celanise. Needless to say, my father had many fond thoughts of her over da years.

Shortly after da 'exposure' incident involving Celanise, Teodore gained employment at Fornerets as a plantation hand, maintaining da stables and amending (making poor soil good for growing crops) da fields wit manure. His skill in planting and producing superior quality sugar-cane had gained him a fair degree of respect in the parish. He was referred to as one of dose 'sugar-maker saviors from the islands.' He was also trusted to secure saddles, horseshoes and bits for da horses from da Carriere Estate (the parish's leading provider of riding equipment) on behalf of Fornerets and other plantations as the opportunity arose.

After da fall of 1815, Teodore never saw Celanise again. He had learned dat she was given to[67] a wealthy planter in New Orleans at one of da weekly 'Quadroon Balls' held at Da Globe[68]. However, he did pay his respects to her mother, Madame Faisse, who passed away da spring of da following year.

On May 16, 1830, my father rode his white horse; he named Sweets. (He had insisted Sweets was a Lipizzan bred from da same bloodlines of da Danish stud dating back to 1765) into New Roads to register as a free person of color. Teodore Bayonne had learned much about horses, particularly da Lipizzan and Andalusian breeds, from his father.,

Suddenly, Jules interrupted himself. He looked as though he was trying to remember something or that he'd left out something that was important to the telling of his story . . . I was right . . . he had. Recovered from his momentary pause, he continued . . .

"Wait a minute, wait a minute, let me back up one generation. It'll make more sense if I do it dat way.

My father's mother, Rose, was a mulatto[69] woman born to a slave mother named Marie. Aldough she was freed at birth by her white father, Jean-Luis Dumonte, she was taken as a mistress by Pierre Cadot, the son of a neighboring planter, Philippe Cadot, at da of age fifteen. Pierre Cadot at only twenty-seven years old was killed during da early years of

---

67 "Given to" suggested that Celanese was a plaçée, usually the case when a wealthy white planter arranges for a free woman of color, quadroon or octoroon to be taken as his *financially cared for* mistress.

68 The Globe was the home of one of the well-known weekly quadroon balls, where the resulting *plaçage* was customary. "places to which these young creatures are taken as soon as they have reached womanhood, and there they show their accomplishments in dancing and conversation to the white men, who alone frequented these places. When one of them attracts the attention of an admirer, and he is desirous of forming a liaison with her, he makes a bargain with the mother, agrees to pay her a sum of money, perhaps 2000 dollars, or some sum in proportion to her merits, as a fund upon which she may retire when the liaison terminates. She is now *'une plaçée.*" Quoted by Marcus Christian (Free Colored Class of Louisiana—14-7) from Frederick Law Olmstead. *A Journey in the Seaboard Slave States* (New York: Dix and Edwards, 1856), Harriet Martineau, *Society in America* (Paris: A&W Galignani, 1837), and G. W. Featherstonbaugh, *Excursion Through the Slave States* (New York: Harper and Brothers, 1841).

69 Rose may have been light-skinned (mullato) but was not subject to the process of plaçage which was apparently a system in operation in St. Domingue (Haiti) at the time she was living.

da revolt.[70] My grandmother, Rose still in her teens, fled to da mountains in da northern territory (just south of Cap François and north of Acul) where she performed da duties of a seamstress and processed laundry for da renegade blacks who had fled da plantations as a result of da revolt.

Rose Dumonte, as she was called, gave birth to a son, Jean François, sired by Pierre Cadot. Unfortunately, her firstborn child, died mysteriously before his first birthday."

Jules didn't explain what he meant by 'mysteriously', but I suspected it was probably due to an epidemic of some kind specific to children which contributed to the high infant mortality rate at the time. My good sense and upbringing told me it would be insensitive to press him, especially about something that he either didn't know or didn't want to talk about; so I didn't.

"Now, my father's father, my grandfather, Ferdinand Bayonne, was born in Saint-Domingue in 1766. He was born a free person of color on da Du Randon Plantation, owned by André Du Randon. DuRandon was a white, widowed sugarcane planter from da Basque Country in France from which Ferdinand's surname (Bayonne) is derived. It is believed dat André Du Randon fathered seven children including Ferdinand, da eldest child, by a Ghanaian slave girl named Effie.

Effie, born 'Asare' from da Southern region near Lake Volta in Ghana, made da journey to America around 1748, with an older sister—'Cembe' on a French vessel originating from LaRochelle, named 'Le Saphire.' Effie and Cembe, abducted by neighboring tribal kidnappers in da fields in dere village, were separated when dey arrived in Saint-Domingue. Dey never saw each other again.

Ferdinand met Rose in 1791 during da original revolt. He brought her down from a village in da mountains south of Cap François where she'd been living wit several groups of other renegade slaves (maroons). Two years later, my father, Theodore, was born in da northern territory of Saint-Domingue on da Du Randon Plantation.

Ferdinand Bayonne was a horse handler. He trained and provided some of da world's finest horses to da generals and high ranking officers (of the rebellion against Colonial France) until about 1801. Toussaint's

---

70   Hattian revolution—see footnote 35 above.

favorite white stallion, a Lipizzan, was presented to him in 1798 by Ferdinand, which he rode to negotiate a treaty wit da British general, General Maitland in April of da same year. Christophe[71] was given da beautiful stallion rumored to have come from da bloodlines of da original Karst and Lipizza stock, and likely to have been sired by da famed Spanish stallion, 'Pluto'[72].

Teodore's account of how Ferdinand came into possession of da horses suggests dat in Andre's attempt to avoid being killed by renegades of da conflict; he fled his beloved, but ravaged Du Randon Plantation, leaving twenty-seven fine horses behind. André left wit several other planters, including da former overseer of Breda Plantation, M. Bayon de Libertat, who was said to have been related to André. No record of André Du Randon reaching his intended destination in da Basque Region of France was ever found. It was rumored he had perished at sea wit several others fleeing Saint-Domingue.

No one ever told me how he did it, but somehow Ferdinand secretly returned to Du Randon and removed five of da horses he'd had to leave behind; and hid dem in da 'high country.' All of des fine horses were said to have been bred from European stock and sent to André between 1788 and 1790. Des horses included a light-grey, seven year-old stallion,[73] (later given to Toussaint). Ferdinand had cared for them right up to André's hasty departure from Saint-Domingue in August of 1797. No one knows for sur, but it seems reasonable dat des poor animals met da same fate as Andre; wherever and watever dat may be.

Ferdinand was a man of many 'talents.' He served his time in da army as well, having fought under da command of Henri Christophe from 1803 through 1807 and supported da first monarchy of Haiti under King Henri I. He also supported da new command by growing sugar, coffee

---

71 Henri Christophe was a key leader in the Haitian Revolution, which succeeded in gaining independence from France in 1804. In 1805 he took part under Jean-Jacques Dessalines in the capturing of Santo Domingo (now Dominican Republic).
72 Pluto: the famed gray Spanish stallion from the Royal Danish Stud, foaled in 1765.
73 Lipizzans are genetically a type of grey (horse). Born dark, black-brown, brown, or mouse-grey, Lipizzans gradually lighten until the white coat for which they are noted is produced somewhere between the ages of 6 and 10. From the Lipizzan Association of North America—Origins and History of the Lipizzan Horse.

and beans on a small 12-acre tract of land from which he provided more dan one-third of his earnings to da new government.

Sometime in 1810, Ferdinand met a peculiar, well-dressed traveler who offered him an elixir (later determined by a friend to be a type of rum). Da man carrying a leather bag with da engraved initials 'MPS', replied when asked his name. "My friends call me Percival." Da stranger, Percival, spoke to Ferdinand about travels to da New World, da colony of our motherland to be commenced by da 'sons' of Dumonte. Strong and brave was Ferdinand, but wary and perplexed by da words of Percival. He listened, finished da drink and endeavored to diligently tell da story of dese events to his two young sons da following year.

Ferdinand died of yellow fever in 1811 and his wife, Rose died in 1812 of a broken heart said to have been from loneliness and da void left by da loss of her beloved husband. I suppose dat dere had been some good times, but both my grandmother and grandfather struggled with da loss of my father's two younger brothers. Da poor little ones never made it much past walking age before dey died of 'consumption.' Nobody came right out and said so, but da tragedy of losing dere children most likely played a big part in da small, dark cloud dat hovered over dere life together."

"Okay enough wit ancient history. Let's move a lil closer to da present day." We both "leaked" a small but perceptible funny little snort; for me it was aimed at the word "present." I couldn't be sure, but presumably Jules' similar reaction was also due to the same reason.

Jules picked up where he left off talking about his father and his horse Sweets as if he'd never segued onto the little side trip he called 'ancient history'...

"How he came to own Sweets, was never told to me, but da rumor around Pointe Coupee was dat he won him in a bet. Apparently, Sweets' original owner bought him as a foal wen he was raven black. My father, having knowledge of da breed, offered to buy him, suggesting to da owner, he would become a spectacular white horse wen he matured. Da owner, agitated by da idea dat a 'black' (anything) somehow, could become a 'white' (anything), bet my father dat dat was impossible!"

Jules grinned widely. There was no mistaking his mood right then!

"I can almost see da steam coming out dat Joker's head wen he had to turn Sweets over to my father! Not only had da unthinkable happened—losing to a black man. Not only did he lose his property but now everybody knew dat da black man was smarter dan he was. Den, to add insult to injury and to put da icing on da cake da black (horse) had now transitioned into white. Now, fooling da whites by passing is one ting 'cuz dey don't know da people be black in da first place; but having something black turn white before your very eyes . . . weeelll; now dat be a horse of 'nother color . . . No pun intended"

Jules could no longer contain his hilarity. He laughed so hard tears slid down his face; and claimed a tenacious hold on his chin before they dropped and disappeared in the plushness of the carpeted room. His laugh was loud and it was contagious. I had to admit that the thought of Sweets, now a white horse and being the prize of the bet ultimately won by Jules' father was more than a bit of irony.

Finally, and not without some difficulty, we returned to our previous somber state. To tell the truth, though I enjoyed the brief levity, I welcomed Jules' returning to the most fascinating story I'd ever heard. I couldn't wait for him to continue; but it was getting late and I knew our visit would have to end soon. Still, Jules got in a little more of this wonderful story, a saga really, before I had to leave.

It made me feel good that Jules wanted to continue despite the late hour. It told me that he was glad to have someone to tell his story to and that he knew I was interested in hearing (and appreciating) it!

"Some folks say my father paid a small amount to da man, aldough he wasn't obliged to, but did so because he knew da horse's original owner was unaware of da rarity and value of da breed and my father was a fair and honest man.

Anyway, it was a particularly warm morning as he and Sweets left da stable. Da morning dew had already evaporated. Theodore Bayonne was always concerned whenever it was hot early in da day. It seemed dat tings had a tendency to go wrong on hot days, so he was a little apprehensive as he started da morning. And, as you'll see, he had good reason for feeling dat way.

Jules' comment about a 'warm morning' reminded me that if an elder from Louisiana—particularly if they were from New Orleans mentioned a 'warm morning', that usually suggested a hot day would result—'all hell is about to bust loose! All you had to do is wait. So I waited for Jules to bring the 'heat' related to Theodore Bayonne.

First, let me give you a little background. By da fall of 1831, Louisiana planters began to tighten dere grip on dere own slaves like never before. Da word came from da east 'bout an uprising attempt led by Nat Turner[74] in Virginia, enraging white folks terribly and causing fierce opposition to da growing antislavery efforts even in Louisiana.[75] After dat Nat Turner fiasco, it was strickly forbidden for slaves to read and write. Dat went for anybody tryin' to teach dem as well. Slave owners and whites in general, even dose who didn't own slaves, were suspicious of all da blacks. Didn't make no difference wedda dey was slave or free. Da owners were more apt to sell a slave dat was difficult rather dan to risk rebellious behavior spreading to da other slaves. Punishment was harsher dan before and whites tolerated less, readily beating da slaves for little or no reason at all.

Da Mayor of New Orleans, Dennis Prieur[76] was beginning to worry 'bout da possibility of slaves uprising due to da large number of free people of color dat had entered Louisiana over da last 25 years. Let me add dis little 'tidbit' here. Ironically, Prieur was carrying on an affair with a woman of color at da very time he was making decisions affecting free persons of color. Later dat fact would cost him da governor's office. But enough of gossip, at least for now. Anyway, let me go on. Dey was particularly interested in dose of us who came from Saint-Domingue after da revolution, which had lasted twelve years and had devastated dat entire country. Da Mayor believed dat dose who had been freed as a result of da revolution on da island might influence slaves and other coloreds on da plantations in New Orleans. Besides dat, many of da blacks who came from Saint-Domingue had fought in da revolution, so dey were seasoned

---

74 Nathanial "Nat" Turner (1800-1831) was a black African-American slave who led the only effective, sustained slave rebellion (August 1831) in U.S. history. Turner led a rebellion of slaves and free blacks in Southampton County, Virginia on August 21, 1831.

75 Jules may have been alluding to the fact that Louisiana's large Creole population, created the 'illusion' of more 'liberal race' relations—the idea that Louisiana negroes were generally. better off than in any other state in America.

76 The tenth mayor of New Orleans, Louisiana, serving ten years from 1828 to 1838., Prieur lost the election for Governor in 1838 to Andre B. Roman by 808 votes. It was suggested that Prieur's openly publicized relationship with his quadroon mistress cost him the 1838 Governor's election.

fighters and was sure to give dem whites plenty of trouble if anyting even resembling a revolt was to break out!

Teodore met wit a man named Norbert Rillieux[77] around da end of 1843 to discuss da process of boiling sugar using condensing coils inside of a vacuum chamber. See, wat I mean? Remember I told you, he was a man of many talents. Now, I'm fixin' to briefly tell you 'bout, yet another of his adventures. Rillieux was da most knowledgeable person he ever met, particularly in da field of engineering. His method for refining sugar was brilliant, but he, like Theodore and many other free persons of color, could never get da white planters to treat him wit da equality deserving of such accomplished men. Theodore arranged for da purchase of one of Rillieux's evaporators on behalf of the Fornerets and was personally involved in da installation of da equipment dere at da farm."

As Jules launched into another subject, I sneaked a peak at the clock on the wall. I hoped he hadn't seen me. He didn't seem to notice. Still, I expected a staff member to come into Jules room to send me on my way. After all, it was nearing the end of visiting hours and I wanted very much to hear the rest of 'this chapter' of Jules' story, although I hoped he would get to the point.

Fat chance, Jules was changing the subject again . . .

"Byron I am aware dat da hour is late and dat I seem to be jumping from one ting to another, but dis story is long and complicated. But if you'll hang in dere wit me, it'll all come together, just like one of dem jigsaw puzzles. Now, I don't remember if I told you precisely, but I'm sure being the bright fellow I come to know you to be, you already guessed dat Teodore could pass.[78] So he had fewer problems dan most of da other light-skinned folks and mulattoes. But da fact dat he held da knowledge of his true race created an internal struggle for him his entire life. Each time he looked at an image of himself, every time he looked in da mirror, he was reminded of da horror dat his mother and grandmothers must have

---

77 Norbert Rillieux revolutionized sugar processing with the invention of the multiple effect evaporator under vacuum,. was born on March 17, 1806 in New Orleans, Louisiana. Norbert was born a free man, although his mother was a slave named Constance Vivant. Norbert was the natural son of Vincent Rillieux and Vivant.

78 One who could *pass*, meant pass as a white person. Also referred to as *passé en blanc or passé blanc*. Theodore Bayonne possessed the appearance of a white person.

experienced when dere French (white) masters forced demselves sexually to da resultant lightening of da skin affecting several generations of wat I call 'in-between-folk.' Dey in-between black and white and contrary to Teodore's tinking dey not a 'true race' at all.

Anyway, let me push on before dey start putting all visitors out 'round here. In da late fall of 1843 Teodore met a beautiful girl he described as 'sweet as morning dew.' Teodore took her glance and slight smile on dis occasion of dere first meeting to be flirtatious and decided dat was an invitation to get to know her better, sometin he wanted to do anyway.

Fanny, dat was her name, was about twenty-four years old wen Theodore met her and her newly freed status was of great advantage to dere union a few months later. She was granted permission to marry by da owner of Riverlake Plantation where she worked in da kitchen sometimes and at other times in da gardens.

My father said he really loved my mother, but according to wat I was told, his marriage to her was not considered legally binding by many folks in da community because of da restrictions concerning enslaved and former enslaved women at that time[79]. This problem proved to linger throughout dere entire lives. As I said before, my mother probably had been freed before her and my father married, but Louisiana and rest of da world had peculiar laws relating to colored folk, especially wen it came to marriage. He had been afforded a small cabin on da grounds of da Fornerets Plantation. *Da* plantation owner kept da cabin dat was originally used by da overseer. My father lived dere for over seven years while he worked at Fornerets where he met my mother.

Louisiana's law allowed for some gens de couleur libré ownership of property, and because he owned a small farm, he had earned enough money to support da young mullato, Fanny. He tought she could help him wit cleaning and cooking while he worked breeding horses and tinkering wit da latest inventions of da day."

I wasn't sure if I was tired or what, but as I strained to focus my tired eyes and mind toward the man seated in the chair across from me.

---

[79] The Black Codes accepted as law for much of the State of Louisiana between 1806 through 1866 (replaced by "Jim Crow" later) were often interpreted to restrict marriage between slaves and former slaves and free people of color.

It suddenly occurred to me that Jules was still speaking to me and that only a few brief moments earlier, it seemed more like I was listening to his father instead of him! I had absolutely no evidence what Jules' father, Theodore Bayonne looked like, but there in the quiet of that little room, another entity was speaking—a different person, yet the same man, whom I thought I'd come to know as Jules Bayonne. But now, I was faced with yet another challenge: the acceptance of the presence of Theordore Bayonne, who was now sitting in the stead of Jules who was there (*I began to wonder, exactly were 'there' is or was or will be; was it the now, the then or the yet to come?*). But how could this be? Did I doze off and imagine this other person conversing in enough vivid detail as if Jules' father were present? Perhaps I did get lulled into another state of 'incredibility' by Jules' soothing and melodic voice and heard him speak of his father. (*It reminded me of the times I'd fallen asleep with the TV on and some of its programming infiltrated my dreams; and actually posited itself there as a 'scene' in the dream*). I started to try to rationalize the strange feeling of the presence of another distinct individual speaking . . . but then my 'rationalization' turned into a why? A what for? Hadn't I already entered the world of 'irrationalization' when I met Jules? The bigger question was: Why start trying to rationalize now? The die had already been cast and if I was going to benefit from this adventure in the personage of Jules, Theodore or anybody else that happened to show up, I need to let go of the 'theory of rationalization' where obviously, in this case, none existed!

It took me a minute to realize Jules had stopped speaking of his father when he, looked at me and asked again the question I'd hoped in vain he would forget to revisit: "So can you tell me a little about your father?"

I responded almost apologetically. "I know *very* little about my father, I'm afraid. You see my mother already had two children before she met my father and I think she was a little surprised to know she was expecting with me. Nevertheless, she never spoke much about my father and I suspect he didn't stay around too long after finding out my mother was going to have his baby. The fact is I'm not sure I ever saw my father."

Jules looked at me almost as though he were disappointed: "You have a pathetic situation, boy! I never met a person who didn't know anyting about where dey came from before. Am I da first person you ever talked wit about family matters such as dis?"

I began again, even more apologetically this time, as I hung my head ever so slightly. "Well, it's true, my background probably doesn't' compare to yours, but . . ."

Jules interrupted. "You don't have a background! Boy, what kind of *'receptive'* are you? No past whatsoever?"

Talking about being ashamed and embarrassed! Jules' going straight to the point really hit me hard! Instead of continuing to feel sorry for myself, I shook off his comment about not having a background. And what was all that talk about being a *'receptive'*? I'd always heard the word *'receptive'* used as an adjective. Now, here, Jules was using it as a noun, a person; specifically used to name me, Byron Marcelle Coleman!

Instead, when I heard the word *'receptive'* used by Jules for the first time, I wondered what he meant by it, but at the same time, I sensed his frustration. I was reluctant to inquire as to his meaning of the word, at least for the moment.

Despite my still smarting from Jules' reference to my not having a 'background,' I found myself defending my position. I insisted (at least in my own mind) that I did have a background. However, my defense of myself proved almost futile. "I have some background, for instance my mother . . ."

Jules stopped me again. "Your mother is my future, and you are too! I'm very aware of dat much. I know more about you dan you know 'bout yourself! Wat I *don't know* is da *other* half of you; dat's makes you whole. Son, you need to know where you come from!"

"Oh, so then Jules, you do *know* that we are related?" I said, clearly realizing there was no getting around *that* mystery any longer.

Jules stroked his well-trimmed beard and remarked, "Byron, It sounds like you were brought up by upstanding people. But as da Count[80] said, " . . . of course, to you, people's positions are important. But such people are only given positions by ministers or kings. God has placed some above

---

[80] Jules had remarkably quoted from the sixth chapter of Alexandre Dumas' The Count of Monte Cristo, a pivotal moment when Edmond Dantes is fulfilling his mission of revenge and announces his entitlement as appointed by Providence to exact such an action on his enemies, although he masks nature of the mission which will be revealed in time.

ministers and kings. He has given dem missions more important." Jules summarized his comment saying, "Your folks do well to be proud of you *son,* but we both *know* why you are having such a difficult time fittin' your upbringing in dis situation wit me."

A chill rocked me to the core when I heard Jules call me son, knowing *now* he literally meant it. For certain, Jules' last comment suggested we would eventually stop the game of charades and confront the subject of reconciliation of time between his present and my past.

After Jules was transferred to the facility in Riverdale, Georgia, the staff over at Grady Memorial seemed to be less concerned about the peculiarity of his case and had resolved that he was more mentally out of touch as opposed to being a person from a past period in time. I could not seem to be able to contact any of the physicians at Grady Memorial Hospital who advised me not to discuss certain things with Jules, so upon inquiring those proposed possible dangers with the physicians at the Riverdale facility, I was assured that no real danger was apparent. Quite frankly, it was apparent to me that Jules' *problem* had been transferred along with Jules to the Riverdale facility and it was no longer a concern of the staff, including Harris, at Grady. But what I was later to find out, Grady, Harris, the hospital staff and the entire incident, now more than two weeks later was only necessary as a means to get Jules and me to meet as a result of *other* plans.

As the gong signaled the end of visiting hours sounded in the corridor and which could also be heard over the facility's PA system, I took my leave for the evening. On the ride home, I had the time and solace to contemplate the fact that at least one thing had been settled. Jules had finally acquiesced to our kinship. I smiled broadly, happy that no one I knew could see that silly Cheshire Cat grin on my face, signifying I'd won that 'round.'

* * *

Back about the fourth visit, I began to take more things to the hospital in attempts at jolting Jules' memory and *easing* him **into** the present current day. On this particular day, Monday, January 15, I brought my family bible, the one which had been given to me by my great-uncle, Samuel Pourciau just after Janice and I were married in 1976.

Jules observed the tattered book I had held together very carefully with virtually 'spit and glue.' "Dat bible has seen better days!" Jules remarked.

"Good evening Jules. How are you doing today?" I asked.

"I'm real good today, tanks. I had eggs, fresh sausage and grits for breakfast!" Jules offered happily. "May I look at your bible?"

I placed the tattered book, held together with extra-wide cellophane tape and my son's stray green permanent marker scribbling over the fading-white Jesus image, on Jules' lap. I sat in the chair not more than three feet across from him, wondering if he was going to reprimand me for not taking better care of the Holy Scriptures. I decided not to give him that opportunity.

"You're so right Jules, my bible has seen better days, many of them which I enjoyed with my children and the great delight we shared in my reading to them from that bible. My son, Derek when he was three years old took the marker to Jesus because he said Jesus looked better green. I had every intention of having it restored in the future, I just ain't got 'round to it yet."

As Jules thumbed through the first few pages of the bible before I realized I could stop talking. He was no longer listening to my explanations or anything else I had to offer. I heard him murmur faintly about the beauty of the writing as he admired the beautifully painted exhibit plates, including those displaying *The Creation*, *Jacob's Dream*, and other popular stories depicted by famous artists.

Jules turned to a plate where Jesus is standing in the court of Pontius Pilate and as he looks out at Peter a rooster, in the background, appears to ready himself to crow. He commented softly, "Dese paintings say a whole lot, don't dey?"

I nodded in acknowledgement as he continued.

"As I said before, some people believed dat da *photograph* has da power to take away part of a person's soul. I heard it said dat some places in dis world it is tought dat a photograph might open da *door* to demons and the like. But I'm certain you don't take any stock in all of dose myths."

My puzzled expression lasted a few seconds before I noticed Jules was waiting for me to respond to his comment regarding photograph myths. I gathered my thoughts and responded.

"Please pardon me, Jules, but I was about to say that I hadn't heard of such myths; but then it occurred to me that I had once read a story by the Irish author, Oscar Wilde, entitled *The Picture of Dorian Gray*. The author's main character, Dorian Gray has a portrait of himself painted. But the *twist* in this story is that the portrait takes on a life of its own. It and not Dorian revealed Dorian's character flaws and sins. As time went on, the portrait aged and became hideous, reflecting his misdeeds, while Dorian remained ageless, handsome and *without sin*."

Jules hummed and rephrased his query. "But, what importance do *you* place on paintings and pictures?"

I wrestled within to provide an intelligent answer. "Well, I guess I had taken the process of capturing a person's image for granted. But as you brought it to my attention, I got to thinking about how a great deal of detail regarding an individual can be surmised from a quality painting, a superior portrait or an exceptional photograph. Much, much more than the obvious visible details the observer can make during a specific point in time is only temporal which depends upon the period in time, the social status, the mood of the subject at the time and place the image is captured." Pointing to the painting Jules had referred to in the old, weathered bible, I continued, but this time in more detail. "Jesus is standing in the courtyard of Pontius Pilate, who is turned away, 'washing his hands' of the complicated matter of deciding the fate of a prisoner accused of sedition. In the foreground is a man trying not to look at Jesus and a rooster looms in the frame as if it's about to crow. The painting in this instance, coupled with a familiarity of the written words related to the incident, offer compelling support to show how dramatic and unforgettable the actual occurrence of the event was."

Jules began, "Well, I do see your meaning. Dese images do seem to say a lot. I also have heard about da *Dorian Gray* writing, aldough I never read it for myself. Da story seems fascinating—a painting dat takes on da characteristics of a man, aging and decaying with da traits of da man while da man himself maintains a flawless appearance. But, I must confess dat

I am more intrigued by your interpretation of da images found in your bible dan dat Dorian Gray stuff."

Then, at last, Jules closed the bible, looked at me squarely and asked; "Wat do you favor most in dis book?"

I thought for a moment, and then *proceeded with caution*. "I think I like the works of First Samuel. In particular, the story of David selecting five smooth stones and slaying the giant Goliath of Gath interest me the most." I thought that my answer had impressed Jules since he did not reply for a few moments. *I should have known better.* Suddenly, as if his *batteries* had been recharged, Jules began to unravel my David story with questions and comments, probing my understanding and instructing me as if he were a seasoned professor of theology.

"So then, are you Catholic?" Jules asked.

"Not really, although I was married Catholic, I am considered a Non-denominational Christian," I replied, not sure what drove him to that conclusion.

"Some would say you are a *heathen*, where I come from." Jules snapped grinning. I laughed, with a smile, hinting I could withstand a little joking.

"Why would you tink a young boy like David would take on a fight wit a giant like Goliath?" Jules queried.

I responded with a half-baked answer, "I guess the noble idea that David needed to protect his people was an adequate reason."

Jules stared at me disappointedly and hissed, "So you really believe dis young boy was developed in both mind and body to aggressively take on da 'champion' of da Philistines?"

I stammered, "I don't know."

"Well," Jules continued, "As I recollect, da two armies were in a ravine separated by opposing peaks when da giant came down in da area reserved for battle. This is where Goliath shouted his famous proclamation[81]. His stature and menacing battle attire undoubtedly presented an awesome sight

---

81 From **KJV**, 1 Samuel 17: 8-51 "... choose you a man for you, and let him come down to me." 10 ... I defy the armies of Israel this day; give me a man, that we may fight together." 16 "And the Philistine drew near morning and evening, and presented himself forty days." 23 "Goliath ... spake according to the same words ..." In summary, Goliath shouted out his obscenities to the armies of Israel for at least forty days until David came up, heard the speech and after initially running away, values the reward and then declares: "... for who *is* this uncircumcised Philistine, that he should defy the armies of the living God?"

for all to see. David was a mere visitor at the site where the army of Israel had encamped. His only purpose for being dere at dat particular time was to bring a basket of food for his older brothers, as he was instructed by his father wen he heard da threat of Goliath. I further recollect dat after he challenged da entire armies of Israel to send dere best to fight. Everyone ran, apparently including Saul and David! So, *nobility* may not have been part of David's reasoning.

Hmmm, that's not quite how I remember the story as it relates to David running away from Goliath. As I recall, the story goes that he ran toward Goliath with a sling and five smooth stones.

"But as you may remember, Byron, David overheard dat da king would give riches, his daughter as a bride and freedom for da family of da man who would kill da giant. David asked da soldiers discussing dis, to repeat what dey had said. Upon hearing dese men repeat da king's reward; David was overcome by boldness and bravely declared da giant was uncircumcised and unworthy of da defiance to da armies of da God of Israel. So, I rather tink, David was moved by da tought of getting da *girl*, da promise of great wealth, or da freedom and most likely **all** of dose tings combined."

"You are probably right, Jules," I answered. "But are you suggesting he was not brave?"

Jules continued: "I guess your contention dat he was noble could be a factor since he also had to address da accusation of one of his brothers who suggested he was showing off for da crowd's (Israeli army) approval. But if so, den his need for da men to repeat what da reward was seems to support my supposition better. I bet David was seeing dat rich daughter of Saul's in his mind's eye."

Jules carefully placed the bible on the small table next to his chair and rose from his seat. With his right index finger pointing near his temple, Jules went on to say: "Keep in mind David's only social contact largely consisted of da incessant bleating of sheep. Now, wouldn't it be nice to bed down with a fine woman in dere palace instead of enduring da natural elements of da environment wit some smelly and needy, woolly varmints? Oh, I tink you see it clearer too, Byron! Most men wen confronted wit even da possibility to win a better status, will usually rise to da occasion and roll da dice. Da kind of wealth that King Saul offered would make life so much better for David and his family. But, I'm not so sure David was tinking about his own family so much as he might have been tinking of da comfort of da beautiful woman he caught a glimpse of before[82]. Possibly, da rumors told by da other men about da pretty princess had been described to David caused da stir in his ambitions of a better life. I have a question for you. Do you dream?"

"Yes I do have dreams." I answered calmly to Jules' curious question. I wasn't sure if he were asking about my aspirations or the dreams I experienced while I slumbered.

"I mean, do you dream? Not just dose dreams you *have* when you asleep," Jules countered.

Aha, clarity was on its way.

"Yes, I responded, I dream mostly of my future and how things might be if I don't stray too much from the goals I have set, and in some instances those goals set for me by my loved ones."

"In your dreams for a better future, so you see other people participating with you—striving with you?" Jules pressed again.

Oops, still did't know which type of dream he referred to, so I opted for dreams of the slumber variety.

I struggled with recalling particular instances of my dreams as I responded. "I can't say for sure that others are there present when I dream those sleepless visions of what is to happen in my future, but I do have something to admit in relation to others involved in my dreams *while sleeping*. Shortly before we met for the first time, I dreamt of an attack in a place I vaguely remember taking place in Denver, Colorado. Janice and I ran, fleeing a large group of armed men who were shouting horrible, hateful and vindictive words as they began to fire their weapons in our direction. I was so afraid, as these awful people caught my wife and were closing in on me when a man I *knew* as Jesse was struck down by the shot one of the men who was doing the chasing. He fell in front of me, only a footstep away, causing my panic to reach the level of paralysis, I

---

[82] King James Bible 1 Samuel 14:49 "Now the sons of Saul were Jonathan, and Ishui, and Melchishua: and the names of his two daughters were these; the name of the firstborn Merab, and the name of the younger Michal . . ."

screamed—Jesse! Then, I suddenly awoke, trembling, drenched with sweat, vividly remembering calling out name of a man I'd never met before. That is, until a few days ago when you spoke of a man you met named Jesse."

"Colfax, the town over in Grant Parish—well, you do dream!" Jules exclaimed.

"Jesse?" I questioned, more confused than before and wondering why Jules was getting so excited.

Jules sat back, looked up at the low hung ceiling and began. "Jesse McKinney *and* Levi Nelson—two men who didn't know each other, so I am told, but da events of da *conflict* in Colfax, which happened da same time François and I bought da farm in Livonia, almost 'nixed da deal.' White folks, all over da state were a little testy wen it came to doing business wit coloreds around dat time. François was so uneasy dat later on, he sold his share to me. Da land—dat is da one ting I tink—I don't' know—maybe dat's it! I can still smell da earth, a ball of dirt I grabbed and sniffed as I closed my eyes and dreamed of my future."

It looked as though Jules was experiencing the moment, eyes now closed, lifting a cupped hand near his face. I refused to say anything, I patiently and quietly listened. In the stillness, white noise prevailed, faintly I could hear Jules breathing, and with the rhythm of his ebb and flow, I closed my own eyes. Now, I too, saw the land, heard the dreams of the ancients whispered through the rustling leaves of the tall cypress trees.

CHAPTER 12

CODE NOIR

When I opened my eyes, I was surprised to see Jules, calmly staring as if he were awaiting my next query. I felt we had not completed the conversation of visions and dreams related to the bible—there had to be more to glean from David's story. I sensed Jules had more to give, if I would only ask. Not wanting to disappoint him, I 'prepped' myself to ask how Jules was able to have solidified his belief in his faith as strong, particularly as a devout Catholic. Cautiously, I questioned him.

"Jules, do you really believe in everything in the bible?"

Jules repositioned himself in the large chair. He appeared to be somewhat perplexed by my question. He stroked his beard, inhaled deeply, and then answered.

"Faith requires me to not understand, yet accept. I am aware dat da bible has had human hands shapin' its form, but I am very certain of da divine guidance dat allowed dose hands to yield a frame for God's peoples' morals and standards. Often, men do not apply da rules correctly, but dat does not make da *rules* wrong. Of da few tings I absolutely understand in da bible, I have faith witout question and da tings I don't quite comprehend,

God is big enough for me to place my faith in da goodness of da intent of da men who were da writers and I accept dat by faith."

"I understand faith," I began. Then I paused, hoping to get a little more understanding of how Jules' embracing of his religious beliefs had come about when Jules continued as if he had read my mind.

"Maybe I have failed to give you sufficient support for my position with respect to faith. My father explained some tings to me wen I was a young boy. As a man, I return to dose teachings wen I am burdened wit toughts of despair or confusion. I was helpin' him to building a small shed to house his garden tools, saddles, bridles and bits. He was faced wit a need to measure a joint comin' to a corner. My father was more than sixty years old by den but even wit his weary eyesight he saw me startin' to fret and walked over and gently took da hammer from my hands and said: *"Dere is an order to wich all things obey. Foundations will determine da strength of all dat is created."* He den showed me how da floor of da small shed had been constructed of rough, thick timbers wich had been secured to four stone pillars embedded in da compacted earth. Da walls we were addin' to hold da tin-covered roof was solidly connected to da floors and was secured at da corners havin' no errors. My father den took me outside dat small shed and sat down on da little steps at da entrance and motioned for me to sit beside him. He moistened his lips as he pulled gently on a grip of grass in front of him, singlin' out a slender straw from the patch of grass and stuck it in the corner of his mouth and said:

"Dis place called Pointe Coupee was settled almost one hundred years before I came from Saint-Domingue. Frenchmen and Africans were here den working da very land we sit on now. With dem came da religion we came to know as defined by da Code[83] wich we were subjected to by da order of King Louis."

My father went on to explain how da *Code Noir* had been forced on more dan four generations of our ancestors, first in Saint-Domingue and later in Louisiana."

---

83   Code Noir, written by Marquis de Seignely in 1683, ratified by France's Louis XIV and adopted by Saint-Domingue Sovereign Council in 1687. The Code Noir defined French sovereignty in her colonies, including the business of slavery and the restrictions relative to the institution of slavery. The Code Noir also forbade the exercise of any religion other than Roman Catholicism in the French colonial empire.

Jules paused for a moment and at that instant, it occurred to me that I had just received a remarkable revelation from Jules—Louisiana, particularly prior to 1803, was a Catholic colony! Furthermore, after 1803, during the time that free people leaving Saint-Domingue; fleeing the chaos resulting from the revolt, came to Louisiana seeking refuge, added to the already largely (black) Catholic population. At the very least, the explanation of the *Code Noir* made me aware of how the '*Cornerstone*' of faith had been laid by our ancestors. I started to connect the timelines of the middle ages, throughout the colonial period where the establishment of power in the church by Charlemagne[84] and Otto III, began cementing the foundation of Christian doctrine, and the vanity of the kings—James, Henry (VIII) and Louis (XIV), who needed to 'translate' the scriptures such that they would shape society to this day.

Jules began to speak again. "During da revolution, Christophe and Toussaint were confronted with da concerns of how Roman Catholicism was da demanded religion over da French territories and colonies. Dey had agreed dat, adhough dere were doctrines manipulated to encourage da institution of slavery and its degrading elements, da underlying message declaring dat *Christianity was good for all people*. Dose men and most of da leaders of da revolt embraced Catholicism in spite of its inherent flaws, contending dat, if applied properly, did much to stabilize moral conduct."

I asked Jules a few more questions, anticipating he would reveal that the decree enacted in 1685 by Louis XIV, the famous French king, was the ***sole*** determining factor as to why more than half of the State of Louisiana's populations are affiliated with the Catholic Church to the current day![85]

I was curious to know more about Jules' understanding regarding the origins of modern Christianity in his region. I ***needed*** to understand how Christianity in general and Catholicism in particular, had shaped our family's lives to this day, in addition to the countless others who faced with similar circumstances, were required to adopt and adhere to religious policy impacting present generations.

---

84   Charlemagne, the Christian Emperor of the Franks between 771 to 814 A.D., also referred to as Charles the great, was one of Pepin the Short's (king of the Franks) sons and the grandson of Charles Martel.

85   Source: Jones, Dale E., et al. 2002. Congregations and Memberships in the United States 2000. Nashville, TN: Glenmary Resarch Center.

Jules responded as if he were reading my thoughts. "I have heard da story of da Council[86] presided over by Constantinople,[87] where da rules of da bible were set for da ages. Are you testing da validity of da written word?"

I was trying to figure out how to answer Jules, hoping not to offend him by my obvious cynicism. But before I could settle on an approach, he spoke again.

"I agree most closely with da sentiments of Frederick Douglass regarding **Christianity of this land** as opposed to da **Christianity of Christ**. He wrote concerning da illegitimate doctrine promoted by hypocrites around da time he was born:[88] *"Da unblemished, good, pure and holy Christianity of Christ requires da practice of law, judgment, mercy and faith."*

Jules seemed in be no hurry to expound on this newly broached subject which gave me some time to give it due consideration. I tried to imagine the frustration Jules and other people of the day who, like Douglass were subjected to the cruelties of a society controlled by ignorant, yet dangerous people. The complexity of the nature of a people who promoted a doctrine contradictory to that of the horrible practices of black slavery, where *hushed* violence inflicted on their own (white) women and children, and unbridled adultery must have been extremely difficult to endure.

Jules began again. "Even dose who were sympathetic to Mr. Douglass were troubled by his candor in his description of da evil associated with man's abuse of Christianity. Men who championed Mr. Douglass when he spoke on behalf of abolition became indignant because of da publication of his narrative, exposing dere evils. So much so, Mr. Douglass was required to explain his writing, which had obviously offended some of his benefactors, as to his love and acceptance of a pure and genuine Christianity.

"Mr. Douglass admitted dat he had spoken in a "tone and manner..." so as to lead many to believe he opposed religion. He attempted to clarify his position by pointing out dat da region of this country holding slaves

---

86   Council at Nicaea

87   Constantine the Great (Latin: Flavius Valerius Aurelius Constantinus Augustus) Roman Emperor from 306 to 337 AD. Constantine was the son of Flavius Valerius Constantius, a Roman Army officer, and his consort Helena. He called the First Council of Nicaea in 325, at which the Nicene Creed was adopted by Christians.

88   The Narrative of the Life of Frederick Douglass, by Frederick Douglass, Boston, MA Published At The Anti-Slavery Office, No. 25 Cornhill Copyright 1845.

was of concern without regard to genuine Christianity. It was necessary for him to distinguish two separate ideals claiming Christianity; da good, pure, peaceable and holy one, and da one dat should be rejected as it is bad, corrupt and wicked. If dere is support for corrupt, slaveholding, women-whipping, cradle-plundering, partial and hypocritical Christianity of dis land, den we must reject dis and embrace da impartial, loving nature of da proper Christianity of Christ."

I listened intently as Jules' support for one of my dearest historic icons poured from his heart with tremendous passion. He paused, his eyes now locked in my direction as if he needed my approval to continue. I nodded, hoping he sensed I was not only in total agreement with his comments, but also, overwhelmed at his detailed familiarity with the written sentiments of Frederick Douglass. I beamed a smile as Jules continued.

"Byron, if you want to know how I feel about da misrepresentation of Christianity, all you have to do is read what Mr. Douglass said. I am in total agreement dat dis country's claim to da religion as Christianity is truly da highest level of deceit! How can men justify da taking by force, da horrid, brutal beatings of another living person, den fervently embrace da bible as clergy and missionaries? I too, detest da beastly inconsistencies of da fraudulent Christianity dis country manipulates for its own gain. At da same time, dere exists, an authentic Christianity—da one where Christ is in da center—demanding dat we love one another! It is not likely dat da Christianity dat harms, commits gross discord and disrupts peace to be da one Christ intended."

* * *

The evening had ended too soon. I was hoping for more but Jules seemed more ready to call it a day than to continue with *my* education. It seemed as if all that talk about Douglass had sapped all his strength. I left, hoping Jules would be as eager to see me the next day as I would be to see him. My sense gates were opened full throttle. I arrived home totally unaware of the time I walked from the building in Riverdale until I had parked my car in the driveway.

Thank God for automatic pilot!

That night, my mind buzzed with anticipation of how much more I was certain to learn from this sage of a man I'd come to know as Jules Bayonne. My mind was a flight as I pondered the powerful emotion of love, intermingled with genuine respect—the kind one should have for a wise family elder. This was a new experience for me—the missing connection for a man who had no ties to his father or grandfather. I never met my mother's father; although I was informed he was alive until I was about thirty-one years old. My mother scarcely knew her father, so it was very unlikely her children would ever meet him, much less have any kind of relationship with him. But Jules, on the other hand, fulfilled *that* role (or at least how I imagined it to be) *perfectly*! But, how can this be?

Sleep, won out at last.

* * *

I returned the next evening, Tuesday January 16th with an unfamiliar, but pleasant energy. Perhaps it was the feeling I had that this was the day something exciting was about to happen, but I liked the feeling, whatever it was due to. I had just entered the room, we exchanged greetings, when suddenly, Jules blurted.

"Byron, I got 'dis newspaper today—no news of President Roosevelt[89]. I'm a little surprised, him being president and all! Instead, The Atlanta Journal-Constitution writes many stories about a 'President Bush'!"

I stared at Jules waiting for his next move. I think he must have been waiting for mine as well . . . He didn't say anything for a few moments.

I kinda felt like we were playing a cat and mouse game . . . I continued to wait patiently for the drama to unfold.

Jules finally eased himself from the chair and slowly walked to the window. I noted an almost imperceptible tremble in his voice as he asked the question I knew was coming: "Byron, how can dis be da year of 2007?"

I finally answered him fearing he might lose his grip on this fragile thread of the 'here and now' saying, "I don't know Jules, but it *is*, and you are here in it." "Can I get you something?" I offered, sensing that he must have been shaken at hearing this news (no pun intended).

---

[89] Theodore Roosevelt, the 25th U.S. President in office September 14, 1901 to March 4, 1909.

Jules turned around and softly spoke "I don't guess you can bring my wife, Victorine here?"

"I don't think we can Jules," I sadly replied.

Although, Jules seemed to have resolved that he was functioning in the present period; a time different from a time he insisted was much earlier, this episode was one of a few occasions where he seemed to reflect, with difficulty, accepting the strangely complex issue of *time*, well, at least as how strangely it relates to him.

Hmm, I wondered, or how strangely it related to me?

Had Jules Bayonne been *interviewing me* all along? One thing for certain, I was getting the education of a lifetime from this man who seemed to keep life simple, and yet offer principles that are boundlessly unlimited by time and place. But how can it be? I questioned, no actually interrogated myself internally. I was still struggling with varying levels of disbelief and denial regarding the possibility of Jules Bayonne from the 1800's being in my (2007) presence.

It also occurred to me that in much of the time in each visit, Jules was aware of the current time period *he was told* we were in. He did not 'meltdown; on the contrary, he appeared to be quite relaxed most of the time, almost as if he understood *how* it was possible.

My instincts told me I would never have to ask *him* how, so I sat back in the comfort of the soft tweed covered chair and looked at Jules and waited.

"I was born in da same year of da *Great Disappointment*[90], so some people tought I came wit special gifts, others tought I was peculiar." Jules paused, took a deep breath and began again.

---

90   The **Great Disappointment** was a major event in the history of the Millerite movement, a 19th century American Christian sect that formed out of the Second Great Awakening. William Miller, a Baptist preacher, understood by studying the prophecies in the book of Daniel (Chapters 8 and 9, especially Dan. 8:14 "Unto two thousand and three hundred days; then shall the sanctuary be cleansed") that Jesus Christ would return to the earth during the year 1844. A more specific date than of October 22, 1844, was preached by Samuel S. Snow. Although thousands of followers, some of whom had given away all of their possessions, awaited expectantly, Jesus did not appear as expected on the appointed day and as a result October 22, 1844, became known as the Great Disappointment.

"My wife's father was a tough man." Jules started to explain. "Old man Randall[91] still reminds me to dis day, dat I needed to provide better for his daughter dan she had been while she was in under his roof and before I convinced her to marry me." "So," Jules continued, "I bought some land wit a friend's[92] help and built a cottage for Victorine, Willie (our first born) and me to start *life's journey*."

I wondered who Jules was referring to when he spoke of 'Willie', but he didn't mention any additional details—leaving me to conclude this was yet another of his unrevealed 'mysteries.'

Jules became reminiscent for a moment as he sat back down in the chair in the corner of the room and stretched both arms out the length of the chair resting his fingers over the edge of its arms. He stared at me with an intense look and asked.

"Can I count on you to keep a promise to me, Byron?"

"Certainly, Jules," of course," I said, hoping I could help relieve this uneasiness he seemed to have at that moment.

---

91 John Randall is Jules Bayonne's father-in-law. According to the U.S. Census, John Randall was born in 1824 and died around 1910.

92 Jules Bayonne and Franciois Francis purchased approximately sixty-six acres of land in 1870 in the Area now known as Frisco in the town of Livonia, Louisiana. Currently, his descendants (including the author) own just under thirty-three of the acres of the original property.

CHAPTER 13

THE PROMISE

"I need to speak to you as a friend, in strict confidence. Do you understand?" He reiterated his concern to confide in me, then stated. "I want you to be truthful wen you talk to me, as I must be wit you."

Jules got up again and walked over to me, leaning down so his face was within twelve inches from mine.

"First ting, tell me, who are you?" He asked this question, staring at me as if he were studying some type of object of intrigue.

"I am Byron Coleman, son of Dolores Washington and B.M. _____" I responded. Jules pointed his index finger at me and interrupted,

"No! I want to know how you tink you are of any concern *to me*! You and I must be able to speak freely now!" Jules hissed. "I would like to tell you someting of great importance. But dere can be no mistake as to whether or not you are supposed to hear dat of which I am supposed speak of." He whispered this as he straightened up from his bent position, walked to the door and quietly closed it. "Let us speak freely now. We have been working very hard, avoiding someting—dere is *someting* of great importance, we both must confront and, by now you know dat we need to use our time wisely. So let us stop wasting time, and let us deal wit wat is important."

Jules returned to his seat and snuggled back in his chair, glancing at the closed door frequently. I couldn't help but wonder if he was looking for some unmistakable assurance from me; or if he was afraid of our conversation somehow being overheard . . . or both.

I pulled my chair closer to where Jules was sitting as I sat down directly in front of him sensing that the time had come for me to assume a posture which required that the strict observance of confidentiality between the parties:

Your daughter, Florence, and her husband, Peter Sorrell gave birth to two daughters, one in 1911 and the other in 1913. The eldest, she named Theresa, the younger Ethel. Theresa Sorrell is my grandmother, who died 1978 in New Orleans, Louisiana.

"Remember, you promised to tell da truth to me yeah, Byron," Jules interrupted, sighed, slowly blinked his eyes and then began again as if I'd never started speaking. I acquiesced into the silence mode.

"I just met a man by da name of Sorrell a few days ago who is very likely a key to my predicament. But dis talk about 1911 and even 1978, is wat *is* to happen, in the future?"

I shrugged my shoulders and looking puzzled, responded. "Well, sort of. I supposed in one instance, *for you*, it is what will occur, and in another sense, *for me* these events have already occurred."

Jules sat back in the old chair and stroked his beard. Now, he was the one with a puzzled look on his face. My mind raced and I thought, this does not make any sense. This *is* the year 2007 and Jules appears to be struggling with events that took place in *his* current year of 1903, which he insists is the year it was when he fell asleep a few days ago. Things that have occurred in my past *historically connect* as far back as Jules's future beyond the year 1903. I began to worry about Harris' warnings that had cautioned me not to discuss *time* or certain individuals with Jules, fearing it might damage him further psychologically. I felt that *I* was becoming damaged psychologically.

"Jules, based on what you are saying and based on what I know from the records, we are related," I said slowly. I pulled out my computer laptop from its case and turned on the power. As I opened the photo files stored on the system's main drive, while saying to Jules, "I want to show you something. Do you remember when this photograph was taken?"

Jules started to laugh, then shortly afterwards he began sobbing gently. I could see how the fears and joy impacted him as he stared at the computer screen.

"Dat photograph is me, taken just 'bout da time I turned forty-five! I understand wat you are saying to me is dat you are my great grandson! No! You actually are my great-great grandson! I don't feel so good right now, Byron," he said covering his face with both hands. I thought he was about to start sobbing again, which signaled that a hasty retreat was required on my part.

"I should leave so you can rest, Jules," I said as I got up and started to put the computer back into its bag.

"No! "Please sit back down and stay a little while longer," he implored.

"Pull your chair closer to me," Jules demanded in a curiously stern tone. "I must tell you wat is on my mind. I believe I have some understanding of how dis ting may be happening. However, I fear dat if I find out da answer to why I am here, right now, den I will cease to have purpose. If I cease to have purpose, den I tink *I* will cease to be here. I have no reason to know for certain other dan some strange instinct dat seems to be warning me dat once I am made aware of why I am here, den all purpose for me to come here ends for me. Perhaps, I tink too much. Dere is an important ting I have to tell someone and I have been fearful about dis and still is, even now. Aldough, I am unable to recall details of da last time I had dis sensation, I know I have had dis *feeling* to occur before."

PART 4

THE JOURNEY

CHAPTER 14

JULES AT THE HELM

Receptives, Gifteds, Guests and . . . Oh My

Jules leaned toward my left ear and whispered as if he were about to share the deepest and darkest of secrets:

"It was an uncharacteristically blustery, late morning towards da end of summer," he began. "Da sweet smell of cane syrup filled da breezy, humid, air wen Marcel P. Sorrell, a tall dark-skinned man walked up to my carriage just as I entered da path to my house on Monday, August 17th, around midday[93]. I was holding da reins, not really tinking about much wen he simply '*appeared*' out of nowhere and slowly strode to da left side of my horse and den he came over to me. Da man was immaculately dressed in a dark gray suit wit da whitest shirt I've ever seen. And dose fine pair of highly polished black shoes he wore was da finest dat I'd seen in a long time. I hoped dat I wasn't staring, even dough I knew I was, at da handsome gold ring on his right ring finger with a gold letter "S"

---

93   Subsequent research noted that the 17th of August for which Jules implied was in 1903, and was in fact, a Monday.

embedded in a deep, red smooth stone. By da looks of dat small black monogrammed leather case, and da way he dressed and da way he talked, I guess you could say he looked like a man having strong financial means. Da young gentleman, I supposed to be about thirty years old, spoke clear and proper English."

Jules settled back in his chair, now sitting about three feet away, facing me. The look on his face told me that he had thought about *what* he needed to tell me, although I sensed he still was troubled as to *how* to continue his *story*.

He began again. "Byron, I was not sure about you a few days ago. Dere were many questions I needed da answers to before I could feel right about how much I could *afford* to offer you."

"So are you saying that you did not know whether you could trust me or confide in me?"

"Not exactly; dere's more to consider dan da matter of *trust* or *confidence*." Jules began, "You see, a few days ago wen you asked me about da name Sorrell, I was reluctant to tell you about Marcel Sorrell because I was still not sure you would *believe* me. Even now as we speak comfortably about dese matters, I still have difficulty coming to terms with da notion dat dis time period—your 2007, makes me a very old man, considering I was born in 1844. Dat would make me 163 year old, not to mention wat Sorrell cautioned me about back den. He said dat I might experience some difficulty discussing da details regarding his visit wit me wit anyone who didn't possess da qualities of my "*Receptive*." I was not certain whether *you* might be da one to give da doctors cause to send me away to an asylum. Anyway, I assure you, I am of sound mind as any person you will ever meet. And presently, it appears that it *is **you*** who are da "*Receptive*" who Marcel Sorrell referred to."

I attempted to persuade Jules that he should continue to tell me what was on his mind without worry that I would make any judgments. Sensing his concern for discretion and trust, I promised not discuss any part of our conversation with anyone he did not approve of. I also had some concerns of my own as I turned my focus on the last comment Jules made.

"But what do you mean by *me* as '*the Receptive*' referred to by Mr. Sorrell?"

Jules continued. "Dis rather strange gentleman carefully positioned himself dat day he approached me, just slow enough to still my horse as I arrived at my home after a brief visit in New Roads. Den, he politely asked if he could have a moment of my time. How could I decline such a well-mannered request? Well, I couldn't and I didn't. His demeanor was most genteel and his soothing nature had a calming, almost hypnotic effect on me as he spoke. So much so, dat I was captivated by da ease in which he was able to complete a somewhat hasty introduction. As I permitted him to speak, I was fascinated by his knowledge of tings dat had to do wit events dat had happened before he said he was born. Da most peculiar ting about dat incident was da length of our discussion. It lasted only a few moments, I am almost certain, but by da time we had concluded our talk, several hours had passed!"

Stunned, for a moment, I asked for Jules' forgiveness and for him to repeat the name of the man again. He hesitated at first as if he sensed my disbelief before declaring in a perceptibly louder voice, "Marcel P. Sorrell!" Dis is da only Sorrell I have ever come to have known. You remember, I told you about him da other day."

Jules seemed annoyed. I wasn't sure if it was because he didn't think I believed him or if it was because he thought I forgot what he'd told me earlier about "da only Sorrell he knew." Not wanting to belabor the point, I nodded, indicating I remembered, and then gave Jules a second nod as a signal for him to continue.

"Dis man also described tings dat I read about—tings dat had yet to happen in da future and quite frankly in da first few moments wen we met; I wondered if he might be *diabolique*.[94] Aldhough I was somewat wary of his intentions, his goodly mannerisms overrode my suspicions and I invited him to come up to da house. He was quick to oblige as he climbed up next to me on da carriage. As we rode toward da stable, he asked if he could trust me to keep our meeting in confidence and not mention anyting we discussed wit anyone else for da time being. I trusted dat any reasons for keeping this information confidential were reasonable, at first, so I agreed."

---

94   A term employed to define a demonic person or one being possessed by demons.

Jules paused. He appeared uncomfortable, for a lengthy moment; and then he began again. "For da most part, yes I needed to be certain to know who would be da one entrusted with da message sent by Mr. Sorrell." At that moment, Jules became very somber as he looked at me with the most piercing stare I'd ever received or even seen for that matter. *I was rocked to my soul!*

I asked Jules what *message* he was referring to, and his response presented the most remarkable sequence of information I had ever personally been *privy* to. I couldn't decide if the information was private or privileged. *My best guess was that it contained some elements of both.*

With an almost, trancelike stare aimed directly at me, Jules began—slowly. "Marcel P. Sorrell became known to me as a '*gifted.*' Dis is da word *he* chose and dat is *wat he* referred to himself as—a '*gifted.*' You see now, since I met Sorrell and conversed wit him on dat day at my farm, I have come to believe in da possibility dat **all** people can access da full potential of da brain (and the mind). I have tought a fair bit about dat day and my understanding of da unlimited power most people possess. It's sad, but I know dat very few individuals will attempt to discover such power—dat is to say, *due to all kinds of fear, not many* will access dose potentials. I understand dat very few individuals will find success after earnestly and sincerely attempting to unlock da mysteries of da lesser-employed parts of da mind, mainly because dey lack belief. Marcel P. Sorrell suggested dat dose few individuals who do access more of da full potential of da brain's capabilities are among dose he called '*gifteds.*' He insisted dat dese '*gifted's* have da ability to 'move about' *before and after certain, identifiable events in time*—witout regard to scientific laws regarding time and space. '*Gifteds*' can (and do) *respond* to transmissions of communication from '*receptives*'—individuals who desire or wish to be visited by '*gifted.*' A '*receptive*' is one who initiates a visit or visits from a '*gifted.*' A '*receptive*', performing in da capacity of a '*guest,*' may also visit another '*receptive.*'

Byron, in that regard, I function as a '***GUEST***' to you," Jules explained.

Taken aback a bit from Jules' complicated explanation and detailed definition, I offered my understanding. "Jules, so . . . I am *your* '*receptive*'—and you are *my* '*guest*'?"

"Yes, it appears so. I'm not sure if I can fully explain it," Jules replied, almost matter-of-factly, "But a '*guest*' " is like a conduit.

"Yet you are a '*receptive*' as well as a '*guest*'—I mean, with respect to your ties to Marcel Sorrell, right?" I asked, with an obvious puzzled look on my face.

"Yes, as I implied before, '*guests*' are not as capable or as likely to employ da more complex mental and powerful potential as da '*gifted*', like Sorrell. But, '*guests*' do possess da ability to 'visit' '*receptives.*' Da transmission from an individual initiating contact, usually a '*receptive*', through *ki gen don* (ones who are '*gifted*') enables a '*guest*' (envite[95]) to appear in wat Mr. Sorrell referred to as *select time dimensions*.

Mr. Sorrell, a '*gifted*', enabled me to respond to your request for a visit—I came because *you wanted me to come*. By my own ability, I cannot *move about*, nor do much of da tings I *knew* Mr. Sorrell could do, but *your requests* seem (facilitated through Marcel P, Sorrell) to make it so"

"I don't know that I buy this!" I muttered, barely audible, as I wondered, *When did I request a visit?*

Jules, apparently hearing my muted comment, snapped back, "I'm not *selling* you anything, but *you* fit da description of Mr. Sorrell's '*receptive.*' Just tink about it for a moment and try to remember da time(s) you prayed, tought, wished or yearned for someone to give you answers to difficult questions during your life. Now, tink carefully and you might *see* dat dis is da *only* possibility for us being here, now, together, in *your* time of 2007. Oh, one other ting; you probably have been experiencing a great degree of recollection of your most significant childhood and early adult *memories*, too! So, now you tell me, has any or all of dese tings been happening to you lately?"

I thought about Jules' proposal and remembered; there was a time—I was not quite a teen, when I wanted some guidance—to know of the last true, 'noble' man who was part of my ancestral background. Who, what man, what person in whose footsteps I could and should follow? Who was worthy of my respect and admiration necessary to make me—an impressionable boy—into a man? Where was the last stable example of a good father figure occurring within *my* bloodlines? These questions may

---

95 Creole spelling of the English word "invite" (invitee).

have been a *call* out (desire, summons) from a desperate little one, afraid of what awaited around the next dark corner. After all, I believed in *prayer*. Shouldn't that belief also extend to those prayers getting answered s? The uncanny, unending flood of memories convinced me—Yes, Jules' proposal was possible! Yes, I did yearn, ask, pray, wish, hope and remember! So now I, a ***'receptive'*** have the answers—in the personage of Marcel P. Sorrell's ***'guest'***—Jules Bayonne!

Jules now had a warm smile on his face. He gazed at me unflinchingly; and as if he could read my thoughts, leaned towards me slightly and declared. "So if you will permit me, I will deliver the *parcel* as instructed."

"What parcel?" I thought to myself but quickly abandoned my thoughtful wanderings as I returned Jules' gaze to show him he once again had my undivided attention. "Please pardon my interruption and continue Jules," I said as I sat back and listened with renewed intensity.

"I can still recall quite vividly dat windy morning wen I first laid eyes on Marcel P. Sorrell. He told me dat ***'gifteds'*** are dose rare individuals who had da ability to identify and recognize traits possessed by persons who are to become ***'guests.'*** Dese are dose who were highly attuned to da 'flow.' Marcel P. Sorrell defined me as a ***'transitional,'*** one in the *transitional* phase or as one who is unable to become a ***'guest'*** until they reach 'metamorphosis'" stage[96].

Jules stopped a moment to catch his breath, and then continued with a new-found vigor. "Mr. Sorrell informed me dat ***'gifteds'*** are destined (called and *required*) to facilitate (yon moun ki fasilite) ***'guests.'*** ***'Gifteds'*** are often erroneously categorized as "angels" (zanj) or seraphim, aldough ***'gifteds'*** have limited abilities, and are unlike da more powerful angelic beings belonging to da Heavenly Father. Nevertheless, much like da angels, ***'gifteds'*** can appear as any normal person."

Again, Jules stopped speaking. This time I couldn't tell if it was because he needed to catch his breath or if he stopped for me to catch mine after having shared this new and remarkable information. Jules stared at me as if he knew I had a question for him. I did.

---

[96] Jules never suggested during this discussion, but it was later decided that the metamorphosis stage was the process of death.

I wanted to ask if he (still) was a '***transitional***' or if he had already progressed, and was now a '***guest.***' I fought the urge to ask and simply gazed back at Jules, hoping he would offer the answer without my asking. He blinked slowly as if to gesture—a whisper, clearly audible poured from his lips. "What is your guess?"

"Guess?" I mumbled. "Guest—no pun intended," I murmured, with a smirk, hoping that it would dissuade him from playing the "cat and mouse" game. It didn't work.

Ignoring my deficient humor and apparent lapse of memory, Jules repeated that '***guests***' have ultimately completed the '*progression*' (morphed) or successfully 'transitioned' from '***receptive***' to '***guest.***' "Additionally, dose who are in da process but not yet having completed da stage, are considered '***transitionals***' (tranzisyon[97]). Dey are usually accompanied by a '***facilitator***' or a '***gifted.***' Now, a '***transitional***' is usually contacted by a '***gifted***' at some point during their life to prepare them to become '***guests.***'"

Indirectly, Jules had defined himself as a '***transitional***', alluding to Marcel P. Sorrell as a '**gifted**', engaged in Jules' facilitation process.

As Jules began to outline his understanding of the process according to Marcel P. Sorrell regarding these entities, he noted that there seemed to be many complex exceptions.

"Now you gotta get dis, Byron. "For example; apparently, not all '***transitionals***' will become '***guests***', due to da nature of 'free will' afforded to everyone. You know wat I mean, some will and others won't respond to da calling and take on da required responsibilities of a '***gifted***', dough, by definition and acceptance of da 'calling', a '***gifted***' must serve as a '***facilitator***' to a '***transitional(s)***' or a '***guest(s).***'"

"And another ting Sorrell told me is dat da activities of '***gifteds***' and '***guests***' go unnoticed or undetected by '*others*', inferring that they (***gifted*** and ***guests***) don't operate using the same rules as earth-dwelling humans."

Jules slowly leaned as far back as he could go in the large chair, and squinting his eyes, he announced, "You do know more about wat I am saying to you, don't you?"

Before I could respond, Jules added, "I am certain dat you are very aware of how dese tings work! Marcel told me dat dose who really *believe*

---

97   Creole spelling for the English word "transitional"

are most likely to be '***transitionals***', or at da very least, '***receptives***'! You understood wat was meant wen John spoke of da 'Comforter' who would abide wit you forever[98]. You knew dat if *His Spirit* would (does), den we, in His own image, might do also! You *did know* dat, right? Didn't you know dat? Otherwise, why or rather, how could you have summoned me?"

Already perplexed by the mysterious nature of the current topic, now heated with Jules' fiery emotions, I attempted to slow the pace to catch up by asking, "Wait Jules! What do you mean, *I summoned you?*"

Jules tilted his head slightly. "*Your increased and intensified memory as of late has some purpose and intent*, so tink! Do you ever recall asking, praying or longing to know about anyone who held da same toughts you did; possessed your same character; your same work ethics—why you walked, talked, smiled, experienced pain—joy, gratitude, love—all dose important tings the way you did? And, did you ever wonder who it might have been, from dose who came before you; who had dose very same qualities? I tink instinctively you knew dat all dose tings dat make up you, had to belong to one who came before you? Tink about it very hard—dose were da times wen you summoned me!"

I was amazed (and believe me that was putting it lightly!) to hear Jules' matter-of-fact declaration of my "increased memory as of late. It was "as if he shared some of my innermost thoughts. Until now, I chalked it up as those traits of mine I wanted to pass down to my children. But, finally I started to grasp the realization that there was much, much more to his latest comment than that—he revealed there was a reason for my 'flashbacks.' It was as if he knew that I had recently I been experiencing more of these memories which had become more frequent and more vivid since just prior to Harris' introducing the two of us a few weeks earlier. As subtle as Jules' suggested "purpose and intent" seemed, I felt as if these recent recollections and memories were preparing (priming) me for something unimaginable and exciting!

I was very young, Jules, I began. I do remember thinking that there had to have been one person—one man in my family's history—a great man who I could pattern myself after. I yearned to know the person of worth who I was destined to follow in their footsteps—to be like that

---

98   *Holy Bible* (King James Version) John 14:16: "And I will pray the Father, and he shall give you another Comforter, that he may abide with you for ever; . . ."

person. I couldn't have been more than twelve years old when I '*longed*' for an answer—who or when was the last righteous man in my family's past?

I wanted to confirm my understanding by talking a little about cloning, but decided against it, as that discussion most certainly would have been way beyond Jules understanding; and very foolish of me to throw yet another foreign object (concept) into a pot that already had as much complexity and mystery as a that of a Northerner trying to make a pot of authentic (Southern) <u>Louisiana gumbo</u>.

Jules had squarely confronted me with the fact that I pretty well understood what he was trying to explain with regard to the '*entity*' subject; and I sensed that he wouldn't discuss it much more anyway. I had pretty much resolved that if I would refrain from pressing the matter, he might voluntarily return to the discussion on his own accord later.

Instead, however, Jules returned to a different, but familiar subject. "So, I believe now would be a good time for us to continue our conversation about your father, including *your* people sharing da Sorrell name."

I pondered the query briefly and Jules must have sensed my reluctance to open dialog about family members whom I didn't quite know much about anyway. So, in a most peculiar manner, and much to my delight Jules also must have sensed my slight discomfort related to my ignorance about my own family. Instead, he did the gentlemanly thing by quickly changing the subject.

"Marcel Sorrell told me dat one of da most bittersweet serendipities of my life journey I would experience, may be dat of feeling an overwhelming presence of da souls I came in contact along da way. So, if *you choose to journey*, Byron, I have no doubt dat you will experience such moments. Do you understand any of dis I am telling you now?"

I tried to mask my lack of imagination. I answered "affirmative," thinking I could figure it out later. "Yes, of course, I do understand. I suspect, you probably experienced something physically more peculiar than anything you ever felt before. I would imagine the nature of what occurred to you was overwhelming."

What a lame reply, I thought. I wondered if Jules detected how dumb I felt after the response I had just spouted. I waited, and then made a barely audible "hmm" hoping Jules would resume discussing the point he had made a bit further. Apparently, sensing I needed a little more understanding, Jules continued.

"Da first time I experienced da sensation, I instinctively knew dat something miraculous was going on. Da uncanny feeling of *Providence* guiding my actions was intense on dat day on which I was found in da rain on the streets in Georgia. I attempted to explain dat my journey as Marcel Sorrell had predicted, had now begun. But all my efforts were in vain and da people at da hospital deemed me incoherent and labeled me a "*buffoon*." I was unfamiliar with dis sort of *travel*, and in particular, I had found it difficult to communicate wit da people I was introduced to up to now—well, at least it is easier to talk to you. I was reluctant to discuss my peculiar visit I'd had wit Sorrell and chose not to mention any reference to da *parcel* I was instructed to deliver during dat visit wit anyone until you came a few days ago. It was on your very first visit wen I felt compelled to reveal dis message (deliver the parcel) to you."

I interrupted by reminding Jules of his earlier comment to me. "But you do recall telling me you didn't trust me at first?"

"Not exactly. I recall saying dat I was reluctant to tell you about Marcel Sorrell because I was still not sure you would believe me. Actually, I had divulged to you dat I experienced a strange feeling of fear, or rather da overwhelming sensation dat some important *purpose* would decide my fate. Matter of fact, dat feeling still looms in my thoughts."

I was not real happy to hear this. I became slightly uneasy and nervously stroked my chin, hoping that Jules wouldn't change his mind about telling me things I so desperately *needed* to know. But as fate would have it, he continued on the subject of this *journey* and the obvious burden he carried in trying to describe this fantastic 'epic' to in a manner that I could 'manage.' I must have stopped stroking my chin. He began again, almost as if he were reading my thoughts.

"Look, your *journey* will most likely be in the *discovery of who you are and how you became*. Whatever you decide it is, you still need to commence it very soon."

"I know, I answered. "Not only do I realize that the journey must be arduous, I'm also faced with the fact that I'm not getting any younger!

I'm also going to take to heart what you told me, and strongly urging me to begin with the *"search for the knowledge of your (my) father."*

With that hint, I now had a beginning point for a series of astonishing events to come which would have remarkable, lasting impact on my future. I began to find the clarification, partly from Jules' soothing tone and largely from the mesmerizing nature of the message he came with. Nevertheless, this day's lesson was far from over.

"Byron," Jules paused briefly. "Mr. Sorrell predicted dat I would travel far west past da Mississippi and south and east of da continent and witness the marvels of machines used to take men from place to place in less time den I could ever imagine! As we spoke, the discussion led to tings I had read in books by another fellow by da name of Jules."

"Another fellow named Jules?" I questioned with a puzzled look. I wondered if he was referring to one of his sons or grandsons bearing the same name.

"Yes, the writer, Verne [99] from France!"

"Have you read works by Jules Verne?" I asked suspiciously.

Jules responded, "The ones he wrote during da war were very popular, so wen I could, I read as many books I was able to get my hands on, including books by Alexandre Dumas[100]. You know, I was born da same year Dumas published his greatest book. Dumas' father was born in a region near my father's family, back in Saint-Domingue. I believe we may be related to da Dumas family as well."

"Incredible!" I hissed. "My wife's maiden name happens to be Dumas!" Her paternal great-grandfather is *Alexander* Dumas. We suspect there is some tie between her family and the author's family—likely going back to Saint-Domingue, as she too has creole ancestry. Both of her parents are children of creoles originating in Saint-Domingue."

Hmm, that would make us double kin . . .

Jules had a queer grin on his face as he shook his head. "Still fightin' da ting, aren't you? I understand. See, now maybe you can imagine how I feel, even dough. Mr. Sorrell explained as much as he could about dese tings I

---

99 Jules G. Verne, well known author from Nantes, France. Works include *Journey to the Center of the Earth* (1864), *From the Earth to the Moon* (1865), *Twenty Thousand Leagues Under the Sea*, (1869-1870).

100 Alexandre Dumas, the French writer, best known for historical novels and high adventure books, including *The Count of Monte Cristo*, (1844-1846) and *The Three Musketeers*, (1844).

am seeing here, now, even wit you here as a witness! Notin' could prepare me for da strange, marvelous, yet frightening events I have encountered since I made his acquaintance! So 'drink up' the experiences, take it in wit me—hold on to da faith!"

I could almost hear Delonde, my niece, laughing heartily saying "I told you uncle Byron, Alexandre Dumas *is* my cousin."

Delonde, my wife's youngest sibling's daughter was a dear, sweet, pretty young girl, who in a very rare occurrence, died from the complications of Lupus in January 2005. Delonde passed away just after her twenty-first birthday and ten years after her mother, Didi passed away from the same dreadful disease. Delonde insisted that Alexandre Dumas was related to her; and I would tease her saying that Dumas was a 'white man' (jokingly) and that it was not likely they were related. When Jules had explained it was because I summoned him, that he came to be, I immediately thought of Delonde. It was comforting to know that I would possibly laugh and talk with my dear niece also.

After taking a brief mental 'excursion' back to the past, I returned my attention to Jules, hoping I hadn't missed much of what he'd said. As Jules continued, I was relieved, my mind picked up to follow Jules exactly where I'd left him: "Anyway, Sorrell and I spoke at great lengths of da written adventures of Jules' (Verne) characters and how much of wat they had experienced would become much more familiar to me not much later. This is wat I meant wen I said, I believed wat seems to be a dream right now, I fear I have experienced before."

I wondered if Jules was experiencing a form of Déjà vu—the phenomenon of having the strong sensation that an event or experience currently being experienced has already been experienced in the past.

"I was convinced dat *dis* Mr. Sorrell understood more about how dis kind of ting might have been possible dan he led on, aldough our discussion remained focused on da subject of me going from place to place in da next century, wich seemed to make less sense—at da time. We discussed da possibilities related to advancements in communication, particularly those of Edison, Maxwell and Bell, who were making significant progress even dough dey experienced great opposition."

"What do you mean opposition?" I asked.

"You remember a few days ago wen we talked about da invention of da telephone, right?"

I responded, easing my chair a little closer. "Yes, I do. We agreed to continue that discussion."

"Well, in a manner of speakin', as you already know, some opposition is always to be expected wen men attempt to improve or make progress using new techniques or methods. Dat is, at least until such techniques passed certain tests or dey have been proven. President Hayes[101] openly stated he did not believe anyone would need to employ da use of a telephone.[102] Around da same time, wen Bell was almost broke, he tried to sell da telephone patent to Western Union. Is Western Union still in business, Byron?" Jules asked, almost in a sarcastic tone.

"Not to the degree that Mr. Bell's business is these days." I responded.

To summarize, the story is that Alexander Graham Bell offered to sell the telephone patent to Western Union for $100,000 in 1876. The committee appointed to investigate the offer filed the following report:

"We do not see that this device will be ever capable of sending recognizable speech over a distance of several miles. Messers Hubbard and Bell want to install one of their 'telephone devices' in every city. The idea is idiotic on the face of it. Furthermore, why would any person want to use this ungainly and impractical device when he can send a messenger to the telegraph office and have a clear written message sent to any large city in the United States? . . . Mr. G.G. Hubbard's fanciful predictions, while they sound rosy, are based on wild-eyed imagination and lack of understanding of the technical and economic facts of the situation, and a posture of ignoring the obvious limitations of his device, which is hardly more than a toy . . . This device is inherently of no use to us. We do not recommend its purchase.[103]"

---

101 Rutherford B. Hayes, the 19th president of the United States 1877—1881.

102 In the 1870's, President Rutherford B. Hayes was reported to have said to Alexander Graham Bell (re: telephone) "That's an amazing invention, but who would ever want to use one of them?"

103 An article recorded in *Familiar Sounds—New Distances; The Telephone* (https://soundsoverdistance.weebly.com/predictions-of-the-telephone.html) Note that no accurate reference has been tied to a particular author of this quote and as of the date of this writing, writer, Phil Lapsley, insists the quote isn't true—"It's a made-up blend of several different,

Had Western Union been less critical and purchased the patent, I doubt that the Bell Systems, and later, AT&T might have had the same story they have today.

Jules continued his discussion.

"Much of da discussion Sorrell and I had didn't make sense at da time we spoke, but later, often before I would fall asleep at night, wen I was tinking on all sorts of subjects dat kept me up until dawn sometimes, den our discussions took on new, clearer meaning. I pondered his comments on da powers of da mind and how much of da wonders of life were not always visible to man through his known senses. He spoke of how da war dat separated da country was formed in da *collective minds of many men* long before it occurred on da battlefields. Of particular interest to me was how he insisted dat everything was following a *natural order* and dere were no *coincidence*. Furdermore, da sooner I accepted dis theory as fact, da more I would be able to comprehend everything around me. I knew he was right, yet my own fears caused me to fight such a belief."

I looked at Jules and asked the question he seemed to be waiting for. "What were you afraid of?"

Jules, sat back, took a deep breath and replied. This gesture of his always put me of 'high alert.' Past experiences with this man told me he was about to 'drop' more of them wisdom nuggets on me I welcomed and had come to expect. I smiled in anticipation.

"Da idea dat dere were no coincidences, changes all of wat I tought I knew. Why did da cane grow better some years dan others? Why did my father come to Louisiana from Saint-Domingue—wen he came? Why did he stay in Pointe Coupee and not in New Orleans? Why . . . how he met my mother and why I was born, where I was born? Why is Victorine eighteen years younger dan me? Da answers to dose questions, confirms dat dere are no coincidences. Why I am here now? Why you are here—tied to me in a way we both have yet to determine? Dese tings are a bit unsettling given dat *none* of dese questions, da related answers, situations or events are coincidences. But dere is no inconsistency in my faith in God, and dis understanding dat dere are no coincidences, because

---

but related, stories." Exploding the Phone: The Untold Story of the Teenagers and Outlaws who Hacked Ma Bell, by Phil Lapsley published Februrary 5, 2013.

we believe dat *God is in control of everyting*. Wat fear I possessed, had more to do wit knowing dat men are granted free choice, and dat da suggestion dat some individuals exercising free choice might give da illusion dat da possibility exists for one to have da power to override divine providence. Dis new understanding clouded my instincts, for instance, da nature of *right and wrong*—sometimes da two change places—dey reverse order. I considered dat dere might not be many *real* absolutes. It also caused me to tink more about everyting. Da more I knew about tings, it seemed da less I really knew."

Jules sighed, and then continued quickly; I supposed he did so as not to lose momentum.

"Sorrell said dat *I* would journey to strange and marvelous places where mountains grew from God's hand, up to da clouds and are peaked wit snow to da lowest levels of canyons and depressions in da earth are spectacular and vast. We spoke of how everyting on earth was made of da same ingredients and dat dose ingredients contained great power if we ever studied da materials earnestly enough. He and I held a brief debate on da subject of da soul of man. Both of us concluded dat da soul does not cease to exist upon da death of a person. Dat discussion kept me tinking for a long time afterwards. Sorrell, however, did not subscribe to da belief dat da soul returns to a particular place, but rather it moves witin da universe and can be accessed by other souls."

I came to the conclusion that for each of the previous half-dozen or so visits with Jules, I found I was more fascinated and mentally stimulated by the topics we discussed. I was listening attentively to Jules' experience regarding Marcel Sorrell, but as if compelled by a mysterious force, I was suddenly mentally catapulted back to a conversation I had nearly twenty years earlier with my mother regarding the existence of the human 'soul.'

Although I was influenced by Houdini's[104] sentiments towards spiritual things, diametric opposition to that more skeptical position lurked in the reasoning segment of my mind. Logically, I knew no one had "come back" from clinical death to report there was an existence, nor had there been the

---

104 Hungarian born, Erik Weisz in 1874, later known as Harry Houdini, illusionist, magician, escapologist, stunt performer and debunker of spiritualists, was one of the most famous entertainers of his time.

charge of Harry's secret code ("Rosabelle believe"[105]), but I never openly admitted my intellectual agreement. Instead, I voiced my heartfelt ties to this controversial subject with my mother as we discussed the matter. She adamantly supported the idea that the human soul was a tangible separate entity, the existence of which remains after the physical properties of a person are no longer present. I, on the other hand, only had an 'inkling' that the soul had substantive, measurable properties.

I was now convinced if we could discover the existence of a quark in 1964—unknown until then, or the notion that a microscopic substance found in the pus of discarded surgical bandages in 1869 which later (in 1952) DNA was determined to play a significant role (genetic material) in heredity, and finally, repeating what was mentioned before (about our thinking we know what we don't know, until *it* is discovered):

"... Fifteen-hundred years ago everybody knew the earth was the center of the universe; five-hundred years ago everybody knew the earth was flat and fifteen minutes ago you knew human beings were alone on this planet. Imagine what you'll know tomorrow!"

Much of what I came to understand as 'truth' has occurred since Mr. Houdini's death (1926), resulting in many former skeptics, including me to use the term 'impossible' less and less as time goes by. That being said, I came back from my little mental meandering and resumed with vigilant attentiveness to Jules' discussion regarding Marcel Sorrell.

Jules appeared unaffected by my brief mental departure. He went on to explain that Sorrell talked more about the unknown abilities of the human person and how the brain held secrets yet to be revealed. "He insisted dat I would experience some of dese wonders and in particular, dat *I* would see other countries and travel in new and different ways unlike anything I had yet experienced. I spoke to Mr. Sorrell for a little more dan an hour that day, but da conversation seemed to have lasted a whole lot longer dan dat. He spent a brief moment assuring me dat I might feel a sensation of distinct well-being, and I must confess, that aldough I expected to have been more fatigued after the lengthy discourse, especially since I'd been

---

105 Excerpts from Arthur Ford's "Nothing So Strange" (New York: Harper and Row, 1958). It was originally titled "A Round with the Magicians"

away from home on business elsewhere for most of da morning. On da contrary, I seemed to possess more energy da more we talked."

"What happened then?" I asked.

Jules sighed and closed his eyes momentarily. He seemed weary, but then, he began again.

"Sorrell den apologized and stated dat he needed to be leaving and I offered to walk him back to da front gates where he originally appeared. When we arrived at da gate, he turned to me and extended his hand and told me how honored he was to have met me, den he looked at me wit a strange grin and witout breaking his gaze on me, reached into da leather case and retrieved a bottle of rum he said was one of tree bottles he was given by a special friend. He offered da fancy bottle of rum and instructed me to toast a drink one day in honor of dis particular meeting between da two of us. He commented dat I would know wen da time was 'right' to take dat drink. As he walked away, I looked at da bottle of rum, impressed wit da label and da bottle, wich had a cut-glass design and a curiously rounded shape."

Jules continued, "Da bottle was labeled *Don Q*."[106] "I had da first drink from da bottle on da evening of August 1, 1903, after a particularly satisfying walk in Victorine's flower garden . . . and so it seems, began da Journey."

I wanted to hear more about Marcel Sorrell and how Jules believed he had some key role in the 'Journey' Jules had decided to define as his *appearance* here in the new millennium.

As incredible as this proposal for Jules' "appearance" in my time seemed, at the very least I had an answer to "how" he might have been able to reach the twenty-first century. I had just about convinced myself of everything I had earlier been reluctant to believe in. But now what was missing was "why" in *my time*? Why with *me*? I never asked Jules, but he seemed to already know what I was thinking when he suggested I also had in all probability encountered one named Sorrell also.

Suddenly, just as I was readying myself for departure that evening, Jules asked another question which I was unprepared for.

---

[106] The author's research reveals that this brand of rum has been made in Puerto Rico since about 1865.

"Byron" Jules spoke just above a whisper. "Why is your television flat? Why is it not made more visible in *form* like you are to me and like I am to you?"

Because I wasn't prepared for the complexity of the questions Jules had fired at me so rapidly, I did what I always do when I need to stall and think about what is presented to me, I answered with a query of my own.

"Are you referring to depth and mass of the television programming?"

Jules picked up a *Time* magazine in one hand and the Rawlings major league baseball in the other from the table across the room and slowly walked over towards me murmuring.

"I am having difficulty explaining..." Reverting back to a whisper, Jules sighed and continued as he pointed to the cover image on the *Time* magazine. "This image of the man—'Dick Cheney' is like a photograph, right?"

I nodded and responded simultaneously. "Yes, it is."

Then he unexpectantly tossed the ball to me, and said. "Now dis is not flat like da photograph!"

I surmised Jules was speaking of three-dimensional projection, but I didn't think he would relate to such a term, so dismissing his inquiry I responded. "That has not proven to be possible!"

As soon as I said it, I thought to myself, "Oops," Jules must be thinking, "Hasn't this idiot been listening to anything I said? Didn't we just spend all that time talking about 'non-coincidences' and 'non-impossibilities?'"

Jules stared at me, shook his head as if in disbelief at my comment and confirmed what I'd been thinking:

"I am surprised you *still* talk of wat is possible or wat is not! You asked me if I believed everyting in da bible. I told you some things dat I questioned, but confided to you dat my faith allowed me to accept it all. Well, I tell you truthfully, wen Jesus walked on water and raised da dead, den told his disciples dat if dey believed in Him, dey would perform greater tings dan He did[107]. So I believe in **all** tings as being possible, through Da Christ. Wat is hard for me to relate to is your disbelief! Wit all this stuff of your world..."

---

107 Jules probably was referring to (KJV) John 14:12 "Verily, verily, I say unto you, He that believeth on me, the works that I do shall he do also; and greater works than these shall he do; because I go unto my Father."

I heard much of Jules' comments; however, a strange feeling came over me as if a voice was echoing the words (again):

"*. . . Fifteen hundred years ago, everybody knew that the Earth was the center of the universe. Five hundred years ago, everybody knew that the Earth was flat. And fifteen minutes ago, you knew that humans were alone on this planet. Imagine what you'll know tomorrow!*"

Almost instantly, as if breaking through a fog, I could hear the volume in Jules' voice rising as he continued to speak of his frustration in my lack of faith and belief.

I understood Jules frustration, but risked asking him for permission to stay a little longer anyway; as I positioned myself towards the chair opposite from where he had been seated. "Do you mind me staying just a few more moments?"

He motioned, pointing to the chair and I sat down. Jules sat down and sighed and with his eyes fixed on me, he waited for me to speak.

"Jules," I paused trying my best to find the right words that might help to explain what I had not understood myself.

"What you sense about me is a fairly correct assessment. I do harbor fears associated with our advancements in science and technology, probably because I *do* believe much of what is considered by many to be theoretical, is in fact, a real possibility. I have considered ***how*** you come to be here now, particularly since I do believe you are from a time past. But this *possibility* is somewhat unsettling if my senses are questioned by others and I am required to tell them what I truly believe."

Jules calmly said "Now den, you do recognize my dilemma—we are now viewing da picture wit a single eye."

I nodded acquiescence. *Duh, why hadn't I considered before now that I wasn't the only one trying to figure this thing out when Jules was really the one trying to figure out, if asked, the "hows" and "whys" of his personal transcendence from my ancestral past to his unfamiliar (my) presence.*

By the time I left Jules, I was more than ready to squeal aloud, "Beam me up Scottie!" It had all been a bit much, but I guess (no "pun" intended) I must be a glutton for punishment—I couldn't wait until my next visit with Jules.

* * *

CHAPTER 15

WADE SORRELL

The next time I visited Jules' hospital room, I came with an agenda of my own. I began to rewind some stuff:

I thought about the summer in a little *arm-pit* section of New Orleans East, where Interstate 10 crosses over Chef Menteur Highway there is a place nicknamed *The Goose* It is so called (named after a well-known juke joint located between Dale and Reynes Streets on Chef Menteur Highway—*The Blue Goose* that had burned down in the early 1950's. This seemed like as good a place as any to recall the details to Jules.

It was there in 1967 when a big, beautiful metallic green Buick Electra convertible pulled up in front of our house in the 4400 block of Reynes Street that I first recall meeting my grandmother's brother, Wade Sorrell.

"Did you say Sorrell?" Jules questioned with a now familiar astonished look on his face. "You do realize dat dere is a great deal more meanin' to dose memories you seem to be havin' lately—fascinatin' ting—da memory, right? Sorry, I interrupted wat you was 'bout to say—please go on."

Jules' comment about my acute recall of events, places and especially the memories of people who seemed to pour from my mind as of late gave me goosebumps. *I forced myself back on track, making a mental note that Jules had touched on something wonderful and enlightening—the gift of memory.*

My great-uncle Wade was larger than life to me as he stood well over six feet tall. Back then, he was probably the tallest of all the men in my family and that statistic probably remains unchanged, even today. He was accompanied by his new and somewhat shy bride, Vera. It was clear from the outset that Wade Sorrell had neither a shy nor timid bone in his body. My mother, Dolores had aptly described him to tee, when she referred to him by the term, '*bull of the woods.*' This term was a name usually reserved for a man of distinction, whose very presence exuded an element of class supported by an upstanding upbringing. My initial impression about Uncle Wade is that he was a smooth operator. He looked smooth; he talked smooth, he walked smooth. Hell, the man *was just plain smooth* by anybody's standard!

He was the firstborn of my great-grandfather, Peter Sorrell and was born in 1910 in New Orleans to a lovely woman named Nora Vance. Peter Sorrell never married Nora, so my uncle Wade secretly wrestled with the legitimacy issue for much of his life. I say secretly because you sure couldn't tell just by looking at him or even talking to him that he had any unresolved issues in his life.

I'm telling you the truth; this guy had swag in his swagger! He had topped the best dressed men in Chicago for more than ten consecutive years before I had graduated from high school in 1972. The man for whom my brother Prentiss derives his middle name (Wade) had come to town! My mother loved her family as evidenced by the fact, like many of the other *greats* and *great-greats*[108] who came to New Orleans, whether from Chicago or New York, my mother's house was the first place they felt welcome enough to come to visit and *rest a spell."*

I had heard about my Uncle Wade for a very long time before that summer in 1967 when he and my Aunt Vera came to visit. He had been particularly well-known as a bartender in the Chicago night-life world in the mid 1930's (after prohibition ended in 1933) through World War II and up to the early sixties. I remember how excited he got when he

---

108 Nicknames used to describe the great uncles, great aunts, great-great aunts and uncles, et cetera.

recalled one of his most memorable nights. It was on December 18, 1943 at one of the clubs where he worked. It involved the settling of a long-time bet between two patrons who were arguing about who the reigning Heavyweight Champion of the World was. Wade Sorrell had received a telegram from the editor of *The Ring* (magazine) indicating that Joe Louis was indeed the World Heavyweight Champion during his stint in the Army during World War II. *Uncle Wade to the rescue . . . problem solved!*

I glanced briefly at Jules, now beaming a broad smile and 'rocking' his head and torso signaling his agreement, but I got the 'feeling' that Jules' gestures signified more than agreement. It was more like he had been there in New Orleans at the same time I had been—he had actually met Wade Sorrell too! At least, so it seemed to me at that moment. I 'broke' my gaze at Jules, allowing for a focus on the dark-brown corduroy slippers on his feet, which permitted me to return to my 'introduction' of Wade Sorrell.

Somewhere around 1965, he bought a small restaurant in the Southside of Chicago on South Halsted. He named it *Sorrell's Original Painted Dall*. It was common knowledge in our family circles that Wade Sorrell was rumored to have served some of the best barbeque in Chicago for more than twenty years. Every year at the beginning of summer, some of Wade's *personally favored* family members (from the time I left New Orleans and moved to Denver, I was one of those whom he personally favored) received a gallon container of his secret barbeque sauce. I didn't know it at the time, but we were soon to find out firsthand of the local fame of Sorrell's Original Painted Dall. That sauce was so good that if my taste buds could talk they would shout, 'Umm good; it ain't no rumor, this sauce is off the hook!'

Janice and I drove from Denver, Colorado to Chicago in a tiny Datsun B210 sedan to visit my great-great uncle Jimmy (Samuel James Pourciau) in the spring of 1978. Uncle Jimmy, who had acted as my spiritual elder and the most critical of father-figures in my life at that time, had recently suffered a stroke. Fortunately, he was recovering under the care of his wife, Americal Jones Pourciau. We received a hearty welcome into their home on this first visit to Chicago. I remember wondering whether or not Uncle Jimmy could drive, as he insisted that Janice and I (mere visitors and first time visitors at that!) take him to (his nephew) Wade's place. We made it to "Sorrell's Original Painted Dall" by early afternoon where Uncle Wade was working very hard. Even though it was only a little past mid-day, his shirt was already soaked with perspiration. I didn't have to wonder why for long; the heat coming from that savory pit tucked away somewhere on the backside of the property, coupled with a rather warm day, told the whole story. Uncle Jimmy really enjoyed himself that day; and not just because we had the privilege and pleasure of eating Chicago's *best ribs* (my personal evaluation). He really perked up as he 'took' the floor during that visit; reminiscing about days long past and how he longed to be back in the kitchen working with Wade and Joe Johnson[109] again.

I may not know my Dad, but these uncles almost made up for that void. These guys were somebody. Ones who could actually say that they personally knew such luminaries like Joe Lewis and Jack Johnson!

That spring of 1978 would be the last time I would see my Uncle Jimmy; he died the following December in Chicago. My Uncle Jimmy's wife, Americal and I stayed in close contact for many years after his passing. One day in the fall of 1985, while we were still living in Denver, she called to tell me that she couldn't get in touch with my Uncle Wade. I felt something bad had happened, so I immediately started calling everyone in the family from New Orleans to help find out what was going on. A few days later, Americal called to let me know that he had suffered a stroke and was hospitalized. I had been at a business convention in Charlotte, but recognizing the urgency of Uncle Wade's condition, I left it early to fly out to Chicago. Boy was I happy to visit a recovering Uncle Wade, who expected full recovery and assured me he would be okay. Sure enough a few months later, I visited Uncle Wade at his home in Flossmoor, Illinois. He seemed much better, as he was trying to get settled in the garden-level of the home which had been converted to a suite to accommodate his recovery and rehabilitation processes as a result of the damage caused by the stroke.

Apparently absolute independent living didn't work out for Uncle Wade. By the winter of 1986, I visited him in a very nice nursing home where he could be assisted in his rehabilitation by medical personnel,

---

109 Joe Johnson, a longtime friend of Wade Sorrell and Samuel J. Pourciau, and a former middleweight boxer.

relieving the burden of his lengthy recovery from his family. You can imagine my surprise when I visited Uncle Wade at his new digs, which were more like a studio apartment, including a fully equipped kitchen, than one would expect in a rehab facility.

It was a cold and very windy day when I made that first visit to Uncle Wade's new digs. The heavy snowfall savagely pelted my face as I hurried along the short distance from my car to the facility's entrance. I wondered what kind of people would settle in a place like this—Chicago was brutal! As I approached his room on the seventeenth floor, about fifty feet from the elevator, I could smell the newness of the carpeted hallway leading to number 1706. Uncle Wade's voice beckoning me to enter the unlocked door seemed so much more resonating than I had been accustomed to in the past. Perhaps the 'hollowness' of the room, magnified his illness since I had last seen him, nevertheless, his voice, though it was unmistakably Wade Sorrell; it sounded more frail and brassy—a lot less warm and smooth as I had come to expect. Uncle Wade sat with his back turned towards where I entered with his legs dangling on the side of the bed near the lone large window. He turned his head just enough to see me and smiling, he motioned to the one of the chairs beside the window, welcoming me to sit.

As I sat there, I observed that the room's light gray walls were clean and held several institutional abstract art pieces, which tastefully hung on each wall. The room was small, but inviting. Surprisingly, its chairs were very comfortable and could easily accommodate three people without looking nor feeling cluttered. To the right of the entrance was a bathroom with the open door revealing crisp, white towels hanging on the wall. At the opposite end of the room, next to the wall of the bathroom was a small gas oven range with four burners; one lit with a pot containing a waft of something that made me forget about the cold, harsh weather of the *windy city*.

He cooked some collard greens and cornbread that day when I visited him at the nursing home and we ate like royalty—two princes, laughing and reminiscing about his early years in Chicago, and the wild parties and galas he had attended over the years.

Little did I know at the time that that would be the last time I'd ever see Uncle Wade. Thinking back on that day, perhaps he knew his run in this life was about to come to an end soon. As the evening came to a close on that last day, he pulled out a large corrugated box from under his bed. One by one he opened several manila envelopes he had taken from the box. Slowly and methodically, he began to identify each article. He sat on the edge of the bed and faced me as I eagerly accepted the offer to sit in the comfortable gray upholstered chair, which was closest to his bed. He hesitated as he slowly began to hand me each envelope. I think I also caught a glimpse of a glimmer of a tear that refused to fall from his right eye. Almost ceremoniously he began with the photograph of him and his first wife. She was beautiful. He then passed a second photograph. It was my Uncle Wade in a pose with another handsome woman; whom he informed me was his second wife. Then yet another photograph of a strikingly beautiful woman, his third wife, Aunt Vera!

I stared in wonder and just before I asked, he replied as if he heard my thoughts. 'Each of my first two wives died very shortly after we were married. I don't talk about them much because of the horrible pain I felt from each of their untimely deaths.' Finally, I mustered the courage to ask with an uncomfortable laugh. 'Were you ever suspected as a contributor of their deaths? I mean, after the second woman's demise you must have appeared to be the male version of the black widow, right?' He smiled as if to accept my offbeat humor, and then replied with amazing class and dignity. 'I loved them.'

I was glad I hadn't prodded him on the names of wives numbers one and two before he explained about how talking about them was very painful. *Thanks Momma for giving me the good sense to think about other peoples' feelings and knowing when to keep my mouth shut!*

I couldn't help but thinking while at the same time confirming what Mom had said about Uncle Wade: He had in fact, again proven to be "bull of the woods." Most people wouldn't have been able to recognize my oftentimes strange sense of humor and that the query was not so strange after all. I'm equally sure that because he considered me friend; not foe helped a lot as well. Whew, bully for me!

'I was blessed to have known and been in love with each one of them,' he continued. 'They were as beautiful on the inside as they were on the outside. They were both so young! If anyone thought I had caused them to die, no one said so; but I truly felt I was a very unlucky man after my second wife died. I was almost afraid to try a third time, but I am happy I tried once more, even though I was much older by then. Your Aunt Vera was the one woman who made my life complete and with her I gained two beautiful children. That just goes to show that we should never let what first appears as setbacks in life to cause us to give up. Sometimes we fall into that ole trap of thinking that maybe we weren't supposed to be happy. Or even that we too old to find that happiness. But look here, what if I had given up? I would never have found Vera and been blessed with those two beautiful children she gave me.'

I watched as tears welled in the corner of his eyes and spilled over onto his weathered cheek as his fingers carefully separated a bundle of photographs and documents and selected two more photographs. Next, he spread out on his bed two black and white photos of three young women posing together. A faint, almost reminiscent smile kissed his lips as he explained that two of the three women in the photos were cousins from New York."

For a brief moment, I wondered why he didn't introduce the cousins; then it dawned on me that he didn't, because he couldn't. He'd forgotten their names but remembered that they were from New York! Hmm, now I didn't feel so bad about forgetting things sometimes. Even Uncle Wade being sharp as a tack forgot things from time to time!

He hurriedly bundled the photos, documents, and other important papers and placed them in my hands as he said, 'I'm passing on the gauntlet to you. Now, you need to keep track of the family!'

I accepted the bundle with pride, knowing that Uncle Wade had entrusted me with the responsibility of keeping in contact with the family on purpose; and not just when, as is the practice in most families, we see each other only at funerals or weddings.

For a time, we continued to engage in a few more awkward discussions about buying back the restaurant and starting operations back up as soon as he recovered. But I knew he was saying goodbye to me that cold winter evening in Chicago at the end of 1986. As I walked back to my rental car parked a few yards away from the building's entrance I thought about how sad I was right then and how much sadder I'd be when he actually died. I didn't have long to wait. My Uncle Wade died the following year in September, 1987.

I often thought about that last visit with my dear uncle, how he had given me those precious documents and photographs that he'd valued so dearly, and his adamant command to 'keep track of the family!' From the look on his face and the sternness of his tone, even as his frail body was declining rapidly, it was obvious he considered those items (and the instructions related to them) to be of major importance.

For more than ten years, I had merely looked at the bundle of documents from time to time after receiving them, until one evening in the middle of October 1997 when I bought a new computer and decided to try a new family tree program. Uncle Wade and his pictures and other documents had provided me with the most complete data I had to input into the program, so that became my starting point. One of my clients had allowed me access to a document scanner which enabled me to scan the few photos I had from Uncle Wade's package, including the heraldry documentation.

And that my dear Jules is my experience and the delightful opportunity I had in spending some of those last days in the life of Wade Sorrell; and those that I shall cherish all the days of my life!

I knew Jules had something to add to my long-winded reminiscence, but still, he paused, then sat back in his chair, looked up at me and declared:

"I reckon you were da one who had da right questions and I am da one who's supposed to give da right answers—you know to set things straight, so to speak. So you make sure you set da records straight; dat is to tell da correct tale about us in its entirety."

Although I wasn't quite sure what Jules meant by this; I was beginning suspect that what he was alluding to was the roller coaster ride he'd referred to earlier as 'my journey.' I wasn't envisioning myself from a distance taking a ride; I was on the ride and experiencing every one of its rises and falls; and therefore, I was to include all facets of "our story" including my "bumpy ride journey" which was as much a part of the story as the story itself.

* * *

Jules was standing now, and as he continued, this time he was more animated than before. The varied crescendo in his voice matched the movement in his hands just like those of a well-rehearsed orchestra conductor. I took this to mean that I needed to pay close attention to what Jules was going to present next. I mustered up a full alert. With Jules there was no such thing as "sleeping on the job"! I never knew where he was going next. He had so many questions as well as so much information to impart. Astonishingly as it may sound, he could talk about my past, which became his present; as well as my present which unmistakably, became his future.

"Between 1850 and 1865, life was very hard for most people where I live. Da most difficult ting to wrap my head around was seeing niggers free and 'slaved' working in da same field."

Now, with tears welling in his eyes again and cracking in his voice as he appeared to struggle for a way to convince me to share what he was feeling, he spoke.

"Da smell of cotton and cane burning in da fields, trying to keep da Union soldiers from taking or destroying property at da Plantation was awful hard. Bodies and limbs of dose young boys being burned and da smell of cotton could make most men sick. And now the unthinkable among southern gentry had happened: cotton was no longer *King* in Louisiana, and da rest of da south. Young boys wit no life in dere eyes and no future to look forward to seemed to be all we saw for a long, long time. Watching da children die from yellow fever or just from not having hope seems to go against everything God made dat was wonderful. A few years ago, someone from Massachusetts[110] wrote about a man's soul weighing a little less dan one ounce and dat wen he died, da missing weight was dat man's soul departing. You remember we spoke before dat some folks say dat having an image of a man takes a part of dat man's soul from him?" Jules shook his head as if he'd suddenly thought about the image I showed him of himself, before he added, "Looking at dat picture of myself dat you showed me, you know da one you showed me before, right now, makes da hairs on da back of my neck stand up."

---

110 According to Duncan Macdougall, MD, Dorchester Massachusetts, reported on April 1, 1901, " . . . The loss was ascertained to be three fourths of an ounce." (Approximately 21 grams)

Finally! Don't know what took me so long to realize that Jules' brain worked much faster than his lips, especially since I shared this same attribute! He had so much to tell me that oftentimes his 'train' (of thought) got disrupted and got off track; sometimes even derailed! Now I could see it.

I began to share some of his pain as I quickly rose and walked across the room saying, "Excuse me Jules, I need to use the bathroom."

The small room offered little, but some, solace as I bent over the basin allowing my face contact with the water running, and attempting to mask the sounds of my muffled sobs and thought, *this is not possible! Here I am with a man insisting he is my great, great-grandfather, One hundred sixty-three years after his birth and more than one hundred and three years after his recorded death! Superficially, I pretended that I was not sure what was bringing on these tears. But deep down, I had to admit that it was my inability to control my thoughts and feelings that really was the largest contributor to this sudden sadness I was experiencing: Jules could say something that made me believe that he was in fact who he claimed to be; and I believed him at the time. Then I started second guessing stuff and I started wondering how the impossible was possible. Man, something had to give. I knew it would, but it was the indefinite when that I found so very troubling. God, I really needed your help on this one!*

CHAPTER 16

FAST FORWARD

And the Beat Goes On

When I returned from the bathroom I found Jules had sat back down and seemed to be a bit more calm than when I had hastily retreated to my personal "weepy" moment. He looked at me with a gentle smile and said, "Well until I wake up or you wake up, one or da other, you should start telling me all about dis future ting and all 'dat's involved in it."

"I promise to start from the beginning tomorrow, Jules. You've already had enough for one day." *As I think retrospectively on that specific day, truthfully speaking, Jules wasn't the only one who had had enough for the day . . .*

* * *

The week had flown by so fast! It was now Friday and I hungered for more of whatever it was Jules had for *me*. I guess, for the first time in a very long time, I felt like *a sponge—soaking up everything* Jules laid before me.

It felt good, but bittersweet. Deep down inside I knew that there was an end, looming on the horizon. And it was approaching far, far too soon!

I left the building, exited into the oncoming darkness of the late-evening.

The weekend came and went pretty much as usual with me teaching a driver safety class on Saturday in Atlanta and returning home late evening physically and emotionally drained trying to heal society of its minor ills associated with young automobile drivers becoming or causing another person to become a statistic of traffic collisions. This had really become an issue recently. Despite all the statistics and warnings from various sources, they just didn't get it: texting and driving is not cool!

I had thought of Jules all day that Saturday, particularly as I grappled with the lesson plan for my Youth Driver Safety Program. The morning's class was scheduled to begin discussing the issue of saving lives to as it relates to the nation's teens and young adults operating motor vehicles. The morning's message to a room full of nineteen through twenty-five year olds, at-risk motorists was to *"choose life[111]."*

I couldn't help smiling a bit when I thought about how much this guy in the personage of Jules Bayonne had so overwhelmed, overtaken and not to mention overjoyed my life in the few days since I'd met him. He was never far from me—if not in my physical presence, he certainly took up a lot of my mental and emotional presence. But it was 'all good!' Thanks to Jules I was finding a whole lot of forgotten peace because of learning about my 'Dots' and the identification of the chief 'Cornerstone,' I could now without a doubt select the correct path that made me choose life.

---

111 The Bible reference Deuteronomy 30:19 is alluded to, which states "I call heaven and earth to record this day against you, that I have set before you life and death, blessing and cursing: therefore choose life, that both thou and thy seed may live:"

PART 5

REFERENCE POINT

CHAPTER 17

CHOOSE LIFE

As I entered Jules' room the next evening, he started firing questions at me before I could get the door to the room closed behind me.

"Does it appear dat a county founded wit so much promise, potential and resource can eliminate war in the future?"

I almost thought this was a trick question until I remembered that Jules had missed "some things," like big worldly events. Besides, before I left him last time, I'd promised to take the lead at our next meeting. So now it was my turn!

America has been deeply involved in two major wars in the twentieth century—World War I and World War II, and several so called military 'conflicts', (including the Korean and Vietnam Wars) since the American Civil War. This news seemed to really disturb him. He wanted to know the specific details.

"World War I, called the *Great War* began in 1914 and ended in 1918 caused nearly 10 million deaths for the fourteen nations involved."

Jules sighed deeply and then replied with tears welling in his eyes.

"Dat many men perished?"

I nodded and waited for Jules to continue. He heaved, paused and then with some difficulty, he began again.

"I supposed at da time da nearly six-hundred thousand boys dat died between da time I was eighteen and twenty-one on both sides—North and South failed to teach men how to settle differences in a sensible manner. I often wondered wat God tought about da horrible change in His plans for dose boys—da children dat would never be born as a result of da carnage left by war. Da families, da generations from dose unborn children dat never became, for dose who da world will never benefit from, was da most incomprehensible waste of lives and life. But now, from wat you say, da devastation of war and da resulting consequences actually pale in comparison to wat I was tinking back den"

I thought about the proposition Jules had just presented and considered that the odds of survival which bring forth generations of a single family over a five-hundred year period would prove extremely rare; given the fact that war is happening or has happened somewhere in this world at any given time during any given five-hundred period. This is mind-boggling even if we cut the time period from five hundred to one hundred years. By now, I had begun to expect Jules had the ability to sense my thoughts. I short-circuited my mental gymnastics for the moment; so I waited, again to give Jules enough time to absorb these factual atrocities.

Jules stared at me for a moment, and then began. "So, just tink about it for a moment, it is remarkable dat you are here, Byron. (*I was right*). Your ancestors from da period just after da war between Lincoln and Davis' armies had to survive not only dat period's devastation from war and famine but also from da diseases dat claimed da lives of a great number of men, women and children. If you factor in all da tings dat could go wrong for each generation leading up to your current living descendant, your being here should be a humbling experience. Don't you agree?"

"Oh, absolutely, Jules!" I responded.

Jules continued. "Conditions surrounding each of your ancestors had to be near perfect or at least relatively uninterrupted for each progression of life, union, den birth of each person, and so on. Just as wen Abraham begat Isaac; Isaac begat Jacob (or Israel); Israel begat da total (twelve) tribes and so on, many complex obstacles were present. Against great odds and perilous daily dangers, dose people persevered, dey survived and in most instances, dey thrived. Dat's wat I meant about folks havin' dere '*Dots*'! Somehow, it seems dat one of da messages from da Prophet, Moses[112] gave instructions to da people (Isrealites) wen faced wit da option of choosing life between and death was by all means, to choose life, so dat not only do you get to live in da present, but you also increase da odds for dose who come after you to get to live in da future!"

Remember, Byron, dat all living organisms contain an element of striving—I like to call it da universal self-preservation switch. Any organism lacking dis element is subject to inevitable attack by resistance or adverse events affecting its survival. Essentially, the recipe for survival is da ability to combat attacks from man and nature and win! Failure to endure and win da resistance yields some form of retardation; often severe and perhaps even leads to da ultimate death of an organism."

Wow! I finally 'got' Jules' dissertation on the subject of '*Dots*'!

This revelation took me back to Saturday's Youth Driver Safety Program. It was all so much clearer to me now. I realized that in the instance of the young people, not only was I to instruct them in the proper use of automobiles, but my responsibility (duly appointed or not) also included the provision, for imparting knowledge to them regarding the vigorous struggle towards the law of survival! And, by making this important choice and commitment increases the likelihood that their *seed* will also have an opportunity to choose life, which in turn, causes *Providence* to move in one's favor.

I don't know how I'd missed it before! Jules had initiated the discussion of the necessity to 'choose life' on at least three of our visits. I just hadn't picked up on it until now. Now, I recall how intense he had become in his attempts to make certain I understood the deliberate choosing of life as a '*Cornerstone*' " element of life and essential to one's philosophy of living. He further noted, Almighty God had given man this incredible gift, but in order to possess it, one had to be aware that the gift of blessing had been given. "Read it for yourself", Jules hissed. "You do have a bible—

---

112 Jules' reference to the biblical "Prophet"—*Moses*. Deuteronomy 30:15-19 King James Version (KJV): "See, I have set before thee this day life and good, and death and evil; . . . I call heaven and earth to record this day against you, that I have set before you life and death, blessing and cursing: therefore choose life, that both thou and thy seed may live . . ."

read it, for heavens' sake" Jules bristled. *This was more a command than a suggestion or question.*

"Do you fancy riddles?"

I nodded simultaneously with a murmured affirmation. But still thinking: *Here come those 'Dots' again!*

"Would you at least be amused by da parables spoken by Da *'Cornerstone,'* Himself from da scriptures?" Jules added.

"In your reference to The *'Cornerstone,'* are you speaking of Christ?" I asked, with an almost arrogant confidence. I was thinking, but did not say: Got this one, this time Jules!

It had suddenly occurred to me that I was obviously becoming difficult, a most unflattering habit I had developed over recent years. I was displaying the very same poor behavior, bordering on a disrespect for which I harbored tremendous disdain when I encountered the same behavior from others directed at me. I was immediately ashamed, as I was raised better. My Mama would not have approved. It was also very obvious that Jules did not approve; nor was he the kind of person who would entertain my psychological jousting for very long. So, defeated and ashamed on two fronts, in an instant after I had responded to Jules regarding Christ being a *'Cornerstone,'* I humbly apologized.

"Please excuse my vanity, Jules; if I my responses seem condescending, it was not my intention to do so, but I often make outbursts without thinking first as a means of masking my own self-proclaimed, but secretly held deficiencies in my personal self-esteem. I admit that I still have a long way to go. This is real hard for me to admit, especially since I thought I had this thing licked!"

"Why do you abuse yourself so?" Jules asked, with that warm subdued, comforting tone in his voice that told me, I'm alright in spite of these little setbacks or quirks as I liked to call them. Then to make sure I got the message, he added, "You are very perceptive in your answer and, equally as perceptive in getting a good handle on who da real Byron Coleman is. Don't restrict yourself—dere's more you have to add, right?"

Now, Jules seemed to slow the pace of our dialog by changing the tempo of the conversation. His words were hypnotically warm and easy to mentally digest. *Good, I needed that!* I sensed that he wanted to have me tell him what *I* was feeling in my *heart* as opposed to what my mind thought, or what was limited to what was in my head. The gentle prompting by Jules caused me to consider the '*Cornerstone*' as a personal entity (person), in addition to those deemed inanimate objects—the literal stones used in architecture, as well as sets of principles, concepts and ideologies, necessary for the functioning of an advancing modern society.

"As you might recall . . ." Jules continued, "Before da creation knew of *He* who was dere at da very beginning, during da creation, so it was told, da placement of da '*Cornerstone*' for da building of everything was through wat was said."

Somewhat confused, I interrupted Jules. "I'm not sure I'm following you, I don't understand."

Jules was quick to respond. "Of course, you do! Remember da one of da *twelve* who wrote it:

"*In the beginning was the Word, and the Word was with God and the Word was God . . . All things were made by him . . . And the Word was made flesh and dwelt among us . . .*"

You know dat some thirty times, da words "*And God said . . .*" appear in Da First Book of Moses (The Pentatuch: Genesis 1). Consider da possibility dat da *Word* for whom da apostle referred to, is probably da same *One* as in "*And God said let **us** make man in our own image.* I merely suggest, just as da *Word* is of major concern, so are *spoken words*. Wat if words do create, or tear down—wat if words are tings dat can actually, for real, do tings? Da placing of da '*Cornerstone*,' even if it is *Da Word*, or words, dey deserve some consideration. Don't you agree?"

"Absolutely!" I replied, now more astonished at Jules' clarification of Genesis (1:26 of the Old Testament and that of St. John 1:1—3 of the New Testament[113]).

But now I realized there was even more to be gleaned from Jules' careful selection of the **word** '*Cornerstone*' and my imagination was in hyper-gear when he pointed out how vital **words** are. As I wrestled to

---

113 Genesis 1:26 King James Version (KJV) "And God said, Let us make man in our image, after our likeness: and let them have dominion . . ."; John 1:1-3 King James Version (KJV) "**1** In the beginning was the Word, and the Word was with God, and the Word was God. **2** The same was in the beginning with God. **3** All things were made by him; and without him was not any thing made that was made."

give some half-assed answer, I sensed Jules had keenly observed I had that 'deer staring in the headlights' look, so again he allowed me to *save face*:

"Don't know—do you subscribe to da rules or roles as dey once related to fatherhood?" Jules asked.

Wow! This guy has *serious* reasoning skills. I had to sorta laugh to myself about how I still get surprised at Jules' ability to 'read my mail!' As I recovered from my amazement in his mental prowess, and began to give his query due consideration, it occurred to me that in the midst of challenges and struggles throughout the history of human existence, *some things* ought not to change.

I took a deep breath, and then exhaled a carefully thought out response.

Well, I am aware that there are rules that dictate how fathers should act and to some extent, there are consequential penalties one must incur if he fails to adhere to or follow the *fatherhood creed* established long ago by our ancestors. However, I am also of the opinion that recent societal and cultural issues have changed the game somewhat. For example, there have been a few changes made to the rules, particularly since traditional roles have been blurred with the enactment of legislature regarding women's rights and laws designed to protect women and children.

"Incredible!" Jules blurted. "So are you saying da cornerstone dat governs fatherhood has been removed? How could dis happen? I suspect dat if dere haven't been adverse effects and dire consequences yet, dere *shall* be sometime soon!"

Well, perhaps you are right, I began. But, I would like to think that the cornerstone may have required amending or adjusting to correct sags in the foundations as opposed to the *removal* of the cornerstone all together as it relates to fatherhood. For instance, the traditional rigidity of the head of the house role was inflexible. The role had to allow for change in circumstances; it required adjustment in the case of widows, single and unmarried mothers. These women now had to assume the responsibilities of the fathers who left their families, oftentimes involuntarily. Such was the instance and devastation caused by the advent of the Civil War, I would think. Right? There were numbers of men who never returned to their homes or to their wives and children as well as those who never got the opportunity of the pleasure and experience of becoming heads households—they perished in battle. The *'Cornerstone'* related to the role of fathers was honed with an understanding that *fathers* and *husbands* would be the rule without regard to the exceptions that would decay this rule over time with increased frequency and impact. Then, of course, there are fathers who share the terms of 'deadbeats', 'absentees', 'sperm donors', 'birth fathers', 'biological fathers' and 'baby daddies.' These men, their personage (appearance) as well as their sense of *duty* (responsibility), would require amending, or possibly even major repair of the foundations that once governed men.

Jules' slightly, but noted, furrowed brow told me he was obviously troubled about something I'd said. I wondered what he was thinking and if we were still on the same page. I watched. I waited. I remained quiet as he walked to the table in the corner of dimly lit room to where a small burgundy, leatherette bible rested. He picked up the *Book* and began to respond with a raspy voice.

I couldn't tell which sentiment had triggered Jules' *raspiness*: was it sadness because of the way things had turned out; frustration in my not grasping what he was trying to say . . . or something else?

"Da idea dat da *'Cornerstone'* was placed without consideration for *da* exception to da traditional role is not a new concept. Keep in mind dat da vast majority of our forefathers were faced wit da problem of being separated or forcefully removed from dere families anyway. Most of da Europeans came to dis new world witout dere women. Consequently, many of dem turned to passé en blanc[114], through plaçage. Da intent was to start wit such a rigid stone, wit da knowledge dat dose exceptions dat might arise still rested on a foundation dat would provide for da return to the da original intent[115] at some point along da way."

---

114   The process whereby light-skinned blacks (literally translated), *pass for white*. Due to the mixing of races, particularly in Louisiana, some people, due to lighter skin tone, were accepted as white. This concept pertains to those possessing the ability to "pass' and exploited their ability to advantageous ends.

115   Jules suggested that the strange new trend of plaçage relationships was introduced often with disregard to those traditional roles (rules) of husbands and fathers. Ironically, today, "intent" with respect to husbands and fathers has been returned to due to the wide acceptance of interracial relationships. " . . . there is evidence to show that race mixing was common for many reasons. For one thing, white men chose their mulatto paramours quite intentionally, and not just because white women were few in number. The precedent for this had been established nearly two hundred years before when the French planters

Hmmm, maybe it was something else. I was thinking Jules was referring to men leaving the home either voluntarily or involuntarily, which resulted in leaving behind fatherless households; but it seems like he was going in a completely different direction. He was talking about the advent of interracial relationships!

I understand. I started, sensing Jules' need to continue his explanations regarding the complex nature of interracial relationships and its evolution, particularly as it occurred in Louisiana. It was also clear he wanted to be certain I fully comprehended how these 'relationships' impacted both of us. Although I felt privileged to get this knowledge from Jules—it was personal to me, it was obvious that the knowledge was *not* for me exclusively.

"*'Cornerstones'* are oftentimes a matter of wat appears to be da most inconsequential in nature. A good example is provided in da instance of da *manners* you displayed. You chose to respect da idea dat I should be addressed as *Mister* until I gave you permission to refer to me by my first name is an exceptional example of 'good manners'—'respect' being da '*Cornerstone*,' da ting, in this instance. I am most impressed dat you possess dis quality. You and I were taught dat a man deserved da consideration to be called *Mister* under most circumstances and certainly for male persons having reached da level of adulthood and if it was not determinable as to da maturity of da man, good 'upbringing' dictated da use of *dat title*. Dat is, at least until da person being addressed offers or suggests da parties should refrain from da *formality*."

I didn't feel I deserved such appreciation, but knew instinctively that I should acknowledge, at the very least, some level of thanks to Jules for recognizing how well I had been taught and that he put me in the same class as himself. Jules' clarity and thorough discourse regarding the importance of one possessing and displaying good manners, was such a remarkable, but not unexpected example for me. There was no doubt in my mind, I was in the presence of a great human being, but, as obvious as it seemed to me, there was a sense of common humility about Jules.

---

from St. Domingue took the finest slave women for their mistresses . . . were brought to Louisiana by the planters when the latter fled St. Domingue" Sybil Kein, editor of "Creole—The History and Legacy of Louisiana's Free People of Color", Chapter 3, Plaçage and the Louisiana 'gens de couleur libre' "How Race and Sex Defined the Lifestyles of Free Women of Color by Joan M. Martin.

Thank you much, Jules. I choked out humbly.

"No! Thank you, Byron!" Jules retorted.

* * *

During those subsequent visits, Jules spoke of 'Dots', choices, boundaries, and emotions. He constantly referred to the 'amazing power of God.' I took notes during most of the visits, but I would have kept a better journal if I had only realized he was providing me an education on life that would provide such a successful guide for my use and others as well. Not to mention the fact that this man held me hopelessly captive most of the time which pretty much precluded my concentrating on taking meticulous notes.

It occurred to me that in the first few meetings with Jules, time seemed to pass ever so slowly. Conversations that lasted only minutes, felt like an eternity—the most pleasant levels of wisdom, fulfilling my hunger, stopping just short of overwhelming. My handwritten notes filled three legal pads within seven visits, but while I was recording key discussion points, I was unaware of the volume consumed. I could almost kick myself that I did not think about recording our conversations instead of trying to memorialize the most salient points of our discussions.

As I took my leave from today's visit with Jules, I started thinking about how much I loved visiting with him, but always experienced a state 'beyond exhaustion' on my way home. Funny thing was, that I didn't know how exhausted I was until the moment the door to his room closed behind me. I'm sure my state was due to the constant firing of my brain cells as I tried to absorb what he had to offer while still contributing my own personal opinions and perspectives. These visits with Jules was what I imagined it'd be like if one could pass through an 'enlightenment portal.' As I entered his room, this whole fantastic world of wisdom and possibilities opened up. In retrospect, it reminded me of an *Alice Through The Looking Glass* experience; but the good thing about my experience was that I brought the wisdom I learned back with me; into 'my own real world!'

I guess what they say about time passing slowly when you're having fun has somewhat of ring of truth to it. I immediately found this to be the case in the first few meetings with Jules, time seemed to pass ever so slowly. Conversations that lasted only minutes, felt like an eternity—the most pleasant levels of wisdom, fulfilling my hunger, stopping just short of overwhelming. My handwritten notes filled three legal pads within the first seven visits, but while I was recording key discussion points, I was unaware of the volume consumed. Needless to say,

I continued to be amazed at the insightfulness of this man on present day happenings, even though he'd been deceased well over a hundred years! I guess this would be enough for anybody to experience that "beyond exhaustion state" including me, Byron M. Coleman!

Today was no exception. After collapsing to a well-needed sleep on the sofa for what seemed to be several hours, I awoke from a troubled nap; surprised to learn from a quick glance at my watch I'd only been out for less than thirty minutes. Not fully awake and trying to figure out whether I should get up or try to get some more sleep, I decided that a glass of wine would ease my restlessness.

I walked to the dining room to find my sister, Deborra sitting at the table talking to my wife, Janice about children and grandchildren issues. As I poured a glass of muscadine wine, it occurred to me that now would be a good time to bring them up-to-date with the events of the last few days. I hoped the girls could take what I was going to say without the proverbial 'grain of salt' when I noted that since by the looks of it, they'd *refreshed* their wine glasses a time or two prior to my joining them, might make *that* 'salt' easier to swallow! Well, here goes. I made room for myself at the head of the table; sat down, and began:

"Deborra, the strangest thing has happened already this year . . . this man can't possibly be who he says he is." Janice offered her input attempting to solve the mystery. "Maybe he *is* some old guy that's just suffering a psychotic episode. Isn't that what the doctors have already said?" I felt obliged to counter on two fronts; not only to champion Jules, but also to justify why I keep going back for more! "Yes, except that he has knowledge about things that only a person studying our family's history would know." During the first thirty minutes or so of my summarizing what transpired between me and Jules, Deborra kept staring at me the whole time. Her only, but repetitious comment was, "You're kidding!" I wasn't sure if I'd convinced Deborra or not until she asked, "Well who do you think he really is?" I thought long and hard about that question and rather than commit to an answer, I gave my sister a 'look' that said nothing, yet said a whole lot.

I was thinking—you really don't give a rats' ass, girl. I'm the one that has to answer that question for myself—but thanks for being a good listener!

Deborra was never was good at solving mysteries, or even attempting to help solve one. In fact, I knew she wouldn't bring up the subject about Jules after the next twenty-four hours, unless I brought it up. For my sister, most things were 'out-of-sight; out-of-mind.' However, for that moment, she listened and, then she asked the right question; not for the benefit of her own self-satisfaction, but for mine, though I'm certain that her query for my benefit was unintentional. The main thing was that now, without a shadow of a doubt, I knew the answer—Jules Bayonne was/is who he said he is—Jules Bayonne, my (second) great-grandfather!

That evening when I had settled in my bed, I again reflected on the **word** and the dynamics surrounding its various meanings—both faith-based and secular. The former led me to the bible where I spent more than an hour reading from the Book of James.

*"If any man offend not in **word**, the same **is** a perfect man . . . But the tongue can no man tame; it is an unruly evil full of deadly poison. Therewith bless we God, even the Father; therewith curse we men, which are made after the similitude of God. Out of the same mouth proceedeth blessing and cursing. My brethren, these things ought not so to be."*

Book of James 3:2 KJV

The Book of James led me to yet another ramification of the **word**. As St James put it: " . . . man can not bless God and curse man with the same instrument-the tongue (and the **word** that springs forth from it though virtually invisible has very powerful effects)." It supports an all or nothing proposition about faith in God: You either have faith in God or You don't!

It was easier for me to have faith in the existence of Christ after seeing the Shroud of Turin displayed at the Vatican collection on exhibit at the 1984 World's Fair in New Orleans. Although I was (am still) aware that the Shroud is not the definitive burial cloth of the risen Christ, presently, the Catholic Church still recognizes it as a relic. I recognized that pending ongoing scientific discussions regarding the authenticity and the dating of the Shroud, my (like many others) faith in the relic is premised on unstable, shakable foundation, at best. Regardless of authenticity, or the lack thereof, the symbolic nature of the Shroud of Turin (added with my puny faith), is compelling enough for me to 'feel' the *message*.

In the small room housing the Shroud's life-sized image, I was overwhelmed by the presence of the awesome spirit of God, as I gazed at the linen cloth and the reverse negative image of a man brutally tortured. The cloth's iron-oxide stains where the wounds were visible in the wrists, feet, side and around the head spoke to me. At that moment, a resounding voice spoke out loudly within my spirit: "Because thou hast seen me, thou hast believed: blessed are they that have not seen, and yet have believed!" I wept there, alone in that dimly lit room, illuminated only by the backlighting of the Shroud. Initially, I thought it was the *tangible* Shroud of Turin, the thing I could see which had bolstered my faith in God. However, it was the intangible thing I could not see when God spoke (**word**) to my spirit, that made me realize the real truth about myself. My belief and faith in God had been dependent upon a wavering faith that depended primarily on the seen rather than the unseen. This truth is what caused me to weep that day in that dimly lit room. Later, I would realize that the incident at the 1984 World's fair was not a coincidence, but rather a deliberate and orchestrated 'coming home' of sorts. You see, for more than a decade I had abandoned my 'Cornerstone' of faith. But it had not abandoned me. The 'foundation *stone*' remained, as well as the major components of the structure which housed my faith. So *that* timely visit to *that* exhibit, was the initial point of my restoration project—a renovation to which Jules added master craftsmanship towards its completion.

Incidentally, it was then—during my reflection of the Shroud incident, where my study on *words* was in 'full swing,' when I had reasoned that the person or persons responsible for the word definition of 'coincidence' was probably riddled with psychological phobias. I accepted (and adopted) Jules' declaration; *"There are no coincidences!"* In other words, events and/or occurrences happening in simultaneous (coincidental) concert do not exist.

* * *

CHAPTER 18

MODERN TIMES

Something Old; Something New

On Wednesday (January 17th) evening when I stopped by to see Jules I was surprised to see how comfortable he'd become with watching television. "Hey Byron! Da lady dat come to take care of me said dis 'teevee' can teach me wat da world is come to."

"Good idea, Jules" I said, trying to convince myself that perhaps this visit wasn't going to be awkward after all, given the apparent ease with which Jules had now adopted 'teevee' as a way of life in these so called modern times.

Thank you Jesus! Looked like my preconceived awkwardness of this visit wasn't going to be awkward after all. As a matter of fact, Jules' ease in accepting 'teevee' even presented the ideal approach on how to start talking about one of the most remarkable inventions in current history and how to use its 'magical powers' to help Jules understand the 21st century now that he was right in the *smack* of it.

I wasn't sure if Jules' experimenting with the remote control had led him to the program guide yet. I took the chance that perhaps he'd not yet discovered this feature by taking the remote control from the side table and switched it to the guide information. I quickly tuned in to the History Channel, hoping to avoid any protests Jules was ready to make before I could 'school' him on this handy feature. The programming was airing the series "Modern Marvels—Great Inventions." The Trans-continental Railroads detailed the post-civil war era when trains were the engineering feats of the day. *Perfect!* Jules looked attentively at the screen. It was obvious that the program *had* him and I suspect filled in some of the gaps (in time) he had. As commercial breaks advertising Yahoo and iPod flashed across the screen, Jules' expression revealed an undeniable curiosity about what they were and the roles they played in our present-day civilization. He seemed to absorb knowledge like a sponge. It was difficult to tell whether he comprehended the information or not. But, I suspected he grasped more than perhaps I gave him credit for. I was most interested in how impressed he was with even the most minor achievements of 'modern times. After about two hours of 'teevee' history and my verbal footnote narration, Jules asked if we could talk a bit without the 'teevee' on.

Before I could prepare for his first question, he said in a calm voice, "Da people of 1903, Byron, wat happened to da people of 1903?" *I had no idea on how to answer Jules' question. It was foolish of me to even think I could, especially since I had no agenda to help me answer any question Jules might pose. Besides, you'd think I would have caught on by this time and recognized that Jules was in control of these meetings. On second thought, perhaps I did realize this fact after all, at least enough to have employed a 'fall back' position* . . . Again, changing the subject seemed to be my best approach.

"Jules," I asked, "How many children do you and your wife have?"

"We have ten children. You have children"? *Just that easily, he took control again!* I hoped that Jules hadn't noticed my raised eyebrow at his response; and if he had, I hoped he took it to be a reaction of surprise and not of disdain. I offered a quick response in hopes of dispelling the latter.

"Yes, my wife and I have a son and a daughter." *We'd talked about so many things that I guessed Jules had forgotten about my telling him early on about my two kids attending college.*

Still, I ventured out nervously as I returned to my inquiry asking Jules, "Ten children?"

"Byron, I married a girl wen I was twice her age at da time." I could tell by that impish grin on his face and how relaxed he'd become that he was enjoying this part of the story. He went on. "She is wat we call "assez noir"[116] Her skin smooth wit da color of maple syrup. Her hair is a fine texture wit thick, curly black locks. She is a small-framed woman, just under five feet tall but she is surprisingly, physically very strong.

My oldest boy, Willie is startin' to spread his wings dese days and little Jules—only two years behind Willie moves at his own pace. Da youngest boy, Leo, clings to his mama. He a real 'Mama's Boy' so I get stuck wit my lil' girls. Dey da youngest and real lil darlings dough. Dey follow me around da yard like lil' ducklins', but I don't mind dat so much. Dey got more spunk dan da boys sometimes. My oldest daughters, Lizzie and Edwige are more like dere grandfather, John (Randall—Victorine's father). Dey look a lot more like him dan me or dere mother. Florence is da quiet one—not physically very strong compared to da older girls, but real smart. Dose two older girls are so 'bossy,' telling all da others, boys included, wat to do.

Hold up! Did Jules just switch up his dialog form? Did I just hear him go from "little" to "lil" and then start truncating 'ing' endings? I know, I promised myself that I'd give whatever Jules said my undivided attention. But I couldn't help getting distracted by what I was hearing! My ears are like finely tuned instruments; finely attentive to whatever I hear. Normally, I'd make a comment to correct one's English, but dealing with Jules this was not an option for two reasons. Number one and most importantly, I didn't want to interrupt his 'flow'; and number two, which I suppose was equally as important, was that Jules could tell me whatever he wanted to say in whatever manner he wanted to say it. Besides, I don't know why I even noted his changed dialog, especially since by all indications of this man's academic prowess, I know he'd write the King's English 'correctly.' I just need to remember that by now, nothing this guy says or does should amaze me.

---

116   "Pretty black" a term used often to describe the finest slave women selected as mistresses two-hundred years earlier (17th & 18th century) by the French planters of St. Domingue. Often described as women of "exotic beauty" resembling the "high-born Hindus of India"

Most of dem, boys included, mind wat da girls say—except 'Man', I mean Noel. Noel, prefers to be called 'Man' rather dan Noel, Fergust or Theodore, his given names. I kinda' like 'Man' too. I'm told he's so much like my father, Theodore—we named him right! He's real strong, firm and sometimes a little stubborn. I tink he has a 'girl' over in St. Francisville, but he ain't serious yet, at least as far as I know.

Anita, Adele and da youngest girl—Jean Elvin, because dey are so lil', and dere da baby girls, dey are more like best friend playmates to each other dan sisters—you know wat I *mean*, no sibling rivalry like dem other ones. Dey so much alike, dey almos' look like triplets. Dey inseparable too, so much so—'da lil' ones' is wat we call 'em."

Just when I began to sense Jules had given me a great deal of information and would soon need to have some answers to *his* questions, he sat back in his chair, sighed and began again, speaking quietly.

He did, but it wasn't what I expected.

Jules' entire countenance changed from joy to sadness with his next inquiry: "What becomes of my children?" Good question, but I had no answer. And, what's more is that my 'change the subject' evasive tactic may very well have led Jules to this train of thought. His pointed question convinced to an unprecedented certainty that I knew for sure Jules had accepted the idea he was presently in a period of time to which he did not belong. I didn't know if he was being rhetorical or whether he needed an honest answer from me. Regardless of his intent, I didn't have any good answers anyway. I think that it was at that point I started to wonder, and frankly, to worry about *what was to become of Jules*. I also seriously wondered what the future held for me as well. I began to wonder if *I* might be the 'one;' the *real* the target of a cruel, elaborate hoax that would ultimately conclude in what I hoped would be a rational resolution—good or bad. Or, maybe there was nothing cruel about any of this. Maybe there was something wonderful, magical—gifts that I needed to accept, embrace, cherish and remember. For certain, at a later date, I would have to try and explain this experience of Jules Bayonne's visit to *someone* else. This experience was much too precious to keep to myself.

Instinctively and reluctantly I knew there was going to be an end to this unusual, strange, yet remarkable encounter. I reasoned that I had better find out as much as I could while the *treasure* was still there for me to feel, see, hear, touch and uncover.

I inched closer to Jules and asked, "What about the farm you bought?" Whew, I mused, yet another of Jules' questions I managed to dodge—*successfully this time, but admittedly I had to be a trifle suspicious that Jules was somehow leading me in a direction he wanted to go. Jules Bayonne was not so easily diverted to a path other than the one he wished to take!* Still, I reverted to my oft used and so far, so good diversion strategy.

"We own a farm in a little town called Livonia, about eight and a half miles from New Roads. You know about New Roads?" Jules asked.

I nodded, "Yes, I know a little about it."

Jules continued. "My house is modest but comfortable. I raise a few heads of cattle, chickens, guinea hens (also called keets), and horses. Da barn is large, but needs work on da structure and could use a little whitewash. Victorine keeps a garden dat yields enough vegetables to feed us and da several families dat live nearby. Pecan trees are producing each year and a few fig trees produce more dan we can eat and give to da neighbors before da birds get dere share. Victorine's garden is one of her great joys. She often said dat laboring in her garden was da most satisfying use of her time because it allowed her to learn valuable lessons about nature. She tought she could be an artist of sorts, mixing da different colors of flowers and she could conduct experiments, testing her ideas about seeds, cuttings and da health of da dirt. Da girls play around in a little patch of flowers dere mother put out. Da colors of da roses and irises look nice until da unfriendly chill of winter sets in. Most of da shrubs and flowers come from cuttings give to me by Madam Parlange. Da one ting my wife and I have been gifted wit is da knack for growin' tings."

Hmm, Madame Parlange again. I wanted to hear about her. But I decided to be patient and hope that it would pay off. I maintained my silence for the moment and did't interrupt Jules' flow, as I tried to think of a way to steer the conversation back to Madame Parlange if that became necessary.

"Tell me about your house, Jules," I queried.

He responded cheerfully. "Well, da land is just off a dirt road about two miles from Parlange Plantation. I cut a path through da first two-hundred-twenty feet from da road and built a six-room cottage and a six stall barn."

I was suddenly overwhelmed with 'bursting' pride by the revelation that Jules Bayonne was the first of my US-born ancestors to have legally acquired land. The value of land for anyone coming to the 'New World' provided for a new kind of freedom not experienced by many people, especially for black people who didn't even own themselves less than ten years previous to the time of Jules' purchase. In the short period of time since I had been introduced to Jules, he seemed to repeat the theme of land ownership very often. The importance of the ownership of land became so clear to me. I began to hear the 'chant' all around me from whom I supposed was my ancestors. I recalled that in the Civil War-era movie, "Gone with the Wind," Scarlett O'Hara's father (Gerald) tells her: "Land is the only thing in the world worth working for, worth fighting for, worth dying for, because it's the only thing that lasts."

After having heard about the importance of land a number of times by the curious and mysterious Jules Bayonne, I suddenly related to Jules Winnfield (Quentin Tarantino's *'Pulp Fiction'* character) when he tells Vincent Vega: " . . . *when I had what alcoholics refer to as a moment of clarity.*" From this moment on, going forward, I vowed to pay closer attention to everything Jules Bayonne was saying! I would hang on to every word uttered from his mouth, as if he were The Dalai Lama, speaking to me alone, without his customary throng of followers. After all, Jules Bayonne had no other visitors, to my knowledge, therefore, the precious time he was devoting, the wisdom and fascinating history had to be specifically for me! And the package was a special delivery, all for me! I had to make sure it was signed, sealed and delivered; and especially for me!

CHAPTER 19

REVELATIONS OF A DOMESTIC SERVANT

Life on the Plantation

"Tell me about Madam Parlange, Jules," I ventured to ask. *Success, hallelujah! I couldn't help but notice how peaceful Jules looked when he was revisiting pleasant times.*

"My employer, Madam Virginie Parlange was married to Colonel Charles Parlange of da French army, who had served under Napoleon. She was a small-framed woman, just over five feet tall and had a pale skin-tone. Her hair was naturally black, but she kept it colored dark brown trying to cover da gray that managed to peek through every couple of months. Madame Virginie was a 'high society' person and took pleasure in having da plantation gardens wrote up in da papers. Da gardeners kept da place in tip-top shape, in accordance wit instructions from Madame Virginie.

She kept a book on everyting on da grounds and constantly made notes about everyting in season."

"You worked on the plantation as a domestic servant?" I asked.

"Yes," Jules replied studying my face as if there was an anticipated expression he could read.

As if he knew what was on my mind, Jules offered more specifics. *And I eagerly obliged him.*

"Nothing we endured during dose days of slavery was more difficult to try to understand dan dat of da nature of a people divided by da evils of separation into opposing groups . . . dose dat was favored and dose dat wasn't. Da idea dat any black man or woman had advantages because dey were closer to da master as opposed to dose living in da quarters is one of da biggest deceptions of all time. Yes, I was employed by da mistress. Yes, I received *wages* for my efforts but I might add, only at da convenience of da plantation owner. Most of da time, Madame Virginie did not pay me, using da excuse dat da war and da support of da Confederacy; or later, wen da North appeared to be winning, dat Union soldiers took her money. Yes, I was made to endure da suffering and torture wrought against my own mother who was not always free. I knew of her work and of how she had 'taken da whip' along wit others of my kinsmen. Sometimes seeing da terrible tings done to my people and not having da ability to do someting about it was just as painful to me as da poor soul bearing da pain. Anyway, dose you might call oppressors, knew da impact of having da more advantaged blacks witness dere harshness to da other less fortunate ones to remind us dat we could get da same if dey chose to do so. Does dat make me wrong because I saw fit to use dis gift or dis *curse* to survive? I put it in dose terms because keeping your mouth shut to save my own skin is da gift of discernment, while at da same time, da guilt of knowing you should have spoken out against the injustice is da curse. Den you start to justify your own action or inaction as in dese cases by tinking dat it's okay not to say anyting because it wouldn't do no good anyway!"

Jules seemed momentarily 'defeated.' He shook his head in sad contemplation as he poured out his emotions regarding the controversial subject of his employment as a house servant. I couldn't help but think how complicated this issue was then and even now. I thought about the black people of South Africa, being a majority but inflicted with the horrors of apartheid. Why could these people not prevail in their own land? For almost fifty years, the black people of South Africa endured the atrocities and hatred perpetrated on them just because it was allowed by whites and sad to say, tolerated by blacks. *This racial recidivism was all much too familiar . . .*

It suddenly occurred to me that Jules and other free people of color were an important and key element in the attainment of freedom by black slaves. The fact that his mother was a slave and his father a free person changed the nature of how they both were treated (individually and jointly) by other slaves and the white plantation owners.

"Da fact dat I was free, had less to do wit wen or where I could go," Jules explained. "I was still suspiciously black to the white folk so to be on da safe side, I carried my 'free man' papers wit me everywhere I went. Dis was especially important because I was not allowed to move about or otherwise mix wit slaves, even from da Parlange Plantation unless requested by Madame Virginie, herself. Even den, I had to have papers in order for slaves to travel wit me. On more dan one occasion, a young slave, usually a male, would ask me to turn a blind eye and let dem escape. Men have an instinct for freedom. Not being free seems to hold a greater harshness for men. Most men would rather run away dan to stay a slave. It was more difficult to stay and not only face da 'whip', but also to watch dere women and children whipped and abused. Women endured more pain, no doubt, and dey had a stronger resolve dan men, I tink. Could be because dey had a stronger need to keep dere children wit dem. Yet, I was always able to convince dem men dat staying made more sense dan running. Wen a man has to ask someone to let him run, he doesn't want to run, he is hoping someone will show him why he shouldn't. Usually, slaves didn't trust me because I worked in da house and was tought to be one who reported any contrary or rebellious activity I might have heard or witnessed. Madame Virginie often asked me 'wat those niggers up to, now?' I always told her dere was nothing stirring in da quarters."

Jules continued. "Wen *I* was about sixteen years old, I started hearing a lot of hushed discussions about freedom for black people. But it wasn't until some years later, as a young man, particularly before I was thirty, I understood dat most our folks, both slave and free, needed to define for themselves wat was meant by "freedom" before dey could long for it. Dis may have been one of da most perplexing issues confronting an oppressed people, considering da only alternative available for us was to emulate whites. Da questions dat arose in da mind of many was would an enslaved black hope to be more like da master? Or should dey even be tinking about acting like a master? After all, his lifetime observations helped set such limitations. He had very little in da way of guiding his future, save da *emulation*. How could a man wish to be a machinist in either the north or south wen dere was no way to even know wat a machinist was, let alone wat he does? And, even if he could figure out wat a machinist does, den he has da problem of knowing how to do da job wit no training in dat area. Da concept of a 'job' had not been clearly defined in da *times* to dose in bondage. Employer-employee relations had not yet evolved, so how could one desire this refined form of labor? Da fact dat one could get paid for working for another was unimaginable! Just tink about it, Byron, for centuries slaves had been in bondage to white masters. Da institution of slavery was borne of ignorance and a presumed laziness basing its success on da idea dat da *robbery and theft of effort* somehow could prevail over equitable progress involving labor. Fortunately and ultimately, da reality of bondage was so repulsive and unnatural, dat its long overdue and impending failure was finally realized. Da fact dat some free people of color engaged in slavery may be da result, as I suggested earlier, dese free blacks had succumbed to da most basic form of emulation and/or assimilation"

I muttered, "You will be assimilated. Resistance is futile."[117] *Somehow I kept forgetting that Jules might not readily grasp these 'modern references.' But, on the other hand, not to worry, Jules always managed to figure out one way or another what I was talking about!*

Jules seemed surprised at my cynicism. "That's an interesting perspective. You should know I didn't personally own slaves. But, I have kinsmen who did. And I suppose, you too have a difficult time reconciling da idea of a man owning another man. Da last of dese big slaveholders—Madame

---

117   Quoted from a fictional species appearing in the Star Trek franchise referred to as the Borg. The recurring antagonists employ "collective audio messages" sent to their target, advising them that their biological and technological distinctiveness will be added to their (Borg) own and that "Resistance is futile."

Decuir[118]—you remember, da one I mentioned before, lost everything at da gavel of da auctioneer da first week in da spring da year after I *bought* my farm from Madam Robilard. Keep in mind, I was born of a free person of color (my father) and a former slave (my mother) so, we probably tink more alike dan not wit regards to da slave *issue*. But I tink I got a slight upper hand here due to my vantage point. I can view dis situation from da slave side as well as da free side."

He was right again. I decided not to pursue his proposition at the moment. I could do that later without his help! Instead, I took the discussion where I wanted it to go by asking Jules, "When did you leave the plantation?"

He stroked his beard, "In 1878, I left my living quarters at Parlange in Mix[119] to live wit Victorine's father and mother, John and Adeleanne Randall, in a small cabin in Oscar (Louisiana). Our oldest, Willie, was born dere and it was dere dat we shared some fond memories and a lot of love. A few years earlier, me and my good friend, François Francis, bought some land together—a few years later he sold his share of the land to me. We built a little house on da (my) property by early 1883 and added on to it little-by-little 'til it was big enough for da whole family.

Da house has three bedrooms, a parlor and kitchen. Da porch has a double entry wit shutter doors flanked on either side by large windows. We had it whitewashed and added a barn to house my three horses and a mule. We have livestock, primarily dairy cows and hogs. We also have a few chickens and guinea hens to provide meat and eggs.

We grow a little cane on da west side, which we sell to da market, including about thirty pounds of unshelled pecans. We also make our own syrup and harvested pecans from wat we keep for ourselves. Victorine is da one wit the green thumb. She plants enough okra to sell two-to-three bushels a year to market, plus wat we manage to keep for ourselves.

You ever had 'smothered okra,' Byron?" Jules broke his discussion to ask.

---

118 Antione and Josephine Decuir, free people of color owned some 1,000 acres of land and more than 100 slaves in Point Coupee Parish, Louisiana. Antebellum Free Persons of Color in Postbellum Louisiana: Loren Schweninger copyright 1989

119 Mix is the name of a community located in Pointe Coupee Parish, Louisiana. It is the home of Parlange Plantation House, a National Historic Landmark. It is located along Louisiana Highway 1, south of New Roads, Louisiana.

"Yes, I responded, I most certainly have, Jules! My mother made it from time-to-time, sometimes with shrimp, sometimes without. My wife loves it too."

"Does she cook it for you?" Jules queried.

"No, she doesn't, *I do*!" I replied, smiling, as I added, "I do almost all of the cooking at our home—the deal we agreed to over thirty years ago, now!"

"Janice, right?" Jules, with his left eyebrow arched and a sideways grin, questioned, adding; "She must be a special girl—sounds kinda like my Victorine! Yes—I cook for da family as well, so, you see we have a few things in common, Byron!" *I wasn't surprised at Jules' latest admission, which again, attested to things we had common.*

We chuckled for a moment, and then as if someone had shouted, " Action," Jules began again.

"Da house *has* a tin roof—really good sounds wen we have light rains—not so much during hard rains and storms, though. At dose times, it can get pretty scary; almost sounds like da roof gonna come off any minute. It never did, but sure sounded like it!

We added palins'[120] around the house, about thirty feet away in da front and forty-five feet past da back steps, so we could keep rabbits and coons away from da small vegetable and herb garden."

We spoke at length about the Bayonne family farm, house and the little town of Livonia before the sun began to set. I thought I should leave before Jules was completely 'burned out,' although he would never have told me he needed to rest. I packed away my pad and pen, expressed my gratitude to Jules, and readied to depart, when Jules remarked:

"When you come back tomorrow, we need to finish our discussion on *cornerstones*." (And then, almost whispering to himself, I overheard him say), "*Time is running out fast!*"

I was thinking the same thing; but I pretended not to have heard him, "Pardon me?" I responded.

"Nutin, I didn't say anyting." Jules remarked quickly, adding, "I eagerly await your return, tomorrow."

---

120 Palings ("palins') are pointed-tipped fences, often fashioned from cedar trees grown in the region as it is abundant, insect and rot resistant.

By the time I exited the building, but for the light of the moon, it was dark as I made the short trip to my car. It felt more than a little eerie. The building, cast an unusual shadow of loneliness—very brief, yet very haunting.

I breathed a sigh of relief as I revved the motor. I felt relieved, from exactly what, I'm not sure, but relieved none the less.

CHAPTER 20

NEVER REMOVE THE 'CORNERSTONE' OF YOUR FOREFATHERS

That night after I left Jules, I experienced a terrible restlessness. I wasn't sure why. Maybe Jules' talk about his family and their fate had triggered questions in me about my own family and how little I knew about my own lineage. I was unable to sleep, so I opened my old King James Bible and started reading from the gospel of St. Matthew. Almost immediately, my mind was fixed on chapter one, which declares that the chapter details . . .

"The book of the generation of Jesus the Christ, the son of David, the son of Abraham."

I realized that the writer Matthew deliberately limited his recognition of 'grandsons' or 'great-grandsons'—alternatively, choosing the term "son(s)" instead,[121] as if to give one cause to reason that all of the individuals within

---

[121] The first use of the words; *grandson, granddaughter,* and *grandchild(ren)* occur in writing between 1580 and 1590.

the lineage are important, but some have historically more definition and add a greater significance or emphasis to the continuity of the family line. It is noted that there are fourteen generations of men between Abraham and David (the King), and an additional fourteen generations between David and Jesus, the Christ.

The passage caused me to recall an incident that occurred about a year ago when I asked one of my ten-year old students if he knew his father's name. He quickly replied, "Leroy Robinson, Sr. My name is Leroy Jr," the boy proudly announced. When I inquired as to his father's fathers' name, he looked puzzled and said "I don't know." As he walked away, I recalled at that moment, pain in my soul, for him. Unfortunately, it was then that I became acutely aware that most black males today, including me, shared the same dilemma or better still, we shared the same shameless, hate-to-admit it phenomenon. At that moment, it occurred to me that I hadn't thought much about it, but I too, didn't know my father! Moreover, I didn't know his father, nor his mother (my paternal grandmother) either! What of his father's father?

This dilemma was not new, on the contrary, our knowledge of our ancestors are often rooted in a place we know little about, or not rooted at all. I am convinced that knowing how one got here gives clues as to where one needs to go next. Each individual within a lineage is necessary. The exclusion of any one individual and the lineage ends there as in the case of a single offspring. Even in the case, where the family name continues the loss of a single individual, at the very least, alters the course of familial direction. At that point I was reminded of the discussion Jules and I had about how many lives had been lost in the Civil War, especially with regard to children that would never be born and the generations from those unborn children that would never be. As usual, I had to agree with Jules. Knowing who you came from is as equally important as the survival of each individual in the 'line.' Jules Bayonne was certain to be a constant and painful reminder as to how little I knew about my ancestors. Ultimately, this translated to a deficiency in the very knowledge of me; who I was and even more frightening who I was to become. I was faced with the same dilemma as Jules: What would become of or happen to my own children?

Whew, enough already. This little exercise required too much mental exercise for this time of night.

I smiled to myself, happy that sleep was at last soon to make its arrest as I turned out the reading light and nestled into the proffered peace and tranquility of my bed . . . and my already sleeping wife.

* * *

I was feeling pretty chipper the next morning as I entered Jules' room despite the fact that last night had met with some fretfulness before I could finally get to sleep. I hoped today's visit wouldn't prove to be too challenging, as I wasn't looking forward to facing another restless night two nights in a row.

Jules immediately 'took the floor.' "My father gave me noting of material value. However, da most valuable ting he did give me was a few principles to live by. Even doh I was only four or five, I'll never forget dat he once told me to '***never remove the 'Cornerstone' put in place by dose who came before me.*** ' Remember I tole you dat he died when I was jus a lil chap, but I still recall wat he said as if it were yesterday" Jules explained his father's reasoning. "Da cornerstone was put dere after careful consideration and, probably disputed and debated by many people through da ages as to its acceptability or necessity, but for certain, it was put dere for a reason by da person most knowledgeable about da structure." I knew what Jules was telling me was important. Though I couldn't fully comprehend its meaning at the time, I dug deeply to figure out where I'd heard those words before.

I was listening carefully to Jules; and then I remembered—It was the words spoken by the renowned Reverend Ellsworth Harris, Sr. from New Orleans, Louisiana's Lowerlight Baptist Church–around the late sixties or early seventies. I don't think I'll ever forget that little shotgun house, turned Baptist church in 'The Goose' where the service was held. That stuffy, humid little one-room building was smaller than the area currently housing my swimming pool. I'm sure its measurements were not more than about twenty feet wide by forty-five feet long, pulpit and choir stand included. I recalled that this particular Sunday was one of those Sundays when at least three or four of the five of my mom's brood made it there[122] to be spiritually enlightened. My mother, much like The Spinners' 'Sadie Mae' [123] made sure we (those of us who were still living at home at the time) hurried to Sunday school (at Lowerlight Baptist Church on Ray Avenue) and 'learned the Holy story.'

Well, like many black Southern Baptist preachers, Reverend Harris employed the timely 'wafting' of the folded-white handkerchief (like he was trying to flit away some pesky flying insect that nobody else but him could see). This action was not complete without the alternating of periodically dabbing the sweat beads off his forehead and upper lip to emphasize critical points during the delivery of his 'heated' sermons. Mind you, these were the sermons that stirred the elders on the second pew into the frenzied 'shouts' you might have heard of (or bore witness to yourselves). And we mustn't forget about the holy dance that accompanied those shouts in perfect syncopation. This particular Sunday was such a Sunday—one for which the amusement factor rivaled that of the astonished crowd present at the Clemmons 'Calaveras County' event [124].

With a slow, methodical wipe of his brow, from left temple to right temple, Reverend Harris stressed: "*. . . **Jesus saith unto them, Did ye never read in the scriptures, The stone which the builders rejected . . .***" Then with a long pause, he turned to acknowledge the choir who were now cheering and blurting "Amen, and "preach brother" (almost forgot—"yes"). Some of the men, most of whom had their own handkerchiefs, used them to mirror back a 'reception' of Reverend Harris' message. The women, most of whom carried fans responded in a like manner. Then came another wipe of the forehead and dabbing of the upper lip. Long pause again, then his

---

122   It was rare that all five of my mother's children were in the home at the same time, because the three eldest, including the author were entrusted with the care of one of the greats (Aunt Bertha or Ma) which permitted for a much-enjoyed absence from the "wrath of fire and brimstone." Note however, we were usually never farther than fifty feet from my mother's home—just the same we were "excused" to go "next door to the greats" on many Sundays. For the record, my brother Richard escaped Sunday school far more than any of moms' five kids!

123   Sadie—a popular R&B song written by Jefferson, Hawes, Simmons for the Spinners' New and Improved LP. The song, Sadie, was released in 1974 and featured Philippé Wynne on lead vocals.

124   Reference intended to *The Celebrated Jumping Frog of Calaveras County* by Mark Twain. 1865

saying: *"... the same is become the head of the corner: This..."* Stop! Extra, long pause, then he repeated: *"This is!"* By this time the organist had joined in to emphasize each spoken two-word syllable. He now shakes his head side to side and prances a bit in the pulpit while simultaneously offering to the congregation a comment: "I want ya'll to hear me now!" More shouts of "amen," "preach brother," and "tell it!" Reverend Harris now in high gear and hoarse from screaming to all thirty-five members in the congregation, reads: *"This is the Lord's doin, and it is marvelous... in our eyes!"*[125] Almost without pausing, Reverend Harris eased into 'the altar call.' [126] : "If you don't know the Savior or if you've been feeling like something is missing in your life, or if you are here as a visitor and need a church home to call your own, then we want you to come today..." One sister, for whom I won't identify, 'came forth' every *single* Sunday I attended in at least a five-year period. *Man! I figured she was devout Christian (or an excessive Saturday night sinner—every Saturday night)!*

I also remembered how it seemed so often Reverend Harris was talking directly to me, particularly on those occasions when he would say: "There's a place for *you* in the eternal fire!" or "*You* may be one step closer to Hell!"

But now, as I listened to Jules, thinking back to the 'good reverend' Ellsworth Harris, Sr., the sermon proclaimed in the 1960's and 1970's made more sense today, at this moment.

Jules explained further, "You see Byron, *only* your father could be *your* father. Witout him, in particular, you are excluded from da structure. How you live your life best has already been figured out before you came along. Changing dem in da slightest could prove to be costly. *Be careful dat you don't mess with Providence.*[127] I was constantly told by my father to always *make da choice of life* as opposed to death and, further dat *I must choose blessings instead of cursing.*"[128]

---

125 Excerpts from Psalms 118:22-23 and Matthew 21:42 KJV. The first mention of the ancestors' wisdom and a principle in terms of an architectural mark is found at Proverbs 22:18: "Remove not the ancient landmark, which thy fathers have set."

126 Altar call or invitation to reconfirm or accept Christ as the Savior.

127 This comment was made by Jules on several occasions. Later I found profound understanding of his meaning and the use of "Providence" to be interchanged with God Almighty.

128 Jules was obviously making reference to Deuteronomy 30:18 King James Version (KJV) "I call heaven and earth to record this day against you, that I have set before you life and death, blessing and cursing: therefore choose life, that both thou and thy seed may live:"

This got me to thinking of my own personal family situation. I asked Jules, "What does one do if he doesn't know his father, or is raised by a surrogate family member?"

Jules appeared to be puzzled for a moment, and then asked, "Are you speaking of stepchildren?"

I replied. "Well, yes but, in particular, stepfathers."

Jules gave me another example saying. "Byron, Madame Virginie (Parlange) was married to her cousin, Claude Ternant[129]. Together dey have two daughters, Marie[130] and Julie and a son, Maurius. Claude died, leaving Madame Virginie a widow and three children behind wit a plantation to run. Dose three children were raised by Madame Virginie and her second husband, and da children's stepfather, Colonel Charles Parlange. Dey changed da name of da plantation to Parlange after dat and added another son, Charles Jr. to da family. Dat would make little Charles half-brother to da first three of Madame Virginie's children, right?"

I froze bewildered—I had no earthly idea where Jules was going with this illustration. "Yes, that's right."

Jules continued. "I didn't notice Mr. Charles favoring any one of da children over da other ones. Madame Virginie wouldn't have allowed any such ting either. But you already know from your bible how Joseph was a half-brother to all of his father's children, except Benjamin, da youngest. So, I suppose you tink dat just because a man marries a woman who already has children, dat he will encounter problems? And, dat dose problems vastly differ from da man who marries a woman wit no children and then bears him children of his own? Of course, the same could apply to step mothers as well as step fathers, but since we're talking about males as being da 'cornerstones' let's leave da women out for da purposes of dis conversation."

Jules waited for me to respond.

I thought long and hard and surmised in my mind that Jules had given me what he thought was a good, but much too brief of an example

---

129   Claude de Ternant was the son of Vincent de Ternant, Marquis of Dansville-sur-Meuse
130   Marie Virginie de Ternant, wife of Anatole Placide Avegno and mother to Virginie Amélie Gautreau (the model for John Singer Sargent's painting Portrait of Madame X). Anatole Avegno, a major in the Confederate Army, died of leg wound he suffered in the Battle of Shiloh in 1862.

of how one should approach 'blended family' concerns. Additionally, it was somewhat hard for me to grasp because I personally was not a stepparent, though I had been a stepchild; and his example was specific to the perspective of a white plantation owner. This perspective was hardly something black folks in the new millennium could relate to, considering most black folks have very little knowledge or concern about the history involving plantation owners. Nevertheless, 'most black folks' were not the issue here anyway; rather, the concern of this particular issue rested squarely on the merits of my ability in considering how a white plantation owner in the early to mid-1800's might deal with children who were not his. I finally spoke, still wrestling with how I could present my situation delicately to Jules.

"I also know that there *are* likely to be problems as was in my case!" I exclaimed. "My stepfather was not a good man!" I continued. "He left very little in the way of a legacy, except for my two younger brothers."

Jules pointed his right index finger upwards as if to interrupt. "Ah but your mother taught you to refer to her youngest boys as your *brothers*, right? She did not 'qualify them' as your step brothers or even as your half-brothers, right? "

"Yes, she did." I replied.

"I would say, your mother is a wise woman, den." Jules stared as if he were looking right through me and then continued. "Keep in mind that colored people faced da problem caused by separation of family members from da time we were taken and put on dem slave ships. It don't really make much of a difference wen you consider dat we all get here wit some help, oftentimes it is not wit da ones we started da journey wit. Your mother more dan likely told you dese tings and gave you wat you needed to be a good, well-rounded, 'salt-of-the earth' person."

At that moment, I felt as though Jules really knew my mother. Initially, I thought it was peculiar that he said she *is* a wise woman, instead of choosing *was*, since I had already told him my mother had passed on more than seventeen years ago. But then I realized he was trying to tell me that even when those pass from this life, they never really pass from our personal presence. They are alive and well in our memories and in the things that they taught and 'abided' in us!

"Well, consider this." Jules began again, "Surrogates as you have suggested calling stepfathers, stepbrothers, stepsisters and da like are family *too*. Dese people could prove to be, in some instances, da very '***cornerstones***' necessary for da survival or continuity of a family."

Still a little unsure of Jules' meaning, I asked him to clarify his comment regarding 'cornerstones' and how an individual might *prove* necessary as such. I'm sure you could see my concerns, as up to this time, I thought 'cornerstones' had to be *full-blood related. Just when I thought I had things figured out, Jules had to go and complicate stuff!*

Jules sighed as if he were growing impatient with my incessant questioning of his lessons.

"*You must take your rightful place within da family!*" Jules blurted, continuing his lesson. "Just as Joseph had to do, you might have to endure evils inflicted upon you from your brothers, or some other family member, maybe even a *surrogate as you called dem*. You are aware dat Joseph's father, Jacob brought forth children from four separate women? Joseph and his youngest brother, Benjamin shared da same mother but da other ten brothers were born to three other women.[131] In spite of all of dat, you are *expected* to take *your* position at da head of your family's table. You may be da *one* necessary for da provision of da whole family to have a meal at dat table, just as Joseph's purpose was ultimately to save his family, *surrogates* included and his father, Jacob. As you might recall, Jacob or Israel is da head of da twelve tribes. Da twelve tribes are represented by da sons of Jacob, fulfilling da prophecy (covenant with God)[132]. Just tink about it. What if Joseph had perished in da desert where his brothers had cruelly

---

131 As written in the Old Testament in the Bible (King James Version), *Rachel* is the mother of *Joseph* and *Benjamin*; *Leah*, Rachel's elder sister, is the mother of Jacob's sons; *Reuben, Simeon, Levi, Judah, Issachar, Zebulun*, and (a daughter) *Dinah* by Jacob. Bilah, Rachel's handmaiden, is the mother of sons; *Dan* and *Naphtali* by Jacob. *Zilpah*, Bilhah's younger sister and Leah's handmaiden, is the mother of Jacob's sons; *Gad* and *Asher*. Collectively, the twelve brothers represent the covenant tribes of Israel.

132 Moses (the prophet) records in Genesis 27:13-15:

> *13* And, behold, the Lord stood above it, and said, I am the Lord God of Abraham thy father, and the God of Isaac: the land whereon thou liest, to thee will I give it, and to thy seed;
>
> *14* And thy seed shall be as the dust of the earth, and thou shalt spread abroad to the west, and to the east, and to the north, and to the south: and in thee and in thy seed shall all the families of the earth be blessed.

abandoned him? Jacob and his entire family might have faced da perilous famine witout da benefit of a favorable alliance in da only country having da resources to help dem survive starvation! Dey was a sizeable group of people, but Joseph fed dem! He fed all of dem, yes he did!"

Jules repeated the verse, this time it seemed with more intensity than when I heard it from Reverend Harris. *Maybe I was just listening more carefully. I connected with the fact that Joseph was a cornerstone—rejected by some of his siblings—the children of Jacob (Israel) who would realize God's covenant (promise) of the land, the numerous seed (descendants) and the blessings.*

"The stone which the builders rejected, the same is become the head of the corner: this is the Lord's doing, and it is marvelous in our eyes?"

"Da *cornerstone* is placed dere for a reason-don't ever remove it. Not you, me or anyone else has da right to remove da cornerstone placed dere by Providence! "

Jules paused, then pointed his finger at me and said. "You need to know *something* about da man who *is* your father. Stand up on your hind legs and go find him. Dere is only one ting I must caution you about finding him—guard yourself so you don't get hurt—be it your father, or anyone else you attempt to 'tie' yourself to, dere might be complications—da kind dat cut emotions powerful deep!"

"I will, Jules, believe me, I will." I responded to Jules, while in my heart I dismissed the idea that I would or could put the effort in this kind of a project. After all, I didn't want 'pain' of any sort.

Jules pulled closer to me and began again.

"You need only a few words of wisdom to go through da journey as I have come to understand, my son:

*Know **where** and **who** you come from.*
***Never** shit or piss where you lay your head or where you eat.*
*Live a **Godly** life.*
*Be truthful **to yourself** and **wit others**.*
*Take care of (love) **you**, then **yours**.*
*Listen for da answer, **then; do** as you're told.*

---

15 And, behold, I am with thee, and will keep thee in all places whither thou goest, and will bring thee again into this land; for I will not leave thee, until I have done that which I have spoken to thee of.

Remember to say **please, thank you, yes sir** *and* **yes ma'am**—*basic manners are always da order of da day.*
*****Your word** is your bond. (Keep your promises)*
***Words** are tings—be careful of wat you say—wat you **give life** to.*
***Never remove da cornerstone** (set by your forefathers)."*

I'll be very candid. At that point, while still in Jules' presence, I was already beginning to regret this 'assignment.' There was stuff in my past that I wanted to not think about anymore, let alone look for more heart ache and possible rejection from my real father . . . Still, just as quickly, I decided to put on my 'big boy pants' and forge ahead . . . No matter what, I had to seek truth . . . " . . . and the truth will set you free" (John 8:32)

CHAPTER 21

GHOSTS FROM MY (OWN) PAST

Revisiting the Dark Side

I forewarn my readers now as the following paragraph is the only segment of my writing which I employ (implicit) vulgarity in an effort to make a point. I will be brief, but in order to describe this one character, I find it important to assume artistic 'psychological nakedness' in an effort to bring forward, the dark side of my personality when confronted by individuals who cause harm to defenseless ones—often the very beings 'they' have been entrusted with and the duty to protect. Although, I have attempted to avoid extreme, explicit profanity, the intent is to have you share my emotion with unbridled, unrestricted understanding. I insist that any latent bitterness you might detect is a due to my direct exposure to one, lone, evil individual. So with my sincerest apology . . .

My stepfather, my mother's husband of more than thirty years, was not a very nice person—he beat my ass (and more so, my brother, Richard's ass) constantly. He justified his actions by suggesting that I because I always stayed in some type of mischief. Thus, the need for numerous ass beatings to keep my behavior 'in check.' I contend that my stepfather needed very little excuse to tear into those of us who were *not* his children—'not of his blood.' As if the beatings were not enough, he was very adamant in proclaiming this fact publicly on many occasions. I suppose, the damage and pain he caused, may have built some character in me, albeit not of the 'good' variety. I didn't take too well to his brand of punishment; so in my very early years, **I actually 'plotted' his murder!** I insist to this day, 'Divine Intervention' kept me from committing one (the fifth or sixth—'thou shalt not kill') commandment. I am ashamed to admit, that I have broken most of the other ones (commandments), but then, I digress.

On one occasion, when was just short of sixteen years old, I threatened to "carve his f——g heart out" if I ever witnessed him beating my mother again. (This guy was a true tyrant through and through—nobody who was not of his blood was safe around him). Those words were the exact terms I spewed the day I stood on that shaky, but resolute declaration of true manhood! I *knew* that a (civilized) *man* need never abuse the woman he is entrusted with the promise to protect! I *despise* a so-called man, who is so small as to beat his wife (or any woman for that matter). I never saw him beat my mother after that particular event but I'm certain the bastard did, **but certainly not while I was around!**

I think Jules Bayonne alluded to his intolerance for abuse of people in one of his 'cornerstone' points—one should care for (love thyself as thy neighbor) oneself, so there is the capacity then, to extend care to those entrusted. I suggest that it's difficult, or rather inconsistent to love yourself, and maintain a 'balance' or inner peace and still extend hatred and discord to those entrusted to your care. My point is that the first tenet where love is concerned is that if you love yourself, it follows that you will also know how to love others. After all, (unselfish) love of self is prerequisite to love for others, especially those with whom there is constant contact and interaction, such as that which occurs between a "trustee" and those entrusted to his or her care.

Anyway, the only good I believe I got out of being in the same world with *that* man, was a clear knowledge of what personal character traits I didn't want to possess. Oh, I understood why those traits surfaced in this "*boy*"[133] my mother had married, who was from rural Mississippi. I didn't know much about his family history, but it didn't take much to surmise that either the 'cornerstone' was missing or he just didn't get the message on how to assume the duties of champion and beloved guardian of the family. And, although I knew why brutality within families occurred, I was naturally, diametrically opposed to the idea that we had merely become like those we assimilated.

In any event, I will not attempt to offer any excuse for any violent behavior inflicted on women and children, especially on those within the family circle. It is a repugnant, vile, vicious offense that is unacceptable in any circumstance. This violent behavior is just as ugly when perpetrated by an adult woman on the children (and/or her spouse). I contend that to bring willful and malicious harm to those souls, entrusted to be protected by one who has a duty to protect, is an abomination and transgressors should be punished severely and sometimes (in many cases) executed.

Conversely, I am immensely grateful and thankful for those who stand against domestic violence, oftentimes to the extent of physical intervention. These 'superheroes' are the avenging angels doing battle with wretched, horrific, demonic assholes. The worst of these worthless, ruinous vermin are those who 'hide' their destructive deeds. They are not recognized as the evil they really are, behind closed doors, sneaking and masking the evil. Often they are attractive to the outside world, and in their hidden world, they wreak, unbelievable, incredible havoc on 'the innocents.' Thus, the 'avenger' cannot avenge what he can not recognize as needing avenging.

I must have said enough. Jules offered a friendly interruption. He continued by adding his comments related to the '*cornerstones*' to the subject of stepfathers or 'surrogates.'

---

133   In rural Mississippi, black males no matter the age, were referred to as "boy." A more important fact is that he was only eighteen years older than me—a mere "boy" when he married my mother.

Again, I marveled at his wisdom. Somehow he figured out that I needed to spout off about the negative experience I'd had with my stepdad, so he allowed me to 'sound off' but not so much as to get off on the wrong path.

"Well now, wit respect to your 'surrogate.' He *did* not have da knowledge you have been given—da 'cornerstones', as a result, you may have had shit or piss dumped on you—often in da same place dis man laid his head." I could feel the puzzled look on my face. Jules obliged me with an explanation, "I suspect dis mistreatment dat you endured as a victim, had just as much of an adverse effect on your younger siblings, his kids. Furthermore, dis wretched man was likely *short* in 'blessings' dat would have otherwise accrued to him. Da right ting for dis man to have done was to have either adopted you, given you his name, and treated you (and your elder siblings) as if from his you all was his own 'blood and bone'! Or, at da very least, he should have encouraged contact wit your 'blood' father, assuming he (your father) was alive when he (your surrogate) married your mother. He went about da whole ting in da wrong way. Dis is exactly wat happens wen da 'cornerstone' is amiss. I am truly sorry you or any of your people had to endure such adversities. You may have heard dat: **'You can be da biggest rat in the barnyard . . .'**"

I chimed in simultaneously with Jules, completing the proverb. **"But you're still a rat!"** Jules winked and nodded an approval at me as we shared a common chuckle.

"So da saying still stands today?" Jules questioned, as we continued to share the levity together, not expecting an answer to the obvious.

Jules' comments gave me a perspective on my past that I had not considered. All of the family is adversely affected by the favoring or lack thereof, specifically, the attitudes of the most responsible family members pass to the children, even if the favoritism is to a slightly lesser degree. This psychological 'wedge'—petty jealousies, rivalries and such, driven by hatred, or just indifference, often occurring between siblings, sometimes continue into their adulthoods. And, even worse, those 'issues' have a toxic impact on *their* (the sibling's) offspring, poisoning untold generations in the future. This wonderful man's guiding words confirmed my need to address the controversial subject of step parents—how serious one should consider the undertaking of the task—and the horrible, inevitable *shame* they should expect to live with in the event they misuse the almost sacred trust they swore to uphold if and when the hell-like consequences are 'brought to light' for all to see. The exposure of a fraud uncovered!

Immediately, upon Jules sharing his list of rules to live by and his thoughts regarding blended family member's roles, I thought of one our dearest friends—*family* by mutual selection—Adelia and some conversations we had more than twenty years ago along the same lines as these spoken by Jules.

* * *

CHAPTER 22

A RETURN TO HAPPIER TIMES

Our Dear Adelia, Family by Proxy

Adelia, born in North Dakota, is a descendant of the Arikara tribe of Native Americans. Presently, there are fewer than fifteen hundred tribe members due to the long-lasting and devastating impact caused by Europeans from the time they landed in and settled North America. One of the first things I learned from 'the horse's mouth' so to speak as Adelia pointed out, Native Americans were not a primitive people. On the contrary, many tribes held a common 'set of truths', developed by a highly civilized and compassionate people. This 'set of truths' were *their* rules to live by:

- Take care of mother earth.
- Honor relations within the tribe (family members and friends).
- Know and respect the "Great Spirit."
- Respect all that is living.

- Take only what you need from the earth and nothing more (hunt, kill only what is to be consumed).
- Consider the well-being of all of the tribe.
- Give thanks to the "Great Spirit(s)" for each new day.
- Tell the truth.
- Get up and go to bed with the sun following the rhythm of nature.
- Enjoy life but do not leave a "footprint" (bad things) when you leave it.

Those words held more meaning today, as I spoke with Jules, than when Adelia had shared them with us (a handful of friends, including Janice and me) years ago, although I had a fairly good respect for what she had said back then. Though the words are different, both Adelia's "rules to live by" and Jules' "few words of wisdom" certainly complement each other and one would do well to incorporate them into their own lives to the fullest extent possible.

Adelia's husband Kalani, is a descendant of Kamehameha the Great[134] and a prominent Japanese family who migrated to Hawaii in the early 1800's. Janice and I met Kalani and Adelia, shortly after the birth of their youngest son (Brandon, aka 'Ski Ray'), in 1986. Our children have grown up to young adults since we met as young adults more than thirty years ago.

The thing I find so interesting is how the '*cornerstones*' (words of wisdom) Jules gave me and the set of truths', Adelia (and Kalani) gave *us* are very similar; even though superficially it appears that their cultural origins are worlds apart. Not only are the guidelines wise, they are very comprehensive for many of life's applications. Nevertheless, they are simple, effective standards, for which any person, without regard to background, ethnicity, social or economic status. These standards are not easy—they are hard, but very plausible and very possible for all to apply. These simple *rules*, rather, noble standards in which to live by, are most definitely worthy of earnest effort.

---

134 Kamehameha I (c. 1736?—May 8 or 14, 1819[1]), also known as Kamehameha the Great (full Hawaiian name: Kalani Pai'ea Wohi o Kaleikini Keali'ikui Kamehameha o 'Iolani i Kaiwikapu kau'i Ka Liholiho Kūnuiākea), was the founder and first ruler of the Kingdom of Hawaii.

The reasons for (Kalani and Adelia) their blessings are discernible—they live by sacred codes of ethics which were passed on to them from their ancestors. Today, more than ever, they are the ambassadors in their family—those we (Janice and I) refer to as 'the ones'—in the application of the principles handed down by their ancestors. Somehow, it became clear that Adelia and her husband, Kalani were those 'surrogate' family members who were 'placed' in our lives for a designed purpose Adelia and Kalani are blessed with two awesome sons who refer to us as 'Uncle Byron and Auntie Janice'! Our son and daughter refer to our friends as 'Uncle Kalani and Auntie Dee'! (Dee is short for Adelia). My wife and I love those guys dearly and because of the understanding and love they gave Janice and I, we hope to never take them or the principles they taught us for granted.

At another (much like the one where we met Kalani and Adelia) independent business owner's seminar in the fall of 1988, a few months after we met Kalani and Adelia, Janice and I were introduced to Eleazer (Ellie) and Ngozi, Nigerian immigrants, who soon also became brother and sister by way of a four-way (one of those rare occasions when four individuals *all* feel good about each other) mutual adoption (choice). It was at one of those seminars where I learned about the qualities of those individuals possessing a 'magnetic personality' (as opposed to a 'repelling personality') and how important it was to surround oneself with magnanimous personalities. Although I don't remember exactly where I got it from, I was reminded of an old saying: "Association brings assimilation" (a *'cornerstone'* principle, for sure).

When I first met Eleazer—I quickly identified him as the epitome of one with a 'magnetic personality.' Until I met Jules Bayonne at Grady Memorial, in the beginning of 2007, no person had challenged, or stimulated me intellectually as profoundly as Eleazer. He knew and shared so much wisdom and knowledge, particularly as it related to improvement or betterment of mankind. He saw the good in every person he came to know, including me. During the time I was introduced to Eleazer and his wife, Ngozi my character flaws were in full bloom. Although I was trying very hard to be a 'better' person, I still harbored rough edges securely knitted in what is known as low self-esteem. Moved by Eleazer's extension of an open hand in unconditional friendship, in spite of my obvious shortcomings, his admiration, love and respect for me caused me to open up and value his sage-like wisdom akin to that of a good older brother. Our children also referred to us as Uncle Byron and Uncle 'Ellie'—the testament to how dear we became to each other.

One of my life's ultimate honor came when I was introduced to Ellie's circle of relatives and friends as 'one from our tribe,' a declaration that suggested I was to be considered Nigerian—a good suggestion, since my DNA results indicate my ancestry hails from West Africa—including about seven percent Nigerian! . At that event, a birthday party for one of Eli's friends, I was invited to partake in breaking, blessing and the sharing of Óji[135] (Kola nut). This is a ceremony for which the honor of participation is usually limited to members of an Igbo tribe. On very rare occasions, a person with no ancestral ties to the Igbo people are welcomed to partake in the sacred tradition, whereby, an elder of the gathering (or in some cases the youngest) breaks kola. Since the Kola does not understand English (or any other language), the prayer(s) on the Kola presented, must be in Igbo (language). Eli ushered me in as his guest—his brother, the elders recognized *me* as among those to receive the Kola—the symbol of life— the ancestral, sacramental communion. I *belonged* to the 'people' from that moment on! I had now truly become Eleazer's younger brother—an honor which I count, as one of the greatest that any man could receive! The Kola was the 'cornerstone.'

A few years later (the year after my friend, Ellie died) I was honored to bear witness to the union (marriage) ceremony of Ellie and Ngozi's— eldest child, my 'niece', beautiful Ihouma, and her new husband, Rob.

The young couple's traditional Nigerian wedding was held in Denver, Colorado and attended by several hundred friends and family. The festivities,

---

135 Óji, (also referred to as Kola nut) is fruit of the kola tree native to the tropical rainforests of Africa. The caffeine-containing fruit of the tree is sometimes used as a flavoring ingredient in beverages. The Kola (and its related ritual) is significant in traditional spiritual practice of culture and religion in West Africa, particularly Niger, Nigeria, Sierra Leone and Liberia. For the Nigerian people, the breaking, blessing and sharing of Óji is a tradition which, it brings a community together and is always done in Igbo (language) to invoke the presence of the ancestors, who do not understand or speak English. The ancestors "ridicule" English as a language spoken through the nose, resulting in the phrase: "Oji anagbi asu Beekee" (The Kola does not speak English) as a chiding to any attempts to perform the ceremony (Breaking of Kola) in English.

rituals, colors, flavors and fragrances made our senses come alive. Janice and I were seated nearly in the center of the large ballroom at a white cloth-covered round table accommodating eight other guests.

From forty feet across the room I gazed at Ellie's son, Obi who was smartly dressed in a khaki-colored linen traditional Nigerian suit which he topped off with a slightly tilted, dark brown cap. He smiled exactly like his father. I guess it was about that time when the apparition of Eleazar emerged—Obi had become Ellie! The smooth, easy grin that Ellie always wore was the very same Obi was now wearing. Obi's face beamed at me. I became convinced of Ellie's presence; knowing fully, in my mind, that my friend's *physical* being had departed at the beginning of the previous year. Vincent, Ellie's younger brother (now assuming the seat as the eldest) sported Ellie's bowler hat. The 'baton' had been passed. On that day Obi's cap seemed more a crown than a hat.

During the wedding reception, I was honored to partake in the breaking of the Kola ceremony. The invoking of the ancestors must claim responsibility for the presence of Eleazer, because Ngozi[136](Ije)—his younger sister excitedly offered to Janice and me as she visited our guest's table that she "saw Ellie" wearing the black bowler hat donned by Vincent! Vincent, dressed in a black, gold and silver traditional Igbo suit, danced and strutted, regally tapping the floor with his walking stick. As Vincent floated about the ballroom floor, captivated by the enchanting sounds of the drums, the black bowler hat was filled with Eleazar's persona!

Many times while speaking with Jules, I could hear Eleazer's or Adelia's messages of truths, and disciplines, pouring out with generosity and compassion as if they were there, present in the room, in perfect harmony, providing the backup voices to Jules' beautiful song.

As I think back on those wonderful times with my Nigerian family, it became apparent to me that Jules was also 'delivering' (or, at the very least, identifying the contents of) the *parcel* to which he referred earlier. It was the unfolding past that shaped my present state, but only momentarily, as it kept evolving into a future that would never quite *arrive*. Interestingly enough *now*, (the present) is always fleeting, as time never 'stands still.' It

---

136 Eleazer's widow, also named Ngozi, shares the name Ngozi with her sister-in-law—Eleazer's younger sister (also referred to as Ije).

is always the past or the future; the *now* exists only for a fleeting moment; if at all.

As I heard my inner-voice reminding me of the importance of life's rules, conventions and boundaries, the concept of the '*cornerstone*' consumed me. More and more, my mind drifted towards the function of this foundational concept.

In modern building structures, it is often included in the planning, the placement of items of interest, trinkets of the time of the construction, sealed inside of the cornerstone to act as a time capsule for future generations to discover. Generations later, upon the demolition of the building, the contents stored in the stone reveal the trends of a generation before. Newspapers with important events headlined, jewelry, popular consumer products, the most recently invented gadget, a bestseller book or form of music, and other time-dated items are among the treasure found within the cornerstone.

In some structures, the location of the cornerstone is obscure, perhaps not identifiable, or even lost to the ages, further adding to the mystery surrounding the cornerstone. Maybe obscurity protects the cornerstone from those who would violate the law of retention demanded by the wise keepers of the cornerstone.

For a brief moment, my mental drifting seemed to be a rude interference of our precious time together, and then . . .

Jules began to speak again. "Just before he died, my father told me:" **"Take care of all of yours, unless you want to be known as worse than an infidel."**

I wasn't sure if I'd been thinking about the past in hyperspeed or if Jules had been caught up in his own reminiscence because it was unusual for him to remain (what seemed to me) silent for such a long time.

Jules looked at me and paused and whispered, "I read it later for myself in the bible the day that Willie (Sr.)[137] was christened."

"You read what, Jules?" I asked a little confused.

---

[137] Jules and Victorine's firstborn. Willie Bayonne and his wife, Theresa Bergeois bore one (documented) son—Willie Jr. who died before reaching adulthood.

"First book of Timothy 5:8!¹³⁸" He blurted as though annoyed. *I was reminded that reading my bible more often and intentionally would have been more profitable when dealing with Jules. Oops too late!*

He then continued. "Don't you folks read your bibles over here in Georgia? Dese instructions were given by Paul to Timothy. You are required to provide for da needs and da protection of dose of your house. For you, it means, da *entire* house of **Coleman**. My father felt dat it was almost a commandment dat *I should never start something I didn't intend to complete*. He told me dat once a man puts his hand to da plow, turning away from da task is not acceptable and dat if dat man transgresses, he den is not *even* useful to Almighty God."[139]

Jules stopped speaking; his face now held a broad smile, as if he was really enjoying 'rattling my cage.'

From the look on his face, I assumed Jules' had concluded his current thought and was waiting for some type of response from me. Then, I spoke, (hoping) intending to make some point of reason, or at least in defense as a response to his stinging lesson. "But my father does not bear the name Coleman. My mother and her first husband, Herbert Coleman is the donor of the name for which my brother Richard and I share. To be accurate, only my sister, Deborra is truly a Coleman, since Herbert is her biological father. After Deborra was born and her father divorced my mother, she had Richard and me. My brother, Richard and I also have different fathers. Afterwards, my mother married Roosevelt Dyer and he and my mother had two more sons, Roosevelt Jr. and Prentiss Wade Dyer. The end result is that the five of my mother's children were partially raised with Roosevelt Dyer, Sr."

Jules, looking perplexed, calmly admitted, "I am somewhat confused about much of what you have said, but it sounds like *you* are also. All of your relatives *are* who dey *are*, but dat fact doesn't ensure you being accepted *witin* family by dem. In other words, some of your family members may not claim you as *deres*, but you must claim dem as *yours*. You have

---

[138] "But if any provide not for his own, and especially for those of his own house, he hath denied the faith, and is worse than an infidel." (KJV) I Timothy 5:8

[139] Jules or his father, Theodore seemed to have extracted meaning from (KJV) Luke 9: 62 ("And Jesus said unto him, No man, having put his hand to the plough, and looking back is fit for the kingdom of God.")

a responsibility to live up to da name you bear, however it was bestowed on you. Wen you do so, you force da *owner* of your surname to proudly claim you as deres."

Wow! I understood exactly what Jules was telling me! This is exactly what I attempted to explain to my children over the years; that their surname name (Coleman) was an assumed name. However, it was more accurate to say that—we are from the Washington clan—the name of my mother's father, Joseph Washington.

Jules wasn't finished yet; he went on explaining, "Da family should be da first *fortress* or stronghold of protection. Its members should be protected from all outside forces of evil and evildoers as well as from dose who may be identified (by blood or surrogacy) as evildoers witin da family ranks. Women and children should be protected from abuse and from da harm of *predators*. Men under duress become more complicated and unpredictable, often confusing emotions to a point where dey harm demselves, and directly or indirectly, bring harm to others—all too often to dose dey have been entrusted to protect. So, we really are our brothers' keepers—Cain's curse all over again. For dis reason, all levels of 'ethics' must be passed on from generation to generation. Generally, women should be da teachers of da tings girls need to know to become women later and men should help boys become da men of da future."

Jules stopped talking as if he had said all he was going to say related to family structure. He arose from the chair and walked towards the opposite end of the small room. His back was turned to me and his shoulders sagged much like that of a man carrying a heavy burden. I quietly got up and accepted his actions as my cue to call it a day. On my way out of his room, I whispered to him, "I'll return tomorrow evening, Jules. Please try to get some rest . . ." He turned around to face me again, neither accepting nor denying my offer.

* * *

PART 6

MY STORY: A PERSONAL HISTORY

CHAPTER 23

MY LETTER TO JULES

Dear Jules

I wrote this, knowing I would give it to Jules only if he promised to read it after my visit during the week of January 22nd (and preferably not before the late-evening of January 24th). I was going to be traveling that Friday, January 25th to Biloxi, Mississippi for a weekend trip with Janice; I intended to return on Sunday, January 28th and looked forward to seeing Jules the remainder of the month to learn more of his wisdom, for which I now yearned more and more.

Dear Jules:

I have truly enjoyed spending evenings with you, learning of our past and how you came to be. However, I am stirred and restless in this effort because I am unsure as to how you might respond to what I have to tell you in this letter . . .

I was raised by my mother, Dolores Mae Washington, the first born and daughter of Theresa Sorrell and Joseph Washington. She was raised by her father's sister, Mary and her husband, William at least until the time she was six years old, somewhere around 1940. I suppose since Joseph and Theresa never married, some agreement between the parents provided for their daughter to reside with an 'able' family member on her father's side at that time—his younger sister, Mary. Sometime prior to 1945, Eloise White Sorrell, Peter Sorrell's wife (my great grandfather) brought Dolores (and her younger brother, Madison Jr[140]) to live with her and Theresa's father, Peter Wade Sorrell, about one-and a half miles east of Gentilly Woods, a community in Louisiana. Peter Sorrell built the little two-bedroom bungalow on the middle street—Reynes Street—of the area in New Orleans in the 'Goose.'

My mother stood not more than four feet-eleven and remained pretty much petite until after the birth of her fifth child, Prentiss, when she was not yet thirty years old. Even then, she still maintained a body that rivaled the sex symbols of that day——-including the likes of Marilyn Monroe and Bettie Mae Page (1950's pinup model; a.k.a. "Queen of Pinups"). Between 1951 and 1954 she even sported a hairdo similar to that of the racy, controversial Page, bangs and all.

I was born on the morning of October 24th 1954 in New Orleans, Louisiana at Charity Hospital. On that day, the thirty-fourth President of the United States of America, Dwight D. Eisenhower, pledged direct support for the South Vietnamese President Ngo Dinh Diem and his government. The resulting Vietnamese War, fought by my father and many other family members and friends lasted so long it threatened to include my own involvement by the time I had reach manhood, twenty years later.

Interestingly enough, this 'war' was considered to be a 'conflict' (not a war despite its longevity and high mortality); not a war simply because Congress never declared (a 'War Powers' constitutional requirement).

In 1954, the cost of a gallon of gasoline, at twenty-one cents, was just three pennies more than a loaf of bread. Earlier that year, (on May the 17th), The Supreme Court handed down the decision to overturn its 1896 ruling of Plessy vs. Ferguson, declaring it to be unconstitutional for separate

---

140 Madison Jr. born two years after Dolores, was between seven and fourteen years old when he resided with his sister and his aunt (Ethel) at his grandparent's home in the Gentilly Woods community in East New Orleans.

educational facilities to continue to exist in America. I expect this one event ties us as much as our blood relationship, considering our 'shared life span' and content of the issue. (We were both living and breathing beings during these periods; you in 1896 and me in 1954). Later that same year, the first successful transplant of a kidney from a live donor was performed.

My mother was my primary caretaker. However, as the third of my (then spouseless) mother's children, I also enjoyed the benefit of the careful and watchful guardianship of my great aunts, Bertha and Dorian (Shosh), and my great grandmother, Eloise Sorrell. That made four generations living under one roof! Four generations of Peter Sorrell's descendants have resided in the little white, wood-framed, clapboard home on Reynes Street between the 1940's through 2002. Ma's (Eloise Sorrell) old house was sold at the end of 2002 and later destroyed by hurricane Katrina in September 2005.

After Dorian (a.k.a. Shosh or Dora), her husband, George, and Aunt Bertha's husband (Gus Robertson), died, by 1956, we all moved to three separate neighborhoods located in the Tremé. Our first apartment was next door to Cohen's Formals[141] on North Claiborne. We stayed there for about a year; then my mother married *that* young boy from Woodville Mississippi in 1957 and we all moved to a small apartment above Peck's Steak House on Basin Street[142], less than two blocks away. My two younger brothers, Roosevelt and Prentiss were born between 1960 and 1962. Then, just before Prentiss was born we moved to a little yellow duplex on the corner of Ursulines and Villerie, less than a half-mile from the apartment on Basin St.

We lived in the Tremé, one of the first African American settlements in America, from the time I was born until the end of 1964. Up to my eleventh birthday, I had become one of so many black urbanites intimately 'tucked in' in this little world of jazz and blues.

---

141   Cohen's Formal Wear was located at 714 North Claiborne Ave. in New Orleans, Louisiana and specialized in tuxedo sales and rentals and was a landmark business establishment during the 1950's through 2004, serving the Tremé and French Quarter communities until August, 2005 when significant damage due to Hurricane Katrina ended all commercial activity. The apartment structure which were next door to the business was dismantled due to irreparable damage resulting from the 2005 hurricane.

142   Peck's Steak House was a small capacity restaurant, originally housed at 1529 Basin St in New Orleans, LA. The building has since (1976) housed several businesses and has been replaced by new a building since 2005.

CHAPTER 24

ELOISE SORRELL

The first of the four (generations)

Born in 1894, the only child of Jennie and Mitchell White from Leesville, Louisiana, Eloise Sorrell, affectionately called "Ma," was the first person I found in our family's history who had finished college. She graduated from Dillard University in 1916 with a degree in Education. She taught elementary school for a few years in New Orleans before meeting and marrying my great-grandfather, Peter Sorrell in 1925. Several years earlier, my biological great-grandmother, Florence had succumbed to tuberculosis in 1918.

Due to Florence dying at such an early age her two young daughters, Theresa and Ethyl, then only five and three years old respectively, went to live with their grandmother, Victorine, who was residing in New Orleans. Theresa and Ethyl remained with Victorine until around 1925 when they moved to live with their father and stepmother, who also now resided in New Orleans' Tremé neighborhood on St. Phillip Street.

Theresa did not enjoy being with her stepmother much and when given the opportunity to live with her father's sister, Aunt Bertha she gladly accepted. At the same time, Theresa's younger sister, Ethyl chose to stay with Ma where she was encouraged to continue her education. She also earned a degree from Dillard University sometime around 1935.

Ma gave those of us who were close enough to her, much love, support and guidance. She raised Ethyl, Dolores, Madison Jr, me then my sister, Deborra's son, Donald Jr.—four generations, for which she received little 'credit.' I am unable to speak with any degree of accuracy on behalf of all of my family with regards to Ma's ability to 'raise' children; after all, I was the fourth generation of five she had a direct hand in forming a productive member of society. So, she gets my vote, hands down for a job well done!

I have never known a more even-tempered, loving person than Ma. Certainly, there are other family members who would disagree, but for those few of us who enjoyed the up-close and personal care from Ma, she was wonderful! Now, her kindness and loving characteristic was not without its 'boundaries' and if we dared to venture beyond her clearly defined limits, we were sure to face the one-half inch, slit at one end, leather belt she kept in plain view in the bathroom hanging from a hook behind the door. I confess, although I never personally experienced a *real* 'whippin' with Ma's strap, I had come close enough to learn how to stay out of harm's way. I had witnessed, on more than one occasion, my brother, Richard taking a very brief 'lashing' for doing something to invoke Ma's ire.

Richard was always doing something stupid, but serious enough for Ma to enlist some 'act right' by way of her trusty, leather strap. Somehow, out of all of us kids, Richard seemed the most likely to push Ma's 'button,' but *that* never surprised most of us. You see, only Richard and Madison (my mother's brother) could challenge any person to the point of frustration, which often required strong discipline to get them back 'in line.' Uncle Madison didn't seem to have much use for an elder who wouldn't 'bust his ass to prove their love for him.' and apparently Richard had adopted a similar modus operandi. I'm guessing that Richard assumed the same 'risky' mind set because he really looked up to Uncle Madison and wanted to be like him in every way. Even so, I can only remember three instances where Ma raised her voice in anger with someone (in our family), and I am glad to report I was not on the receiving end of her 'wrath' on any of those three occasions.

I point out these observations of Ma's loving demeanor to magnify a most significant fact. That is, Ma did not bear *any* children of her own. She was the only 'constant' in our lives during the period beginning in 1930's, for than more five decades. She provided us with the place we all called 'home.'

* * *

The smell of fresh cantaloupe was the sensation that left the greatest impression on me during those summers I spent with Ma, my great-grandmother. After my mother built our home next door to Ma's house, I was blessed even more. Now, I could spend much more time with Ma than those intermittent visits that only summers could provide.

The back door from the dark-green painted kitchen at the east end of the house led to a double room—enclosed porch. From the window in each segment of the porch I had a great view of the backyard (years later I came to realize how small the yard really was—what had seemed like several acres was actually less than twenty-five feet deep by twenty feet wide), where peach, pear and fig trees produced fruit to support Ma's annual preserves efforts. The first segment of the room held all of Ma's canning and preserves, neatly placed on wooden shelves against the farthest wall. The next segment of the back porch held Peter Sorrell's old tools and work items.

Eloise Sorrell ran a small 'sweet shop,' which was more than a place where cookies, candy and soda could be purchased by neighborhood residents and visitors. Ma's 'sweet shop' was also a place where patrons could also get freshly sliced deli meats, cheeses and sandwiches. The shop was conveniently located next (attached) to her home. It was attached to the south side of her little two-bedroom clapboard bungalow style house. Peter Sorrell had the 'store' built around 1935 so Ma could work her budding cottage industry from home. Ma had decided teaching school had become more stressful than she imagined, so she and Peter resolved her problem with the sweet shop idea. Ma had operated the store with fair success until about 1948, when a young fellow from the neighborhood robbed the store.

He accomplished this horrific deed by forcing himself through the door just as she was closing for the evening. He backed her into a corner, cleaned out the cash register, and then he turned the .22 caliber pistol aiming at Ma's face. He fired the pistol just as she raised her hand to shield her face. Fortunately, the bullet grazed her hand just at the end of her palm, but the force knocked her down, breaking her wrist below the point of the wound. She passed out as the robber fled the store, but not before she could identify him as one of the neighborhood youth. His father begged his son's forgiveness and vowed to punish him. Ma's kindness and forgiving nature blossomed once again when she decided not to press charges. Unfortunately, Ma never reopened the store for business; and by the time I was born, the store had sadly faded into only remnants of what it had once been. The meat refrigerators, slicers, beverage tubs, cookie jars, display props and counters was all that was left of a deteriorating inventory until the structure was razed in 1967.

During those wonderful, annual summer visits between 1961 and 1963, I would go into the store, scavenging for toothbrushes, *Ace* hair combs, and any other novelty items I could forage from the dusty shelves. That old place had become a grand source for my imagination and the visions I entertained of someday reviving the old store to its former splendor.

I experienced bay leaf tea, *Rock 'n Roll Stage Planks*[143] with sharp cheddar cheese slices, green "Depression Era" glass bowls, "Ball" and "Mason" canning jars—some empty and many filled with figs, peaches, pears and pickled watermelon rind made by the loving hands of Ma. The yellow "Arborite" table with chrome legs and matching marbleized print upholstered chairs was always the center for the fresh cantaloupe or honey dew melons to which I was first introduced in those long ago-past, blissful days of my summer visits to Ma's house.

---

143   Rock 'n Roll Stage Planks were cookies originally made by Jack's Cookie Company. Packaged in waxed paper wrappers, the twin rectangular cookies measured about six inches long by four inches wide. A similar product called "Uncle Al's Stage Planks are sold currently. They are a thin gingerbread cookie, with scalloped edges and holes in the middle, with a very thin pink icing coat.

Ma had a picket fence, which she insisted was made of Cypress (the best kite stick material). It probably was, but all I knew for sure is that it did not make the best kite sticks, contrary to Ma's insistence that it was in fact a Cypress fence. To find the best homemade kites, we—me and one or more of the neighborhood ('backdoor') kids hanging out at the time–somehow convinced Ma that we needed to go to see Mr. Guidrot. So, Ma walked with us, southwest about five blocks (on Chef Menteur Highway—Highway 90) to Mr. Guidrot who shaved balsa wood to form the frames of his Japanese "hummer" kites. They were made of lightweight, colorful 'tissue' paper. They were beautiful, but unfortunately they were quite fragile and subject to frequent, devastating 'mishaps,' as the fragile paper tore or became useless at the slightest contact with moisture. Old man Guidrot whose kites sold for seventy-five cents in 1963 had a fantastic repeat business. We stopped buying them from him in about 1967 when Ray (one of our neighbors, who resided two houses away) started making bigger and better kites for us if we 'sprung for' the cost of materials and perhaps a "Big Shot" root beer, or paid him about fifty cents total. Ray's deal was a tad bit better than Mr Guirdot's kites. It was closer to home for those of us who lived in the 'Goose,' and most importantly, they lasted longer.

Ma and I ate Cracker Jacks for treats after grocery shopping (referred to as 'makin' groceries' by folks from New Orleans and originating from a direct translation of the American French phrase "faire l' épicerie'") at Schwegmann's Super Market on Old Gentilly Road, about two miles away. At that time, it was the largest supermarket in the world. The Cracker Jacks 'prizes' were so cool back then and Ma always made sure *I* got the prize out of her box!

Yeah, those were among my most precious memorable times—the good as well as the not so good.

CHAPTER 25

THE MAKING OF BYRON MARCELLƟ[144] COLEMAN

It was probably sometime in 1959, when I grabbed a glass from the kitchen table and scooped up a glass full of water from the bathtub in the apartment on Basin Street. Of course, the water was being prepared for a later soaking of some white linens and 'venetian blinds.' There was a strong smell of chlorine bleach coming from the water; which I apparently ignored. I wasn't the sharpest tool in the shed, but I at least had enough sense to tell my mother after I drank the water. So, I was rushed to the emergency ward at Charity Hospital to have my stomach pumped. That is among several incidents that I'll never forget, though I don't remember what prompted me to get the water from a bathtub already filled with

---

[144] The symbol at the end of the author's middle name is known as a 'Latin capital barred letter O.' The Ɵ is used because the authors' birth certificate shows the 'o' with a 'strikethrough'—the assisting nurse added the o in error (according to his mother), then she attempted to 'correct' it. The author has indicated he "rather liked the flaw and decided to embrace it this way."

chlorine water. Perhaps it was because my 'almost' five-year old stature wouldn't allow me to reach the kitchen faucet. What *I do remember* is how disappointed I was that I was rushed to the hospital in the family car instead of a careening ambulance ride with its sirens blaring at full blast. An ambulance ride would have made me feel important because every other vehicle in its path had to pull over and stop. Even red lights couldn't stop me. *I was only almost five, but I felt like a big, grown up king . . . everything had to pause for me and my make believe royal entourage.*

That incident would prove to be the first of many annual 'stints' of hospital visits I would have just before the start of the school year. My 'brush' with unfortunate events' *prevailed* up to my sophomore year in high school in 1970. My mother insisted that I was the only 'accident prone' child she had. *I can only imagine her sigh of relief at this prospect. And, I certainly couldn't argue that point!*

The same year I drank bleach water; I turned five years old and was 'sentenced' to elementary school. By all accounts (my own) I had been snatched from the loving and caring arms of my mother to trudge all of (less than) one-hundred yards from our apartment above Peck's Steak House to Joseph A. Craig Elementary School. There, I was introduced to my first nemesis, the formidable Principal, Ms. Dedeaux. For four and a half years, through the first half of the fourth grade, I got to know *my sweet* Ms. Dedeaux much better than my two elder siblings. Mind you, teachers could 'discipline,' no, back then they could flat out whip your ass. And they did! They really did, indeed! I might also add, they did so without the slightest hesitation, provocation or parental consent!

This may very well be why so many of my annual hospital visits 'coincided' with the advent of returning to school. Jules would say, "There's no such thing as a coincidence!" I think he was 'right on' in this situation as well as the many other times his wisdom had proven to be 'on point.'

Things calmed down for me by 1960, when we had moved to Ursulines Street and my two younger brothers were born. Good thing too, because our house on Ursulines Street was even closer to the school and if I'd been acting up, my mother would know it immediately and there was no such thing as 'waiting 'til I got home to get it.' No, not so! Punishment was swift and immediate! My mother had no problem with 'meting' out punishment right then and there and in front of all my friends. It was like getting penalized twice—once by my mother; and then again, later by my friends' teasing me. Unfortunately, this 'double jeopardy' wasn't enough to convince me to submit to 'apparent' authority. Thank God for my two brothers who proved to be more 'hard headed' than me! My two knucklehead younger brothers replaced me as the baby, in more ways than one. Now, it was them that caught hell, if not from my Mom or their father; they caught hell from me—a lot. But I figured it would help build character (*who was I kidding?*) in those boys, for the most part as well as helping me adjust into the big brother role!

But even at 'my best' in teaching my brothers 'a lesson in life,' I was no match for my stepfather's tyrannical reign' over our family . . . and that was putting it mildly. Things were bad . . . and we needed a 'superhero' in the worst way, quick fast and in a hurry.

As I look back on these unfortunate circumstances, I wondered if Roosevelt was ignorant, just plain evil or perhaps the fact that he hadn't 'gotten the memo': I was once told that: "Hurt people, hurt people." I realize that, we as a people (black folk), historically had been, almost summarily, 'beaten.' So, once a societal hierarchy was established, which now allowed *us* the ability to exercise control over those entrusted to us (our own families), we mimicked the only thing we knew to do to ours—beat them. There is and never was any excuse for beastly behavior based on the premise that the evil deeds of those who once controlled us, is now the root cause for us to inflict such atrocities upon others, especially our own families. There simply is no excuse for *this* horrible behavior!

God didn't let us down. He gave us what we needed when we needed it. He gave us our own 'homegrown superheroes.'

Years ago, during my childhood, the 'superheroes'—those 'good guys' came in the form of 'visiting' uncles and great or grand-uncles. My Uncle Jimmy was my super hero, "in the flesh." He came to New Orleans with that special flair. The kind that exuded so much self-confidence and strength from his mere presence, it was undeniable. We felt safe from the terrors of abuse at the hands of the tyrant stepdad. On those visits, which lasted at least a week, in just about every year in the 1960's and 1970's, Uncle Jimmy showed up at my mother's house bearing trinkets of candy, courtesy of the candy factory in Chicago where he was employed for several years. Along with his infectious smile and a gritty laugh, loud and robust, he also brought the feeling that 'nothing bad was going to happen' to any of us while he was there for those few short days. I don't know if he was really aware of the hopelessness we experienced at the hands of Roosevelt, nor was he necessarily made aware of how much he neutralized the violence in our home simply by his mere presence. But there was little doubt in our minds his persona was our gift from God Almighty, as Roosevelt assumed the duplicitous, 'out-of-character' role of the loving and doting stepdad who any kid would be blessed to have.

Alternately, about half of the family 'visitor appearances' to New Orleans, and only on rare occasions during the same time frame Uncle Madison and Uncle Jimmy visited at the same time. Uncle Madison's visits, much like the visits from Uncle Jimmy seemed to neutralize Roosevelt's wrath, temporarily. I suspect my uncles intimidated him to some extent. Whether or not this was truly the case, it didn't matter. The important thing was that we didn't experience the harsh, biting, stings of his unwarranted meanness. I think Uncle Madison was aware of his impact—he was definitely the 'alpha male.' And, he knew it! I think he even relished the notion that he could get Roosevelt to let him have some of his garments without resistance. All he had to do was proclaim: "Roosevelt, you need to let me have that shirt and the matching pants—I like the way they fit me and you don't need them . . ." And, Roosevelt always acquiesced . . . without protest.

Curiously, Uncle Madison had the utmost respect and admiration for Uncle Jimmy—also his great uncle—the younger brother of Peter Sorrell. After all, Uncle Jimmy, just by virtue of being the older of the two, demanded the utmost respect in its own right. On those rare instances when Uncle Jimmy and Uncle Madison were in the same room at the same time, it was evident who held the esteemed position of 'alpha male.' Equally as curious, I could only recall a few times when those two men actually shared the same room in my presence. While these two men had the same effect on Roosevelt—the 'small player among the big dudes', Uncle Jimmy was a bit more wily, yet really smooth, more likened to a 'big cat (lions and tigers) trainer' in a circus act, minus the customary chair, pistol and whip. Instead, he relied on his soothing firm tone of voice, commanding respect the whole time as he 'stroked the hair of the beast;' He literally reduced his subject into something so passive that one could almost hear a faint whimper from the vicinity of the subject (Roosevelt). Uncle Madison, on the other hand, was a bit brasher in his role as a 'suppressor of tyrants.' He was more comparable to a young bull in heat among a small herd of heifers, snorting, and huffing so you could be made aware he was entering or leaving the room. Testosterone seemed to pore—from his pores like sweat from a Louisiana longshoreman on a hot summer midday at the wharf.

These were *crazy times* indeed! In the middle of all our personal or familial madness, the tension of the (second) African-American Civil Rights Movement in the south, and The March on Washington,[145] gave rise to increased unrest in our household. I'll never forget that fateful day which rocked all of America; and I'd go as far as to say, the whole world on its heels. Evening was approaching early that day in the living room of the yellow 'shotgun duplex' on Ursulines and Villerie. Mom and us, kids were all huddled together in front of, a tiny Emerson black and white television on November 22, 1963 as Walter Cronkite[146] reported: "From Dallas, Texas, the flash, apparently official, President Kennedy, died at 1:00 p.m. Central Standard Time, 2:00 p.m. Eastern Time, some thirty eight minutes ago . . ." Before we could catch our breaths and begin to digest the passing of our beloved president, two days later, we watched (on "live" television) in horror along with the rest of the world, as Jack Ruby, a prominent Dallas night club owner, shot and killed Lee Harvey Oswald, the accused lone assassin of President Kennedy!

Christmas 1963 was hardly a joyful time as I recall, due to the foreboding uncertainty just over a month after the assassination of the 35th President of the United States of America. By New Year's 1964, we were beginning to recover. We had just moved into my mother's new home

---

145 The March on Washington, D.C. took place on Wednesday, August 28, 1963. At the steps of the Lincoln Memorial, Dr. Martin Luther King Jr. delivered his famous "I Have A Dream" speech.

146 Walter Leland Cronkite Jr. (November 4, 1916—July 17, 2009) was an American Journalist often referred to as "the most trusted man in America" and best known as the anchorman for the CBS Evening News from 1962 to 1981.

at 4455 Reynes Street, which unfortunately meant, we were leaving our beloved Tremé for this new rural community east of the "Big Easy"—a place in the notorious ninth ward. That New Year ultimately brought a renewed excitement into our new home just east of the Gentilly Woods development in what is known as Plum Orchard. More notably, our old neighborhood survived Hurricane Katrina and is still endearingly referred to as 'The Goose.'

In February of 1964, a young black fellow from Kentucky provided us with a renewed pride. At first, we didn't know for sure if the source of our pride was due to the quickness of his fists or the glibness of his tongue. We later learned that it was both! It was the next day, Wednesday, February 26th after the big fight between Clay and Liston that prompted the excited school yard buzz about "Cassius Clay," the twenty-two-year old Heavyweight Champion of the World. Everyone wanted to go 'bear-huntin'[147] because of that fight! In 1964, Clay, was quoted as dropping his "slave name" to become who we now recognized as Muhammad Ali. He emerged as one of the most electrifying, positive figures America—black or white—had seen in quite some time.

1964 was a black 'stride' (pride) year. Sidney Poitier[148] became the first black person to win the Academy Award for Best Actor. The Voting Rights Act of 1964 was passed in July and in early December of that year, Dr. King, became the youngest recipient—black or white—of the coveted Nobel Peace Prize. The "British Invasion" of America by England's Beatles caught some of us (including my sister, Deborra—the quintessential "Beatlemaniac") off guard, while others like myself, would much rather listen to Curtis Mayfield's "Keep on Pushing," "We're A Winner" or "People Get Ready."

As much as our pride swelled in 1964, 1965 brought its own 'deflations' and nightmares for black people. That year 'Malcolm X' was assassinated

---

147 In a documentary film (Convention Hall in Miami Beach) on February 25, 1964 that featured an interview with the colorful sports writer Bert Sugar describing the first fight between Clay and Liston, we hear Clay (Muhammad Ali) come in and he's running around saying, "I'm the greatest! I'm the greatest! I'm goin' bear huntin' tonight! Although the challenger, Clay entered the ring as a 7-1 underdog, Sonny Liston, nicknamed "The Big Bear" suffered a humiliating (TKO) loss when he refused to answer the seventh round bell.

148 Sidney Poitier, born February 20, 1927, an African-American Actor won the Academy Award for Best Actor for role in *Lilies of the Field*

on February 21st. The Watts Riots—five days of hell, claimed thirty-four lives, thousands were injured and resulted in more than 40 million dollars in property damage. Hurricane Betsy flooded our home and buckled the floors in my grandmother's home. In spite of it all, James Brown gave us a glimmer of hope with his "I Got You (I Feel Good)" and Stokley Carmichael's whisper of "Black Power" became the loud and clear shouts for the next year.

By 1966, I learned the most important thing I would ever learn in my life; it became my 'mantra': It is crucial that *you* (I) survive!

The kids in this new neighborhood—more than ten miles away from our beloved Tremé were a rougher breed. Fights occurred daily and we were 'new meat,' so it seemed that for me and of all of my siblings it was us against the world. I fought the most. I should rephrase that; I received a lion's share of beatings at the hands of my enemy-peers. The last beating in 1967, by a kid called "Moosey," who had somehow managed to take my (wooden) "Junior Louisville Slugger" baseball bat from me, and beat me with it, for what felt like hours, above and below the neck. That was the last fight I ever lost! In fact, I became more aggressive, almost enjoyed starting a fight. The fact that I'd also become good with my fists helped fuel that aggression. Despite my newfound courage and 'pugilistic prowess,' there were two families in our neighborhood, however, I steered clear of. I avoided confrontation at all costs with the Monroe's and the Cloud's. These folk were the most notorious group of guys in 'The Goose' in those days; and probably still are to this day as well.

If 'The Goose' was the armpit of New Orleans East, then America Street is/was the odor emanating from that armpit. The farthermost east street ending 'The Goose' is America Street. Countless crimes have been committed on America Street long before Janice and I arrived there and long since our departure from the neighborhood. Law enforcement did not protect and serve the inhabitants of 'The Goose.' Law enforcement *did* frequent 'The Goose' from time-to-time, not to protect and serve, but to heap strong-arm tactics and injustices on neighborhood inhabitants. Shame on America for having a place such as that street representing her name! However, I have always had a rose-colored view of this country— overlooking her faults, awful history, and horrible inhabitants, past and present. But, I am reminded by a popular musician from one of his 1970's recordings—Lenny Williams wrote, "We're sons of thieves, slaves and braves" in this country, and even with its faults, I still believe that America is the best place to live on Earth!

* * *

My hormones were beginning to go 'whacky' that year and I fell in love with a twenty-five year old woman, a songstress, whom I vowed to take away from her abusive husband. I knew I could care for her better, and someday, I would *prove it* (no pun intended, Aretha—you know "Prove It"–smile). Until then, I guess all I could do was just stare at her strikingly beautiful (slightly saddened) face with the violet backdrop on her breakthrough album cover. I was thirteen years old and a young Aretha Franklin was my secret love. I knew her songs would have better meaning with me as her lover—much better than that bad husband she put up with. Anyway, I stayed hopeful until I was in my junior year in high school, and finally realized I was never going to wed Ms. Franklin regardless of my good and noble intentions. I bounced from one short-time (term) girlfriend to another; having my heart broken time after time. I made it through high school and then it was off to college.

I stopped selling *weed* (marijuana) my freshman year in college—all of an entire year had passed since I'd started my enterprise—and began to think about leaving the "Big Easy." One of my fondest mentors, Gilbert Smith Sr told me I might need to get far away so I could 'repackage' myself. I was carrying ('packing') a gun almost always. I knew I would have to use it one day and something inside me kept telling me I wasn't built for killing another human being (nor doing time for the crime). The month after I graduated from Southern University in New Orleans in May, 1976, I left New Orleans for Denver Colorado. (And I stopped 'packing' as well).

A young fellow, fairly new to the old neighborhood, whom I will call "Jerry" (not his real name) came to my mother's house the morning of my departure and asked if he could share the drive with me to Denver on his way to Los Angeles. He had heard from the 'rumor mill', I was leaving to make a new start away from some 'minor unrests' I had helped to create in our town. Like me, "Jerry" wished to escape the evil he'd also help create. As I look back on the situation now, I wasn't a bit concerned about this guy's character—perceived or real—nor was I concerned for my safety in taking this relative stranger along for the ride. Besides, he was just like me; looking for a way out of New Orleans and on to bigger and better things . . . and his offer to chip in with the fuel costs appealed to me, it just served to sweeten the pie!

We hadn't driven very far when "Jerry" and I began to realize that our 'motor trip' was much more than a journey from one place to another. It was also a journey into the deeper reality of what it means to 'man-up.' We both conceded that many of our deeds caused damage to those inhabitants in our tiny community. Ironically, "Jerry" and I had heaped quite a bit of that same evil damage on ourselves in the process. It was more 'eye opening' than funny, yet laughingly we had to admit: "*We have met the enemy and he is us!*"[149] Thus the need for our escape included heartfelt repentance for the commission of the 'havoc' we had formerly wreaked on our fellow man was our decided remedy. Interestingly enough, neither one of us had figured out how we were going to make up for our misdeeds. But we needn't have worried, as we soon learned that "Karma"[150] would find its way to setting things right.

We started out, towing a small U-Haul trailer, hitched to my 1974 Pontiac Firebird, but by the time we reached Alexandria, Louisiana, about 200 miles from home, the transmission seal broke on the car. Fortunately, we were able to trade the trailer for a 26-foot truck and hitch the Firebird to the truck. No way was I going to abandon my two-year old, almost new vehicle so far from home.

In Salina, Kansas, about 940 miles into our trip, after we had succeeded in clearing the overhang at the gas station after being told the truck could

---

149 A quote from a 1971 comic strip written by Walter Crawford Kelly Jr. (25 August 1913—18 October 1973) the American cartoonist morphed the quote from the famous statement of Commodore Oliver Hazard Perry on the "War of 1812": "We have met the enemy and they are ours." It appeared in a "modern day" anti-pollution poster for the first Earth Day in April 1970 and again in the (Earth Day) daily comic on April 22nd, 1971. It is thought that this quote reflects Kelly's attitude towards the shortcomings of mankind and the nature of the human condition.

150 Karma–the spiritual principle of cause and effect where intent actions and of an individual (the cause) influences the future of that individual (the effect)) will have its way.

make it—we got stuck! It seemed like "Karma" was 'hot on our tail! But, I wasn't willing to let it 'get me' and win! No problem, I got the 'bright idea' to let some air out of the truck's tires to enable us to fit under the overhang. It worked; I filled the gas tank, cleared the overhang, and then re-inflated the tires. *Guess "Karma" wasn't going to go 'full blown' on us after all.* However, the owner's threats that we would have to pay if the overhang fell must have shaken "Jerry" up quite a bit! Just as we were pulling out of the station to embark on the remaining 400 plus miles on Interstate 70 West into Denver, "Jerry" confided in me the real and specific reason why he'd left New Orleans. He had loaned his handgun, to a mutual acquaintance who used it to kill another man we both knew. "Jerry" was concerned the incident would implicate him some way. He decided not to wait around to find out, so he left fearing for his life and his freedom; quick, fast and in a hurry. We arrived in Denver late that evening and stayed at the Holiday Inn in East Denver until early the next morning when I whisked "Jerry" off to the airport. To this day, that was the last time I saw him. I'm not sure what happened to him, but sending him packing early that morning, intuitively, seemed like the right move to make.

Two months later on Thursday, July 29th, 1976, I went back to New Orleans from Denver to marry the prettiest woman on earth on Saturday July 31st—no, not Aretha, but Janice Dumas, also from 'The Goose.' She had lived on America Street, only a little more than two blocks (two-tenths of a mile to be precise) away from me in the little pink house that survived Katrina and is still there.

I met Janice in the summer of 1966 on the corner of Reynes and Ransom Streets—years before the Haydel Heights apartment complex was built there. The empty, square-block lot was employed as a playground, pending development of the low-income apartments. The playground's merry-go-round, temporarily placed on the playground, served as our neighborhood's social gathering point. Both Janice and I were fairly 'green' adolescents at that point, so that meeting was nothing more than an exchange of first glimpses and not very well concealed smiles at each other. It was on that day—Frankie Beverly referred to that kind of day as "Golden Time of Day"—you know, at the end of the day! I was only eleven and she was only nine, so like kids at that age, I did what was expected and grabbed the bag of potato chips she was munching on. Janice pretended to be annoyed by my playfulness, yet she obviously enjoyed the attention I was paying. Anyway, the attraction blossomed in 1971 while I was a popular high school football player and Janice was one of the team's cheerleaders. By the time I was a junior and Janice was a freshman in college—now 1975, our romance was well on its way to 'full bloom,' and led to our eventual wedding ten years after grabbing those potato chips.

It's hard to believe that I was restricted from going two streets east of my home street (Reynes) to America Street; or even two streets west to Ray Avenue (unaccompanied by my mother—our church was on Ray Avenue, so usually, only on Sundays Dolores' kids would be allowed on that street). Interestingly, Janice's parents had restricted her (and her siblings') movement to not past Dale Street—only one street west of America Street. Three streets, running north and south (plus one half-length north/south street—Haydell Street), split Ray Avenue and Reynes Street), bound by two major thoroughfares (Chef Menteur Hwy and Dwyer Road) marked (marks) the area known as 'The Goose.' It had to be 'fate' that we even met at all, given the restriction we had to observe.

The faint, welcome, fragrance of sweet olive (Osmanthus fragrans—an evergreen shrub or small tree, bearing small clusters of tiny white flowers in the late summer and autumn known in most of the world for its deliciously fragrant flowers which carry the scent of ripe peaches or apricots) wafted the air as Janice and I checked our luggage in at New Orleans International Airport on Monday morning, August 2nd, 1976 to embark on the 'House of Coleman' journey through life. Our first destination—nearly 1,300 miles away—Denver, Colorado was culturally opposite form anything we both were accustomed to! It was bittersweet that morning. The adventure ahead, we knew would prove to be challenging, but exciting and somewhat sad as we left the comfort of family and friends . . . and of course, our beloved 'Goose' and all that had been familiar to us for our entire lives.

In Denver, I worked as an accountant for a worldwide CPA firm conducting reviews for Fortune 500 companies for five years. I enjoyed a career in the Oil and Gas boom before its decline in 1982, and then I spent another five years as a Banking Regulator for the State of Colorado. For those eleven years between 1976 and 1987, I witnessed firsthand (and in some instances, reluctantly assisted in) corporate corruption and the 'white collar' crime that went on unpunished and unnoticed until the new millennium around 2001 with the first major bust of Enron). At that point, I resigned from the State of Colorado when it found itself in the heat of Senate investigations of the Division of Banking. I figured I'd better get out while the "getting was still good!" I knew I'd made a sound choice when my boss, the Commissioner, came under fire for mishandling the banking crisis.

I had personally assisted in the supervised closing of fourteen thrift (Industrial Banks) institutions in the late 1980's, placing Colorado second in the number of financial institution failures that year. The sad fact is, three or four years earlier, I had warned the Division's leaders, by publishing a list of thirteen of the fourteen that were eminently failing and subject to severe regulatory corrections which would either extend the life or possibly save them from failure. However, during the State Senate investigation of the Division, my reports *mysteriously* disappeared. The Commissioner took the blame, the Division was reorganized, leaving me status quo, but with new, unpredictable and incompetent leadership. These moves confirmed *my insight* that imminent danger was on the horizon and fast approaching. I walked away unscathed; and with the added bonus of knowing I'd done my part to try to avert this catastrophe—I could sleep again at night. I had witnessed thousands of depositors lose life savings, property and in some instances, even their lives as a result of this calamity. I believed that Providence and divine intervention were the only reasons I could rationale the moving of my family out of Denver to Atlanta by 1990.

Still having a connection to the banking system, I secured a position with a major banking system in Georgia while building up my small business consulting company until 1996. At that point I was able to leave "Corporate America" for the second, and final, time to focus on my small enterprise. Which now brings me to where we are today in 2007.

... Based on all the information I have gathered and all that you have provided me with during our visits at the clinic in Riverdale, Georgia, I *am* your great-great grandson.

You once asked, "Who are you?" I did not know how to respond at that time, but due to the lessons, I learned from your patient and eye-opening teachings each time I was with you, I learned that I am *you*—that is I am, because you were here—before, I mean—in your—my time! What I am trying to say is that, your past and my future are the continuation of a journey that began long ago with your ancestors (and mine) and travel today with your descendants (also mine), already born and those yet to be born.

CHAPTER 26

THE MYSTERY:

A Day of Reckoning

I returned to the clinic the late evening of Monday, January 22nd with my letter to Jules. I was openly explaining to him who I was and how we were inseparably linked in 'the journey.' I was apprehensive but excited to present my lengthy letter, hoping we would get 'closure.' Now, the thought of 'closure' disturbed me just a bit. Earlier that day, I began to experience a strange uneasiness, not unlike the feeling I had when I said goodbye to my Uncle Jimmy for the last time; or my last visit with my Uncle Wade; or the last time my sweet, lovely mother looked at me during Christmas dinner in 1990. (Sadly, the next month she went to be with the angels).

When I entered the clinic's lobby, I noticed the position of the reception desk had changed and the carpet looked different—a new color. I thought, *Wow! They did all this rearranging and refurbishing in the short time since my last visit! Think I need to find out who their contractor is!.* I approached the desk and announced that I wished to sign in as a visitor for Jules Bayonne in room 1106. The receptionist, a beautiful young woman whom I was sure I'd never seen before at the desk, looked puzzled at my inquiry. She checked the computer monitor on the desk and with an almost apologetic response, she murmured, "I am not familiar with a person by that name, sir."

I thought maybe I was at the wrong place and turned to look at the doors to see if the signs read: "RiverWoods." It did, so I turned back to address the receptionist, who had by this time, excused herself and was on the telephone as she stared at some papers on her desk. I started to walk down the strangely unfamiliar hallway looking for room 1106 . . .

Jules was gone without a trace!

Or had he never been here to begin with?

I once was told that the more you studied a person's past, the more that person will seem alive to you. *Had I spent the time knowing this wonderful person to such a degree? But I took notes! Jules was most certainly here. Otherwise how could I have so many details?*

Not only that, I now knew Jules was there with me all those other times, like when I felt the granulated gypsum tickle my feet at the White Sands; as I gazed in awe at the massive sculpture of Rushmore; as I stared in amazement at the formations at the Garden of the Gods; when I was intrigued by the voids of the souls of those who perished at Pompeii at the advent of the eruption of Vesuvius; and while I marveled at the ancient leaning bell tower at Pisa. During those visits as I imagined the horrific blood sports that took place more than 1930 years earlier at the Colosseum in Rome Jules was there with me as I experienced the events of the past. Jules was with me when I looked upon the Monument of Washington and heard him whisper; "It took thirty-six years—too long to get this memorial completed—it is as grand as I imagined!" I felt his presence when I felt the fear that caused me to knuckle-grip the hand rests as I sat in the seat for my first airplane ride to Peoria, Illinois in 1975. He was there the time his saving grasp caught me as I stumbled on loose pebbles—which kept me from falling towards a vast trout stream in Toponas, Colorado. In all of the wonderful places I have traveled, I now realize, Jules was there with me.

Jules smelled the same enchanting fragrance I had smelled when I held Wanda, my arms trembling in embrace with a sweet girl—my very first dance partner at Valena C. Jones (an elementary school in New Orleans' 7th Ward).

Jules was with me in New Orleans on Christmas Day at dinner in 1990 when I kissed my mother, then full of life, goodbye a short time later. He rode in the car with me back to Georgia after *that* Christmas Day; then back again two weeks later, in January to put her lifeless body to rest in St. Louis No. 3[151]. Jules steadied me and provided me with surreal comfort as I choked back the tears when it finally hit me some two years later that my mother was actually gone from this life.

I knew, at that moment, Jules was there when Wade Sorrell (Marcel or Percival) handed me the 'seeds' of what became our family tree, a few days before he died in Chicago in 1985. Just as the covenant was made with the grandfather (Isaac) and fulfilled with the son (Joseph), I witness that which was to be experienced by my forefathers. The spirits (souls) of our ancestors bare witness through our sons and daughters.

I may never be able to convince you, my friend (reader), but both Jules and *I* know.

I hesitated before I entered room 1106. As I stood there I stared at the room number and squared my shoulders as if I was trying to prepare myself for what did or did not lie just beyond the room's door. I entered the room without knocking, as if good manners were no longer required . . . Just as I feared, the room was empty.

. . . I searched hopelessly about the dimly lit room. No Jules, no one, nothing! My heart sank, then I directed my focus to the left side of the warmly upholstered chair to the side table—there it is! The little book—*Dreams from My Father*! I started towards the table when my foot struck an object. I faintly sensed its shape on the tip of my shoe. First my eyes followed its movement, then I rushed in the direction of the rolling object. The *baseball*! I bent down and seized with some degree of urgency the worn, leather ball, as if the still rolling object would vanish from my reality . . . just as Jules had done.

As I clutched the book, my undelivered letter and the old baseball, my eyes welled up; I could no longer contain myself. I was not sure I wanted

---

151 A landmark burial ground established in 1854 having elaborate above-ground mausoleums, tombs & gravestones located on Esplanade Ave. in New Orleans, Louisiana.

to anyway. I sobbed openly! My vision became blurred by tears, as I left room 1106. I closed the door gently behind me as if to make certain to not disturb *anyone* left behind; and the knowledge that I'd never again visit room 1106 again deepened my sadness. I weakly moved down the unfamiliar corridor towards the entrance. I could feel the young, attractive woman's perplexed gaze on me as I hurried past her desk. I did not return her gaze. I didn't care what she was thinking. I was glad she didn't ask. My response probably would have been less than polite and certainly would not have made any sense! I was too caught up in my sadness. I was leaving RiverWoods Psychiatric Center for the last time—and with quite the heavy heart.

I was kind of glad that the evening was growing dark when I left, which meant less of a chance that anyone would ask me why I was crying in the first place. The darkness was a good cover for the sadness I felt. My tears continued to flow almost to the point of my wondering if they would ever stop. I placed the book and the ball I took from the room on the empty seat beside me and sat in that parking lot outside the clinic a long time. I cried in grief for the first time in over sixteen years; since the passing of my wonderful mother. I missed her so much. But now, I had something more—something new! Jules had given me the knowledge of how I might again feel her hands holding mine, her comforting words, and endless, nurturing love. My tears of sadness and despair miraculously became the overwhelming joy and hopefulness; I needed so much at that time and place!

I filed away my seven and a half page letter that I was hoping to give to Jules. At the time I thought it all had been a waste of effort. I had momentarily forgotten that nothing happens in a vacuum and without purpose . . . the letter had a purpose. I was satisfied that its purpose would be revealed to me sooner or later as I traveled on my 'journey.'

CHAPTER 27

THE PARCEL

I struggled through the remainder of the winter, spring and summer of 2007. My mind seemed to have the tenacity of a guard-dog grip on one comment Jules made during our brief encounter. He said he was to "deliver the parcel."

It is June 27th 2007. Another phone call! This time it was *'The Wolf'*—my Uncle Bennie; he had left a voice mail that morning while I was out running errands. Bennie's father, Bennie Francis, Sr (whom we called *'Pops'*), referred to Bennie Jr as *'Wolf'* for as long as I can remember. I never asked either of them why, but Bennie Jr, a man of large stature wears the name very well.

"Byron, this is Bennie. I called to inform you that my dad passed away this morning. He had been visiting us for the last few weeks and so I had gotten into the routine of waking him to come to breakfast. This morning when I knocked on the door, he didn't respond the way he usually did. When I touched his shoulder to awaken him, I could tell he wasn't breathing. He had gone to sleep last night and passed away sometime very early this morning. I will be working on the funeral arrangements and once I have the details, I'll let you know. I hope you can make it to New Orleans and be a part of his home going celebration."

Uncle Bennie is three years older than I am and one month younger than my sister, Deborra, As we were growing up, he was more like a big brother to me than my uncle. He was a great example to follow when we were kids, down in New Orleans. I think that it was probably due to his father, Bennie Sr, setting such a fine example for him (and us) to follow. The younger Bennie was just 'paying it forward' in how he dealt with the rest of us kids. He left such a powerful and lasting impression on me that even now, I still seek his guidance and, sometimes he unknowingly mentors me. From 1976 to 1989, when I lived in Denver, on every visit back home to New Orleans, my mother would insist, "You need to go and visit Bennie!" I didn't see what my mother saw back then, but when she passed away in 1990, I finally understood a great deal more. My mother was very loving to her siblings, and much later I was pleasantly surprised to learn that Bennie found comfort in my mother's encouragement during his difficult years, especially during the challenges he faced with his first marriage. Bennie, much like me, had missed her infectious laughter and warm gentle words that made you feel so good, long after she was no longer in your presence.

I always understood that Bennie Sr was my mother's stepfather, although, my mother always referred to him endearingly as 'Pops' so, my siblings and I followed suit and also addressed him as 'Pops.' My mother and Pops had as great a relationship as any daughter and father could, and largely due to their example, I believe Bennie Jr is the best *surrogate* big brother I could ever have.

Bennie Sr and my mother faced the challenge of the 'rightful' place of Jules' daughter, Florence with respect to heir-related interests. As is the case in many large families, the 'runt' of the litter doesn't always get to share in the spoils of the hunt. Sometimes due to smaller stature, or inattention on the part of the offspring (or the parent), regardless of the reason, the 'undernourished' sibling in this example seemed to befall Florence (and ultimately to her descendants). Florence's siblings may have been more aggressive in getting the feast than she was and by the time she died, just after she was twenty-five years old, her two young daughters had not yet established strong ties to the Bayonne clan. It may have been partly as a result of the girls' father, Peter Sorrell, taking work in New Orleans, relocating the family away from Point Coupee. Perhaps Florence's siblings established rank based on age; she and younger brother, Leo being among the last born. Whatever the particulars surrounding Florence's position within the family, her descendants would need to restore their 'rightful' place later. I was delighted to learn that 'Pops' and my mother documented much of the 'fight' back to the feast table. Jules' lesson regarding 'surrogates' was a treasure. I have gained so much respect and admiration for 'Pops' role in the family. He has been, and is certain to continue to positively impact our family in the future.

I called Deborra and told her about 'Pops' passing and invited her to come along with Janice and me to New Orleans to attend the funeral. Her response was an immediate, "Let's go celebrate 'Pops' Home Going."

Deborra was real 'easy' when it came to going back to New Orleans, fondly referred to as "*The Big Easy*" by most of the people (including me) I knew who were natives of New Orleans. For some reason, there was a mysterious, magical attraction, which always magnetically brought many people , some of whom after having left for a period of time, back home. I concluded over the past thirty years since I left New Orleans that the *'magnetism'* causing folks having roots in one of the most unique cities in America, was largely due to the historical and cultural ties of a distinctly unique group of people.

Many people born in Louisiana are tied to generations of people who are native to New Orleans. Much of the population, particularly *black* people, creoles and French descendants, have ancestral ties to the original European settlers of Louisiana. Sometimes these ties extend as far back as the early 1700's. Prior to the *'founding'* of New Orleans in 1718 by French colonists, (although already inhabited by the Chitimacha[152]) the city had already set down native *'roots'* still recognized today through the tribute paid to the native Americans as evidenced by the *'Yellow Pocahontas,' 'Wild*

---

152 Chitimacha, also known as Chetimachan or the Sitimacha, are a Federally recognized tribe of Native Americans who live in the U.S. state of Louisiana, mainly on their reservation in St. Mary Parish near Charenton on Bayou Teche. They are the only indigenous people in the state who still control some of their original land, where they have long occupied areas of the Atchafalaya Basin, "one of the richest inland estuaries on the continent.

Magnolias,' 'Creole Osceolas,' 'Flaming Arrows,' 'Red Hawk Hunters,' and the other fifty to sixty Mardi Gras Indian[153] 'tribes' who still perform in annual Mardi Gras ceremonial celebrations. I am more convinced than ever, that the historical ties of a people lay psychological claims to their people often so strongly that its attraction is almost comparable to a genetic trait. I suggest that it is the reason that my children—who, even though they were born in Colorado, have a romantic fascination with Louisiana.

During much of the seven-hour drive from our home in Fayette, Georgia to New Orleans, Deborra, Janice and I spoke of family (mostly about Jules). I felt an uncanny, but familiar 'presence' as we spoke of family members that had departed from *this* life. I wondered if they were having the same feelings of the invisible, but very powerful 'presence' riding with us, to our temporary return and regrasping of our roots in New Orleans.

Deborra and Janice had fallen asleep as I transitioned from I-65 leaving Mobile, Alabama to I-10 West. We checked into a suite not far from downtown New Orleans and I watched television until just past midnight. Early the next morning, the History Channel was airing a special on the Discovery Channel, entitled "Egypt's Ten Greatest Discoveries." This sort of thing was right up my alley. I watched the one-hour program, narrated by Dr. Hawass[154], one of my favorite television personalities. He was Egypt's 1st Minister of Antiquities. He resounded excitedly: "The bloodlines of the Pharaohs of Egypt can be traced back to more than 3,000 years . . ." I was struggling to have known of only three of my own family's generations on my mother's side! I thought of Uncle Wade's 'appointment' in 1985 of me as the family historian, "the person to keep up with the family's history." I felt ashamed that I had let him down.

---

153 The *'tribes'* of the Mardi Gras Indians are organizations of African Americans, who parade, dance and perform publically in tribute to the Native Americans, who were often supporters of fleeing black slaves (runaways), and provided safe harbor to many en route to the *'Underground Railway.'* Most famous for their elaborate, colorful ceremonial apparel and their competitive appearances on during Mardi Gras, the tribes are a major tradition dating from the mid 1800's (possibly earlier).

154 Dr. Zahi Hawass ,then serving as the Secretary General of the Egyptian Supreme Council of Antiquities, and currently Egypt's Minister of State for Antiquities Affairs. Dr. Hawass is the foremost authority on Egyptian mummies.

Later that day, as I participated in the funeral services, reading from Ecclesiastes 3:1-15, I experienced what is termed by Samuel L. Jackson (as 'Jules in the film; *Pulp Fiction*), '*a moment of clarity.*'

As I read from that bible in that warm little AME church down in the Tremé, overlooking the vessel that cradled the remains of the *only* grandfather I had ever known in my life, tears welled in my eyes. The *life events* occurring after Jules Bayonne had departed that I thought I'd lost that spring day in 2007, had begun to reveal the *contents* of the *parcel* Jules had *delivered* to me:

1. *To every thing there is a season, and a time to every purpose under the heaven:*
2. *A time to be born, and a time to die; a time to plant, and a time to pluck up that which is planted;*
3. *A time to kill, and a time to heal; a time to break down, and a time to build up;*
4. *A time to weep, and a time to laugh; a time to mourn, and a time to dance;*
5. *A time to cast away stones, and a time to gather stones together; a time to embrace, and a time to refrain from embracing;*
6. *A time to get, and a time to lose; a time to keep, and a time to cast away;*
7. *A time to tear, and a time to sew; a time to keep silence, and a time to speak;*
8. *A time to love, and a time to hate; a time of war, and a time of peace.*
9. *What profit has he that works in that in which he labors?*
10. *I have seen the task, which God has given to the sons of men to be occupied in it.*
11. *He has made every thing beautiful in its time: also he has put eternity in men's hearts, so that no man can find out the work that God does from the beginning to the end.*
12. *I know that there is no good in them, but for a man to rejoice, and to do good in his life.*
13. *And also that every man should eat and drink, and enjoy the good of all his labor, it is the gift of God.*

14. I know that, whatsoever God does, it shall be forever: nothing can be added to it, nor any thing taken from it: and God does it, that men should fear before him.
15. That which has been is now; and that which is to be has already been; and God requires that which is past.

I heard the faint prompts echoing in my mind from Jules Bayonne, commanding me to **"plant, heal, build-up, weep!"** At that point in the reading, I became a blubbering, snot-dripping mess! I don't know how, but I continued, choking through the **words**: **"laugh, mourn,** *and* **dance!"** I may have even shuffled a bit too! I regained my composure as I read and *heard*: "Gather **stones!**" "Now **embrace, get, keep, speak, love,** be at **peace, work and labor, eat and drink . . . know that He has made everything beautiful** *in its time***!"**

The most obvious of the *parcel's* contents was the acute, undeniable recognition of the marvels and miracles when I remained open mentally, and without resistance. Now I understood the inevitability of the phrase Jules repeated: *"Relax and enjoy the journey!"* And with the subtlety of a prayer answered by the Almighty, acute vision, heightened hearing and unbridled understanding came to me freely as whiffs of refreshing oxygen.

On the way back from New Orleans, I suggested to Deborra that I would take my 'appointment' more seriously. I not only told her of my plans to have another Family Reunion in 2008, but more importantly, I would be more involved in contacting those members of the family we had lost touch with. As if on 'spiritual cue', Deborra asked, "How is Cousin Mable related to us? Who are her parents? And what about Cousin Curley?" She was putting me to work already! I didn't mind her queries, as a matter of fact, I added to the conversation, my own musings, "I'm still trying to find out how they fit in the family tree along with Udell Mays and many others who lived in Chicago. I wonder what happened to Aunt Dee's kids—Vivien, Vicki, Joi, Kelley and Craig? Oh, I really need to contact Michael and Kelly—Uncle Wade's kids!" I was getting excited about my new role and all the 'uncovering' it was sure to bring!

I hope to not insult you, my reader, as to infer that Jules Bayonne was also riding with us that day we left New Orleans, but we all admitted to each other, a feeling of 'someone' else riding in that car with us. Even weeks later when I asked both Deborra and Janice about discussions we had on the way there and back, they asked if there were four of us that had taken that trip. I constantly thought about what Jules said about the parcel during our trip to New Orleans and back to Fayetteville.

Jules' parcel's contents had become apparent, including the fact that its contents though personally delivered to me, could also affect the lives of others, as was the case with Janice and Deborra on that revelatory return trip from New Orleans.

* * *

The evening we got back, I sat at the dining room table with my laptop computer and began a search for B. M. _____, my biological father, with whom I had no personal recollection of at all. The last time I initiated any effort to locate my father was in 1976. At that time, personal computers were not as accessible by the general public for securing information; and the methods of searching had not advanced to include current technological tools (such as the internet, social media, DNA 'kits,' et cetera.). Much of my knowledge regarding B.M. _____ came from conversations with Eloise Sorrell, my step-great-grandmother. Sometime between 1970 and 1972, she told me: "Your father is a very good-looking man. You favor him a lot, except he's a little darker and a little taller than you. Your mother met him on the army base, here in New Orleans. He was in the army and the last we heard from him, he was living in Newport News" (Virginia). Suddenly, I heard Jules say it again, this time, very, very clearly (although still inside my mind), "You need to know where you come from!" I thought and thought about those words, turning them over and over in my mind. How can I find out? *Rhetoric*! . . . "Take your rightful place in your family!"

Within thirty minutes from the time I sat at my dining room table, determined to follow Jules' instruction and make contact with my father, I found a promising lead. I had a phone number. I made the call immediately thinking I had to be very tactful if someone answered. What if my father's wife or their children answered? (What if they didn't know about me; how would I explain my existence to them?) What if he's no longer alive? I braced myself for everything and nothing. I had failed, perhaps on purpose, in this quest before. I resolved right then and there that this would be my final attempt to make contact with a person I knew virtually nothing about, and who knew very little about me. I also considered the possibility of being disappointed in what might be said between two persons facing a discussion of this nature, needed *this time*, to be the time I had tried my best! After all, without my father, there'd be no me.

The phone rang several times! There was nothing, then finally the answering machine picked up. "You have reached _____, I am not available at this time. Please leave a message at the tone of the beep."

I left the message. "Hello, this is Byron calling for B.M. _____. I am related to some people you met years ago when you were stationed in New Orleans back in the fifties. I am calling to touch base with you and let you know that the folks you knew back then are doing fine and thought about you. Please give me a call when you get a minute and I'll give you a status update on all of us from down in New Orleans. I can be reached at . . . goodbye."

Immediately after leaving the phone message Sunday evening, I felt heaviness as I trudged upstairs to my bedroom where I found Janice and our daughter, Erin; both half-awake in our bed watching television. (More accurately, TV was watching them).

They didn't seem to notice, so I blurted out, "Guess who I just left a telephone message for?"

"Who?" They answered in unison, obviously more interested in what I had to say than snoozing or the television program they'd been watching with sleepy eyes just moments before I entered the room.

"B.M. _____!" I replied, almost matter-of-factly. I was trying not to sound too enthusiastic, hoping they wouldn't ask too many questions. I couldn't give them more . . . I had nothing else to offer at that time.

"You're lying, right?" Janice yelped.

"No, I'm not. I got his answer machine, so I left a tactfully, ambiguous message, requesting a return call." I responded to my wife and daughters' partial disbelief.

"Do you think you really found him this time?" Janice asked.

My wife had witnessed me agonizing in my earlier attempts to establish contact with my biological father from about the time we first started dating in 1974, and to a large degree, throughout our first year of marriage. I had not been successful in getting in touch with my father back then, and my failure to do so ultimately yielded bitterness. I had begun to think that it was too late for us to have any meaningful relationship anyway; after all, I was a grown man—I had graduated from high school and even college! Now, I'm a man, well over fifty! What would I need with a Daddy at this point of my life? Based on the obvious pain I experienced in those years, long, long ago, there was no doubt (and with good reason), Janice was concerned about any false hopes I might entertain this time around. But, the difference this time is that in 1974 and through 1976, I had no knowledge of *Jules Bayonne*—and this event (the earnest attempt to contact my biological father), as I would come to understand in a short time, would present a major consequence on my future and the future of my family!

"Well, I did my part." I muttered as I headed back down the stairs. I wanted this recent action to set awhile . . . I needed to think about what I'd just done, pondering if I'd made the right move or not, fully realizing: right or not, I couldn't undo what I had already done. "Hmm," was all I could manage audibly, even to myself and to my own queries.

CHAPTER 28

B. M.

I don't think I'll ever forget that fateful morning of July 2, 2007. I had been conducting a four-hour training seminar and while I was taking my first ten-minute break, around 9:00 a.m., my mobile phone rang. I remember thinking, *'Now, who in the world could that be calling after I had already started class? I had begun assuming who it might be—a late student calling to give me some excuse for why they couldn't get to the café class; or perhaps it was a court official checking to see if a particular student was taking today's class, et cetera.*

I answered in the most serious voice I could muster up, expecting that the caller had to be a telemarketer. I needed to convey in no 'uncertain terms' that the call was unwanted and unsolicited! Besides, I was on my break and I didn't want to spend any of it talking to person or persons unknown!

"Byron Coleman, How may I help you?" I was surprised to hear the gravely-voiced man at the other end of the call. He answered my less than sincere inquiry, "This is B.M._____; I'm returning your call. I know who you are! You are Byron, my son! Your mother is Dolores! I am glad you called! I run the bingo for my club most weekends and I was away Sunday night, until late when I got your message."

I was caught a little off-guard, first by the returned phone call, then at the unexpected joyful mood the man on the other end of the conversation. So many things were running through my mind—both fact and query! Was this someone's idea of a joke? I wasn't amused. Then I thought, it probably wasn't a joke considering all the information he delivered in all of ten seconds! *Damn*. Talking about inopportune moments. I had waited for this call for a long time, but right then I needed to get back to conducting the second half of my class, scheduled at the Panera Bread Café in Lennox Mall. Fortunately, the fact that I'd done this class so many times, I could teach it in my sleep, proved to be quite an asset! My head was cluttered with the one simple question I had to ask; and the kind that I desperately hoped would be answered in the affirmative. The kind that I was not sure what I'd do or say next if the answer were "No." But I took the risk and asked it anyway, "May I call you back later this evening?"

I breathed uneasily or perhaps I even held my breath. It seemed as though it took a long time for his response. I thought: *Oh, oh, now he's gonna be lost to me again.* After all who'd say, "Yes" when I hadn't even offered him an explanation as to why I couldn't take his call right then and there. A call that I'd waited far too long for and hoped he wouldn't be put off by my, "Can I call you back later?" I felt *that* kind of 'stupid' when long after the opportunity passed, I finally came face-to-face with all of those personal "shoulda, woulda, couldas," I told myself, "at least I wasn't completely taken aback and left the 'door open' by asking if I could call back later."

I must have been holding my breath. I finally breathed an audible sigh of relief (which I hoped he hadn't heard), when he reiterated his being so happy to have had me call and asked to "please call back this evening!" He didn't seem to want to hang up. Neither did I. I promised I would call back later, but for the time being, I had to get back to my seminar. I had already exceeded my break by more than five minutes. I smiled to myself as I replayed my own 'mandate' of cautioning the participants about returning from break on time . . . now my own tardiness had made me the subject of 'clicking tongues,' impatient glances at the large, black clock on the wall and frequent 'sneak-a-peeks' at wrist watches and cell phones.'

I had difficulty focusing on presenting the dry and uninspiring subject matter of driver safety for teens and young adults after that phone call from B. M. _____. Not a surprise . . . given the magnitude of the event and the undeniable excitement of making the call back to him later that evening. To tell the truth, nothing could have inspired me more than getting back to my Dad. Inside my mind resided the eerie echoing of Jules' encouraging words telling me to "enjoy the journey!" The rest of the day lingered on tortuously as I encountered a nervous anticipation of what was to happen when I finished the seminar and returned home to make a *promised* phone call. From all indications, if I correctly read the joy in my Dad's voice, during our earlier conversation, I should relax and enjoy the ride. It was all good. Still, I was afraid I hadn't gotten it *right*, even though I'd rehearsed this scene in my mind at least 1,000 times over what seemed like 1,000 years.

Promptly, at 5:15 that evening, I called and B. M. _____. I was relieved when he answered with the same excitement I had picked up on in his earlier phone call. "Boy, I was so glad to hear from you! Where are you living now? I didn't think you were calling from a New Orleans number."

As I listened to his rush of questions, I began to wonder when I was gonna get the chance to slip in an answer. His questions were coming so fast, I didn't know where to start. I was reminded of those job interviews where the questions are so compound in nature that you invariably forget all of its parts, and have to ask if you fully answered whatever was asked.

Finally, I was able to respond, "I live in an Atlanta suburb, just south of the airport in Fayetteville, Georgia. So, see you're right, I wasn't calling you from a New Orleans number. As a matter of fact, I've been away from New Orleans for quite a while." I felt a little uneasy—still a little unsure as to why *I* had to find my *Daddy*, as opposed to my *Daddy* finding *me* impeded my timing, somewhat.

Self-preservation is just that and in large part it's all about timing . . . "knowing when to hold 'em and knowing when to fold 'em." In this case, it wasn't quite yet time for us to run towards each other in slow motion through a field of golden wheat to end up in a "drippy embrace." I'd been without him this long. As badly as I wanted to talk, see and touch my Dad, I wasn't sure it this was the right time to do so. Even though I had been the one to make the first move; I could wait little longer and see how this thing was gonna play out.

As I paused, hoping I could gain some control over my emotions I tried to mask my nervousness. He didn't seem to notice. *Good. I didn't know where to go from here.* He pressed on, "We were all worried about you—wondering if you got messed up with that storm (hurricane Katrina) back a few years ago. In fact, 'Tine[155] and 'em, in Easley contacted the Red Cross back then trying to locate you!"

Now, it was my turn to speak. I wasn't sure how to begin, I was still a bit uneasy and had to talk to myself. *"Calm down B, after all this is your Dad you're talking with, not Dostoevsky's Grand Inquisitor."* My self-talk worked and moved me to the point where I figured out that the only sane thing to do was to start at the beginning; or at least with some *recent* history.

"I left New Orleans in 1976, shortly after graduation from college. Soon after, Janice and I got married and moved to Denver, Colorado. We stayed in Colorado until 1990, then moved to the Atlanta area where we've been since. So, thank God, we avoided Katrina directly, but we had quite a few family members who remained in New Orleans and were devastated by the storm. Consequently, many of them relocated near us, here in Georgia."

"Good! So everybody made out okay then?" More questions . . . but what else did we have to talk about . . . we were 'catching up!'

"Hey!" I managed before he could continue the conversation. "I hope it was okay for me to call. Since I didn't know the 'whos,' 'whats' and 'hows' of your household composition, I tried to use some discretion by leaving you a rather cryptic phone message so as to not cause you or your family any problems."

At last, I found my footing—and my voice. No more small talk: "First off, let's get the 'elephant *out* of the room.' I'm sure you're wondering, as would any reasonable person would wonder, why I'm contacting you now, after all this time. I didn't call because I wanted or needed anything. We are all fine here, and I promised (thinking of the promise I made to Jules Bayonne, earlier that same year) that I would try to contact you."

---

155 Clementine ___, B. M. _____'s younger sister, whom I lovingly refer to as Aunt Tine.

I was glad he didn't ask me to recite the promise nor the name of the promisee. That would have required a whole lot of explaining which I was definitely not prepared to do. Instead, he put my mind at ease.

"Well, there's no problem at all." He began again, "It's just me here anyway, since my wife passed away a few years ago. But she knew about you, so there wouldn't have been any problems with you calling me. That ain't the kind of thing you fail to *mention*. Momma[156] worried and wondered about you and how you were doing all the time, too! She passed away in 1995."

"I'm sorry to hear . . ." I thought about how I would have loved meeting my paternal grandmother. I'm sure she would have readily filled in some of the 'history gaps' that my Dad couldn't do simply because some of the times she experienced would have even preceded stuff before my Dad was born. Not to mention, being able to compare what she told me with what I'd learned from Jules. I could only imagine how this conversation with my Dad would have been so different if I'd talked with her *prior* to meeting Jules! Those familiar 'shoulda,' 'woulda,' 'coulda' ghosts of missed opportunities resurfaced—Big Time!

Without breaking the flow of the conversation, B.M. _____interrupted with a proposal better than I had hoped for. "Look, we're having a family reunion at the end of July, in Greenville, South Carolina, and you and your family need to come and be with me and all of the rest of our *other* family. You also have uncles and aunts and cousins in Easley who will be very excited to meet you at long last. I know, I'll have to 'face the music' for not keeping in touch with you, but it'll be well worth it! Greenville is only two hours from Atlanta, so it won't be too far to come—not like coming all the way to Newport News (B.M. and his family resided in Newport News, Virginia since the late-1950's). I would be proud to have you come; it just might provide me some redemption. I'll cover registration so bring *all* of your family."

Whew. Now I was *really* uneasy. I hadn't expected more than a quick phone conversation consisting of exchanging a few niceties, ending with the proverbial "take care of yourself—let's stay in touch . . ."

---

156 B.M. _____'s mother, and my paternal grandmother Hattie

I didn't know what to say or do at that point. My best way out of this situation was to do just that and 'sign off.' I quickly made up an excuse to end the call, promising I would earnestly try to make the trip. The truth of the matter was that I wasn't even vaguely interested in considering going to that *Family Reunion*! I didn't know those people and they didn't know me! After all, I was fifty-three years old! For the second time in less than 24 hours, I asked myself, "What did I need with respect to a 'Daddy' at this point in my life?" I didn't think about it at the time, but looking back at that first encounter with B.M., Jules would have been sorely disappointed, at the very least.

After I hung-up the phone, I turned and looked eye-to-eye with my wife, who had been staring at me in disbelief the whole time. I knew Janice pretty well, especially when she eyeballed me eye-to-eye. I was pretty confident in presuming that I knew what she was thinking; because admittedly, I was thinking the same thing: Why contact him in the first place? What the hell was I expecting? What was I hoping for?

"What?" I said. I didn't have to look in a mirror to know I was wearing that stupid, defensive look on my face. You know, the one where you deny having your hand in the cookie jar despite the fact that crumbs and smeared chocolate ring your mouth and cling to your fingers and the front of your shirt.

"I don't think going to that family reunion is such a good idea!" Janice blurted, she also wore a worried look on her face.

I was a bit taken aback by her unsolicited response. I thought she would have been elated at the prospect of my meeting my Dad and the rest of my family. I retorted with a blank gaze, " You didn't hear me make any promises, either did you?"

I shouldn't have answered Janice so harshly. I could understand how she would be worried about how I, her husband and best friend, might be overwhelmed and perhaps even disappointed in the long run regarding the potential reunion with my Dad and the *other* side of the family.

For the moment, I didn't think much about the reunion, except for thinking "no way, Jose." Still, I was perplexed by the unfolding of events. It was almost as if Jules had a hand in the outcome at each turn, subtly directing the players and circumstances. I remembered that he said: "There are no coincidences."

About thirty minutes after speaking to B. M. _____ the phone rang again. I glanced at the caller ID which read: "B ____." I almost didn't answer, thinking it could only be a telemarketer call. It turned out it wasn't another telemarketer and I was so glad I was already sitting down. I was about to meet another one of those *non coincidentals*. I answered. The unfamiliar voice on the other end introduced himself to me as my brother, Ben. *Who? I didn't even know I had a brother named Ben!*

"Hi Byron, I'm your brother, 'Ben.' I just called to tell you we knew about you. Dad told us about you years ago. We all really look forward to seeing you at the reunion in Greenville. Don't worry about a thing, you'll feel very welcomed—we look forward to having you join us!"

I asked a few questions about his family and he told me he was married with a son and daughter, all of whom we'd meet at the reunion. We talked for about ten minutes, trying to garner as much information as possible from each other, including the 'coincidence' that we shared an identical family composition, before concluding our conversation with an agreement to keep in touch.

Less than ten minutes after I got off the phone with Ben, the phone rang again. This time I didn't even check the caller ID. I was getting a bit irritated. These phone calls were *disturbing my peace! I* answered the phone rather tersely this time. I was in for another shock.

This time it was Ron, the youngest of my father's sons. He called to reassure me that we wouldn't regret coming to Greenville. He also encouraged us to come and meet the rest of the family who was expecting and hoping to see us that weekend for the very first time.

At that moment I decided not to answer another call that night! I could hardly contain myself. I was literally undergoing emotions which up to that time had been completely foreign to me. It felt strange to experience first-hand another person, so responsible for my very being, attempting to fill a void that had existed for more than fifty years. A mixture of both excitement and apprehension was overflowing from me. It quickly became contagious among the others in my presence; and soon our little house was buzzing with the possibility of newfound adventure.

The phone calls from my brothers were among the most uplifting and positive, life-changing events I have ever encountered. Just prior to my *interviews* with Jules Bayonne, I had thought it important to define the level of relationships I had become a part of over the years as a result of damage done between and among people in the course of human interaction. I had realized that just because we grew up in the same neighborhood, saw each other every day, or went to the same school—even had the same teacher, shared similar interests, our parents knew each other well, it still didn't necessarily make us *friends*. What that meant, I learned, is that these *relationships* are merely superficial, at best. The fact that we just happened to grow up in the same neighborhood, saw each other every day, went to the same school—even *shared* the same teacher, shared similar interests, and maybe our parents knew each other is just that—a superficial *sharing*. No more, no less.

* * *

Monday following my phone conversation with (my father) B.M. _____, I felt a real need to talk to a friend, someone other than a blood relative; and so, I turned to Joan. I went to visit, her at her office in Marietta, Georgia. Joan, and her husband Shawne, are included in the handful of rare individuals I refer to as friends.

Her eyes lit up when she saw me. A good sign that she was glad to see me and knew that I needed her to 'unburden' myself. In other words, although I hadn't previewed her on Fridays night's events, Joan knew something serious was going on with me. She led me to the conference room instead of her office.

"Hey B, what's going on, Brother?" she asked as she ushered me into one of the armless chairs lined up in front of the rear wall of the huge room. *I knew better, but secretly I prayed that she wouldn't regret asking me that question.* I took the proffered seat. She sat down beside me to where she could hold my hand and look at me eye-to-eye.

I'll never forget the look on Joan's face as I related the events which had unfolded before me on the previous Friday evening. Interestingly enough, although I couldn't clearly read her, what I did feel certain about is that she believed me, incredible as it was. And, she was going to come up with that uncanny wisdom that no one else I knew possessed. I could always depend upon Joan to point me in the right direction. After explaining what had occurred the previous Friday, Joan went into her pensive mode. I always relished this time with Joan. I knew she was carefully 'digesting' all she had taken in from me and my accounts of what happened on Friday. (*I would later learn just how fateful that Friday would turn out to be.*)

After listening to me for about an hour, Joan arose from the armless chair she'd been sitting in next to me and walked over to close the massive glass door. I could tell by the familiar tilt of her head and partially furrowed brow, things were about to get serious. Joan retreated to a leather chair positioned it at the middle spot of the heavy mahogany conference table directly in front of me and said:

"B, you *have to go* to that family reunion. *And,* you need to take Janice, Derek and Erin so they can meet your father!" I wanted to protest with a lot of "ifs", ands "buts" and the proverbial excuse of all times: "You just don't understand what it was like growing up without my bio father when I needed him all those long years ago when I was growing . . . and now that I'm grown and don't need him anymore, here he comes . . ." I didn't open my mouth. I said nothing. I knew she was right; after all the reason I came to visit her in the first place was to get her opinion, which I greatly valued.

Joan stared at me for a long moment; a confirmation that meant she was as serious as I had suspected. Then, without breaking her stare and still not speaking directly to me, she pressed the intercom speaker button on the phone to call her husband, Shawne into her office.

Oh, oh, this was fixing to get real serious now . . . Joan was calling in reinforcements . . . as if she needed to do so. As far as I was concerned, she was doing quite well on her own! I turned my attention to the phone's intercom speaker button as if it somehow represented Shawne 'in the flesh.'

Shawne answered Joan's intercom page very quickly, as if he had already anticipated it. "Hey Baby! What's up . . . is this about . . . ?"

I wondered if Shawne had seen me entering the office earlier or if Joan had already 'previewed' him on the matter.

Joan cut him off before he could finish his inquiry, which I suspected was of a more *personally, private* nature. Joan quickly responded before he could say more.

"Shawne, Byron's here I'd like you to listen to this and tell me what you think . . ."

Joan's nod signaled me to tell Shawne the story of the phone conversations with B.M. _____.and my 'brothers.'

As I reiterated the details for Shawne, Joan listened as intently as she had done the first time she heard my account of the phone calls and then interjected again.

"Shawne, I told Byron he needs to go and meet his father, but I wanted him to talk to you too. Byron, not long ago, Shawne reacquainted with his father, who had not been a part of his life for most of his adult life. I encouraged him to make contact and he did. Additionally, your children need to know their grandfather, particularly since he asked you to come and bring them along too. I know it will mean a lot to Janice too. Besides, she just might find out that Erin looks like Aunt So-in-So who has no children of her own; or why Derek laughs the way he does . . ."

Shawne interrupted, and I redirected my attention to Joan, staring intensely at her; still not quite wanting to do as she suggested; and trying to rack my brain regarding whether or not I knew about Shawne and his father.

"Yea baby, but remember, my biological father and I did not know each other at all. We did not have a relationship, positive or otherwise; it was my stepfather who was the positive male role model in my life. As a result, meeting my biological father was not as likely to happen or be a positive event because I already had a great relationship with the only man I ever knew as a father. In fact, I thought meeting my biological father would probably be at best, very awkward. In my case, I was right, it was at best awkward. Now, in all fairness, I have to admit that I really didn't want to re-acquaint, reconcile or any of those other 'niceties' that are supposed to manifest in situations such as these. I wasn't interested in seeking my 'real' father, as my stepdad had proven to be a more than adequate surrogate. Truthfully speaking, I didn't want to jeopardize our relationship in any way, form or fashion by entertaining an interloper who I didn't even know!

So, Byron, you know Joan and I are family to you and Janice. I know I don't have to tell you this, but I feel the need to say it anyway. I just want you to be prepared and not walk into this situation blindly. You should go to that reunion, but guard yourself so you don't get hurt. I know that it seems what I'm saying is diametrically opposed to Joan's recommendation, but don't take it that way because my intent is purely cautionary. Whatever you decide, remember Joan and I will pray for you, Janice and the kids to have a safe trip and that reuniting with your father *adds* to you. Be sure to give us a full 'report' letting us know how everything turned out, when you guys get back"

I remembered hearing those same comments of caution from Jules only a few months earlier.

"Thanks, man; I'll seriously take under consideration all you said. I'm pretty convinced after talking to you and Joan which way I should go." He and Joan exchanged loving words and terminated the intercom connection; I waited for Joan to say more.

"B, you need to go! I feel it in my spirit that you will not regret it. You will get to meet your brothers for the first time. Didn't you say your father has siblings?"

"Yes. I believe he has sisters and brothers who live somewhere near Greenville, South Carolina."

As we both stood, signaling it was time for me to leave, Joan added her own good wishes and intent to include us in her prayers as she repeated Shawne's assurances to do the same.

I left Joan's office with a little more confidence than I had before our visit. I felt that going to Greenville was more than just a good idea, more than likely. As Jules would say, "It's Providence."

It took a bit, but a few days later, I had decided we would go, pursuing the *journey* as it seemed to naturally *roll out* before me.

I convinced Erin and Derek to 'clear their calendars' to accompany their mother and me to that 2007 reunion in Greenville, South Carolina. It was held the weekend of August 31st through September 2nd, which I'm sure would afford us an experience quite different from that of our traditional, backyard family barbeque.

CHAPTER 29

THE REUNION

The Journey had begun . . .

We arrived at the Hilton Hotel in Greenville about 7:30 pm on Friday. As we entered the parking garage, my cell phone rang. I handed it to Janice to answer so I could focus on finding and pulling into a parking spot.

"We are just pulling into the parking garage now!" Janice reported to the person on the other end of the call. "Okay, we'll meet you in the lobby in a few minutes", Janice excitedly announced and turned the phone off. Janice, Derek, Erin and I engaged nervous chatter about nothing in particular, as we lugged our bags through the garage to the entrance of the hotel. We made our way to the lobby and I instructed Janice to check us in while I paced the center of the lobby looking for B. M. _____I hadn't thought about it earlier, but I hoped he was wearing a name tag. I had to chuckle to myself as I thought that the least we should have done was to describe what we'd be wearing. The last thing I wanted to do was to go up to strangers asking them if they were my Dad. I don't remember seeing any pictures of him—so I had no description to refer to. A gentleman came out of the elevator alone. After I gave him a quick once over, I decided he couldn't be B.M. He might have been old enough to be my brother but not my father. A few minutes, that seemed an eternity, went by when another man exited the elevator. He was accompanied by a girl who appeared to be about eleven or twelve years old. He walked slowly in my direction. He looked as if he was trying to figure out who we were. The man, about six feet tall, dark-skinned, and dressed to the nines, strode across the floor towards us. He was sporting a white Ivy cap, emerald green golf shirt, dress slacks and black shoes. I was a tad disappointed when he glanced at me and then turned away. I should add, I was disappointed, but not deterred. I'd come all this way and I wasn't going to let another wasted moment go by. Something more than courage and curiosity rose up in my gut at that moment. I approached this man and at about three feet away I spoke.

"Are you my Daddy?"

He laughed heartily along with me and replied. "I think I am!" I'm not sure what I was thinking at that moment. However, I was surprised that I had reverted to the more infantile, familial address of "Daddy" referring to this 'stranger,' whom I did not know and couldn't figure out what else to say at that moment. So, I did the next best thing. I excused myself.

"Okay, let me go help my wife and kids settle in and then I'll call you to come visit with us."

The Journey had begun.

We found our room and after settling in, I called my father to come over and spend a little time getting to know Janice, Derek, Erin *and me.*

I started out by bringing out photos of my mother, me and a copy of my birth certificate. I thought introducing things that we had in common would be the best approach to our getting to know each other. My additional motive in starting this journey was to present them to my father in an attempt to settle any concerns as to the validity of my identity. He looked at my mother's photo and smiled. This was all Janice needed to know. It was *safe* to satisfy her curiosity regarding how my father came to know my mother.

Janice's burning question had been the focal point of most our discussion during the two-and a half hour drive from Atlanta to Greenville. It was one, among many, I could not answer. The timing was ripe. At the first opportunity, in that fine hotel room, she boldly queried.

"So, how did you meet my mother-in-law?"

B.M. _____ seemed to have been prepared for the question, but appeared surprised that I wasn't the one asking the question. With a moistened gleam in his eyes, he cleared his throat and started.

"I was stationed at Camp Leroy Johnson (New Orleans Army Air Base) in 1951 through 1955. It was the summer of 1952 that we met . . . Well your mother came to the movie theater with a friend of hers, whom I had met sometime before that evening and she introduced her to me. I ran the projector on the base and I saw her come in the door in a red dress. She looked so good! I asked for her phone number and she gave it to me, but for several days afterwards I was afraid to call her. You see, I didn't think she would have anything to do with me. So, after a few weeks had gone by and I heard that Johnny Ace was coming to town for a concert. I finally got up the nerve to call and ask her if she wanted to go see Johnny Ace and she said 'yes.' I was more than overjoyed! Man, I was so proud!"

As my father spoke, I recalled that Jules, in one of our last visits, had suggested there was a calculability of the odds related to the union of two people, who upon yielding offspring; survive to encounter a union with someone, et cetera. It was at that moment, I grasped the depth of meaning in Jules' comment—the 'Divine Strategy,' which was constantly working like a complex machine with its intricate gears engaging, turning processes on, positioning, placing, adapting to adversities, correcting glitches, while maintaining movement with progression of time and space from the timeless beginning seeds of our ancestors to any given precise moment in that continuum we know and call time. All of this motion—without human intervention or 'interruption,' produced up to that present time the remarkable 'products' we call human beings! The *Dots* connected in each instance and B.M. and Dolores' meeting was far from a 'chance' incident! At that moment, I was again struck with the profundity of Jules' insight; and of his uncanny ability to share the complexity of that insight in an understandable way for others to grasp!

In all likelihood, my attitude about meeting my father that weekend had already experienced the range of emotions of disappointment, then anger, associated with a boy growing up without his father. It had been resolved by the time the phone call was made a few weeks earlier, that at that point in my life, my father and I owed each other absolutely nothing, except mutual respect. After all, I was grateful that my mother and father had that moment, which ultimately resulted in my very being.

While my father was reminiscing about my mother and their relationship, I have to admit I was not fully attentive to all he had to say. My thoughts were elsewhere. There was a question I needed answered . . . finally, I asked him, "What did he do to get my mother to drop her panties . . . ?" Somehow, I managed to ask it audibly, but I cannot recall how I posed the question. I hoped, given that we were in the presence of Janice and the kids, my query has some semblance of 'respect!' Regardless, of how my question appeared to B.M., he defended his actions and partly, my mother's honor, saying:

"Your mother and I stayed together for over three years. I used to go over to your great-aunt's house and help turn your uncle over in bed to relieve his bed sores. I got to know your great-grandmother real well. She was a real nice person to me. But your mother didn't want me to meet your grandmother—her mother for some reason. She didn't feel it would have been a good idea for me to meet her."

I never asked B.M. why my mother did not feel it 'a good idea' for him to meet my grandmother—her mother. I assumed my mother had some reluctance in exposing the details of her relationships with men, to her mother—perhaps she felt like she wasn't obligated to divulge her affairs or maybe she harbored some 'self-esteem' concerns being that she was in her early twenties and was a single-parent to two children, and an 'unexpected' third child coming shortly.

B.M. continued for a long time, to speak about his family, past and present. I was happy with his approach, including the fact that he introduced to the souls of his mother, Hattie and his father, N.Z who had already passed on. It helped me to better understand the 'other side' of where I'd come from, as up to that time, I'd only known my mother's 'side' of the family.

A hint of an early morning, southern-style breakfast as a continuance to the 'welcome to the family' process and a declaration that it was late—'we all needed to get some rest'—B.M. moved smoothly from his seated position towards the door. It was on that note that B.M. and I said our good nights and he departed to his hotel room, one floor below.

It was well after midnight, but I was much too worked up to bed down for the night, even though I knew there was a big day ahead after sunrise with all the reunion's planned activities.

Janice, always the level headed one between us, sensing there was no calming me down from all the excitement, said her goodnights to me and the kids, hardly got those words out of her mouth before she was out like a light. I watched television a little while with my kids. Sleep was still evading me when I finally decided to go for a walk. As I walked the streets of Greenville, South Carolina alone until 4:00 a.m. with mixed feelings of confusion and fears, I realized I was *overwhelmed!*

John Richard (Ricky), the following morning at breakfast, my father's middle son, extended a most heartwarming welcome to me and my family. It was then that I felt genuinely a part of something I hadn't known I had been missing most of my life. The connection between him Ricky and me was immediate and *strong.*

I belonged to *this* family! It was this group of people from whom I had been missing! I felt like Tigger![157] I was so glad I'd stepped out and taken the chance to meet the other side of my family. Joan had been right, as usual. Shawne was a little more cautious, but most importantly, he had encouraged me with his urgings for me to step out and to take a chance . . . just be careful. I smiled then as a vision of Shawne suddenly appeared to me in my mind's eye cautioning me 'not to drink the Kool-Aid!' It struck me at that moment how very blessed I was: Not only did I have brothers of another mother; but in Shawne I had a brother of another mother and father!

* * *

During that reunion weekend it occurred to me that my children, it seemed, were on a 'journey' of their own at the same time. Initially, I

---

[157] Referring to *Tigger*, the main character in *The Tigger Movie,* a 2000 American animated film co-written and directed by Jun Falkenstein. Part of the Winnie-the-Pooh series, this film features Pooh's friend *Tigger* in his search for his family tree and other Tiggers like himself.

hadn't considered how, like me, they also must have been overwhelmed by the 'newness' of having suddenly acquired an extended family. I had no idea how in the following months we would experience the wonders of getting to know the people we belonged to. Then I would begin to have those strange feelings of being overwhelmed. So many faces, attitudes, characteristics and obligations to care for fret over. Maybe it was the 'newness' of the idea that I really had family to belong to that was both burdensome and blissful. This journey was taking me to the place where I could understand the bittersweet feelings Jules had referred to.

Over the next year, the journey continued with frequent visits from Janice and me to South Carolina with Aunt Jane, Uncle Scuddy, Uncle Willie, and Aunt Juanita. I enjoyed home-cooked meals and restaurant outings with Aunt 'Tine, Uncle Clarence, Aunt Dot and Aunt Clara. I felt the stinging void created by the absence of my father's brothers, the late (Uncle Shiny—Curtis) James and the late J. D. (Jake), but I also felt their presence in getting to know them through their sons. The thing that stood out most often and most vividly came from the wild and curious tales about these larger-than-life men to whom I now belonged as well. And then there was the sweet, but so brief encounter with my father's sister—the one they called 'Cat'—she proudly proclaimed herself as "N. Z's only daughter," for whom I deeply regret I didn't get the chance to really know (she died shortly after we met). Along with my father's siblings and their spouses, their children and grandchildren—my cousins became much more like my siblings because of their close ties to our grandmother, Granny Hattie. As a result of this 'closeness,' I can genuinely refer to each of them as 'brother' or 'sister.'

CHAPTER 30

GRANNY HATTIE

Missed Grandmother

My last visit with Jules Bayonne had been over a year ago but I still felt his presence, heard his hearty laughter and could hear his smoothly toned wisdom. I was most often aware of his presence when I was introduced to family members I had not known previous to meeting my father. I experienced this presence anew each time I met a relative for the first time. I became profoundly aware of the vast combinations of interesting and important individuals who were absolutely necessary so that I might exist. Such was the case of my father's mother, Hattie.

Unfortunately, I reunited with my father's side of the family twelve years too late to have met Granny Hattie, as she is fondly referred to by all of her grandchildren. Aside from having last seen my father when I was three years old, I did not know any of his siblings or their children until the mid to late 2007. I am absolutely certain Jules Bayonne was somehow responsible for uniting me with Granny Hattie. I will explain later, my rationale for why I am so certain of Jules' involvement, but for now, I will stick to the chronology of the *miracles* which began in 2007.

My father's youngest sister, Evelyn Jane (Aunt Jane) was introduced to me as a part of the chain of events, related to meeting Hattie's remaining relatives shortly after Jules *left* in March 2007. Although I first met many of my father's relatives on Saturday, September 1, 2007, at the family reunion in Greensboro, South Carolina, I was actually introduced to Granny Hattie a few months later at Uncle Scuddy (Aunt Jane's beloved husband) and Aunt Jane's residence in Easley, South Carolina—my father's birthplace. I 'met' Granny Hattie by way of photographs and the vivid retelling of her life via the stories told by Uncle Scuddy and Aunt Jane. These stories presented a graphically powerful picture of Hattie and spoke volumes of her acceptance of and performance in the matriarchal role as well as her confidence in leading the family. The description of Granny Hattie's persona coupled with photographs—posed a subtle displayed of a powerful tribe leader and provided a clear explanation as to why she was spoken of with such reverence and respect. In Easley, South Carolina Aunt Jane and Uncle Scuddy, carefully sorted a package of old photographs, finally settling on four as they jointly declared; "These are for you—your Granny Hattie kept these all those years until just before she died, then she gave theme to me."

The first of the photos Aunt Jane presented to me, the largest—an eight by ten sepia tone photograph was of me as a two or three-month old infant. I couldn't be sure, but I imagine the hands holding me, probably belonged to my father. They looked strong and young; the hands of somebody just starting out on his own journey and firmly grasping at his future. This photo must have been of major importance, as my mother once had a wallet-sized copy exactly like it, but had lost it when her wallet was stolen around 1969. I recalled her being so distraught because that was the only photo she had of me as an infant. Receiving that photograph was one of what I would later refer to as "one of life's little miracles." Keep in mind, that prior to 1969, obtaining a copy of a photograph was a costly and difficult process, and unless one possessed the 'negative' of the print, getting a copy required a professional to achieve a reasonable likeness to the original. There were no scanners available to laymen, no personal computers, no e-mail, no downloads, et cetera.

The second photograph Aunt Jane handed me, an original portrait of my mother, taken when she was fifteen years old, came as a tremendous surprise. I thought it had been lost, but much to my delight here it was in my very hands, before my very eyes! This muted color image of my mother showed her dressed in a wonderfully flared, chiffon, white floor-length gown. A strand of medium-sized graduated pearls, framing the tip of her collarbone hung gracefully around her neck,. A large orchid corsage draped the modest neckline of the gown, resting just below her left shoulder and slightly above her heart. She was clutching her ribbon-tied high school diploma with both hands; a dainty lace handkerchief rested gently at her left wrist. A simple light blue-gray drapery and a colorful, rose print carpet framed the backdrop of this classic portrait taken in the spring of 1948, captured in time, the young lady, who would give birth to me six years later. I had seen this identical portrait hanging on one of the hall walls at my mother's home in New Orleans until shortly after her death in 1991. Somehow, my mother's favorite portrait of her high school graduation from Booker T. Washington High School in New Orleans *disappeared* with all of the other family photographs that had also once covered the beige painted walls of that little white brick duplex in Gentilly Woods. I had often wondered what had become of that portrait. It had been more than sixteen years since I had last seen it. I had thought many times about how nice it would be to have the portrait—where could it be? Again, I was astonished; and my heart raced, at this wonderful discovery of that long lost, beloved portrait. I didn't admit it at the time, but I got kind of 'puffed up' with pride, as I was the only one of my mother's children to have that prized image of her in my possession. I felt like I have rediscovered a *buried treasure* that wasn't really buried, it just needed to be <u>unearthed</u>!

I eagerly awaited as Aunt Jane handed me the next photo. It was a five-by-seven black and white Kodak print of my father's 1949 Chevrolet Fleetline—his first automobile. My father told me that my mom looked so good driving his car—it made him proud when, the guys in his outfit would tease me, saying, "Here she comes, B.M.!" This photograph, as did many of the others, stimulated the memory of people like Aunt Jane and

Uncle Scuddy to share the fondness and warmth of treasured, firsthand experiences they had with loved, departed ones who had passed on before the present generation had the opportunity to do likewise. These would have been the untold stories, which ultimately would have been lost forever with the passing of the elder generation, were it not for the urging of Jules Bayonne during his fateful, brief, miraculous visit in early 2007 to 'make the journey.'

Finally, the last photo Aunt Jane handed me was the one I found most impressive. It—also a five-by-seven was of my mother, Dolores, hugely pregnant, standing in front of my father's prized automobile, which was parked in front of Eloise Sorrell's home in Gentilly Woods. This fourth photograph has become one of my most treasured possessions. The story depicted in this single relic is so comprehensive in that it inherently contains the historic evidence of what was both past and present (me before I was born and me now as a grown man). For example; my brother Richard is silhouetted inside the car, (my sister, Deborra is not visible in the photo, but probably nearby), and my mother is just twenty-one years old and probably within a few months from delivering me. Estimating from the vegetation and the warm weather clothing (sandals) she is wearing, it's summertime in New Orleans, and the small, vacant, overgrown patch of land behind and to her right is the site of the future home she had built in 1965. Additionally, the unfinished home of Joseph and Eva Garnett, who became our wonderful neighbors for decades, is also present.

The same weekend (a few months after the Greenville reunion) I received the photographs from Aunt Jane and Uncle Scuddy, Janice and I was driven a few miles away to Aunt Clementine's ('Tine)' house. Although I had met Aunt 'Tine' a few months earlier, I still hadn't realized how incredibly important her role was relative to my father's getting to meet with my family—and to a greater extent my father's only daughter. Janice and I had only been seated a few seconds before she grabbed my shirtsleeve and pointed to the wall to the left of the entry of her home. Aunt Clementine also had an eight-by-ten copy of the photo of me as an infant hanging above her mantle in her living room. As Aunt 'Tine' pointed it out to me as she commented, "Mama always wondered about you, where you were, how you were doing!"

As I reminisced about how I felt when I received those photographs, I could truthfully say that I had gained much more in the way of value and appreciation since Jules' visit. I could see why he was so intrigued with the invention of photography and the 'captured image.' I have been blessed with the patience and appreciation needed to carefully observe the fine details I once overlooked and/or ignored as inconsequential. The value of keeping a record of a loved one's life, especially through the medium of a 'captured image,' proved to be an incredible and indelible resource in preserving the cornerstone of 'remembering' (honoring) those who came before we did.

For as long as I could remember, even as a young boy in elementary school, I had this feeling that there were people praying, looking out for me, interceding on my behalf, and even dispatching spiritual forces to protect me from evil. I realized that Jules Bayonne must have been one of those souls who did not know *of me in his present time*, but had great concerns for those who would come later through his *seed*. But Hattie, my paternal grandmother *did know* who I was. She spoke to my mother via telephone about me. She cherished my image and despite never having physically gazed on my face, loved and fretted about her first grandson! My soul bore witness to that kind of love one has for their own. As my own grandchildren arrived, I became aware of the importance—no, the absolute necessity to pray for their safety and protection; and for their future, including their (prospective) children and children's children whom I may not see in *this* plane of life.

As I got to know my father's children, siblings, nieces, nephews, grandchildren and cousins, I was also solidifying my ties to Granny Hattie. Most of my *new* family—they who always were there but I did not know until after Jules *left*, presented or introduced Granny Hattie to me through wonderful, humorous and fond stories about her. They knew and loved Granny Hattie, and through their fond memories, reverentially *spoke* her name and breathed life into her which especially allowed me to *know* her. This was incredible stuff! Her photos and portraits, the memories of those who spent time—my father's love, admiration, respect, honor and memories of her placed me in the undeniable embrace with *my* Granny Hattie. This is what I alluded to earlier regarding my certainty that Jules Bayonne was somehow responsible for uniting me with Granny Hattie. Through Jules, the connection with my family, including my father, continued with my introductions to (great) Granny Ida—Hattie's mother; Granny Ida's husband (great) Grandpa Drayton; Granny Ida's parents—(great-great grandparents)—Riley and Hulley; as well as to all of the young children, born in 2007! Again, I was overwhelmed, but for an entirely different reason. All of these 'discoveries' and new experiences were remarkable—particularly since I was presented photographs of Granny Ida and portraits of her parents, Riley and Hully! Within the twelve months of the 2007 reunion I learned about my ancestry dating back to the mid1800's—the same period in time Jules Bayonne first breathed the air on Earth!

Thanks again, Grandpa Jules! God bless you on continuing your journey!

During that reunion weekend in Greensboro, South Carolina in September 2007, Aunt 'Tine' made a passing comment where I learned that I was my father's eldest *boy*, but not his *eldest child*—there was another—my sister Patricia who held the position of 'first-born.' Somewhat matter-of-factly, Aunt 'Tine' announced this fact in my father's now crowded hotel room. I was beginning to learn who Aunt 'Tine' was: A woman of few words, but one who said what she means and means what she says.

"Byron, you know you aren't the oldest—your sister Patricia came before you did!"

Another 'shocker'! After all that's happened, I don't know why anything should continue to take me, the family historian, by surprise. I realized then that a true historian knows the whole story . . . and I'd only known one side of the story——Mama's side. Turning to my father, who smiled mischievously as Aunt 'Tine' announced in a demanding tone, "Bus,[158] it's time all those children got to know each other!" I couldn't have agreed with her more, especially since the reason many black families starting having reunions is so that everybody knows who everybody else is. A friend of mine once mentioned how with kids going away to school and traveling around, there have been times when these kids "meet and greet" their own cousins without the slightest knowledge of their kinship . . . if you know what I mean.

Although, implied in much of this summary of events, the visit from Jules in 2007 triggered my decision to take the journey. I must confess,

---

158 A few family members and close friends of my father employed the nickname; "Bus."

however, it was actually that *cold winter evening in Chicago at the end of 1986* while walking to my car with a few, seemingly insignificant relics (photos) just entrusted to me by my Uncle Wade—a dying old man's final wishes as it were—which started the mental *quest*. I was the self-appointed family historian. The journey started then, but I didn't know it. I was oblivious to the sound of the *ignition*. I was unaware that the plane was boarding, the busses, were ready to go and the trains were loaded with the baggage. Uncle Wade had given me the *passport* and told me to *get on board*! However, *the journey* actively began with Jules, the mystery surrounding his arrival (and departure), his mesmerizing disposition, and his uncanny power to convey love with *steel* and *velvet* balance. As you will see, every event surrounding my introduction to my father's firstborn, proved to have overwhelming evidence of Jules Bayonne's orchestration.

CHAPTER 31

TRISH

Stories from the Other Side

I'm not sure what I was doing, but I'm pretty sure it wasn't thinking about the recently revealed family dynamics when ironically, I received another telephone call. This time it was Aunt 'Tine,' which would result in a milestone introduction; second only to my introduction to Jules and the extraordinarily wonderful occurrences along *the journey*.

"Byron, this is your Aunt Clementine." *That's how she started out, not even a "Hello" or asking if she could speak to "Byron" as 'normal' people do. But then again, that's Aunt 'Tine,' a woman of few words. I'm glad I 'peeped' this fact early on in our relationship . . . otherwise my feelings would truly have been hurt; which I believe would have gotten in the way of my receiving the vital information she was about to share.*

Just as expected, I sensed that Aunt 'Tine' had something of great importance to share with me. First of all, she rarely called to be sociable—

not her modus operandi—she doesn't *do* 'sociable;' and secondly, she used her full first name, Clementine instead of the more familial, 'Tine.'

"Yes ma'am, how are you?"

"I'm fine." Without changing her tempo or tone, she ordered. "Take this number down. I need you to call your sister, Trish, that's a nickname for Patricia, and tell her who you are. Let her know that we all look forward to seeing her at Cora Lee's birthday party in Easley."

"Call her? Why do I need to call?" I asked, before realizing that I already suspected what her answer would be. It was already too late—my stupid question was met by an answer I somehow knew would be returned by my Aunt 'Tine.'

"Because I said you need to call!" She sternly responded. Then she added, "Cora Lee invited you to the party too." *Huh, I wondered when did that happen?* "You need to be there with the rest of the family to meet that girl since she couldn't make the family reunion. Your invitation is being mailed to you by my *sister*, Cora Lee so be on the lookout for it. Call Patricia when you get off the phone with me—today. You can call your daddy afterwards if you want to and let him know that you called Trish to tell her you and your family will also that party, that's up to you."

"Okay Aunt 'Tine' I'll call her." Her insistent tone told me I had better answer in the affirmative. Moreover, both my ears were ringing and stinging as if she had clapped me on both sides of my head at the same time.

Aunt 'Tine' had said what she intended and made the correct assumption that I'd understood her instructions very well. After I hung up the phone, I sighed deeply, as I still wondered, 'why me?' I had to remind myself that I'd started this part of the journey when I had chosen several months earlier, to meet all the family my dad wanted me to meet. This thought calmed me little, at least to the point where I began to rationalize that although Trish didn't know me, I was certain she had heard about me. This thought comforted me as I allowed my fingers to dial the phone number Aunt 'Tine' had given me a few moments earlier. It took a lot for me not to hang up the phone before it was answered; instead I waited as the ring began so at least if Aunt 'Tine' asked, I could tell her I'd made the call. I was hoping the answering machine would pick up instead a 'live person.' I still hadn't put a dialog together that made sense in order to explain the reason for my call.

No such luck or as Jules would have convinced me, it was neither luck nor coincidence that Trish had been home to answer my call!

"Hello." The sweet, firm voice of the woman answering the phone *had* to be Patricia's. It was pleasant and inviting enough, but I had half-hoped to get her voice message request instead. I was caught off-guard.

I rebounded quickly, and composed, I asked. "May I speak to Patricia, please?"

The strong, sweet voice responded, "Speaking."

I inhaled deeply and then nervously exhaled my rehearsed message.

"Patricia, my name is Byron Coleman. I live in the Atlanta area with my wife and children and I got your number from your aunts Clementine and Cora Lee. I am calling you to introduce myself to you and to let you know that our *entire* families are very eager to see you at Miss Cora Lee's birthday celebration which will be held in Easley, South Carolina."

Just before I could catch another breath to inhale and continue, Patricia asked "Wait a second, who is this?"

Forcing myself to slow the pace, I began again, "My name is Byron, my Aunt 'Tine'—Clementine, and yours also, gave me your number. I am having a little difficulty telling you this partly, because I'm a little nervous. I don't often make these kinds of phone calls, particularly since there are so many scams and fraud attempts made by telephone these days. I am also a little excited because I have been given the honor of being the first of our siblings to announce to you, the eldest of our father's children, that I am your brother. If I have your permission to continue, I will, but I assure you, that if I were in your position, this call would seem strange and even a bit 'prankish' to me—I wouldn't blame you for hanging up, but please don't hang up, not just yet."

"Yes, it sounds a little strange, but do continue, I promise, I won't hang-up," Patricia offered. I gladly accepted, which allowed me to relax a little more.

I explained that I had reunited with our father, B.M. after more than fifty years, and met his three sons—our brothers as well as most of our father's side of the family. I briefly interjected my mother's relationship to our father, which bound us together through the common ties of our father, siblings, aunts, uncles, et cetera.

Patricia listened intently. I didn't know what she looked like, but I could imagine her furrowed brow as she tried to take in all this new and surprising information. I imagined how she must also be wondering how come this was the first time she'd ever heard of a Byron Coleman? I'm just guessing, but if I were in her shoes I'd be wondering if this person calling himself was some kind of family secret 'revealed,' scandal or both; especially since I, a stranger to her, was introducing myself for the first time, instead of a family member she already knew,

* * *

On the day (around the middle of January, 2009) of Miss Cora Lee's birthday celebration, I fussed with every detail of the trip to Easley, South Carolina. I was nervous the whole day of the party, apprehensive and worried about how things with meeting Trish would turnout. I only knew a few details about her, and the little I did know, intimidated me just a little. It might have been because Aunt 'Tine' had informed me that Patricia had held a very high-level position with the United States Postal Service just prior to her retirement a couple of months earlier. And to top it off, she handed me a copy of the program from Trish's retirement commemoration which listed so many of her career awards and commendations I couldn't read them all in so short a period as would seem appropriate. So, meeting this celebrity of the family, for the first time was particularly unnerving. I wasn't sure why I was feeling that way. Perhaps, with everything else going on, it somehow made me feel 'inadequate,' a sensation I definitely wasn't familiar with!

The thing that really frayed my nerves about meeting Patricia was the fact that she had never seen our father—ever! Obviously, or so it would seem, he'd never seen her either. At least, I'd met the man before, even though I didn't remember those meetings due to my being so young. I knew little else, at that time about why our father had never met his first child. I also knew he wasn't going to be in Easley the evening of Miss Cora Lee's party—this major snafu was the primary reason for my great angst. Thoughts about Jules came shining through my person and spirit as I reminisced about all he had taught me about the importance of never removing the cornerstone. Another concern I carried to the celebration, was the limited knowledge I had regarding Patricia's life aside from that of her (our) father's lack of involvement. I didn't know what to expect when I would soon be in the same room with Patricia's *mother* and her mother's sister, Miss Cora Lee. Regardless, of a possible diverse consequence, I would follow wherever the *journey* led, good or bad. Jules had suggested there might be some complications along the way, but that "ultimately, good will always prevail over evil," so I proceeded to join the party, despite my many apprehensions; especially since with Dad being out of town, I needed to represent! Still, admittedly, I steadfastly held on a bit to my 'wait and see' attitude.

I hurried Janice. I prompted her to get dressed far ahead of the time, required to make it to the party early, so we could stop at a florist to get a dozen pink roses. I made a conscious decision that roses for Patricia would make a favorable impression on her, even though she could not claim the present festivities as its celebrant. I was careful to not let the gift of roses upstage the beautifully, especially gift wrapped present for Aunt Cora Lee. (I think I need to set the record straight here: Aunt Cora Lee is actually blood-related to Patricia through her mother and not 'blood-related' to me. But in black families, as a matter of course, we neither acknowledge, nor differentiate 'half-bloods' and 'step-kin.' In other words when an individual is related to one family member, they are related to all!)

We had high hopes as we left the flower shop, confident that we could get to the party without incident. We started our trip, prepared with the address to the banquet facility in downtown Easley, but in keeping with my usual habit after numerous visits to my father's hometown, I got lost! Hooray for Uncle Scuddy. As he had done so many times before, when he learned that once again I was lost, he unselfishly said over the phone, "Stay where you are, I'm coming to get you kids!" I think he got a big kick out of coming to our rescue.

We welcomed the familiar ritual of the little blue Ford pick-up arriving, and when headlights flashed by Uncle Scuddy, signaled for us to follow. Wow! We were less than a block away! The closer we got to the venue, butterflies and shattered nerves tried to overtake me, but I choked back that unpleasant taste lodged in my throat. After parking the car, I grabbed the gift and flowers from the back seat and walked slightly behind my wife who had already started walking toward the party's venue.

As we walked towards the entry door, we ran into Uncle Clarence, my father's youngest brother; and engaged in a brief discussion as he handed me a framed photograph of my father and all of their brothers. At that moment I knew Jules was in the midst of that event, because the photograph held the only images of two of my father's younger brothers, Uncle Curtis (Shiney) and Uncle J.D. (Jake) whom I would *never* have the honor of meeting personally—both had died more than ten years before we attended that *first* family reunion in Greensboro. I was *introduced* to these two special men and later came to really *know* them through Uncle Clarence's various amusing and fascinating stories that evening. I'm not sure how long we stayed in that parking lot listening to Uncle Clarence's witty and at times very animated stories before Janice gave me the look that signaled 'we'd better get to the party—the *real reason* for our being there in the first place!' I agreed a secret reluctance, but she was right. We had to retire to the hall's parking lot for these stories, some of which, I dare say, raised more than a few eyebrows, if you know what I mean.

As we entered the banquet hall's main foyer, we were greeted by a cheerful, young woman attired in a beautiful, pastel green-colored chiffon 'party' dress. She directed us to a lectern which held a similarly pastel-colored covered 'sign-in' book designed to facilitate the 'thank you' card process. Afterwards, she escorted Janice and I to a closed door leading to the banquet room. She gave the door several sharp little raps before returning to her 'duty station.' The door was eased open by another greeter, attired much like the first, who initially opened it just wide enough for us to peer inside. As we entered the basketball court-sized room it was such a beautiful sight to see it filled with people already seated eight-to-ten per round, white tablecloth-topped tables, which extended from one end of the room to the other. All-in-all, more than three-hundred people, most of who were somehow related to one another. The room buzzed with excitement, as we were shuttled near the back of the room, located on the same side of where we entered. As we approached our table, we couldn't help but notice the attention focused on a woman standing and speaking in the center of four other women seated at the head table located at the opposite end of the rectangular room. Miss Cora Lee was laughing heartily, at the woman standing who had just described a funny incident involving the honoree when she was a young girl. As I gazed to the left side of the opposite corner of the room, our eyes met, almost simultaneously! The moment I saw her, I knew she was my sister—we looked so much alike! It was hard to wait patiently for the event's formalities to end. After the speeches ended, the music played and people began to dance and move about the room. Patricia made her way towards the corner where Janice and I were standing. We moved toward the entrance of hall and met my sister with a warm embrace. Tears of the joy of a young boy overcame me as I blubbered out how happy we were to have finally met *'the first born!'*

As I held my sister's hand, I kept repeating that I would never let her "go again." Although I still didn't know her *story* on that beautiful night in Easley, South Carolina, something instinctively led me to believe that she also, had been *away* (or, perhaps, the *family* had been away from us) for far too long.

Trish, my long, lost sister and Janice, my wife flanked me on either side and held my hand the entire evening, as Trish led me around to meet all my kinfolk. I felt like the kid who was lifted up to swing between the arms of the two parents who flanked him on either side. Patricia introduced me to (her mother's) family members she had met and I was honored that I was able to, introduce her (the 'missing link') to our father's family members. Everyone (almost) in the room shared the happiness that filled the room, first for Miss Cora Lee's seventieth birthday celebration, and then also, for Patricia's presence.

I thanked Jules several times that evening, but he still wasn't finished *'working his magic!'* Just when I thought things couldn't get more exciting, suddenly, a handsome, petite, light-complexioned woman, briskly walked up to me and asked: "Are you B.M.'s son?"

"Yes ma'am, I am! I am Byron," still beaming the wide smile, which did not disappear the entire evening.

"Well I'm your aunt! I'm the one they call 'Cat'! I'm your Aunt Catina—the only daughter of N. Z.! You know who N. Z. is, don't you?"

The sweet woman's bold announcement was more of a proclamation than an inquiry.

I replied, not quite as boldly, "Yes, N. Z. is my father's (late) father—my (paternal) grandfather!"

"Well I'm your Aunt 'Cat'!" She again declared, robustly, as she hugged me first, and then Janice and Patricia, as she announced, "I expect us to get to know each other better!" That was the universal vow we all shared.

My life has been enriched tremendously due to that evening in a banquet room in Easley, South Carolina. Meeting Trish and all of my family I hadn't known a few short years prior to our recent family celebrations reminded me that *Jules had been there, urging, prodding, suggesting and encouraging—at times it was as if he 'arranged' some of those encounters!*

CHAPTER 32

AN AMAZING SECRET

"... greater works than these..."

I believe that Jules was there, the morning of October 24th, around seven twenty-seven a.m., the same year of the overturning of Plessy vs. Ferguson with Brown vs. Board of Education—the year of my birth. I suspect Jules saw to it that the young mother—my mother and his great-granddaughter, a frightened twenty-one-year-old girl, would recover completely from the circumstances that brought forth largest of her five babies.

Jules was there when I cried out for help, desperately struggling with evil, as an adolescent down in the 'Goose.' Jules was there when I asked myself, "Who will step-up and be the real man in my family—the guide with the 'steel disposition' and the 'soft touch'?" I felt that '*what* I wanted to be when I grew up' meant a lot less to me than *who* I wanted to be (*if*) when I grew up. I didn't hear Jules' affirmative answer; though I now know in my spirit he did answer in the affirmative—Jules was the man who fit the description to a '*T*'—boy, did he 'step-up' in a big way!

Jules smelled the same enchanting fragrance that I did, when I held Wanda, my arms trembling in embrace with a sweet girl—my very first dance partner at Valena C. Jones. Jules was with me when I snatched those Dickey's potato chips from the 'skinny red girl' that day on the corner of Ransom and Reynes (Streets) in the summer of 1967. I'm almost sure, I heard Jules as he laughed in my ear, "You have no idea what you just did!" Jules let me know that Ms. Finley was 'right' for paddling my ass raw for misbehaving that day in Mr. Hart's (the substitute teacher) history class. "So, screw Amerigo Vespucci!" That was my battle cry! After all, by the time we were twelve or thirteen years old, well at least among my peers, we knew this country was inhabited long before Columbus or Vespucci. But that was no call for us to abuse Mr. Hart. I believe Jules also told me that I would need that information from the class at a later date. Now, history is my favorite subject! Go figure! Anyway, Jules may be the one responsible for me feeling so much remorse for my horrible mistreatment of Mr. Hart—It was rumored he retired from education and took a job delivering milk for Brown's Velvet[159].

Later, (in the same year) Jules, no doubt, kept Freeman[160] from doing real damage to me in that fight after school in 1967. Actually, Freeman 'bit off more than he could chew' that day—he got *his ass* handed to him by me instead of the projected other way around. I always felt that someone or something was protecting me during that incident—I say Jules was there!—this is my story—I'm sticking with it!

—I, myself, didn't have the character, maturity or wisdom to do any real good—I know it was Jules there who was whispering comfort to me, calmly, gently and certainly.

Jules is the reason I remember stuff that I thought was once forgotten; Jules is the reason I like *Big Luke, Keyser Soze, Muhammed Ali, white horses and eagles too!*

---

159 Brown's Velvet was the oldest and largest dairy company in New Orleans. The ice cream division was purchased first by Marigold Foods In 1993. The dairy division was purchased by Southern Foods and subsequently became Brown's Dairy, a line of Dean Foods.

160 Freeman was a bully the author encountered in junior high. Freeman caught the author attempting to avoid the confrontation after school by arranging an early dismissal. Failing to escape and agreeing to the bully's insistence that we "go into a nearby garage and shut the door—'so no one will stop us'"—was "all over that guy"!

Never Remove the Cornerstone

I have *'Dots'* because Jules said so—I got them from him!

One of the greatest serendipities I discovered tied to **this** phase of my journey through life is that I now *know* how to 'visit' and communicate with love ones we commonly term as 'departed,' thanks to Jules Bayonne. Another valuable 'discovery' is to know that one should *"Never Remove the Cornerstones"* in life which were (are) placed where they are for good reason.

The spirit world is efficient. It has made provisions for the problem that over-population will one day confront the world. I am of the opinion that a human-based entity which does not *appear* to consume physical space and known resources, offers a profound, yet possible (efficient) alternative. However, I do not suggest we rush to become part of the spiritual world, rather than that, I strongly recommend we become better stewards of this world, as well as enhancing our abilities relative to our currently, underdeveloped spiritual potential.

Jules Bayonne's 'visit' at the beginning of 2007 gave me an understanding of how profound the miracle of life is and how its cycles move beyond what we see, feel, smell or taste, or in most cases, can truly comprehend.

I now know how critical it is for people to 'build' as opposed to 'tear down' and the power that transcends both, the builder and the one who is 'built.'

Jules gave me a renewed appreciation for the technological advances into the new millennium, particularly as it relates to film, photography, recorded music, radio, and television and travel modes.

If one used the auxiliary tools available for the television, the medium becomes a very powerful source of self-education. I had learned to edit, compose and produce my video-based education via select scientific and historic programming. I employed video discs, 'on demand' programming and personal video projects as 'staple mental diet' input. I started to experiment with film, directing and producing home movies using my family and my gardening hobby as my most popular themes. I ceased using television to merely entertain me by 'veg'ing' out on reality shows or sitcom-streaming without purpose; into my head and bolstered my input with programming that would stimulate my imagination, exercise gray matter and cause me to question everything. My only limitation to unbridled travel on this 'journey' was truly tied to the limitations of my own imagination.

I didn't have time to indulge in the trendy reality programs and I accepted the new understanding that there is no such thing as a coincidence when the almost supernatural inklings to turn on the television and a relevant program was airing at that precise moment. My newfound appreciation for television embraced the amazing idea that this form of media is accessible at all times and can be 'programmed' via direct World Wide Web.

Viewing movies on television, on other hand became my passion, so *Ruby Sparks*[161] was easy for me to comprehend. Kazan's protagonist was very real, although fictional—Jules is absolutely real, more so than Ruby—I have (am) the evidence of Jules' existence.

The most rewarding revelation, gained from Jules' 'visit' was the heightened senses I had been miraculously given. I was able to 'see' things, to smell and to hear more than I ever had. I discovered that even my dreams were more vivid and those 'gates' were unlocked, leading me to places within my subconscious, in particular the area of memory, was enhanced remarkably. I was astonished to be able to recall events I hadn't been able to previously remember for decades. Jules had stimulated my creative abilities, giving me a burning desire to encourage others around me to 'see' the greater potential spiritual embrace offers.

I am convinced that an open mind can receive more than one that is non-receptive. Had it not been for the lessons Jules taught me that fantastic winter in the beginning of 2007, I might not have experienced so many major *rewards* during 'the journey' and as I continue, miracles abound, no doubt, largely due to my having acquired an *opened* mind. Jules and the incredible, ongoing journey I joined have opened my mind!

A few years later, while looking over my notes I had written (*much of which had been written when I was with Jules during one our visits—most likely this was recorded at the Riverdale Center*), I came across the following statement:

---

161 A 2012 romantic comedy-drama film (fictional). Directed by Jonathan Dayton and Valerie Faris. Written by and starring Zoe Kazan

"Although I do not agree with much of Eagleman's[162] views with respect to God (I realize the book is a speculative fictional work, but poses interesting concepts relative to possible afterlives) and especially those of his concepts of 'love', I think he may have stumbled on a point of truth as it relates to death in this quote:"

"*. . . Our deaths will occur not just once, but in this series of three stages:*
*. . . the **first** is when the body ceases to function and the **second** is when the body is put in the grave.*

*The **third** is that moment sometime in the future when your name is spoken for the last time.*"

Upon hearing Eagleman's quote and recalling one of the last visits with Jules where he pointed out to me that I had *summoned* his presence. Is it possible that in **remembering**—no, rather, the **speaking** of his name, I had given Jules life?

My children, Derek, the elder, quiet, tall, pensive—more like his mother, and Erin, the beautiful younger, gregarious one—more like me, cornered me. I was not surprised; whereas both were very inquisitive about my encounters with Jules Bayonne, I knew Erin would be the first to query me about my motives and personal proclivities.

Erin, more grounded in reality and substantive tangibles, worriedly questioned me as to whether or not I was experiencing some *psychosis*—(oh, I forgot to mention, Erin is in graduate school earning a masters' degree in Psychology)—and wondered if I might become her first patient. I warned her if that turned out to be the case, there will be no fee paid for her eager (and perhaps premature) diagnosis. I know she believes that my experience with Jules is real, but her slightly cross-eyed stare signaled the tell-tale sign of my daughter's cynicism. Erin boldly stated, "So, daddy, has anyone else been with you during one of your visits with Jules, or were you there alone with him each time?" *Yep, that cinched it . . . she was already thinking how many billable hours she could get outta all this, even though I wasn't going to pay her a plug nickel! I will have to admit that I did find it amusing she was thinking about her professional future.*

---

162 Excerpts from *Sum: Forty Tales from the Afterlives* by Neuroscientist, Dr. David Eagleman. Pantheon Books, copyright 2009.

As I endeavored to support my claims, she paternally offered that they can prove to be healthy as long as I *feel* 'good' about interacting with *this person*, ('a normal aberrant experience'), if they occur within professionally established safety guidelines and pose no danger to yourself or others Sometimes, my baby girl can make me feel like such a moron, especially if I wasn't sure whether or not she is serious.

Derek, on the other hand, offered his support in a much more detailed and convincing manner; "I think it's amazing how much I resemble Jules Bayonne, daddy."

I think Jules is one of those rare entities who has been able to transition to the 'fourth dimension'—which we, in the three-dimensional existence, have difficulty perceiving.—It is not visible to us because of our limited optic and mental senses. But, still, they somehow manage to '*visit*' us here from the fourth dimension. Just as you and I are able to *tap* into (through transcendental meditation) other levels of consciousness, very few other people can comprehend, or even believe the possibility exists, Jules has found a way—maybe even accidentally found the way—to '*come through*'!"

Yeah, I hummed quietly, "He sees it!" We continued our discussion of the possibility that *life continues through dimensions*, the technological advances in genetics and recent scientific discoveries brain and mind capabilities, I was encouraged.

"Take a look at this photograph of our cousin, Derek." I offered, knowing he would see the same thing I did.

"Wow! He looks a lot like Jules! But then again, daddy, I *am* Jules. So *is* our cousin, and so are *you*, and so *is* Erin . . . and so on! All of us are Jules! Don't you see?" *I suspect Derek was trying very hard to convince me he understood and concurred with my assessment of the 'apparition' of Jules—it was logical, it was rational. On the other hand, I wondered if in his query of my 'seeing,' he was trying to convince himself more than convincing me that this all made sense!*

Photographs became more meaningful than ever before! Particularly those (old and new) photos of people—they're somebody! Cinematography as an extension of the invention of capturing images is probably taken for granted more than most creations in the last two centuries. I don't think we have exhausted the remarkability of photos and film yet! As I sat down

Never Remove the Cornerstone

in the comfort of my beautiful, serene little home down in a *lower town* in Georgia, I pondered the future of my two little grandchildren, playing on the floor in that same deep, honey-colored room where a few years earlier, I had received that peculiar phone call which would highlight the road map leading up to now for them (and for me too). I knew they were equipped with all the necessary tools to survive and further *the 'journey'* of Jules—his ancestors and his descendants! I would see to it that they would know and never forget the *'Cornerstone!'* I vowed that I will not remove the *'Cornerstones'* left by Jules or those other beloved ancestors who preceded me. For now it is still *my time* to continue the journey and to invite those who I knew shared the same vision.

I picked up the phone to call my cousin, Pat! She is another of Jules' heirs and a family historian in her own right. I only hope she doesn't get too upset that I'm just now talking to her about Jules and 'Dots' and Big Luke and all the ingredients to make up the 'Gumbo' I call The *'Cornerstone!'*

It seemed like it took Pat an extra, long time to answer her phone. Finally, she answered. "Hi Byron! What's up?"

"Girl, I got some news for you! You'll never guess . . ."

CPSIA information can be obtained
at www.ICGtesting.com
Printed in the USA
FSHW020439161119
64118FS